DIE
LAUGHING

STEVE ALLEN

DIE LAUGHING

KENSINGTON BOOKS

http://www.kensingtonbooks.com

KENSINGTON BOOKS are published by

Kensington Publishing Corp.
850 Third Avenue
New York, NY 10022

Library of Congress Card Catalog Number: 97-072052
ISBN 1-57566-241-8

First Kensington Hardcover Printing: January, 1998
10 9 8 7 6 5 4 3 2 1

Printed in the United States of America

chapter 1

Although I had already sent word ahead through Roger Morton, the agent of legendary comedian Benny Hartman, that I was coming to visit Hartman in his hospital room at Cedars Sinai, I didn't look forward to the experience. I have never approached a suffering person without a feeling of intense discomfort, a reaction perhaps affected by my first such experience. When I was about eleven years old, my mother took me to visit an old man she had described only as "a friend from years ago." She was silent during the long streetcar ride to a part of Chicago I had never seen before. The hospital itself smelled strongly of ether. When we entered the room of the man we had come to visit, I was shocked to see that under his blankets the flatness of the covers made it evident that the poor fellow had lost most of both of his legs. My second shock came a moment later when my mother spoke to him, saying softly, "Hello, Gus." As his eyes met hers, they immediately filled up with tears. I never did learn, then or subsequently, what the relationship between the two was. Had they once been lovers, or just old family friends?

Now, as I walked in upon Benny, his face was pale and wrinkled; there was an IV needle sticking in the back of his left hand and assorted beeping devices monitoring his vital signs. But though he might be dying, the man was chewing on a huge cigar. The cigar was my fault, I'm afraid. I had had it smuggled into Cedars Sinai Hospital earlier at his request, and against my better judgment. It was his trademark, after all; four generations of Americans had watched Benny Hartman stand onstage with a cigar in hand, a prop he had used to punctuate a lifetime of jokes. His doctor had told me that Benny probably wouldn't survive the day, so it didn't seem a cigar would hurt him much.

Another shock came from seeing Benny, for the first time in my life, without a hairpiece. There have been comics who have made comedy out of their baldness but a far greater number have chosen not to. Benny still had a lot of hair on the sides and reminded me of Red Skelton a moment after he does his marvelous sudden-sneeze bit. So even as he lay dying, the old man looked ridiculous. He had always been a good face-comic anyway. The initial endowment, of course, came from Mother Nature and/or the genetic pool, and to his slightly goofy, off-center combination of facial features Benny had added a collection of tricks and shticks borrowed from other, more original funnymen. From the great Harry Ritz he had taken the eyeball-rolling, from Jack Benny the slow, blank-faced take, from Myron Cohen the ability to lower one eyelid at a time in a world-weary manner. And—at least during his early burlesque and Broadway days—from Bobby Clark the gimmick of drawing horn-rimmed glasses on his face with a black grease pencil.

Benny was a comedian of the old school. His humor went all the way back to vaudeville, where he had begun his long career. From then he had gone on to radio, television, movies, and countless club dates, from the Borscht Belt to Vegas. Over the decades he had been in and out of fashion and had lived long enough to find himself rediscovered by yet one more generation—and popular all over again.

"Here's a story," he began, puffing furiously on his cigar. But then he started coughing so badly I thought for a moment he was about to expire in front of me. I was about to ring for a nurse, but then he sighed and caught his breath.

There wasn't much I could say to that, so I sat with Benny

for a long moment in mutual silence, both of us listening to the slow ticking of a small clock on his bedside table. *Tick . . . tick . . . tick.* The sound of a lifetime running down. Benny's hospital room was full of flowers that had been sent by half the celebrities of Hollywood. He had pointed out to me a bouquet which had arrived that morning from the President of the United States. The aroma in the room was a little too sweet and cloying for my taste, but Benny seemed to find satisfaction in the evidence that people were thinking of him. Outside the window I could hear the soft drone of L.A. traffic. In the hospital people might be busy dying and being born, but out in the city it was just a normal May afternoon, smoggy and warm.

Then he paused for a minute and shifted himself in bed, wincing with pain as he did so.

"You want me to crank the bed up or down?" I said.

"Nah, to hell with it," he said. Old age is something you never become completely adjusted to. The adjustments do come to particular infirmities and problems, but overall the situation seems an inconvenience and annoyance. "You know," Benny said, changing the subject, "it took me a long time to get used to being eighty-four and then, about the time I did, they switched the goddamned year on me."

I had never known Benny to be the philosophical type, so his observation surprised me. More oddly, I had never known him to have the gift of wit either, something that will surprise his millions of fans and, for that matter, probably ninety-nine percent of the American people, who evidently assume that all comedians are witty. Actually wit is only one aspect of the ability to amuse others and some enormously successful comedians have not been blessed with it. One of my own favorites, Jack Benny, who was an absolutely delightful performer, depended upon gifted writers for his material in precisely the same sense in which actors—talented or otherwise—depend on those who write plays and film scripts. My motion picture favorites, Stan Laurel and Oliver Hardy, too, were sidesplittingly funny but their genius involved physical horseplay, not what Mark Twain, Will Rogers, Fred Allen, or Groucho Marx did for a living. As regards television, I have publicly maintained since the first night I saw him in action that Sid Caesar is the most brilliant practitioner of the comic trades. He is fully worthy of being described by the word *genius* but he, too, does not employ witty, spontaneous repartee to make us laugh. But that old Benny Hartman had always depended on his writers was as certain as, to Charles Dickens, the fact that old Marley was dead.

"I don't really have a hell of a lot to complain about," Benny said, "as I look back," a line he followed by a quick twist of his head to the rear as if literally looking back. I laughed and even gave him a verbal rim-shot, not at the inherent funniness of the line, but because it was an instance of his trying to make me laugh with what was my own material. He had, needless to say, forgotten its source, or perhaps had bought the bit of business, in good faith, from some writer who wanted him to think it was original.

"I've been rich, I've been poor," he added. "Rich is better." Again I laughed because he expected me to, as he probably also expected me not to remember that the line was created by the great nightclub comic of the thirties and forties, Joe E. Lewis.

"I've outlived three wives and five agents," he went on. "I've seen good times and bad, but you know what I feel best about— I mean of all the things I've ever done or seen?"

"What, Benny?"

"That I've made people laugh."

"That you have, pardner," I said.

"Damn right," he responded. "As a matter of fact, that's why I asked you to drop by today."

"To make me laugh?"

"Nah," he chuckled, "but I hope you'll do me a little favor after I take a cab."

The phrase, originated by comedian Sid Gould, a dear fellow, had become something of a cliché referring to death. *To take a cab, to buy the farm,* were modern equivalents of *to kick the bucket.*

"What was it that you wanted me to do?"

"I want you to help me give something back to comedy. What I have in mind is something that'll honor all of us lucky schmucks who had the gift of making other people laugh. I'm proud and honored that I was a small part of it—and as a matter of fact, that's why I asked you to drop by today."

"To tell some jokes?"

"Yeah, well—that, too. But to be honest, I'm hoping you'll do me a small favor after I'm dead and in my grave."

"Sure, Benny. I will if I can."

"No, this is something you *gotta* do for me. There can't be no *maybes* about it."

"What do you have in mind?" I asked guardedly.

"I want you to help me give something *back* to comedy—this thing that's given me so much. What I have in mind is for you to organize an award ceremony that will honor all those lucky people in the world who have ever made other people laugh."

"*All* the people? That's a tall order, Benny! Do we start with Aristophanes? Finish with Larry Gelbart?"

"Well, okay—we'll narrow down the field a little. An awards ceremony that will honor English-speaking comics of the twentieth century. Is that better? We'll have different categories for living and dead, as well as vaudeville, radio, TV, movies, nightclubs . . . the works."

"Are you talking only about performers, or writers as well?"

"Sure! Let's give some awards to writers, too! Why not? Those poor schmucks need a pat on the back now and then, just like us. We'll give the winners a little bronze statuette—we'll call it the 'Benny.' "

"The Benny," I repeated skeptically.

"Hey, why not? They have an Oscar, Tony—why can't there be a Benny?"

"Well, all right, then. A Benny."

So it was going to be, in large part, an ego thing. At that moment my internal computer punched up the recollection of a phone call I'd gotten, years earlier, from Alan King. "You know Groucho pretty well, don't you?" Alan had asked.

"Yes," I said, "we're close friends."

"Great," he said. "Would it be possible for you to set up an appointment for me with him? Maybe the two of us could go see him together."

"Glad to," I said. Subsequently, arrangements were made for us to talk to Groucho at his home in Truesdale. By that time he was quite old, of course, and on the day in question he was in one of his less-than-charming moods. When Alan told him that he hoped to name an annual comedy award after him, calling it "The Groucho," I expected one of America's favorite comedians to beam with pride and immediately grant permission to be so commemorated. To my surprise, Groucho said, "How much?" Alan's perplexed surprise was expressed in his answer: "What?"

"What's in it for me?" Groucho said. And something in his tone told me he wasn't joking.

"Well," Alan ad-libbed, "I hadn't really thought about that part of it." Both parties agreed to rethink the matter. Needless to say, Alan's idea went no further.

It has never been clear to me, by the way, why Julius Marx called himself Groucho. We all know, of course, that it was just one more crazy name that had to end with the syllable "o" to match Harpo, Zeppo, and the rest, but my point is that of the various attributes of the outrageously funny character he played, grouchiness was at no time included. Irreverence, yes, and a certain cutely naughty rudeness, but such qualities have nothing in common with grouchiness.

"Ya see, Steve," Benny was saying, "we'll give out a whole bunch of 'em. I mean there's no reason in the world to be stingy with the little mothers—they're only bronze. But I want to have one very special prize—a prize to top 'em all—for the Funniest Person Alive. And you know what this prize is going to be? The *grand* prize for this one award?"

"A life-sized Benny?" I suggested.

"A million dollars!" he whispered. His ancient blue eyes lit up so that for a moment he almost looked like a kid of eighty-five. "This is going to grab the world's attention, my friend. I mean, to hell with little statuettes! We're going to do something major league here!"

I studied the old pro for a moment. "Where, may I ask, is this million-dollar prize going to come from?"

"From *me,* babe. Where else do you think it's gonna come from? Santa Claus? Yesterday I had a whole damn team of lawyers in here rewriting my will. I'm donating the moolah myself. After I'm dead, of course. And I'm giving another ten grand to pay for the statuettes. You'll have to raise the money for the awards ceremony itself, Steve-o, but that shouldn't be a problem. Listen, with a million-dollar grand prize, we're going to get tons of attention. The way I see it, we'll broadcast the whole thing live on primetime TV. In fact, if you play your cards right, you should be able to make a bundle out of this yourself. And . . .''

"Whoa, Benny!" I said, holding up a hand. "I'm not sure what I think about any of this. First of all, I can't really believe you're going to give away so much money."

"Why not? I'm a millionaire, Pops! Ya hear about it? Rich guys leave money all the time to universities and art museums and stuff like that. So why can't *I* leave my money to the Funniest Person Alive?"

"But you have two children and a young wife. They aren't going to be too happy about your posthumous generosity. What about them?"

Benny made a dismissive gesture with his hand as if he was brushing away a fly. "My children are grown and doing very well on their own. Jonathan's a big-shot Wall Street lawyer, earning half a mill. a year. And Jennifer's married a guy who owns a ten-thousand-acre ranch in Wyoming. Neither of them needs me. And as for Gloria, the present Mrs. Hartman—well, let's just say I'm takin' care of her in my own special way." Benny smiled in a manner I didn't much like. "Believe me, Steve-o, Gloria's getting exactly what she deserves. Not a penny more, not a penny less."

"The last thing I want to get involved with, Benny, is a family drama."

"There won't *be* any drama. You can forget the family side, Steve. All I'm asking you is to be in charge of the awards ceremony and make certain it's the classy event I have in mind. You're the only one I trust to organize the Benny Hartman Memorial Comedy Awards—that's what I want the thing to be called, by the way."

"Benny, this is a lot to ask. Who's going to judge this contest?"

"A panel of experts, naturally. I've already chosen them, as a matter of fact—you'll find the list of names in my will. After I'm gone."

"Benny—I'm flattered you asked me, but . . .''

"Don't give me no buts, Steve. And don't do it for *me*. Do it for comedy. I've read your books about it—*Funny People, More*

Funny People, How To Be Funny—all that stuff. And I hope you'll do it for all those young kids out there who need some encouragement. Comedy can be a pretty rough field, ya know, when you're just starting out.''

I took a deep breath.

"I'd like to help you out, Benny. But I'm simply too busy."

He reached over to where I was sitting next to his bed and grabbed hold of my wrist with his claw-like hand. For a dying man, he had unexpected strength.

"Steve, please, I'm beggin' you. I can't die in peace unless you promise you'll do this one thing for me. It's like my whole life will be wasted if you don't."

"Benny, there already *is* an annual Comedy Awards program, produced by George Schlatter. And there was another one some years back that I helped produce with Alan King. And Jim Lipton, the producer, and I once proposed one to ABC."

"None of 'em were in the same class with what I've got in mind. Look, Steve, this is not going to be annual. It's a one-time-only extravaganza. You'll be *glad* to be part of it, I promise you!"

It's not easy to turn down a dying man's final request. Benny and I went back and forth about it for some time. He reminded me that he had once helped me land a radio job in 1949, playing on my sense of gratitude. When this didn't work, he offered a specific fee for my service, and a high one, but I still told him no thanks. The Benny Hartman Memorial Comedy Awards sounded to me like a giant, time-consuming headache, and anyway, my schedule was full. Finally, Benny had another coughing fit, and this one made bells ring and nurses come rushing. I was certain I was tiring him out so I tried to sneak out of the hospital room quietly while the nurses were hovering around his bed. But Benny was watching with an eagle eye and wouldn't let me go.

"Steve!" he whispered. "Promise me you'll do it! Do a favor for a dying man!"

So what could I do? "Okay, Benny. If it means that much to you, I'll do it."

"Promise?"

"I'm on board," I told him. "I promise."

Benny sank back into his pillows. "Thank you, Steve." His

voice was very faint now. "You're a true friend. I'll put in a good word for you with St. Peter . . ."

"Benny," I said, "you don't even know St. Peter. You're Jewish."

After a raspy laugh he muttered, "So when did the goyim take over heaven?"

A young doctor told me I had to leave. Benny was fading fast. But it seemed to me there was a sly smile on his lips as I slipped from the room.

chapter 2

I had not lied to Benny Hartman when I said I was busy. It was one of those years when it seemed that Jayne and I hardly had time to unpack between trips. It was all a good deal of fun, but demanding. Each day, I scanned the newspapers and tried to catch the evening TV news for word of Benny's condition. There was no word at all, so I assumed his situation must have stabilized. Maybe Benny, like his friend George Burns, would decide to reach one hundred after all.

Then on May 18, on the final Friday of our tour in *Love Letters*, Benny's death was the lead story on every TV news broadcast. Both Tom Brokaw and Peter Jennings devoted a significant amount of time to the passing of one of America's great entertainers. Dan Rather ran a film clip featuring highlights of Benny's long career, including a segment from a silent film made in the early twenties. Commentators paid tribute—even the President issued a statement from the Oval Office, and the country mourned. It was as if a page of American history had been turned. Knowing Benny, I'm sure he would have enjoyed all the fuss. Naturally, I remembered my promise to him about the awards ceremony, but at the moment I was too busy to give the matter much creative thought. It occurred to me that it might be appropriate to hold the ceremony on the first anniversary of Benny's death, twelve months into the future. Meanwhile, I had a play to do.

On Saturday afternoon, the day after Benny's death, Jayne and I were resting in our dressing room at the theater during the intermission of the matinee performance. Touring on the road is hard work and we were exhausted, glad that this was the last day of our gig, and happier yet that on Sunday we could fly back home to Los Angeles. Jayne was stretched out on the sofa and I was semi-comatose on an overstuffed armchair, my feet on the coffee table. Ten minutes from now we would be back on stage, full of pep and dazzle. But at the moment, we were vegetables.

Then the phone rang.

"Who can *that* be?" said Jayne, yawning.

"I'm not moving," I told her. "If it's important, they'll call back."

We didn't have an answering machine in our dressing room, and few people knew the number. Frankly, I would just as soon no one called us at all. The phone rang seven times and then went silent. But two minutes later it rang again. Finally, it seemed less trouble to pick up the receiver than let it continue to ring.

"Mmm?" I said into the receiver.

"Steve? . . . Steve Allen? Is that you?" came a male voice I didn't recognize.

"Mr. Allen isn't here at the moment," I assured him. "Can I take a message?"

"It *is* you! Thank God! We don't have much time and I want to get on this thing right away."

"Which thing do you have in mind to get on?" I inquired gently. "And *who* are you?"

"You don't recognize my voice? This is Jerry Williams. Remember? We met at the Emmys last year."

"Ah, yes. At the party afterwards." Jerry Williams was one of the top TV producers in Hollywood. A nice young man, I remembered, prematurely gray and a tad frantic. "So what can I do for you, Jerry?"

"Well, I'm calling about the *thing,* of course. Benny told me he spoke to you about it before he died, and that you were on board."

"Are we discussing the Benny Hartman Memorial Comedy Awards by any chance?"

"You bet. Didn't Benny tell you? I'm going to produce the two-hour TV spectacular. The mechanics of the ceremony itself will be up to you, of course, but I'm in charge of the actual broadcast. I've been on the phone the last twenty-four hours and things are coming together pretty good. Unfortunately, the Bolshoi Ballet isn't available, but I'm hopeful about Ringling Brothers and Barnum and Bailey. I'll know tomorrow . . ."

"Whoa! You're going a little too fast for me, Jerry! What about the Bolshoi?"

"Didn't Benny tell you? We thought it would be cute if maybe they'd deliver some of the envelopes onstage. You know. Dress up like Western Union and do a big song and dance giving the envelopes to the celebrity presenters. Unfortunately, they have a date in Australia just at the time we need them . . ."

"Jerry, slow down . . ."

"So Ringling Brothers is our second choice. The way Benny visualized this, a guy would come down from the rafters on a trapeze to deliver the envelope for Best Stand-Up Comic. Maybe a trained seal for Best Female Performance in a Sitcom . . . but surely Benny told you about all this?"

"Surely he did not. Personally, I was thinking of a more modest ceremony, perhaps a year from now on the anniversary of Benny's death. Something along the lines of the Kennedy Center honors. And to tell ya the truth, Jerry, I was thinking of working with Dwight Hemion and Gary Smith, with maybe my pal Bill Harbach brought in as co-producer."

"Those guys are great," Jerry said genially enough, "but Benny did ask me to do this and I think that settles it, don't you? And besides, I see this thing in really big terms. After all, a million-dollar prize to the funniest guy on earth—"

"Or woman" I added, every inch the non-sexist.

"Or kangaroo," Jerry added. "If we need a publicity office at all, it'll be to fight off all the people who want to do stories on us. Hell, we can pick our own network. All of them are going to want it."

Maybe it was because Benny had always been able to get big laughs without resorting to the sort of low-class smut that is the stock-in-trade of so many of today's younger comics.

Jerry laughed. Generally I'm a great advocate of laughter, but there was something about his tone that bothered me.

"Why are you laughing, Jerry?"

"Steve, get with it, man! This thing is going to be *huge*. A million-dollar prize to the Funniest Person Alive—can you *imagine* the monstrous publicity we're going to get? More people are going to watch this show than were tuned in for the O.J. Simpson verdict!"

"I'll have to think about this, Jerry. Frankly, you got me at a bad time, between the first and second acts of *Love Letters*."

"There's no time to *think*, Steve! This is the moment to exchange your slippers for running shoes, baby—this show's going on the air the evening of September 2, live from the Dorothy Chandler Pavilion."

"Impossible," I told him flatly. "That's less than three and a half months from now. The kind of event you're talking about will take six months of planning. At the least."

"No, no, no . . . listen, Steve, we got our time slot fixed with the network, and Benny's already arranged things at the Dorothy Chandler. Everything's in motion. We're moving, man!"

"When exactly did Benny make arrangements for a night at the Dorothy Chandler?"

"More than two months ago. Frankly, I wasn't all that interested in the project to start with, but when Benny came up with the idea of the big prize, and said you were going to be the emcee, I started thinking, maybe we got ourselves a huge hit here."

"The *emcee!*" I said. "Did I hear you right?"

"Benny sure was grateful. Look, Steve, I gotta run—give me a call tomorrow and we'll start to work on some of the nuts and bolts. And relax! We're going to have a ball!"

When I put down the phone, Jayne was smiling at me from the sofa.

"From your face, dear, you've just had a rather big surprise," Jayne remarked.

"And not a pleasant one, either!"

I told Jayne all about it, and she agreed that Benny had his nerve. And that it was impossible to put on such a huge undertaking in less than three and a half months. And an imposition to boot.

"Well, you could always break your promise to Benny," Jayne suggested.

"Break a promise to a dead man?"

"He wasn't entirely frank with you, dear. Do you really owe him anything?"

"No, I suppose not," I sighed. And yet I *had* promised and I knew I'd probably go ahead and do my best with the show anyway. There didn't seem to be any alternative.

I just wondered what other posthumous surprises Benny had arranged for me.

chapter 3

Benny was buried the following Wednesday at Forest Lawn on an overcast afternoon. His grave was situated on a rolling green hillside within sight of eight lanes of congested L.A. freeway. From where we stood, we could hear the soft swish of traffic below. Forest Lawn is the great California supermarket of death; one might choose a more tranquil or secluded spot, but Benny had always loved his pulic, so it was probably appropriate that a few hundred thousand fans would pass within honking distance of his grave every day.

The funeral service was scheduled to begin at one o'clock, but when Jayne and I arrived at ten after one, it still had not started. We stood on a knoll at the rear of a large crowd of several hundred mourners. I was wearing a dark suit and Jayne looked stunning in black, just as she is stunning in red, blue, and several other colors as well. She stood next to me, her red hair spilling out from beneath a broad-brimmed black hat. A broad-brimmed hat that reminded me of the type worn by attractive women in MGM films of the forties, her complexion pale and soft in the gray light of the afternoon. I squeezed her hand and she flashed me a brief smile that was full of shared intimacy. A funeral makes you appreciate the people you love who are still at your side.

Benny's death moved me in a way that is not easy to describe. He had lived a long and successful life, and you don't mourn the death of a man of eighty-five in the same way you miss someone cut down in his prime. But Benny Hartman had been a fixed star in American life for so long that his passing marked the end of an era, particularly for those of us who earn our living making other people laugh. Back when I was a young man coming up in show business, Benny had seemed to me the pinnacle of success, almost out of reach. I'll never forget the first time I met him at a party in Beverly Hills—in 1952, I think it was. Benny stood with me for a moment after we were introduced; he cracked a joke and treated me like a favorite nephew, and I felt I had really arrived at the heart of things in Hollywood. It's not that I ever thought Benny was all that funny, or even saw him as a particularly wonderful human being. A lot of his jokes seemed dated even thirty years ago, and in person he could be an egotistical son of a bitch, if you worked with him. But he was an institution nevertheless and I found myself unexpectedly saddened by his death.

Public figures who remain in place, so to speak, for long decades come to be part of the national psychological furniture. I recall the precise moment when, in 1945, I was on the air at a Los Angeles radio station, KMTR, when the shocking news of the death of Franklin Roosevelt came in to the news department. I knew close to nothing of political matters when I was very young— young people rarely do—and had no particular sense of identification with the Democratic Party or, for that matter, with Roosevelt himself. Nevertheless, an instant after I heard of his death my eyes welled up with tears and my voice—I was broadcasting at the time—choked up.

Standing at the rear of the crowd I saw a number of celebrities and Hollywood power brokers. This was decidedly an "A-event," as the expression goes in this town. I noticed four movie stars and six important comedians, including Jay Leno, Barbra Streisand, and a number of producers, writers, and agents—and this was only the show business contingent. There was also a senator who had once run for President, an oil tycoon, a man who owned a chain of department stores, and all sorts of people who *looked* important, whether they actually were or not. Close to where Jayne and I were standing, a youngish man was whispering loudly into his cell phone, saying he absolutely would *not* pay Demi Moore

three-million-five for a four-day cameo. Funeral or no funeral, the
wheels of Hollywood deal-making never run idle.

Waiting for the service to start, shifting from one foot to another,
I noticed that some people in the crowd were getting restless.
Glancing at my watch, I saw it was one-thirty-five. Then a long,
black stretch limousine came up the narrow cemetery drive. When
the chauffeur opened the car door Gloria Hartman stepped out,
accompanied by an elegant, silver-haired man I recognized as
Roger Morton, Benny's agent of the past dozen years. Quite a few
eyes watched Gloria as she made her way from the limo to the
coffin. She was a buxom blonde, thirty-something, with Big Hair—
elaborate blond swirls spilling down over the tightest figure-hug-
ging black dress I've ever seen on a grieving widow. Her eyes were
obscured by huge dark glasses and her lips were cherry red. Gloria
had an interesting way of rolling her hips as she walked that got
the attention of the male mourners.

"Still stacked, isn't she?" I heard someone say into my right ear.
Turning, I saw it was Terry Parker, the comic actor. "But you
gotta wonder about a dame who marries a guy fifty years older
than herself."

"Perhaps it was true love," I suggested.

Terry grinned. "I'll handle the jokes."

"I'm serious," I said. "Why should a big difference in age
automatically mean she didn't love him?"

Terry kept grinning—a bit too fiendishly, I thought. His tie
was askew and there was a delicate aroma of gin combined with
Listerine on his breath. Twenty-five years earlier, Terry and his
partner Barry Silver had been the most successful comedy team
in the movies. In their routine, Terry was always the slapstick idiot
and Barry the suave, good-looking straight man who got all the
girls. Terry and Barry; it was hard to think of one without the
other. But then Barry split up the team to pursue a singing career
on his own and everyone thought it was over for Terry Parker.
Terry surprised everyone by continuing to make successful movies

on his own. In appearance these days, he was the same as ever—
the same impish smile, silly crewcut, square all-American face, but
he was stouter and up close you could see the gray roots of his
dark hair and his face showed the ravages of booze.

"Hi, honey, how's my favorite redhead?" Terry whispered to
my wife.

"Just fine, dear," Jayne told him, reaching to straighten his
tie.

Jayne's the only person I can imagine getting away with something like that. Terry stood still for her and looked momentarily
like an overgrown schoolboy. "There, now, you look almost
respectable," she said.

"I guess I've had a few," he admitted with his disarming
grin. "But what the hell—this is quite a bash, isn't it, old Benny
Hartman's goodbye party? I guess it goes to prove the old saying—
give the people what they want and they'll come to see!"

"That didn't become an old adage," I pointed out, "until
after Larry Gelbart originally said it," which he had—years earlier—about the funeral of Harry Cohn, a rude, abusive, and
classless movie mogul who had ruled as president of Columbia
Pictures for some years.

"I'll pretend I didn't hear that," Jayne said sternly to Terry.
"Benny was a close friend of yours."

Terry put a finger dramatically to his lips. "Shh!" he whispered. "I'm going to tell you guys a secret . . . wanna know a
secret?"

"Not particularly," I said.

"This is it," he continued anyway. "Nobody *has* any friends,
not in this town. Not real friends anyway . . . Oh, everybody pre-
tends to be all palsy-walsy, at least when you're riding high. But
deep down everybody's out for themself. So I say, to hell with it,
let's have another drink."

Terry produced a silver flask from a breast pocket. He brought
it out like a magician making a rabbit appear, looking to us for
applause. When Jayne and I declined his offer, he unscrewed the
cap, raised the flask to his lips, and drank quickly and greedily.

Meanwhile, Gloria had arrived at her husband's casket and
the presiding rabbi, an earnest young man, had begun the service.

Jayne and I struggled to hear him, but it was impossible with Terry talking.

"There's more to this than meets the eye," Terry assured us with a broad wink.

"Shh!" Jayne chided. "Behave yourself, Terry!"

He chuckled and swayed in our direction. For a second, I thought he was going to fall flat on his face, but he managed to steady himself. "Gotta go see a man 'bout a dog," he said. Then he staggered off across the lawn in a southerly direction, away from the funeral gathering. As Jayne and I watched with some concern, Terry made his way toward an elaborate marble mausoleum about twenty feet away and disappeared around its far side.

"Do you think he's going to be all right?" Jayne asked.

"I don't know. But I came here to pay my last respects to Benny Hartman, not worry about Terry Parker. The worst that'll happen, I imagine, is that Terry will stretch out on a nice comfortable grave and sleep it off."

"I suppose you're right," Jayne said. "Funny, I never thought of him as someone with a drinking problem."

"It's been a few years since Terry's last film. Semi-retirement is rough on some people."

Jayne put her arm through mine. "Let's *never* retire," she whispered. And then we settled down to hear what the young rabbi was saying. Unfortunately, he was not a great orator and we were far enough back so that we caught only occasional phrases divided by incoherent mumbles: ". . . the gift of humor . . . a man leaves his mark upon the world not by . . . but the love he leaves behind . . ."

What I could decipher sounded sensible and comforting, but it was frustrating to miss so much. After fifteen minutes of straining to hear, my attention was beginning to wander. I began to think of Benny, picturing him in his different guises: clown, warm friend, impossible egotist, great star. I was saying goodbye to him in my own way when I was startled to hear a garbled cry. It seemed to come from the direction of the mausoleum where Terry had disappeared earlier.

"Did you hear that?" I whispered to Jayne.

"Hear what?"

Perhaps I had imagined it. My thoughts were back on Benny a few minutes later when I heard the cry again, this time slightly louder. It was an eerie moan.

"I *did* hear that," Jayne assured me. Without wasting another word, we hurried across the lawn toward the mausoleum where the sound seemed to be coming from—a small marble necropolis, neo-classic in style with miniature columns and an ornate statue, an angel of death, standing guard by the wrought iron gate of the crypt. It was the sort of mausoleum wealthy people used to build fifty years ago to commemorate their dead. As we drew closer, I saw a plaque above the front door: HORACE J. LIVINGSTONE, 1864–1935. I heard the moan again and for a wild moment I toyed with the idea that old Horace was trying to speak to us from his tomb. But then we came around to the far side of the crypt and saw Terry Parker. He was stretched out on the grass, lying in a kind of fetal position on his side, hugging his legs with his arms. I was about to remark to Jayne that it was pretty damned sad to see a man as talented as Parker fallen down drunk, but then I saw that booze was not Terry's immediate problem. There was a kitchen knife protruding from his back.

Jayne and I ran the last few feet and knelt by his side. At first I wasn't certain if he was alive or dead. But then his eyes fluttered, he saw me, and he tried to speak.

"Ham!" he whispered, very faintly but insistently.

"Ham?" I repeated.

Terry was apparently struggling to tell me something important, but he didn't have much strength left.

"Ham," he whispered one last time. But as he said the word, all the breath seemed to wheeze out from his body, like an old tire going flat. He did not inhale again.

chapter 4

The Los Angeles Police Department appeared within minutes. Jayne had been the one to go to the Forest Lawn administration building to make the initial phone call, while I stood guard over the body. At first only four officers and a detective appeared, but when they saw the large gathering of celebrities—most of whom still did not suspect that anything was amiss—they quickly called for a busload of reinforcements. The LAPD has been under a great deal of negative scrutiny the past few years—Rodney King, O.J. Simpson, and all that—but in this instance, at least, they were fast and efficient.

Nearly twenty officers stood in a large ring around the crime scene, forming a perimeter that encircled Benny Hartman's freshly dug grave, the mausoleum of Horace J. Livingstone, and the spot where Terry Parker had been stabbed to death. All of the mourners, Jayne and I included, had been herded inside this circle and told that, for the time being, we were not allowed to leave. There was no place to sit and some of the older visitors were visibly unhappy to be left standing on the lawn. But apparently all of us were suspects—all two hundred or so—and we would be questioned individually before we would be released. I couldn't help thinking that Benny would be furious to find his funeral upstaged by a murder.

As Jayne and I watched, an unmarked police car pulled up and came to a halt behind Gloria Hartman's stretch limo. Two men stepped from the car and walked purposefully across the grass toward Benny's grave. One of the cops, the driver, appeared quite young, in his early thirties, a good-looking man with closely cropped blond hair. The second was older, in his early fifties I guessed, a giant of a man who had the saddest, most morose face I've ever seen. He was dressed in a gray suit and reminded me slightly of Bela Lugosi. From the way the other cops made room for him, I sensed he was the person in charge of our immediate fate.

"Officer, this is really *intolerable!*" Gloria Hartman, the young widow, said in a loud, irate voice to the unhappy-looking giant. Her voice had a certain moneyed, trans-Atlantic lilt, but there was a whiff of the Bronx underneath.

"Are you Mrs. Hartman, ma'am?" the giant asked.

"Indeed I am," she replied unpleasantly. "And I demand that you release us immediately. My husband has just been *buried,* for God's sake—this is a funeral for a *very* important man, in case you haven't noticed. And you simply cannot keep us here a moment longer!"

"I'm awfully sorry for the inconvenience, ma'am. And I want to offer my condolences for your loss and tell you what a fan I've always been of your husband. Nevertheless, a murder's just been committed here so we can't let anyone leave until we've sorted things out. Perhaps in your case, you can wait someplace more comfortable—back in your car—or in the room we're arranging to take over in the main building. It'll just be a few minutes more, if you'll be so good as to bear with us."

The gloomy giant was doing his best to carry out his official duties in a polite manner, but Gloria Hartman was still indignant.

"Do you *know* who these people *are?*" she demanded, gesturing to the crowd of mourners gathered around. "These are some of the most famous people in America! You can't just leave them standing here on the goddamn *lawn!*"

"I recognize all the celebrities, certainly. And as I say, I'm extremely sorry. But ma'am, in a case like this where a crime has been committed . . ."

"What exactly is your name?" the widow asked icily.

"I'm Lieutenant Kripinsky, ma'am."

"Well, Lieutenant Kripinsky, by the time I'm done with you, you're going to be *Private* Kripinsky. Do I make myself clear?"

"Yes, ma'am, perfectly. But as it happens, there *aren't* any privates in the LAPD, so if you're going to demote me, it will have to be down to just plain Officer Kripinsky, I'm afraid. Meanwhile . . ."

"Are you being insolent?" Mrs. Hartman demanded. "Because if you are, I have to tell you that the President of the United States telephoned me this morning to offer his condolences. The President of the United God-damned *States*," she repeated, just in case anyone had forgotten what country we were in. "And do you know what the President is going to say when I inform him how we were treated by some lieutenant from the LAPD?"

I was liking Mrs. Hartman less and less, and so, apparently, was Lieutenant Kripinsky.

"Yes, yes," he interrupted. "I'm sure you can get me fired in a flash. And frankly, ma'am, I'd be grateful if you did, for this is a thankless job, and the money's no good, and it's dangerous as well. But *meanwhile* . . ."

I felt for the gloomy lieutenant, I really did. Not only did he have an angry widow to deal with, but a few hundred other people who were unhappy to be detained. While the lieutenant was doing his best to handle Gloria Hartman, Harvey Roth, the writer-director-star of so many funny movies, came forward with some complaints of his own.

"Look, Lieutenant, I absolutely *must* be at Paramount in half an hour for a production meeting, so I'm afraid you're going to *have* to let me go. You can call my secretary for an appointment, and I'll be glad to meet with you another time—say the week after next?"

"Mr. Roth, I'm sorry . . ."

Unfortunately, Harvey Roth's demands had let loose a floodgate of other irate big shots, each of whom had some urgent thing that he or she had to do. In a moment there were several dozen people gathered around the besieged lieutenant, each clamoring to be heard.

"I'd love to help you, Lieutenant, but Bob Redford is waiting for me at . . ."

". . . I need to be on the set in forty-five *minutes.* In make-up . . ."

". . . I never should have come to this funeral. I *hate* funerals . . ."

"Are you listening? The studio's going to lose two and a half million dollars if I'm not there by three-thirty . . ."

". . . Do you know who I *am*?"

And on and on. A sea of self-important voices, each of whom was accustomed to getting whatever he wanted. Finally, Lieutenant Kripinsky put two fingers into the sides of his mouth and let loose a Bronx whistle that probably could be heard all the way to Beverly Hills.

"Listen up!" he shouted. "I don't like keeping you here any more than you do, but that's the way it is. I'm going to have some of my officers bring folding chairs so you'll be more comfortable, and we'll get on with this as quickly as possible. Anyone doesn't like it, we'll bring him downtown and hold him in a cell as a material witness . . . you got that?"

I was impressed. There was not a murmur from the crowd. The man carried with him a real sense of authority. They got it.

"Okay, now that we've got that straight, who was it that found the body?"

Jayne and I meekly raised our hands.

"Come with me," Kripinsky ordered.

chapter 5

"**L**et me get this straight—the last word out of Terry Parker's mouth was *ham?*"

"You got it, Lieutenant." I assured him.

"You're saying *ham* might have been only the *start* of what he was trying to tell you?" said Lieutenant Kripinsky. "Maybe the prefix of a longer word?"

"Precisely," I told the gloomy giant, who looked even more put-out by my news. "Terry didn't have much strength left. He used up everything he had just to say those three letters."

"So he could have been trying to say *hamburger,* maybe? Or a name, like Hamlisch. Or Hammerstein?"

"I believe so. Yes."

"But he actually said the word twice? And you heard it, too, Mrs. Allen?"

"I did. Steve was a little closer to Terry's mouth, and probably heard the word more clearly than I did. But I heard it, too. It was unmistakable."

Jayne and I and the lieutenant were seated on dark red leather armchairs in an oak-panelled room in the main administration building of Forest Lawn. There were a few tasteful, vaguely nineteenth century paintings on the walls—scenic country lanes, tranquil meadows, languid lakes and such. I had a suspicion the room that Lieutenant Kripinsky had requisitioned was generally used to meet with grieving clients. Everything was soothing, even the muted lighting. In the distance I heard the sound of an organ playing.

We had been going over our brief encounter with Terry Parker for the past half hour. The lieutenant had us repeat our statements twice in chronological order, from the moment Terry spoke into my ear while we were standing waiting for the service to begin, to his final mysterious word. Now the lieutenant was trying to mix us up, asking us to remember different parts of our story in jumbled order, backwards and forwards. If I was the paranoid sort, I would have to say we were getting the third degree.

"Now, Mrs. Allen, when did you first notice the brandy on his breath?"

"It was gin, as I've told you twice already. Really almost as soon as he started talking. Wouldn't you say, Steve?"

"Don't ask your husband, Mrs. Allen. I'm asking you."

"Then yes. When he came up to us at the service. He was obviously a bit pickled."

"Exactly how drunk was he?" the lieutenant threw at me.

"Moderate to very," I replied. "One moment he seemed okay. Then he would say something that was off the wall."

"Would you describe him as upset?"

"That's not quite the word. He was more . . . emphatic. A bit secretive, as if he knew something we didn't."

"And what was it again that he told you just before he staggered off?"

" 'There's more to this than meets the eye.' "

"Interesting! And what do you think he meant?"

"I have no idea."

"And then he said . . ."

" 'I've got to see a man about a dog.' "

"Even more interesting! Was he by any chance *looking* at anybody in the crowd when he made that statement?"

"Not that I was aware of. But it's only an expression, a switch on an old line, from the thirties I think. 'I've got to see a man about a horse.' "

"*Only an expression!*" the lieutenant repeated. "You have to understand, Mr. Allen, that a detective investigating a murder can't take anything for granted. Did you by any chance *notice* a man with a dog anywhere in the crowd?"

"I did not. It's not usual for people to bring pets to a funeral."

"It's not usual for someone to be murdered at a funeral either. What about you, Mrs. Allen?"

"No, I'm sorry. There was no dog anywhere in sight."

"Are you saying that Mr. Parker was the type of individual who might just wander off while a funeral was in progress?"

"It's possible," Jayne told the lieutenant in the regal manner she has when someone is starting to annoy her. "But of course, he was drunk."

Lieutenant Kripinsky, Jayne, and I went around in circles in this manner for quite some time. I suppose there was a purpose to his method; after repeating the same story enough times, you start to doubt the truth of it yourself. Given enough time, you're tempted to confess to anything simply to have the questioning end. I felt sorry for the other mourners who were waiting by Benny's grave to be released. If Kripinsky took this much time with each person in the crowd, they'd be here all night.

"Well, that's it then," the lieutenant said finally, flipping his notebook shut. "Please don't leave town without clearing it with me first. I'll want to talk with you again."

"We're suspects?" Jayne asked.

"Well, *someone* stuck that knife in Mr. Parker's back," he said, almost angrily. But then he sighed and added. "But no, you're not suspects—you're witnesses."

Jayne and I walked from our long interrogation into the gray afternoon. Across the green lawn, we saw that a number of uniformed cops were taking brief statements from our group of mourners and letting people go. The near-third-degree, oddly, had been reserved for Jayne and me alone.

chapter 6

Normally celebrities have nice, quietly tasteful limousines, generally black. Jayne and I, on the other hand, have at our disposal an absurd burgundy-colored Cadillac of uncertain vintage, since it has been mongrelized over the years, taken apart and put together again with new parts countless times. I gave this eccentric vehicle years ago to Jimmy Cassidy, our equally eccentric driver.

"Imagine going to a funeral and finding a dead body!" Cass said in quiet amazement as he drove us down the winding drive from Forest Lawn toward the freeway. "I was starting to get worried about you guys—that lieutenant kept you so long, I thought I might have to go out and scare up bail!"

"He wanted to go over every last detail until I thought I was going to scream!" Jayne told him.

"So who did it, Steve?" Cass asked, glancing at me in his rearview mirror.

"What do you mean, who *did* it? How should I know?"

"Well, you're going to find out, aren't you? I mean, Terry Parker was a very funny man—I've always been a big fan of his, as a matter of fact. It isn't nice that someone should just stab a funny guy like that in the back."

"I agree it isn't nice. But we'll let Bela Lugosi do his job and wish him the best of luck with his investigation."

"How did Dracula get involved with this case? He wasn't even a comedian."

"Sorry. That's my nickname for Lieutenant Kripinsky. The

man wasn't exactly a ray of sunshine, though I have the feeling he's a good cop.''

I happen to be pro-cop, by the way. Every society needs police protection and that's why they all have them. The most dangerous animal on earth is, of course, the human, and if there's somebody trying to invade your house in the middle of the night, with all due respect, I don't think prayer will quite cut it. Don't try to tell the thousands of people who dial 911 daily that we don't need police men and women. They know we do. Needless to say, my admiration for law enforcement troops does not extend to bad cops, the southern sheriff bully-types, the sadists, the racists, and the others who disgrace their badges. But they're the bad apples. We need good apples. They're poorly paid and most of them literally risk their lives daily to protect the rest of us. "Meanwhile," I said to Cass, "we're too busy to get involved in a murder investigation, so we'll happily mind our own business.''

I had that blank sense you get when someone isn't listening to you. Cass, I should say for the record, is a wiry old cowboy who came to Hollywood originally from a ranch in Wyoming, hoping to be a star in Westerns. But his timing was off—he arrived in town just when Westerns had gone out of fashion, so he came to work for me instead. A few years ago, when they started making cowboy films again, I asked Cass if he'd like my help with an introduction to some casting agents I knew. But he said, naw, being a movie star probably just wasn't for him after all. He'd learned that living in Hollywood these many years, seeing a number of real movie stars come and go through our lives. Cass said he figured he was doing fine as he was, and probably Jayne and I would be lost without him—which, in fact, was perfectly true. So he continued to live in the apartment above our garage and make certain we didn't get into too much trouble. Which was very decent of him.

At the moment Cass was studying his side-mirror.

"I don't want to alarm you guys, but I think we're being followed," he said. "There's been a green Landcruiser on our tail ever since we left the cemetery.''

Jayne turned and peered through the rear window. "Oh, yes,

I see it, Cass! What a nice car—but you know, I always wonder why people need a four-wheel drive like that in an overcrowded city like Los Angeles.''

"They're a fad," I said. "But that's not the point. The point is it's probably a completely innocent Landcruiser, minding its own business. Life has enough drama as it is. So let's not pump up the adrenaline unnecessarily by imagining things."

"That Landcruiser's following us, Steve," Cass said grimly.

"How do you know?"

"I feel it in my bones."

"Well, I'm *sure* you must be right, then," Jayne agreed in all innocence. "He feels it in his bones, Steve . . .''

I rolled my eyes in exasperation. But I was patient. "I'll tell you what. We'll run a little experiment and see if we can get to the bottom of this."

"Gee, what sort of experiment?"

"Very simple, Cass. Get off the freeway at the next exit. I'm sure the nice green Landcruiser will go happily on its way."

So Cass got off at the next exit, which wasn't particularly convenient in terms of where we were going—home—but I was willing to put up with mere inconvenience in order to squelch any more talk of being followed. But the Landcruiser took the exit, too, and stayed on our tail.

"You see?" said Cass.

"Could be coincidence," I said. "Why don't you get onto the freeway again, and this time we'll really lose him."

When we returned to the freeway, the Landcruiser was still on our tail. There could no longer be any doubt that we were being followed.

Cass and Jayne were pleased with themselves.

I was now alarmed. There was, after all, a killer on the loose. Whoever had placed that kitchen knife in Terry Parker's back had been close to us at the funeral—so close that he certainly knew Jayne and I had been the ones to discover the body. Perhaps he was worried about how much we had seen or heard, and was anxious to eliminate the threat we might pose. I peered into the rear window, trying to make out who it was in the car behind us, but the daylight was reflecting on his windshield in a way that made it impossible to see who was within.

"Cass, maybe you should speed up a little."

Cass stepped on the gas and the old Cadillac shuddered forward. Our burgundy limo, I'm afraid, is not precisely a Ferrari; it's built for comfort, not for speed. Nevertheless, there was a determined expression on Cass's face as he lurched into the far left lane, got the old girl up to 80 mph, then cut to the right once again, narrowly missing a bakery truck.

Despite Cass's theatrics, when I looked behind us the Land-cruiser was still in place. The green machine had a more powerful engine than our old Caddy.

"Hold on, everybody," Cass said, enjoying himself entirely too much. We were approaching one of those cloverleaf freeway interchanges for which Los Angeles made itself famous in the fifties. Cass had slowed down, thank God, to a slightly more reasonable 70 mph. We were in the second lane from the right, appearing as if we were heading straight. But then at the last moment he cut wildly to the right, put his foot down on the pedal, and took a high-gravity turn onto the exit, sending Jayne into my arms. It would be difficult for me to entirely recount our route from this point; as far as I can make out, we looped-the-loop around the clover, got off one freeway, sped onto another, went one exit south and then did the same thing again. After a while, I wasn't certain in which direction we were headed—San Diego, Santa Monica, or outer space. I was hoping a cop would come along and throw us all in a nice safe jail. But as they always say, cops are never there when you need them.

"We lost the bastard!" Cass crowed.

"You nearly lost me, too," I admitted.

At least Cass has always had a good sense of direction. Some-how we had arrived at the Ventura Freeway and proceeded in a more dignified manner to our normal exit, Sepulveda Boulevard in Encino. Cass left the freeway and we were cruising on the residential streets toward our home when he said abruptly: "Son of a bitch! That guy has some nerve!"

"Which guy is that, Cass?" I inquired. The man has a knack

of making me feel like the straight man in a comedy team. But this turned out not to be so funny.

"The guy who was following us fifteen miles ago. He's there again."

I strained my neck and peered at the road behind us. Sure enough, like a recurring hallucination, the green Landcruiser was once again on our tail. Cass put his foot down hard on the gas and we lurched forward, speeding up one hill and down another, racing through the sleepy residential neighborhood like a roller coaster run amuck. This was not my idea of a good time.

We nearly had a head-on collision with a BMW that was pulling out of the driveway of a house Shirley MacLaine used to live in, and then a too-close encounter with a Volvo station wagon full of kids. I had reached my limit.

"Cass! You're going to get us all killed—slow down and pull over. We'll simply ask the guy in the Landcruiser what he wants."

"Is that a good idea, darling?" Jayne said. "What if it's the killer?"

I did my best to explain, patiently, that the killer wouldn't have anyone left to kill unless Cass changed his pace, but my household is a democracy, and nothing is easy. We continued to discuss the pros and cons while squealing along the streets at a great rate of speed.

Finally Cass said, "Oh-oh!"

"Oh-oh, what?"

"Oh-oh, the green Landcruiser went straight at the last intersection."

"But it was impossible to go straight at the last intersection," I objected. "The road went either right or left."

"That's why I said oh-oh," Cass agreed.

We slowed to a blessed stop and turned around. The intersection to which Cass was referring was a "T." At the top of the "T," we had drifted momentarily in a four-wheel slide, and had then continued to the left. But the Landcruiser had missed the turn entirely and gone straight through a redwood fence into someone's backyard. We parked the limo and jumped out to investigate, following a path of destruction through the fence, a flower bed, and a ripped-up patch of lawn. The Landcruiser was at the bottom of a swimming pool, and when Jayne and I and Cass arrived, we encountered a truly bizarre scene. At the side of the pool stood a very wet Harvey Roth, the writer-director-star.

Harvey is a small individual with fuzzy brown hair who has capitalized on his nebbishy appearance; at the moment he resembled a drowned rat. He didn't particularly notice our arrival because he was having a terrific fight with Melissa Courtney, who was equally wet. Melissa, as you probably know, is the pretty blond actress, the co-star of the last two Harvey Roth films.

"You are an absolute out-of-control maniac!" she was shouting at him, which seemed a reasonable assessment of his character, as far as I could tell.

"I am *not* a maniac," he shouted back. "I am merely obsessive. Which is not the same thing at all. And a person *has* to be obsessive to succeed in the entertainment industry—am I right, Steve, or am I wrong?" he asked, turning my way for a moment. "I wouldn't be where I am today if I wasn't driven to succeed."

"Driven?" she shrieked at him. "Your driving almost got us *killed,* you maniac!"

"You see what I put up with?" Harvey asked, appealing this time to Jayne. "She's supposed to be my *girlfriend,* for God's sake. But listen to her—she sounds like my mother!"

"Ha! If I was your mother, I'd have put you in an orphanage," Melissa shouted at him. "But since I'm your girlfriend, I'll just say adios, Harvey! This is where we part paths, amigo."

"Whoa!" I shouted. "Time out! What the hell is this all about, Harvey? Why were you following us like that?"

For a second I thought he was going to turn his anger on me. But then he did his world-famous shrug, and his equally famous how-can-you-be-mad-at-little-ol'-me smile. He looked cute all of a sudden, but I wasn't buying it.

"Well?" I demanded.

"I only wanted to catch up to you so we could talk," he said sheepishly.

They were both shivering from the wet and cold, and looked so miserable it was hard for me to remain angry. Meanwhile, an alarm was sounding from the nearby house whose backyard had been violated and I did not relish another encounter with the police.

"Well, you'd better come over to our house then," I offered reluctantly. "If I'm not too turned around from that crazy drive, we live just a few blocks away."

chapter 7

Twenty-five minutes later, we were seated comfortably in our living room while Jayne and Cass served hot tea and slices of fruitcake.

I have never understood, by the way, all the recent critical jokes about fruitcakes. As far as I'm concerned, the only accurately negative comment one can make about fruitcakes is that they are fattening, but they are also delicious, substantial, and emotionally satisfying. Those made at home are often true works of culinary art, but even the least desirable commercial versions are fun to eat, especially if served with a glass of cold skim milk or a nice hot cup of tea.

I suspect that anti-fruitcake comments are attributable in part to the herd instinct. There seems to be no fad or trend so inane that it cannot sweep through an entire society, transmitted by word-of-mouth, the idle jokes of television talk show hosts, faxes, and other random forms of communication.

Another example concerns the kind of chicken served at public dinners and other banquets. With rare exceptions it is wonderfully prepared—tender, meaty, and eminently satisfying. Yet ever since essentially unfunny if amiable people like Ronald Reagan began to do lines about the "rubber chicken circuit," some public speakers have been putting down banquet dinner-fare, quite unmindful of the fact that the implied criticisms are simply not deserved.

Harvey and Melissa had taken a shower in one of our guest bathrooms. They were dressed in the thick terrycloth robes we had provided, and their wet clothes were tossing in our dryer. But they still hadn't told me what was going on.

"Okay, now give," I said. "What did you want to talk about?"

Harvey slumped forward, looking miserable.

"I just feel so damn guilty!" he sighed.

"About what?"

"You know. The thing."

"What thing?"

"Harvey feels guilty about a *lot* of things," Melissa offered. "And frankly, he *deserves* to."

"I've been in analysis for twenty years," he sighed. "And I still can't kick the guilt habit."

"Poor Harvey!" Jayne consoled.

"Well, it's my mother's fault," he told Jayne.

"No, Harvey, it's *your* fault," Melissa said.

Getting factual information from Harvey and Melissa with their constant psycho-talk was not easy work. "Let's start this again," I said. "What precise guilt did you want to discuss when you were following us at eighty miles per hour?"

Harvey shook his head. "Now that I'm here, I feel so foolish it's hard to begin."

I could see I was going to have to coax it out of him. "Does it have anything to do with Terry Parker's murder today?" I asked.

He nodded.

"You feel guilty about Terry's murder?"

He nodded again, refusing to look me in the eye.

I took a wild shot. "You feel guilty, perhaps, about Terry's murder because *you* were the one who stabbed him in the back?"

He covered his face with his hands.

"He's always looking for sympathy," Melissa said in a stage whisper. "But don't give it to him, Steve."

"Talk to me, Harvey. *Why* do you feel guilty about Terry?"

"Well, it's *like*—like I killed him," he said at last. "I killed him in my heart. Like Jimmy Carter lusted in his heart."

"You *wished* him dead? Is that it?"

"You're so understanding, man."

"And *why* did you wish him dead, Harvey?"

"Because he was a dirty rat fink with absolutely *no* sense of humor. And not only that, the son of a bitch kept trying to steal scenes from me. We had a big fight about it two days ago on the set."

"On what set?"

"Didn't I tell you? On *Flowers in the City*. It's my new picture."

"You're writing and directing?"

"Yeah. And I'm the star, too. My usual thing, you know. Frankly, I have to do everything myself because I can't trust anyone else to."

"I *beg* your pardon!" Melissa shouted.

"Melissa, calm down, please. Now back to Terry Parker. Tell me about your fight on the set."

"Well, he only had a two-week part, you know. To tell the truth, I only hired him because I felt *sorry* for him. I mean, he hasn't worked in years. So he has his role, he's supposed to play the hero's older brother—*I'm* the hero, naturally. But he won't do a thing I tell him. He keeps trying to insert these dumb sight gags into the story. Tripping over chairs, walking into trees—that sort of thing. I keep telling him, we're striving for *sophisticated* humor, Terry. We're appealing to a hip, urban, well-educated audience. We are *not* trying to be the Three Stooges. But he just doesn't get it. The problem with Terry Parker, you see, is he was just so out of date. So finally I exploded."

"You yelled at him?"

"Yeah. You see, the story's about this out-of-sync guy who spends his life growing flowers in a New York tenement—we're doing the interiors here in L.A., right? Well, the day before yesterday, Terry had this really dumb idea—a sight gag he wanted to pull where a flower pot drops on someone's head. For me it was the last straw, one dumb idea too many, and I guess I kind of exploded. What I said was, 'Terry, if you come up with one more slapstick idea, you might as well drop dead yourself, you son of a bitch, because I'm going to kill you!' So you can see how guilty I feel about it now!"

"He doesn't *really* feel guilty," Melissa said to Jayne and me in her stage whisper. "What he's afraid of is what the cops are going to think!"

"Well, *sure* I'm afraid of what the cops will think! Who wouldn't be?" Harvey agreed unhappily. "I mean, I threaten to kill the guy, and the next day someone sticks a knife into his back! Talk about bad timing!"

"As always, you're only thinking about yourself," Melissa told him—this time, directly.

"What have I done now?" he cried in anguish, turning to her.

"Harvey, a human being has been killed. Can't you forget yourself just long enough to show an ounce of ordinary human compassion?"

"Of course I can! Am I made of stone? I'm grieving . . . but meanwhile, I'm terrified of what I'm going to say to the cops. I mean, I don't *like* cops! They're terrible authority figures—they remind me too much of my father."

"He killed his father," Melissa said to Jayne.

"Yes, well, I *did* kill my father," Harvey admitted. "But that's neither here nor there. The old man dropped dead of a heart attack when I decided to become a comedian rather than a doctor, like he always wanted—*more* guilt in my life, dear God!"

"You had to follow your own path in life," Jayne told him gently. "I'm sure your father would have been proud to see how successful you've become."

"Don't let him off the hook, Jayne," Melissa said. "He broke his father's heart. Literally. The poor guy just keeled over one day."

"You're saying I should have become a doctor? What—a gynecologist? A brain surgeon?" Harvey demanded. "What kind of idiot would come to me to cut his tumor out?"

Harvey and Melissa were starting to give me a headache. I heard the chime of my front doorbell and a moment later Cass came into the room.

"There are two policemen at the front door, Steve."

"Oh, my God! Hide me, Steve—I can't face them!" Harvey cried.

"Harvey," I said firmly, "shut up. Did the cops say what they wanted?"

Cass grinned. "They're looking for information about a Land-cruiser that's sitting at the bottom of a swimming pool a few blocks away."

Harvey begged me to invoke the Fifth Amendment—anything at all, but not to let the cops in. He was just playing the clown, of course. Maybe he thought he was being funny. But as far as I was concerned, he was ready for the hook.

"Show the officers in," I told Cass. Without mercy.

chapter 8

We had planned to take the next day off, a small vacation after working so hard. The morning sky was crisp and eggshell blue and the birds were singing in the trees. I stretched in bed with that luxurious feeling of free time ahead.

"So how are you going to spend your indolent day, dear?" I asked Jayne.

"Indolently," she answered. "Actually, I have an appointment at the beauty parlor at ten, and then I thought I'd wander down to Neiman Marcus. How about you?"

"I'm going to stay at home and read and play the piano. I owe Allan Jay Friedman three new songs for the musical we're doing."

"Really? Then you're not going to do anything about Terry Parker?"

"What's there to do? The police have it under control."

"And what about poor Harvey Roth? Aren't you going to at least telephone and find out if he spent the night in jail?"

"I'm sure poor Harvey, as you call him, is doing just fine. Despite his helplessness routine, this is a guy with a team of lawyers at his beck and call and enough money to buy a new Landcruiser if he can't get the one he already has out of that swimming pool."

"Then you're truly not going to involve yourself in the murder investigation?"

"Truly," I assured her. "Too busy."

So Jayne went to have her nails done while I settled in at the piano. But strangely, I couldn't quite concentrate on the melodies

I was fingering. My mind kept wandering. Finally, I gave in: I picked up the telephone and set up an appointment. Then I buzzed Cass in his apartment above the garage.

"What are you up to?"

"Nothing much. I was about to wash the car," he said.

"Well, leave it dirty. I have a small errand to run."

"Where are we going?"

"The Chateau Marmont Hotel."

The Chateau Marmont is an old fashioned castle-like building overlooking Sunset Boulevard on the Strip, one of Hollywood's landmarks. In the old days, people like Garbo and Dorothy Parker stayed there. Nearly all the rooms have kitchens and it's always been primarily a residential hotel, a place for show business people to spend extended periods of time. John Belushi died here, and as you walk through the languid, Spanish-style lobby, you have a sense that this has been a setting for countless tragedies and dramas, successes and failures, a slice of Hollywood itself, sometimes seedy, sometimes grand.

Cass remained with the limo downstairs as I made my way in the elevator to a penthouse suite on the top floor where Terry Parker had spent the last eight months of his life. He had moved into the Chateau following his most recent divorce—number five, I believe. I had an appointment with Terry's personal secretary, who had introduced himself to me on the telephone only as "Dick." When he answered the buzzer, I found myself facing a preppy-looking young man, late twenties, short blond hair combed to one side. He was dressed in beige slacks and a blue long-sleeved shirt that had a Ralph Lauren Polo logo on the pocket. There were dark shadows beneath his eyes and after I had studied him a moment, I saw the eyes were red, presumably from recent weeping.

"Mr. Allen, please come in." His voice broke for a moment, then he cleared his throat in an effort to hide his emotion. "This has been an awful morning. Just awful. I'm Dick Hamford, by the way."

"Dick *Ham*ford, you say?"

He looked at me, startled. "That's right. Do you know any

other Hamfords? We're quite a large family, actually—from Maryland mostly.''

"No, it's just that the last word out of Terry's mouth was *ham*. That's what I understood, anyway. It's possible he was trying to say something longer but didn't quite have the strength.''

"My God! Do you think he was trying to say my name?''

"I don't know. Can you think of any reason he might?''

The young man shook his head. But he seemed uncomfortable with the thought that the last word out of his employer's mouth might have had something to do with him.

"Maybe he wanted me to do something for him at the last moment . . . but I wasn't there!''

"Were you particularly close with your boss?''

"Not really. I've only worked for him a little over six months. But I liked him. Sure, he was a bit . . . well, I shouldn't say it.''

"A bit of a lush?''

"Well, yes. But he was so talented and basically well-meaning it was hard not to forgive him.''

"He had a kind of little-boy charm, didn't he?'' I suggested.

"Exactly. I don't think Mr. Parker ever entirely grew up. He needed other people to look after him. I tried my best, but I guess I let him down.''

"May I come in, Dick?'' I asked, since we were still in fact standing by the front door.

"Oh, yes! Of course! I'm sorry, Mr. Allen—I'm really a space case today.''

Terry had occupied a large suite facing Sunset Boulevard below, with side windows overlooking the swimming pool on the east side of the hotel. I could see a living room, kitchen, dining area, bar, a half-open door to a bedroom, and a terrace overlooking the street. Everywhere I looked there were cardboard boxes filled with papers and various personal belongings.

"I'm packing up everything,'' Dick told me, following my gaze. "It's damned sad to pack up the belongings of a dead person. I came across his favorite coffee mug, you know . . . and I had to sit down, I was just so overwhelmed. It's hard to believe it's all over.''

"What do you mean exactly, it's all over?" I asked, helping myself to a seat on a white sofa.

Dick sat across from me on a chair. "Well, it was just such a constant adventure, you know, working for a man like Terry Parker. There was never a dull moment. Sometimes I'd get a call in the middle of the night and he'd ask me to pick him up at some bar or party where he'd be too drunk to drive home. I never knew what to expect—sometimes there'd be some horrible moments. But I'll never forget a second of it. I grew up in Baltimore, you understand, far away from anything to do with show business. So it was exciting for me to work for someone like Mr. Parker. Probably now I'll get a dull job working for some bank president. It just won't be the same."

"So you came to work for Terry after his last divorce?"

"That's right. He and Jean split up almost exactly a year ago."

"Did he talk about her?"

Dick shrugged. "Occasionally. Jean was twenty years younger, a stewardess he'd met on a plane flying to Vegas. She took him for quite a bit of money in the settlement, but he didn't bear her any ill will."

"So you'd say it was an amicable divorce?"

"On Mr. Parker's side, sure. He used to say they were just not well-matched, and probably they would never have gotten married in the first place except for one round of martinis too many."

"Was he in touch with her in recent days?"

"No. She got married again, just about a month ago, to somebody in Philadelphia, a lawyer. Mr. Parker sent her a wedding present—I was the one to buy it, as a matter of fact. A nice silver martini shaker. But she didn't bother to respond . . . why are you asking these questions, Mr. Allen?"

"I'm trying to get a sense of Terry's life in the last month or so. Whether he had any particular problems, on-going feuds. That sort of thing."

"You mean, did anyone have a reason to kill him?"

"Exactly."

Dick frowned, deep in thought. Finally he shook his head. "Well, Mr. Parker rubbed some people the wrong way, of course.

There's a guy who lives on the third floor, for example—he has his Mercedes in the parking spot next to Mr. Parker's. A couple of times, Mr. Parker sort of crunched the guy's fender pulling out."

"This happened a *couple* of times, you say?"

"Yeah. It was what you might describe as an on-going situation. Last week, Mr. Parker smashed the guy's right taillight when he was pulling into his spot, coming home late from a party. They had some words about it the next day."

"Strong words?"

"The man telephoned and did a lot of screaming. Mr. Parker offered to buy him a new Mercedes, actually. But the guy shouted he didn't want a new Mercedes, just a parking place as far as possible from Terry Parker! Well, in the end he got his wish—the hotel gave Mr. Parker a new spot all by himself at the far end of the garage, where he couldn't do much damage."

"Very understanding of them," I murmured.

"A place like the Chateau Marmont is used to dealing with some fairly eccentric types."

"I can imagine. Still, a broken taillight doesn't sound like a motive for murder. Can you think of anything else?"

"Mr. Parker had a fistfight with a waiter at Chasen's about two weeks ago," Dick said helpfully.

"Goodness, what about?" I asked.

Dick shrugged. "The waiter refused to serve him another drink."

"Sounds like a wise waiter to me! What about the movie Terry was working on? I've heard there were some problems with Harvey Roth."

"Mr. Parker thought Harvey Roth was a real bastard and used to go out of his way to annoy him. But it wasn't anything too serious."

"What did Terry have against Roth?"

"They just had a different style, that's all. Mr. Parker thought Roth was awfully full of himself, too arty for a comedian. So just to bug him, he'd try to put these really dumb sight gags into his scenes—slipping on banana peels and stuff like that. It drove Roth nuts."

"And you're saying Terry thought up these routines only to annoy Harvey?"

"Right. Terry was a smart man and he had a subtle sense of humor. He liked to play little practical jokes on people. But he wasn't really vicious. Deep down, he didn't have a mean bone in his body."

"Why do you think he drank so much?" I asked—to myself as much as to Dick Hamford.

Dick shook his head in bewilderment. "Stress. Insecurity. I don't know. A guy like Terry Parker just doesn't fit in with the everyday, practical world somehow."

We talked another half an hour or so, but as far as the secretary knew, Terry had no real feuds or problems going, beyond the relatively minor ones he had told me about. I wrote down the name of the man in the hotel with the Mercedes Benz to be on the safe side, but wasn't hopeful it would lead to anything.

Just as I was about to leave, the young secretary frowned and said, "This is probably dumb. I shouldn't even say anything . . ."

"No, please—I'm interested in any small detail you can tell me."

"Well, it's about Mr. Parker's last word, *ham.*"

"Go on."

"It's a funny thing. About a week ago we were talking about the singer, Mama Cass. Do you remember her?"

"Of course. From The Mamas and The Papas. She died in the early seventies, didn't she?"

"That's right. Well, I didn't know too much about them myself—The Mamas and The Papas were before my time. But Mr. Parker was telling me how Mama Cass died—she choked to death on a sandwich. A *ham* sandwich, as a matter of fact. Mr. Parker found that fascinating somehow."

"Did he really? Did he say why?"

"It was because it was such an ordinary, everyday thing— a ham sandwich. You wouldn't think it would kill somebody. I remember he said, 'No one tells you to look out for a ham sandwich, Dick. But if it's your time to die, it can be every bit as lethal as a gun.'"

"And that intrigued him?"

"You bet. He brought it up a few days later, like he'd been thinking it over, how unpredictable death was. How absurd—almost comic, he said. That you could be walking along, or sitting down to lunch . . ."

"Or even attending a funeral," I added.

"Exactly. Just an average moment. Maybe you're spreading mustard on your rye bread, never suspecting it's the last time you'll ever be doing such a casual thing, you're minding your own business, and then out of nowhere, a ham sandwich . . . and you're dead."

"You know," I said again. "I've often thought that one of the most dangerous things in the world is minding your own business."

"What do you mean?" he said.

"Well," I said, "practically every time you hear on the TV news about somebody who was wiped out and they're interviewing a bystander or a friend, he's saying things like, 'Geez, I don't know. The poor guy just got out of his car. He was minding his own business and suddenly—whap! He got struck by lightning or whatever. Or the guy was just coming out of the gymnasium, he was minding his own business and suddenly this golf ball hit him right in the head—' "

chapter 9

"...**O**ut of nowhere, dead! Just like that!" the salesgirl was saying to Jayne about the same time I was finishing up at the Chateau Marmont.

Jayne had wandered down Rodeo Drive, making a leisurely circuit from Elizabeth Arden to Neiman Marcus on Wilshire Boulevard in order to buy a few new frocks. It was awful, of course, to have "nothing to wear," and Jayne was doing her best to remedy the situation, as well as put a major dent in our credit card account—which reminds me of a line I sometimes do when people in my audience ask a question about Jayne. I refer to her near-perfection but explain that she does have a tendency to spend too much money on clothing. "I'll tell you how bad it is. About six months ago somebody stole her American Express credit card and so far I have *not* reported it to the police—because the thief is spending a lot less money than Jayne was. So far I'm about $1800 ahead on the deal."

"But, it's just so hard to believe—a big star like Terry Parker actually getting murdered!" the salesgirl chatted, while pulling out a beige cocktail dress from the rack. She lowered her voice, paving the way for serious gossip: "I used to take care of Mrs. Parker. Wow, was she gorgeous! But I read in a magazine that she used to be a stewardess—can you imagine that?"

"Hmm . . . I like the cut but not the color," said Jayne, discouraging gossip. She held up the dress in front of her body and studied herself in the mirror. "How much is it?"

"Only seventeen ninety-nine," the girl said brightly. Alas, at

Neiman Marcus when they say "seventeen ninety-nine," they do not mean $17.99, but rather $1799.—the decimal point moved two rather crucial points to the right.

"Steve will kill me!" Jayne murmured.

"Oh, but I think it will look *very* flattering on you, Mrs. Allen!" said the horrid salesgirl, hoping to worm her way into my wallet.

(Like a Greek chorus of ancient times, I wish I could chant at this point: "Resist, Jayne! Resist! Do not give into foul temptation!" But Jayne was wavering.)

"I'm not sure . . . let's see what other colors you have."

"I probably shouldn't say this, but she came in here one afternoon about a year ago and spent almost twenty thousand dollars in a few hours!"

"Who, dear?"

"Mrs. Parker. The ex-stewardess. She wanted to put it on her Neiman Marcus card. But you know, even for someone like *that* we have to check with the business office before approving such a large amount. So I called my friend Agnes upstairs and *she* called Mr. Parker at home to get an authorization. You'll never guess what she told me afterwards."

"I'm sorry. I'm not following. Who told you what?"

"It's what *Agnes* told me—my friend in the business office. *After* she phoned Terry Parker. She said it was *obvious* he was sloshed, even though it was only early afternoon!"

"Agnes was sloshed?" Jayne inquired, looking up from the two dresses. She had not been paying strict attention.

"No! Terry Parker was!" said the salesgirl in a dramatic whisper. "The comedian!" she added, for some reason—as though Terry might have a twin brother somewhere, a tragedian who was sober. She went on: "He said to Agnes, 'Let her buy whatever she wants. Hell, she doesn't love me, so she might as well get something out of the marriage.' . . . Don't you think that's an odd thing to say to a stranger over the telephone?"

"Quite sad, really," Jayne said. She looked at the salesgirl more closely: a skinny young woman with a bad complexion and a bird-like nose.

"Go on," said Jayne, paying more attention.

"Well, it's very sad!" the salesgirl whispered. "You see, Mrs.

Parker wasn't alone that day. There was a *man* with her! Very good-looking, and young."

"Here in the store, you mean? Perhaps it was only a friend keeping her company while she shopped."

"Yes? Well, what kind of *friend*, do you suppose, stays with a woman in her dressing room while she tries on different clothes?"

Jayne was liking the young salesgirl less and less. Nevertheless she smiled blandly and said only, "As you get older, my dear, you'll see that there are many different kinds of friendships, and it really isn't our place to judge . . . and now, speaking of dressing rooms, I would like to try on the blue."

But the blue wasn't really blue enough, once it was on. And the amber was . . . well, too pink really, quite hideous. Ten minutes later, the salesgirl was running back and forth from Jayne's dressing room to the showroom, fetching a rainbow assortment of colors and sizes. It isn't so much that my wife is a difficult shopper as the fact that she knows that if she's going to spend a mere "seventeen ninety-nine," the thing had better be right.

Jayne was studying herself in the mirror, deciding what she thought about a color the salesgirl had described as "Rambling Rose," when the dressing room door opened behind her.

"No, it's not really *you*," said a woman's voice. "The wrong choice entirely."

"You think so?"

"Absolutely. You'd be better off in black."

Jayne turned from the mirror and was surprised to see that it was not the salesgirl after all, but Gloria Hartman who had entered her dressing room. Gloria was wearing tight black jeans, high-heeled shoes, and a violet cashmere sweater that was snug enough to leave little to the imagination. Her blond hair tumbled down her shoulders in a sleepy, sensuous manner. Jayne had only seen Gloria once before, at the funeral, and that had been at a distance. Looking at her more closely, it struck Jayne that Gloria wasn't really pretty; there was something rather coarse about her features.

"Gloria! What a surprise!" said Jayne.

"I know we've never actually met, but I recognized your voice when you were talking with that gossipy salesgirl—I was in the next dressing room trying on slacks. I thought I'd say hello."

Jayne smiled. Polite, but not encouraging. Jayne was in a mood to finish shopping and get home.

"Do you mind if I sit down?" Gloria asked. Then, without waiting for an answer, she plopped down on one of the two chairs in the room. "God, I was on my feet forever yesterday. First, that endless service, then the cops, then the reception afterward at my house . . . as a matter of fact, I was disappointed that you and Steve didn't stop by."

"We were planning to, my dear. But that LAPD detective kept us for a very long time. By the time he let us go, we were exhausted."

"Yeah, that Kripinsky was a real pain. I was pissed, I can tell you," Gloria said, "I mean, there I was putting my husband in the ground, a *funeral!*"

Gloria sighed and fumbled for a cigarette in her handbag.

"They won't let you smoke in here," Jayne told her. Firmly.

"No? I guess you're right." The young widow sighed once more and threw the cigarette back into her bag. "All these damned rules drive me crazy! Sometimes it seems like you can't do *anything* anymore."

"This must be a difficult time for you," Jayne said.

"That's for sure! It's bad enough that Benny goes and dies on me—but I was expecting that, of course, what with our difference in ages, and all. But all these lawyers, and the cops yesterday, and people asking all kinds of things. And then Benny's children *hating* me like they do . . . I tell you, Jayne, sometimes I feel like just getting on a plane to St. Tropez and saying screw it all . . . I mean, I'm too *young* to be a widow and take on this kind of responsibility! I deserve a little fun!"

It was quite a speech and defied an easy response. While Jayne sat wondering what she was going to say to Gloria, the salesgirl came back into the dressing room with three new dresses draped over her arm. She stopped in her tracks and said, "Oh!" when she saw that Jayne was not alone.

"What a small world! Can you imagine? I ran into a friend,"

Jayne said breezily to the salesgirl. "You can leave the dresses and come back in five minutes or so. We need to have a little chat."

When they were alone, Jayne arranged the second chair so she could sit next to the widow.

"Now, Gloria, perhaps you should tell me exactly what it is that's bothering you."

"*Everything's* wrong!" the young woman pouted. "I hardly know where to begin!"

"Well, what's this about Benny's children hating you? They're grown up, aren't they?"

"Grown up? They're older than *I* am! Do you know what that's like—to have stepchildren old enough to be your parents?"

"It can't be easy," Jayne agreed.

"They treat me like I'm some kind of golddigger bimbo! And they think it's *my* fault—can you believe it? Like *I'm* getting something out of these damned comedy awards!"

"Ah!" said Jayne. Suddenly she had a better idea why Gloria had come into her dressing room. "You're referring to the million-dollar prize thing?"

"You *bet* I'm referring to the million-dollar prize! I only learned about *that* little shocker last night. From Don Mulberry of Bernstein, Hughes, Mulberry, Mulberry, and Johnson—Benny's attorneys. Don told me about the money after the reception at my house. I said, you gotta be *kidding!* Benny *loved* me—he wouldn't leave me penniless like that. I mean, what kind of joke is *that?*"

"He didn't leave you anything?"

Gloria waved the question aside impatiently. "Just the house in Beverly Hills, and a few stocks worth about one point two mill.—but with inflation and taxes, that's hardly enough for a girl to go to the powder room these days!"

"People *have* been known to live on less," Jayne remarked.

"Well, hooray for them. Personally, I didn't spend the best years of my life on Benny Hartman to be brushed aside like I was dirt." Gloria's mouth was set in an unpleasant sneer. Then she seemed to force herself to put on a softer expression. "You understand, Jayne—don't you? It's not just the money, though I admit it *is* a disappointment to inherit only half of what I was expecting.

It's more the emotional thing, the idea that Benny didn't really care for me like I thought—though I can't believe that. I know there was a lot of talk when Benny and I got married, that he was old enough to be my *great*-grandfather. But you should have seen us together. We were two lovebirds. And that's why I'm positive poor Benny just wasn't in his right mind when he wrote that final codicil to his will, giving away a million bucks like that.''

Ah-ha! thought Jayne, seeing more daylight all the time. "So you're planning to contest the will?''

"Sure, I am! And I'm right, too. He only wrote that change about a month ago, when he was already sick and in the hospital. He was a dying man, Jayne. Probably having hallucinations, even— who knows what crazy thoughts were passing through his mind? That's why I'm hoping you can convince Steve to help me.''

"Help you? But what can Steve do?''

"He's known Benny for ages. Surely he can testify that Benny was confused toward the end, and that no normal person would give away so much money. That's all I'm asking. And it's the truth, too.''

Jayne shook her head. "Well, I'll tell Steve about our conversation, but I don't know if he can help. I think this matter rests between Benny Hartman and his lawyers, and there's not much anyone can do to change it.''

Jayne hadn't promised much, but Gloria took her hand in a gesture of gratitude.

"But you'll try, won't you? You'll speak to Steve? I just *gotta* have that money! Honest, I'm desperate for it—and it is mine, after all.''

"I'll speak to Steve," Jayne said.

chapter 10

"**S**teve, maybe Benny *was* a little crazy to give away so much money," Jayne said. "I don't think so. Eccentric, yes."

We were having a cozy dinner at Chasen's later that night, comfortably ensconced side by side in a red leather booth. I had the grilled salmon, and Jayne the Scampi Provençale—all delicious, but somehow the talk kept returning to two dead people, Benny Hartman and Terry Parker, which spoiled the romantic atmosphere.

"After all, it's not uncommon for rich people to give their money away to various worthy causes," I said after a few more bites. "Andrew Carnegie, Vanderbilt—*they* founded entire universities with their dough."

"Yes, but Benny wasn't *that* rich. What do you think he was worth, Steve?"

"His total estate? No idea."

"Go ahead and guess."

"Okay, just as a game, then. Benny was successful for a good number of years. But he was married a bunch of times, he lived it up, and he earned most of his money back before stars received the huge salaries they get today . . . I'd say if he invested carefully, he was worth ten million."

"Try four and a half million," Jayne said with confidence.

I raised an eyebrow. "That's from the horse's mouth?"

"That's what the salesgirl told me at Neiman Marcus. After Gloria left my dressing room. While I was paying for the little dress I bought . . . it was on sale, sweetheart, so don't frown like that—it was only seventeen ninety-nine."

"That *is* cheap," I admitted, in innocence. "But Jayne—how the hell does a salesgirl know how much money Benny had?"

"Believe me—the salespeople at Neiman Marcus *know* these things," Jayne assured me, a wise look on her face. "You spend enough time in dressing rooms of expensive Beverly Hills shops, you learn what's *really* going on in this town . . . anyway, if you take four point five million as a ballpark figure for Benny's estate, you can see that the million dollars he gave as prize money is a huge percentage of his worth. Once Benny took care of his children, I'm sure there wasn't much left for Gloria. She mentioned the Beverly Hills house and about a million-two in stocks."

"Poor Gloria. Perhaps we can take up a collection for her!"

"Admittedly, she's not going to starve, but I feel a bit sorry for her."

"You do?"

"I'm not saying I *like* her but I *do* see her point. It was a slap in the face for her husband to give away such a large portion of his estate to . . . well, a stranger, basically. I bet Benny's children feel slighted as well."

"So you think I should testify that Benny wasn't in his right mind when he made that bequest?"

Jayne sighed. "Oh, I don't know. Honestly, I wish you hadn't gotten involved in this . . . it's sort of icky, families fighting over money after someone dies."

"I agree entirely. So why don't we talk about something else . . . like what we're going to have for dessert."

Jayne gazed at me with almost sinful lust. "Cheesecake!" she said suggestively.

"Smothered with cherries? . . . Do we dare break our diet?"

"Let's dare," said my wife. "For a single night we'll throw Pritikin to the winds."

So there we were, having a grand old time eating cherry cheesecake, talking about a sea cruise we planned to take to the South Seas—maybe next year, if we could make the time. But then we saw the unmistakable form of Roger Morton walk into the restaurant. Roger is a Brit—one of the English members of our Hollywood community. He's been in California as long as anyone can remember, but he becomes strangely more British with each passing day. Until recently, Roger was Terry Parker's agent.

Roger was with two men I know, a producer and a studio executive. When he saw me and Jayne, I heard him say to his companions: "Look, why don't you order me a whole steer, not too rare—I'm starving. Meanwhile I need to have a chat with the Allens."

Roger headed our way. Jayne and I tried to continue with our cheesecake feast. But it was no good.

"My God! Look who's here! Steve and Jayne Allen!" he bellowed. Roger looks like a character out of Dickens—stout with a florid red face and oversized body shaped like a pear. He dresses elaborately in three-piece suits, sometimes even a bowler hat. "Mmm, what *is* that sinful thing you're eating?" he cried. "Here, you'd better let me taste it for you, make sure it's all right."

Without further ceremony, Roger picked up a coffee spoon from our table and proceeded to attack our cherry cheesecake. He took a huge bite, nearly half of what we had left on the plate.

"Roger!" Jayne cried, more than a little annoyed. "You can't have dessert until you've eaten your main course! Particularly when it's *our* dessert."

"Don't be selfish," he chided. "Anyway, I'm doing you a favor, saving you from caloric overload."

Roger has a certain charm but I've always been annoyed by the volume at which he speaks. In fact, I think I may be the only person in the country to have detected an incipient and, sad to say, fast-growing problem: people talk too loud. The first offender, at least on the public stage, that came to my attention was Robin Leach, the host of "Lifestyles of the Rich and Famous." For reasons that have never been made clear, he literally shouts rather than speaks. Then there's the otherwise amiable football coach who does TV commercials, John Madden. It made sense for him to shout when he was a football coach, but when his mouth is four inches away from a radio or television microphone, the same doesn't hold true. Regis Philbin is another shouter. And, of course, we must mention John McLaughlin, the host of "The McLaughlin Group" in this connection.

In the context of late-night TV shows, David Letterman and

Jay Leno seem to speak at at least three times the volume that sufficed for Jack Paar, Johnny Carson, Merv Griffin, and myself. Perhaps the reason we spoke at a conventional volume is that we were all graduates of radio whereas today's talk show generation came out of comedy clubs where it's sometimes necessary, I suppose, to dominate an audience by sheer volume if not necessarily by talent. Back in the days of vaudeville—the twenties and thirties—before public address systems were introduced into theaters, it was necessary to speak loudly so as to be heard in the last row of the balcony. The puzzle is why so many people are shouting and screaming today when there is no justification for it whatsoever.

"Why don't you sit down, Roger," I suggested sarcastically since in fact he had already begun to squeeze his stout body into our booth. "Can I order you something to eat?"

"No, no, no! Thanks, Steve, but my associates are awaiting. Anyway, food is the *last* thing on my mind," he said dramatically—eyeing the plate of cheesecake. "You can imagine my distress, what? Terry popping off like that! At a funeral, no less! Great God, these colonies *are* a violent land! We don't have quite so many maniacs running about with guns."

"The maniac in question had a kitchen knife, not a gun," I mentioned. "And second—exactly how long have you lived in Los Angeles, Roger?"

"Thirty years!" he said sadly. "Too long. A wonder I haven't taken up surfing, or some equally barbarous pastime."

Roger Morton wasn't quite the clown he pretended to be. He gave me a cunning look. "They tell me you discovered the body, Steve."

"Jayne and I did. Yes."

"And he was still alive when you found him?"

"Barely."

"But he spoke? He actually *said* something before he died?"

"Yes."

"What exactly did Terry say?"

Normally I'm a helpful type, but with someone like Roger Morton, information was like currency—a special Hollywood currency you needed in order to survive. You did not give it away without getting something in return. "Tell me, Roger—you know everything in this town. Who had a reason to see Terry dead?"

"Steve, what a question! Terry was a kind and gentle human being—for Hollywood, almost a saint! We're talking about someone who never hurt a soul . . . except himself. He didn't have an enemy in the world!"

"Yet someone stuck a knife in his back," I reminded.

"It must have been a maniac. A psychopath who happened to be lurking nearby."

"Lurking in Forest Lawn?"

"What better place than a cemetery for a psychopath to lurk?" he asked, lowering his voice. "It's a miracle more people aren't killed at funerals!"

"Come on, Roger—tell me who might have a reason to kill Terry."

"I'm serious, Steve. Sure, Terry drank too much and he rubbed some people the wrong way—we all do—but I can't imagine anyone wanting to kill the poor fellow. He was harmless, really. You know that."

"When I spoke to him a few minutes before he was murdered, he acted as if he had an appointment to meet someone. Do you know anything about that?"

Roger shook his head. "Not a thing. Actually, I hadn't spoken to him since last week, when he fired me."

"Fired you? What for?"

Roger shrugged. "It was a game we played. Generally Terry would fire me three or four times a month, then hire me back with a big show of affection. It was mostly an excuse to hoist a few drinks and get weepy with emotion."

"So you really don't know a thing? I'm disappointed, Roger." Throwing this out was like waving a red flag at a bull; Roger Morton was the sort of Hollywood insider who hated to admit he didn't have the scoop on everything that went on.

"Well, just between you and me, there *is* one individual who's not exactly weeping about Terry's death," he confided, moving closer. "If I were the cops, I'd certainly be interested in the movements of a certain funny fellow by the name of Harvey Roth."

"I know about all that, Roger. Harvey and Terry were feuding about the movie they were working on together—arguing about some sight gag. It doesn't seem such a big deal."

"Oh, I'm not talking about that. I'm talking about—move closer, please, and don't say a word of this to *anyone*. . . I'm talking about . . ." To stretch out the drama, Roger silently mouthed the letters of a name: "M-E-L-I-S-S-A."

"Melissa Courtney?" Jayne asked. "Harvey's girlfriend?"

Roger put a finger to his lips. "Not another word!" he insisted. Then he added, indelicately, "Terry was sleeping with her, of course."

"No," I said.

"I kid you not. Terry Parker was an old scoundrel who had seen better days, but women adored him. They were always trying to save him, or mother him, or foolish things like that. Harvey caught Terry and Melissa going at it in her dressing room one afternoon. There was quite a scene, I understand."

"Who told you about this?"

"Terry, of course. He always bragged about his conquests. Anyway, you asked who might have a reason to wish him dead, and Harvey is the only name that comes to mind. And now it's your turn, Steve—what did Terry say to you before he died?"

"Only a single word. Ham. He said it twice, actually." I explained how Terry was fading quickly and that perhaps he was trying to tell me a longer word or phrase.

"Ham!" Roger repeated with a puzzled expression

Roger sat thinking for so long that I flagged down the waiter, asked for my bill, and put out my credit card. Finally, Roger shook his head.

"Ham!" he said again. "Isn't that the damnedest thing? I draw an absolute blank. Unless, of course . . ."

"Yes?" I prodded.

"Well, there's this. Terry was born in a small town in upstate New York, almost on the Canadian border. Hamburg, New York. He used to speak of it sometimes with nostalgia. Maybe as he lay dying, he saw it again in his mind, the town where he was a child."

"In other words, *ham* was Terry's *Rosebud,"* Jayne suggested.

"Rosebud! Yes, exactly! Just like Orson Welles when he died in *Citizen Kane* . . . maybe Hamburg, New York, was everything

that Terry had run away from. And everything he wanted to return to once again, now that he was dying.''

So we had one more explanation of Terry Parker's final word to go with all the others. Not much of a clue at all—just simple nostalgia for a childhood that would never be found again.

chapter 11

I had a breakfast date the following morning at the Beverly Hills Hotel. After the cheesecake extravaganza at Chasen's, I wasn't in need of more calories. Fortunately "breakfast," in Hollywood parlance, has come to mean an early meeting rather than a meal.

I was getting together with TV producer Jerry Williams and his assistant, Susan Lake, at the Polo Lounge. This would be our first chance to discuss the Benny Hartman Memorial Comedy Awards since our brief phone conversation the day after Benny's death. Jerry stood up and greeted me as I approached the table.

"Hey, Steverino!" he cried, a bit too jolly for eight AM. "How's the kid?"

Jerry was in his early forties, gray-haired, nerdy, but full of energy and even a certain warmth. There were stylish glasses perched on his nose. He shook my hand and introduced me to Susan—straight blond hair, late twenties, with a long, wolfish face.

"I've heard *so* much about you!" she enthused, taking my hand next and pumping so hard I was afraid my arm would become disjointed from the socket. Her voice was nasal with a touch of East Coast money. "You've always been like an absolute *legend* to me!" she said. I could imagine her riding with the hounds in Connecticut in sadistic pursuit of a cuddly fox. I managed to summon a smile and sit down.

The table was inviting. Sunny and crisp with white linen and a vase of freshly cut flowers in the center. A waiter appeared with a silver coffee pot even before I was fully seated.

"Maybe we should order before we get down to business," Jerry suggested. "What are you having, Steve?"

"Just a half-grapefruit and a glass of orange juice."

Susan was having the same, along with a dish of non-fat yoghurt. Jerry was going to stick with coffee. People in Hollywood eat a lot more simply than they used to; except for a few culinary dinosaurs like Roger Morton, gone are the days of Eggs Benedict and pancakes smothered in butter and syrup.

We made precisely five minutes of small talk, mostly about the recent multi-million-dollar renovation of the Beverly Hills Hotel, which is owned by one of the world's richest men, the Sultan of Brunei. Jerry and I both agreed that we had liked the hotel better in the old days, back when it wasn't quite so frenetically fancy, but Susan was too young to know what we were talking about. A few moments of small talk is *de rigueur* at occasions like this, to show that we weren't really obsessive show business types who didn't know how to schmooze and relax. But then, as if a bell had sounded, Jerry smoothly brought the conversation around to the award ceremony, Susan took out a legal pad from her briefcase to take notes, and the meeting was underway.

"So! September 2!" Jerry said, as if it hadn't been on his mind until just that moment. "We got a little less than three and a half months to put together a monster of a show! It's not nearly enough time, but we're all pros here—so what the hell! I feel good about this—what about you, Susan?"

"We're going to blow 'em out of the water!" she said with military enthusiasm.

"With a million-dollar grand prize, how can we lose?" Jerry demanded. This was part of the ritual, too. Revving ourselves up, like bulls pawing the ground before charging the matador. All done to disguise the basic insecurity of show business, the fact that no one has a surefire formula when it comes to the intangibles of entertainment.

"No one's *ever* given away this much money on TV before!" Jerry enthused. "Are you as excited about this show as I am, Steve?"

"Well, to tell the truth . . ."

"I've already gotten most of our sponsors lined up," Jerry

interrupted. His eyes were just about doing the cancan as he mentioned one of the two big cola companies and the second most popular long-distance phone network. "Not only that," he whispered, but *maybe*—it wasn't signed yet, but he was getting *very* positive vibes from the fast-food chain that has sold so many hamburgers that if you could line them all up together, bun by bun, they would stretch to the moon and back.

This was pretty exciting, I suppose. I tried to get in the spirit, but it eluded me.

"Why do I sense an undercurrent here of doubt and negativity?" Jerry said finally, peering into my eyes.

"Jerry, I've had my doubts about this from the beginning. The only reason I'm here, frankly, is that Benny made me promise on his deathbed."

"But why, Steve? *Why* aren't you excited?"

"To begin with, the million-dollar prize seems like overkill to me. It's just too damn much money—it's almost obscene. But I guess I accepted that when I signed on. Mostly at this point, it's hard for me to imagine we can do a quality production in three and a half months. For one, all the top people are going to be booked up. It's not enough notice to get a really talented group together."

"Steve, for us the top people will *un*book their previous engagements—I guarantee it. I keep telling you, this show is going to be huge! There are people out there who'd kill their mother just to get on the air with us!"

"Well, frankly, Jerry, that's another concern I have. I'm going to be very uneasy until the cops find Terry Parker's killer."

Jerry made a gesture with both hands, appealing to the heavens to deal with me. "My God, Steve, do you *like* to worry, or what? Sure, it was a terrible thing, Terry getting killed like that—as a matter of fact, he was a dear, dear friend of mine. But what does his death have to do with our show?"

"Possibly a great deal. Remember, he was murdered at Benny's funeral."

"A coincidence!"

"Was it? The point is, until we know for certain who killed him, and why, we can't ignore any possibilities."

Jerry smiled patiently and decided to humor me. "Okay. So we'll be *very* careful—maybe increase the security around the show—make sure nobody gets within half a mile of Dorothy Chandler Pavilion who's not supposed to be there. Would that make you feel better?"

"A little."

"Great. Now, let's make sure we know who's doing what. Me and my people, we'll take care of the nuts and bolts. Your job, Steve, is to organize the show itself and be the emcee—get all the talent together, the skits, the presenters, the music, and what not. Obviously some of our responsibilities will overlap, so we'll stay in close touch. You're also one of the thirteen judges, right?"

I shook my head. "I can't be both a judge and the emcee. Conflict of interest."

Jerry made another gesture of supplication to the distant heavens. "Steve! You're taking this too seriously! This isn't the Academy Awards! It's a one-shot deal where we'll honor comedy and give away a truckload of statuettes to just about everyone who wants one. What we're going to do, we'll just relax together and have a good time, and do our best not to step on anybody's toes."

"What about the million-dollar prize for the Funniest Person Alive? Don't you think there are going to be a lot of people in the audience, Jerry, who are going to be extremely disappointed if they don't win the big one?"

"Well, sure—we gotta have *something* worth competing for. This will be the climax of the night, of course, and everybody will want the big prize. But giving away statuettes right and left will do a lot to soothe various egos."

"I still can't be a judge."

"But we gotta have thirteen judges! They're all picked—Benny chose them in his will. Critics, writers, professors—a lot of very sharp people. But twelve won't do. We need an odd number to break a possible tie."

"Then pick someone else."

"It's not that easy. Benny had this all worked out very carefully in his will, and we have to do it his way in order to get the money."

"Then I'm out," I said firmly. "I won't be part of any award show that isn't legit. Not even for Benny."

I was about to stand up from the table, but Jerry held onto my arm.

"Whoa! Hold on . . . I'm sure we can work this out with Benny's attorneys. So let's say we get you off the hook and find a thirteenth judge to replace you—you'll just stage the thing and be the emcee. Will that make you happy?"

"Happ*ier,*" I said.

Jerry sighed. And Susan sighed, too. By their standards, I suppose, I was being difficult.

"Okay," he said. "But we have to get a new judge right away. Any suggestions?"

A smile came to my lips. As it happened, I knew a very smart and funny person who had entirely too much time on her hands to spend money in expensive stores.

"How about Jayne?" I suggested.

Oddly enough, I had been a Jayne Meadows fan long before I met and married the lady. She had distinguished herself as a very young actress on Broadway, which led to producer Pandro Berman bringing her out to Hollywood where she delivered a number of dazzling performances in films. Not long ago our friend Carl Reiner called us out of the blue one night to share his excitement at just having seen Jayne's performance in *Lady in the Lake,* a film noted also because it was apparently the first instance where the protagonist, the fictional detective Philip Marlowe, had been represented by the camera so that everything appeared to be seen from his personal point of view. Then there was Jayne's performance in *Enchantment,* Samuel Goldwyn's last big picture in which, although hardly more than a teenager at the time, she played David Niven's mean *older* sister.

I didn't say any of that to Jerry, of course, partly because his slight smile suggested that he saw virtue in my suggestion. Susan, on the other hand, I assumed might not be familiar with Jayne's Broadway and film work. To my surprise she said "Oh, I love what Jayne's been doing on her television show 'High Society.'"

* * *

"I certainly have no objection on principle," Jerry said, "but I have to run right now."

I had been at the point of asking him about his earlier enthusiasm for the involvement of circus stunts, but since we were already into the see-you-later mode, I left the decision about the thirteenth judge on hold.

chapter 12

I walked out of the Polo Lounge, across the lobby, and out the front door of the hotel toward the valet parking area, hardly conscious of my physical surroundings. Nothing about the Benny Hartman Memorial Comedy Awards felt entirely right to me, though I couldn't put my finger on just what was wrong.

As I stood at the curb musing on possible disasters, I noticed an ancient, black '58 Cadillac El Dorado convertible, complete with rocketship fins, arrive under the covered part of the drive in front of the hotel. It was an even more eccentric vehicle than Cass's burgundy-colored limo, and everybody stared—particularly when they saw who was driving. It was Darryl Mann, who used to have a popular TV show in the sixties and didn't look a day older, at least from a distance. He let the valet attendant take his car, then saw me. He did an elaborate double take and stepped my way with his big, trademark toothy smile. A smile that has always reminded me of Bugs Bunny.

"Hey, Steve-o! What a coincidence!" he greeted. "You're just the guy I was hoping to see! Got a minute?"

"Not really, Darryl—there's my driver now, come to pick me up."

Darryl turned and waved at Cass, who had just pulled up to the curb. "How ya doin', Cass? Look, I need to talk with your boss."

Darryl took my arm and led me along a garden path toward the side of the hotel. After we had walked together a few steps, I realized he was using my arm for support. We came to a stone bench, and he sat down wearily. Up close, I could see how old he had become. His complexion was slightly yellow. He gestured for me to sit next to him.

"Just for a moment," I agreed. "Then I do have to run."

"Run!" he said wistfully. "Personally, I can't get around as good as I used to. I had a damned hip operation a few months ago. They put in an artificial joint."

"A lot of people have that operation," I told him.

"Do they? God, I hate getting old!" he said. "You know what I hate about it most? It's not the creaky bones—it's how the young chicks don't even *see* you anymore. You know what I mean? You're over a certain age, it's like they look right through you, like you're a ghost . . . *unless,*" he added with a cunning smile, "unless you happen to be famous. *Then* they do a kind of double take, their pretty little eyes seem to focus. And they say to themselves, oh boy, *that's* Darryl Mann. Or *that's* Steve Allen or Donald Duck. Suddenly you're not invisible anymore."

Darryl was right about that. Exactly when the American people went totally overboard about celebrity I don't know, but they certainly have. There are, God knows, celebrities who deserve their fame and good fortune. They are true achievers with actual accomplishments or talents of which they can boast. To that point the thing makes sense. But now anybody who attracts public attention is immediately considered a celebrity. People begin asking for his autograph or standing next to him to be photographed. It is just one more sign that we're living through a very goofola age.

Darryl agreed and held up two fingers. "There are two things, Steve, that a guy has got to have in America if he wants to get along. He has to be young, or he has to be famous. We all know that youth, good health, is the best deal of all. But since time stands still for no man, personally, I'll take fame."

He was so serious that I didn't laugh.

"How about money?" I suggested playfully.

"A distant third . . . money, even a schmuck can make! But it won't buy you love."

"But you think fame and youth *can?*"

"Absolutely!" he said with an intensity that surprised me.

I smiled and said mildly, "You don't think, then, that maybe being a decent human being has anything to do with it? That maybe loving someone gets you loved in return?"

"Youth or fame!" he insisted. "Either one or the other. And since neither you nor I, Steve, will ever see the right side of thirty-nine again, that leaves just one option . . . am I getting through to you?"

"I'm not sure, Darryl. Maybe you should just tell me what this chat is all about."

"The Benny Hartman Memorial Comedy Awards. That's what we're talking about."

I had guessed as much. "Ah!" I said with a weary sigh.

"I'm hearing rumors, Steve, that *you're* the guy in charge of this thing. Is that true?"

"Only partly. As a favor to Benny. I'm organizing the production itself, but Jerry Williams is producing the TV show around it . . . but let me tell you from the start, Darryl, I have absolutely *nothing* to do with the judging. Anyway, I doubt if the ceremonies will interest you much—the grand prize is only money, a mere million dollars. And since that's a distant third . . ."

"Steve, my friend . . . money, as I said, is of no concern. But the Funniest Person Alive Award—*this,* I admit, has some interest for me. Young women *like* a guy who makes 'em laugh. And the Funniest Person Alive—this will be a guy who will be very, very famous."

"Sure," I said. "For about a week. Until the next award show comes along. I'm surprised you take this so seriously, Darryl."

"I take *nothing* seriously, man. Nevertheless, the Funniest Person Alive is something special. Something they'll put on my tombstone."

"When you're dead," I told him, "you won't be the Funniest Person Alive, Darryl."

"Stop trying to confuse me with facts, babe. I've decided I'm going to win this thing, and that's all there is to it."

"Well, I wish you lots of luck," I told him, standing up. "And now I really must run."

He held onto my arm. "Pal, I just want to ask one little favor—

give me a list of the judges who are going to decide the contest, okay?"

"I can't do it, Darryl. I'm sorry."

"Look, I'm not going to bribe them, for chrissakes. Or apply any strong-arm tactics. I just want to . . . well, lobby them, I guess is the right expression. Send the judges some video tapes of my old show. Just in case anyone's forgotten how I used to have all of America in stitches every Saturday night. You know damned well everybody does this kind of stuff for the Oscars, the Emmys, too—so why not the Bennys?"

I was shaking my head. "You're a legend! Your place in American comedy is secure—you don't need to do this!"

"Don't I? Let me tell you a story, Steve. I have a grandson named Tony, he's eleven years old—he goes to the Hawthorne School in Beverly Hills. You know what happened the other day? He was with a bunch of his friends and he said, 'My grandad is Darryl Mann.' And you know what happened? *Nothing* happened. A big blank. None of those eleven-year-old bastards had ever *heard* of Darryl Mann!"

I shrugged. "Probably they haven't heard of Einstein either. Or Hemingway, or Picasso. So you shouldn't take it so bad."

"But I do, Steve. That's the thing. I take it bad. 'Specially when I know that with just one little award, the Funniest Person Alive, my grandson will be able to hold up his head in school again. It's that easy. So give me a list of the judges."

"Darryl, I can't. My advice to you is forget the eleven-year-olds and relax. This award isn't *that* important. And now, I really do have to go."

I left him and walked back down the path.

"Hey, don't worry about *me!*" he cried out after me. "Hell, I'll just stick my head in the oven and turn on the gas! . . . Maybe *you'll* be a has-been one day too, Steve!"

I suppose I should have laughed. But frankly, the Benny Hartman Comedy Awards were starting to be not even remotely funny.

chapter 13

Jayne was fairly pleasant about finding herself elevated to the position of judge, all things considered.

"But you owe me, darling," she said, eyes smoldering.

"Benny Hartman owes you," I corrected. "From wherever his new address happens to be—and I'm starting to suspect it *isn't* heaven."

Jayne received a phone call later in the day from Jerry Williams to invite her to an initial get-together with the other twelve judges. The meeting was scheduled to be held at Troy Smythe's house in Coldwater Canyon. Troy, of course, is the respected, and feared, film critic for *The Los Angeles Times,* a man whose casual pronouncements have been known to make, or break, a career. When the time came, Jayne dressed for the meeting in a severe gray pantsuit which she thought judge-like.

Finally, Cass drove her to Coldwater Canyon Boulevard, a twisty road which navigates the hump of the Santa Monica Mountains, up from Beverly Hills on one side and down into the San Fernando Valley on the other. The Smythe residence was at nearly the top of the mountain on the Beverly Hills side, on a short, dangerous side road aptly called Cliffhanger Loop. Even Cass slowed to 10 mph while navigating the narrow turns. The inhabitants of West L.A., I should explain, can be divided between two distinct types: hill people and flatlanders. The hill people tend to drive little sports cars and actually seem to enjoy their terrifying roads, where a wrong move can send you and your automobile tumbling down a hillside.

Troy Smythe lived in one of those modern hillside homes built mostly on thin air—hanging precariously on the side of a cliff, and looking as if it might shake loose at the first hint of an earthquake. Jayne was relieved to see that one edge of the house, at least—a few vital feet—actually rested on California ground; the rest of the building was supported by long, metal stilts. She rang the doorbell carefully, hoping not to disturb the delicate balance. A gray-haired man opened the door. He was thin and aristocratic, as Jayne told me later. He had bushy eyebrows knit closely together in a sort of permanent scowl, as though finding fault with everything and everybody around him.

"Yes?" he said, not in a friendly manner.

"I'm Jayne Meadows," said Jayne.

"I recognize you, naturally. But I was expecting your husband."

"Steve *was* going to come," she told him, "but he thought it wasn't appropriate to be producer, emcee, *and* judge. So I got elected."

"Did you now? But do you have any experience in judging things?"

"Don't we all?" Jayne said. "Actually I've always thought that the best judges of actors are other actors, and the same goes for comedians, violinists, and other creative people. But excuse me, Mr. Smythe, I've apparently knocked on the wrong door. I hope you'll find someone who's more qualified."

"Just a minute! Ms. Meadows," he cried, when Jayne turned. "Excuse me if I've seemed rude, but this whole thing has been a nightmare. But please come in. Please . . . we're all just getting acquainted . . ."

Jayne entered the precarious building, into an airy living room that had large windows overlooking an undulating landscape of brown and green hills, eucalyptus trees, and more houses hugging the hills in the near distance. Six of the judges were already seated in a loose circle around the living room, and within the next twenty minutes, four more arrived.

The judges (I think it's best I list them now) were as follows.

Troy Smythe, in all his critical glory. Along with his bushy eyebrows, and a short well-groomed beard, he drove an old MG and smoked a pipe.

Jimmy Preston, film critic of *The New York Times*—Troy's professional rival, an overweight, jolly-looking person. Troy and Jimmy, of course, do a weekly TV show together—"Smythe & Preston"—where they give their opinions of new movies, and by no means always agree.

Donald McCurdy, a large, ponderous-looking man who was a professor at the UCLA film school and the author of a well-respected study of comedy, *What's Funny?*, a book that ran to nearly 500 pages and dissected comedy with such scholarly precision that its readers would possibly never laugh again.

Iris Rainier, the aging screenwriter from the golden days of Hollywood, a thin, white-haired woman who had a merry twinkle in her eye. Iris had written several of the sophisticated, zany comedies of the forties.

Carl Horne, a friendly-looking, balding person—a director of several of the successful comedies of the Rock Hudson/Doris Day era.

David Zephyr, a gaunt man with the fit body of an aging tennis player. David was the popular director of TV sitcoms in the seventies and eighties, but had been in semi-retirement in recent years.

Janet Christianson, a pleasant-looking blond woman who was a critic for *TV Guide* and the author of three books on the history of television.

Graham Madden, the British playwright/director who won critical acclaim a few years back for his play, *Life—Who Needs It?*, which satirized nearly everything. Graham is a lanky individual with large ears, a pointed chin, and a somewhat self-satisfied smirk—as though he was laughing at some joke that only he could understand.

Beverly Nash, an elegant young black woman, very sharp—a TV critic for *Time* magazine.

Marvin Blackstone, the renowned New York drama coach who had a particular reputation for teaching that most intangible of things—comic timing. It was said there were a dozen top movie stars who never accepted a role without discussing it first with Marvin.

Winston Crampton, a languid Southerner, a film critic for *The Atlanta Constitution*.

And last of all, an empty chair for Prof. Harvey Williamson III, from the Yale Drama School, a man who once suggested that there hasn't really been anything notably funny in the dramatic arts since Shakespeare. Prof. Williamson, who rarely left New Haven, had telephoned soon after Jayne arrived to say that he was lost somewhere in Benedict Canyon—one Canyon over from Coldwater—and that if he ever figured out the damnable Los Angeles roads, he would be there eventually. Troy spent ten minutes on the phone giving detailed directions to his house, but fifteen minutes later, when the lost professor still had not arrived, he suggested to the others that they had better begin without him.

It was an eminent-enough group of judges, and Jayne was impressed.

"Let's discuss our basic game plan, shall we?" Troy began. "How we're going to nominate candidates for the various categories, and all that. Benny gave us a good deal of latitude as to how we choose to proceed. The only award we *must* give is to the Funniest Person Alive—and that's the grand million-dollar prize, of course. As for the rest, the so-called Bennys, I've made up a list of categories I'm going to pass around. You'll see how I've divided this up: 'Best Actor in a Television Comedy Series,' 'Best Comic Actress in Films,' 'Best Stand-Up Comedian in a Nightclub Venue,' 'Best Comic Actor in a Theatrical Production' . . . etcetera. I've come up with thirty-three categories in all, and if anyone has any suggestions for some area I missed, we can discuss it. My thought is that it's best to keep the thing simple: each one of us will simply write down our first three choices for each category. We'll tabulate the results and put all the names on a final ballot, and then we'll simply vote for . . ."

"Wait a second," said Jimmy Preston of *The New York Times*, raising his hand. "First of all, if you'll forgive me, I'd like to know, Troy, who exactly it was who put you in charge."

Troy smiled with strained patience. "I'm not in *charge,* Jim. I'm simply offering a few guidelines so we can get started."

"Didn't Benny assign one of us to be in charge?" Carl Horne asked. "A kind of head judge?"

"No. I think that was Benny's little joke. We've got to get along," Troy said.

"We'll, let's get along then," said Iris Rainier, irritably. "I suggest we each spend the next week studying the categories Troy has suggested, as well as various rules of order for us to proceed. I agree with Troy that we should keep this simple. After all, these awards are entirely honorary—it's not as though we were electing the Pope!"

"I'm not sure I agree," said Graham Madden. "With a million-dollar prize at stake, we're going to be under a great deal of scrutiny. There'll be a tremendous hue—and possibly cry as well—if we make a peculiar choice."

Everyone began speaking at once, each with a different idea of how the grand prize should be handled.

"Excuse me," said Jayne modestly, raising her hand.

"Let's listen to Ms. Meadows, shall we?" Donald McCurdy said loudly.

The noise in the room ebbed slightly. "Personally, I think it's absurd," she said, "to allow thirteen people to decide who is the Funniest Person Alive. It can't be done."

"And why not?" Graham Madden asked with a sarcastic smile. "After all, we're a bunch of bloody geniuses!"

"You may be—I don't claim that honor myself," Jayne answered. "But nevertheless, humor is an entirely subjective thing and there's no way for *any* thirteen people to decide definitively what's funny and what isn't. Even for each of us, what makes us laugh changes from day to day. When I'm in a bad mood, the funniest person in the world—if indeed, such a person could be found—wouldn't bring a smile to my face. On other days, when I'm in a giddy mood, some very innocuous comment can put me into stitches."

"So what are you saying? We should just *disband?*"Troy asked her.

There was an out-rush of comments from the twelve would-be judges. Finally Beverly Nash stood up and said loudly: "Shut up, everybody! I want to hear what else Jayne has to say!"

Ms. Nash spoke with such authority that everyone did indeed fall silent.

"Perhaps," said Jayne," we should open up the voting to the general public—at least for the Funniest Person Alive award. It would be ridiculous, as I say, for any thirteen people . . ."

"A general election is impossible to organize," Troy said flatly. "Not with the amount of time we have."

"Another problem-factor," Donald McCurdy added, "is that as soon as you let the public into it you run the risk of having them vote not on the important factor of funniness, but popularity. Whoever is hot this year could easily win and then two or three years down the line be out of the business altogether."

Graham Madden, the Britisher, said, "I quite agree. The history of comedy is studded with examples of men—and women, too."

"Then let's at least open the voting to the show business community," Jayne insisted. "Surely there's time to put the question of who is the Funniest Person Alive to the members of—the Academy, the Screen Writers Guild, Screen Actors, Equity, etc."

In the midst of a chaotic twelve-way discussion, something extraordinary occurred: an automobile appeared briefly in the living room window, where no automobile should be. Apparently it had crashed through a guardrail on Cliffhanger Loop. As Jayne and the other judges watched in horror, the car tumbled a hundred feet down a steep embankment, crashed headfirst into a large eucalyptus tree, and burst into flames.

The police, fire trucks, and an ambulance were on the scene within minutes after Troy phoned 911. Unfortunately, the driver of the car was dead by the time they arrived. It was Professor Harvey Williamson III, lately of the Yale Drama School.

It seemed that thirteen was an unlucky number, even for judges.

chapter 14

Cliffhanger Loop was as crowded with emergency vehicles as a narrow hillside road could be. There were two cars, an ambulance, a tow truck, and two fire trucks, all with their red and blue emergency lights revolving, sending out crazy patterns of colored light against the canyon landscape. The twelve remaining judges stood watching the proceedings on the road outside Troy Smythe's home, along with two neighborhood kids on bicycles.

Fortunately, there was an eyewitness to the tragedy: Jimmy Cassidy. Jayne stood next to Cass as he narrated what had happened to a uniformed cop. Just when he was wrapping up his account, a new official appeared and Cass had to start all over again. The newcomer was Lieutenant Kripinsky of the LAPD, the tall, gloomy man we had last seen at Forest Lawn.

"Okay, here's what happened," Cass told him. Fortunately, Cass is a born storyteller, and he welcomed the opportunity to elaborate on the tale—as if the first time through had been only a rehearsal: "I was stretched out in the front seat of the limo, reading a book and waiting for Mrs. Allen to appear . . ."

"You were completely awake?"

"Of course. I was reading a Zane Grey western. As a matter of fact, I was at a good part of the story, just where the hero's been bitten by a rattlesnake and he has to fight off these three brothers who are trying to kill him . . ."

"Mr. Cassidy, I don't actually need the plot of the novel."

"Okay, and then I saw this car coming along the street. A late-model Chevy. But there was nowhere to park because there were already a bunch of cars in every available spot outside the Smythe house. As you can see, the road's pretty narrow here.''

"You assumed the Chevy was coming to visit the Smythe house?''

"That's what it looked like, yeah. I glanced up because the guy in the car was obviously not accustomed to these hillside roads and he seemed to be having trouble. He went past the Smythe place, then spent about five minutes turning around, an inch at a time, in the next driveway. When he came back my way, I saw he was sweating and looked pretty stressed-out. When he saw me, he rolled down his window and asked if I knew anyplace to park. I said he should continue up the road about fifty feet—there was a wider spot around the next curve and maybe he could park there. He shook his head and said, 'I'm from New Haven. We don't have roads like this back East.' ''

" 'I'm from New Haven.' That's what he said?''

"Yeah. Then he said, 'I suffer from acrophobia. I have a terrible fear of heights.' I felt pretty bad for him and said he shouldn't be driving around in the Hollywood Hills if he didn't like heights. He said, 'Believe me, if I ever get back to Connecticut alive, I will *never* set foot in Los Angeles again!' Kinda sad, when you think about it. Anyway, that's when I offered to let him have my parking spot.''

"That was very nice of you," the lieutenant said, but there was a note of suspicion in his voice.

"Well, why not? I said I'd park around the next bend, and I asked him to tell Mrs. Allen where I was so she could find me when she was ready to leave. And that's when the accident occurred.''

"Describe it for me.''

"Well, it happened awfully darn quick. Out of the blue. He thanked me and then said he'd back up to let me out. He put his Chevy in reverse and backed up maybe five, six feet—just so his taillights were almost touching the guardrail there by Mr. Smythe's driveway. I called out the window that he shouldn't go back any further because there was a cliff behind him. He said, 'Oh, my God! A cliff! Maybe I should pull forward a few feet.' I could tell he was really spooked, poor guy.''

"He sounded frightened?"

"You bet. The next thing I saw, he stepped on the gas—but he just went the wrong way. He meant to go forward, but the car was still in reverse. He seemed to panic. He gunned the damn thing when he should have put on his brake. So that's how it happened. He went backwards through the guardrail, and over the cliff. It was awful."

The lieutenant looked skeptical. "That was a metal guardrail he went through. It should have stopped him."

"Well, it probably would have, except, as I told you, he was freaked out. He stepped on the gas hard. Probably floored the damn thing, thinking it was the brake. I could hear his wheels layin' some rubber before he broke through."

"Mr. Cassidy, in your opinion, could it have been . . . suicide?" the detective asked unexpectedly.

Cass shook his head. "No, I don't think so. The way it looked to me, the poor guy's acrophobia was actin' up so bad, he didn't know if he was comin' or goin'. When I told him he was close to a cliff, he just panicked and did the wrong thing . . . I feel kinda responsible, actually. Maybe I shouldn't have tried to give him my parking spot."

"You're saying it was your fault?"

"Cass was merely trying to do a kind deed, Lieutenant," said Jayne quickly, entering the conversation on Cass's behalf. "Obviously this was nobody's fault—only a tragic accident. When people are frightened, they can often panic and do the wrong thing."

Lieutenant Kripinsky moved his gaze from Cass to Jayne, as if he had just noticed her presence and it disturbed him in some way to find her there.

"Mrs. Allen, please come with me a moment," he said irritably.

The lieutenant led the way to the far end of a patrol car, where they were out of earshot of the various officials and spectators. Jayne was bewildered but had no choice but to follow.

"I want to ask you a question about the funeral the other day. When you discovered Terry Parker's body, did you get a good look at the knife that was in his back?"

"Not a very good look. But I saw it, of course."

"Did you recognize the knife?"

"No. It looked like an average kitchen knife, like thousands of others."

"It's what's usually called a chef's knife," the lieutenant continued. "It was ten inches long, with a teak handle. Do you still claim you haven't seen this knife before?"

Jayne shook her head, more bewildered than ever. "As far as I know, never. I don't believe Steve and I have anything like it in our kitchen."

Lieutenant Kripinsky smiled. "The Mug and Barrel," he said mysteriously. "Does that name mean anything to you?"

Again Jayne shook her head. "Is it a pub?"

"No, it's an expensive kitchen shop on Madison Avenue in New York, at East 63rd Street. It's where you and Mr. Allen bought a set of knives twelve years ago. Knives with teak handles . . . are you beginning to remember now, Mrs. Allen?"

Jayne *was* retrieving a faint memory now. But it was a bit like a car radio late at night on the highway when you are miles out of town—faint and far away.

"You know, I *do* remember that store now. Yes, the Mug and Barrel. They have lovely things . . . oh!" Jayne said, as the memory began to come in more clearly. "I had forgotten, it was so long ago. But yes, we *did* buy a set of expensive knives there years ago. It was a present for someone, but I can't remember who."

"Try, Mrs. Allen. Try to remember who you gave those knives to."

"My God, they were for Benny Hartman!"

Kripinsky nodded sagely. "Exactly," he said. "Go on, ma'am."

"There's not much more to go on about! They were a birthday present for Benny back when his wife Gladys was still alive! . . . Are you telling me that one of those knives was the murder weapon?"

"Curious coincidence, isn't it? You and your husband discovered the body, and you were also the ones who originally purchased the murder weapon."

"Lieutenant, do you really suppose that when Steve and I gave those knives to Benny twelve years ago, we were planning a murder in the distant future? How in the world did you ever find out about that birthday present anyway? It was so long ago, I'd forgotten it entirely myself!''

Lieutenant Kripinsky allowed himself a small smile. ''It wasn't very difficult. The knife was hand-forged and quite special—not an average kitchen tool at all. It had the name of its British manufacturer and a serial number stamped in very small letters near the handle. A phone call to the maker in England gave us the name of the few specialty stores in the United States which sold its product. The rest was easy. Fortunately, the Mug and Barrel keeps good records of their customers.''

''Imagine that!'' Jayne said thoughtfully. ''The murder weapon! I presume you've asked Gloria Hartman about those knives?''

''Of course. She says the entire set was stolen during a burglary at her house six months ago. Quite convenient for her, I should say.''

''Did she report them stolen at the time?''

The lieutenant nodded unhappily. ''Her husband did, apparently. The Beverly Hills Police Department took the call and made out the incident report. An intruder broke in through a window and took a number of things—some jewelry, a stereo, a fur coat. And, oddly enough, the knives.''

''I'm surprised the Hartmans didn't have some sort of electronic security system like most people in Beverly Hills these days.''

''Oh, they have a system, all right. But like a lot of people, they often forget to turn it on.''

''How curious!'' said Jayne. ''Well, I suppose you only have to find the burglar and you'll know who killed Terry Parker.''

''Oh, we'll find him,'' the lieutenant said, narrowing his eyes at Jayne. ''Or her.''

One of the officers called Lieutenant Kripinsky away, leaving Jayne to her thoughts. A tow truck had finally succeeded in getting a line down to the crashed car, and with a loud wrenching of cable, it began to haul the Chevrolet back to the road. Jayne rejoined Cass and together they watched in silence as the death machine was raised slowly back through the shredded guardrail. The body had already been removed by the firemen, but there was blood on the cracked windshield, making for a gruesome sight.

"It wasn't your fault, Cass," Jayne said gently, watching Cass's stricken face.

"There's something pretty terrible about dying in the way you're most frightened of," Cass remarked somberly. He was pale.

"Let's go home," Jayne told him. "And drive slowly, please, around the curves."

chapter 15

News travels fast in Hollywood. The following day, a small army of UPS trucks, FedEx vans, and special delivery messengers showed up at our house with parcels addressed to Jayne. When she tore off the wrapping, she discovered a variety of press kits, all of them touting the talents of different comedians. Some of the offerings were modest, little more than recent press clippings stuffed into an envelope; others were quite extravagant, complete with photographs, posters, cassette tapes, you name it. Most came from professional publicists, but a few had been sent directly from the artists themselves, along with a handwritten note asking Jayne to keep them in mind when it came to voting for the Funniest Person Alive.

Minnow Weinstein, the African-American star, sent a video of her new movie—which was a treat, because the film wasn't even in the theaters yet. Django Roberts sent an invitation for an all-expenses-paid trip for two to see his new show at Caesars Palace in Vegas, airfare included. Cricket Johnson—it seems odd names are "in"—enclosed an invitation to a private showing of his three last films at the Bruin Theater in Westwood, with a champagne reception afterward at his house. Somehow the names of the judges had been mentioned in Army Archerd's column in *Variety* and everybody was lobbying hard so that their talents would not be forgotten.

"This is getting to be a problem," I growled, after tripping over a basket of fruit by the front door that had been sent over by a new comedian we had never even heard of. "We're going to need a dump truck to haul all this stuff away!"

As far as I was concerned, the Benny Hartman Memorial Comedy Awards were becoming a real annoyance. I spent the day on the telephone trying to line up a wide assortment of friends and colleagues to act as celebrity presenters of the statuettes. Then I talked with musicians, dancers, choreographers, scenic designers, and singers until I was tired of it. The worst of it was that I knew I'd be doing this every day for the next three months.

"Why did Benny do this to me?" I complained at dinner.

"Because you were his friend," Jayne suggested.

"Some friend," I mumbled. "And I wish we hadn't given him those damned kitchen knives that time . . . remind me in the future *never* to give another birthday present!"

"Darling, be reasonable—there was no way of knowing one of the knives would end up in someone's back. Anyway, look on the bright side—at least we know where the murder weapon came from."

"Yes. But I only wish it hadn't come from *us!*" I grouched. "By the way, how many knives were there in that set?"

"Four, I believe, of different shapes and sizes. If I remember, the set came with a tempering steel and a wooden box to keep them in."

"So there are three knives still missing! That's a cheerful thought, isn't it?"

"Perhaps Gloria faked the burglary to collect insurance money on her furs and jewelry. Maybe *she* was the one who stabbed Terry."

"Darling, Gloria Hartman was standing by her husband's coffin at the time of the murder. And besides, what possible motive could she have for killing Terry?"

"I'm only trying to be helpful, Steve."

I was in a lousy mood, I suppose, but my life hardly seemed my own anymore, thanks to Benny. The death of Prof. Williamson was apparently a freak accident, but it added to my sense that the comedy awards were somehow ill-fated. I spent most of the evening making yet more phone calls about the show, and glowering every time I heard the front doorbell ring with yet another special delivery gift for Jayne. I was glad finally when bedtime came and I could stretch out and forget funny people for a few hours. But the damned show even followed me in my sleep. I dreamed that a life-sized "Benny" was chasing me around a vast auditorium. At first it seemed harmless enough, almost a game. But then the statuette turned into Benny Hartman himself, back from the grave—a grim, wraith-like figure. He was carrying three knives of different shapes and sizes—the missing knives from the set we had given him—and I knew that if he caught me I was dead. I ran with that terrible dream-sense that I was on a treadmill and going nowhere fast.

I woke with my heart pounding. But there was worse to come: something had awakened me, a soft noise in the room, though I wasn't certain what it was. I had a decidedly uncomfortable feeling that Jayne and I were not alone in the darkness.

After a moment, I heard the sound again—the soft pad of a cautious footstep somewhere near the foot of my bed. I was terrified but did my best to continue breathing deeply, faking the regular rhythm of sleep, even adding a few soft snoring sounds.

Our home, I should mention, had been invaded, burglarized, on three earlier occasions, even though we live in what would be described as an upscale neighborhood and are protected, to a degree, by the Westec security service. In only one of the instances was any property stolen and that was almost certainly an inside job involving a young woman who worked for us at the time and who knew we were out of town. For quite some time thereafter I kept a small baseball bat handy for protective purposes. Eventually somebody stole it. The Winchester people had presented me with a gift of a 22-caliber rifle but I never fired a shot with it in anger, as we say, and it too was eventually stolen, almost certainly by another employee.

Jayne, bless her heart, was sleeping blissfully at my side. I don't ever remember feeling quite so vulnerable or alone. My mind struggled to form a plan—any plan at all to save us. Was there a weapon I could use? A chair? A lamp? None of these items filled me with much optimism, particularly if the intruder had a gun. I lay in bed straining every nerve to hear. I was starting to think I had imagined the sound—or dreamed it somehow—when it came again. The footsteps were moving very quietly closer toward the bed.

I came up with a vague plan, born of desperation. I would let the footsteps approach nearer, as close as possible, and then spring upon the figure at the last moment. It wasn't much of a plan, but I couldn't think of anything else. At least if the intruder believed I was asleep, I'd have the element of surprise.

Closer . . . closer . . . one footstep after another. The hairs on the back of my neck were sticking up like fur on a frightened cat. I waited as long as I dared, until I thought I could hear the stranger's breathing almost directly over my head.

Then I sprang.

"Yeoww!" I roared, like a jungle beast, attacking with every ounce of strength I possessed.

To my surprise, Jayne sprang a moment after I did—she had not been asleep after all. The intruder was a large, dark shadow of a man. I got him around the waist and tried to push him backward onto the floor. Jayne pulled his hair and boxed his ears. The man bellowed in pain and carried us with him into the center of the room.

We all wrestled and swore and grunted and punched and kicked. It was not an elegant battle. Somehow Jayne got hold of a bedside clock and managed to smash it over the man's head. He was strong, but getting hit on the head disoriented him enough so that we managed to wrestle him to the floor. Then Jayne used the electric cord from the lamp to tie up his feet while I sat on his chest to keep him from getting free.

"All right!" the man cried finally. "I give up already! You people are maniacs!"

Jayne switched on the light and we had the first look at our intruder. He appeared to be in his mid-thirties, overweight, unshaved, with long, greasy hair. He was dressed in jeans and a ratty old sweatshirt. To be safe, I remained sitting on his chest

"Call 911," I told Jayne. I was out of breath, and saw my hand was bleeding from a small cut.

"Wait a minute. Let me explain!" the man said.

"Explain what? You've come to burglarize our house and you can tell your story to the cops."

"I'm not a burglar, for chrissakes . . . I don't even have a gun."

"Don't trust him, Steve!" Jayne warned. She had the portable telephone in hand, ready to smash it over his head if he showed any inclination to restart our wrestling match.

"Let's hear him out," I said to Jayne. "Okay, explain and do it fast," I told the guy.

"Well, get off my chest so I can breathe!"

"Not a chance. You're breathing just fine. Now, how did you get in here?"

"Easy. I climbed up a tree and forced open a bedroom window."

"How did you know which was our bedroom window?"

"I was watching from across the street when you went to bed. I waited until you turned off the light."

"A Peeping Tom as well as a burglar!" Jayne cried. She was not amused.

"I'm *not* a Peeping Tom. And I'm not a burglar either . . . I just work for a guy who . . . well, wanted me to deliver a message."

"A message, huh? What is it?"

"I could deliver it better if we changed positions."

"I'll bet you could!"

"I was going to scare you a little, but I wasn't going to hurt anyone. Anyway, my message wasn't for you—it was for the missus."

"Ah!" I said. The light was dawning. And it wasn't a very pleasant light, either. "Somehow I think I know what this is all about!"

"I was supposed to tell Mrs. Allen that she'd better vote for a certain someone in this comedy award thing. Or else."

"Or else what?"

"I was going to leave that to your imagination. The idea was to let you know I could get to you any time I wanted—creep into your bedroom, even—if you didn't vote the way you were told."

"Now comes the million-dollar question. *Who* sent you?"

"A guy. I don't know his name."

"I don't believe you."

"It's true. It was just a stranger. He knew where to find me, and he gave me five hundred bucks to do the job. I'd never seen him before."

"All right, I'll pretend I believe you for the time being. Now let's hear who my wife was supposed to vote for."

"Billy D'Amato," said the man sullenly.

Jayne and I looked at each other in disbelief. Billy D'Amato was a very funny and talented individual, a short, round comedian who ten years ago had used a small part in a TV sitcom as a vehicle to catapult his way to film stardom. I had never met him in person, but it was difficult to believe he would stoop to something like this. After all, he was incredibly successful—why would he bother?

"You're certain this was the message. A man you never met paid you to terrorize us and tell my wife she should vote for Billy D'Amato—or else?"

"That's it, swear to God. I mean, nothing personal against you folks—but five hundred bucks is a lot of bread for a cat like me, if you can dig what I'm saying. I got a kid to support, and two ex-wives."

"Get a job," I said sourly.

Even someone who breaks into your bedroom can become more human, once you listen to him talk. I had relaxed a little, and wasn't bearing down upon his chest with quite the same angry intent as I had done at first. So I wasn't prepared when the man lurched furiously and threw me off, the way a bucking bronco might shed his rider. Jayne was quick. She swung our phone down on his head, but he was able to deflect the blow with an arm. Before we could do anything more, he was out the window from whence he had arrived, and was climbing, half-falling, down the tree—an old maple. Jayne and I watched helplessly from our second-story window as the man hobbled down our driveway and disappeared into the dark residential street.

"Should I call the police?" Jayne asked.

"Why bother? By the time they arrive, he'll be long gone. And I don't relish the idea of filling out yet another police report."

"But, Steve—that was a terrifying experience. We can't just let him get away with it!"

"Believe me, I don't plan to," I assured her.

I'm a mild-mannered fellow and it takes a lot to get me riled. But I had reached my limit.

chapter 16

Hollywood celebrities guard their private phone numbers carefully, but I was able to get Billy D'Amato's without too much trouble. In the morning, I phoned my agent, who in turn made a call to Mr. D'Amato's agent, who quickly called us back with his client's home number and address to boot. None of us had mentioned the Benny Hartman Memorial Awards, but everyone knew that Jayne and I were involved. It was astonishing how important people were suddenly eager to accommodate our slightest wish.

"Hey! If it isn't Steve Allen!" said Billy in a surprisingly friendly manner when I reached him over the telephone. "You know, I've always wanted to meet you. I used to watch your show all the time. Funny stuff! And yours was the show that featured jazz!"

"Hmm," I hummed with displeasure. "Wish I could return the compliment, Mr. D'Amato, but not after last night—"

"I don't quite follow."

"Cut the crap. You know what I'm talking about. Fortunately, the guy you sent over to frighten us got a dose of his own medicine—he told us everything."

"Wait wait wait wait *wait,*" Billy said quickly. "You'd better start from the beginning, tell me everything that happened. Someone's got to be trying to frame me for something I didn't do."

There was indeed an honest quality about Billy D'Amato's denial that made me pause. Even last night, I had had trouble believing he would pull such a stupid stunt. So I gave him the benefit of the doubt and described how Jayne and I had awakened in the middle of the night, and the story the intruder had told before he had disappeared out our bedroom window into the night.

"Incredible!" Billy said when I had finished.

"You didn't pay to have this done?"

"Steve! I swear on my children! You think I'd give some jerk *five hundred dollars?* Everyone knows I'm cheap . . . and besides, I've got a shot to win this award without needing to strong-arm the judges. So why should I bother?"

I was thinking hard. Billy D'Amato would indeed be a contender for the Funniest Person Alive. On the final list, at the very least. So why should he risk alienating one of the judges? Was it possible that someone had given five hundred dollars to a young thug to spoil, rather than help, Billy's chances?

His mind was working along similar lines.

"Look, someone's doing a number on me, and I don't like it," he said. "Sure, I've been tough at times during my career— I come from a rough neighborhood. But I'd never pull a thing like this. Particularly for some dumb award that I don't even care about that much in the first place!"

"This particular dumb award has a million dollars attached," I pressed, not entirely ready to let him off the hook.

"I already *have* a million dollars, Steve. Quite a few million, as a matter of fact. Look, why don't you come over to my place this morning and we'll talk about it. This bothers me a lot and I want to get to the bottom of it as much as you do."

"I'll be over in an hour," I agreed.

Billy gave me his address in Brentwood. About an hour later, Cass and I pulled up in front of an impressive colonial-style mansion off Sunset Boulevard that could have been a set from *Gone With the Wind.* There was a wide sweep of green lawn and white columns holding up the facade; all it needed was Scarlett on the front porch. Cass parked near the front door and I hurried up the red-brick path and rang the doorbell. From deep inside the house I heard a door chime play the opening bar of the old Beatles tune, "Help, I need somebody." It seemed as good a way as any to summon the people of the house, but nobody answered. I rang again and waited, and still there was no answer. Since I had just spoken to Billy on the phone, this seemed strange. After my third attempt, I walked to the side of the front door and peered into the living room window. What I saw made my heart lurch. The room looked as if a hurricane had come through. A white settee was knocked over, a lamp shattered, and a coffee table turned upside down, spilling a vase of long-stemmed roses on the carpet.

"Cass! Come here!"

Cass heard the urgency in my voice and came bounding out of the car. He stood next to me and peered into the window.

"This place is a mess! Looks like something bad happened here, man. No one answered the doorbell?"

"No," I said. "I think we need to have a look around. See if you can jimmy the lock."

Cass set to work on the front door with his Swiss Army knife, but after five minutes we were still very much on the outside.

"This is a good lock, Steve. I'm not getting anyplace with it."

"Let's go through the window then."

"Smash it open?"

"You bet! I don't like the looks of this at all!"

Cass got a tire iron from the trunk of the car, wrapped his windbreaker around his arm to protect himself from flying glass, then smashed his way through the window.

"Careful!" I told him, belatedly.

"Piece of cake," he muttered, knocking some jagged edges aside and stepping through. Cass went around quickly to the front door and I entered in a more traditional fashion.

"Hello! Anybody home?" I cried. I felt silly about it—if Billy hadn't heard us by now, it was doubtful my hello would do any good. We glanced at the wreckage in the living room, then moved quickly through the dining room into the kitchen. Everywhere we looked, tables and chairs had been overturned by some destructive hand. In the kitchen, pots and pans and canned goods had been scattered across the floor. But among all this wreckage, there was no sign of Billy—or any other person, either.

"Let's try upstairs," I suggested.

Mounting a broad, curving staircase to the second floor, we found four bedrooms, a master suite, a home office, and a small gym with exercise equipment and weights. Everything was neat and in good order in the upper part of the house, but there was no sign of life. The silence was beginning to feel unnatural.

"Hey, look, Steve! Someone's swimming in the pool."

"That's odd!" I peered through a window from the master bedroom down onto the large swimming pool in the backyard. There was indeed a figure in the pool, but something seemed wrong about it. Cass's eyesight is worse even than mine, so he wasn't the one to ask. I adjusted my glasses, squinted a little, and soon realized what it was about the figure that was not right. The person was fully dressed and floating facedown.

"Come on!" I cried, rushing down the grand staircase and moving quickly through a patio into the backyard. Cass and I jumped into the pool and pulled a limp form up the steps to the dry cement. It was Billy D'Amato and there was no need to try mouth-to-mouth resuscitation, for a kitchen knife was protruding at an ugly angle from his back. The poor man was very dead. I forced myself to examine the knife itself. It had a teak handle.

Cass and I were staring at the body when we were startled by the sound of a scream, a high-pitched shriek from a dozen feet away. Our nerves were shot anyway, and this was the last straw. Cass and I were so frightened we yelped right back.

The new arrival was a small, redheaded woman who was standing at the edge of the lawn. She was quite young and probably attractive when her mouth was not wide open and her eyes nearly bulging from her head. For a moment or two, she screamed at us, and we shrieked at her. It sounds funny now, but at the time we were all in a state of shock. Then I got a hold on my emotions.

"Let's calm down," I suggested.

"You killed him!" she cried, only slightly calmer. "You murdered Billy!"

"No, ma'am, you've got it all wrong. We only found him this way . . ."

"You murdered Billy!" she screamed.

I tried to approach her in a gentle and reassuring manner, but she ran from me as though I was Jack the Ripper. After a moment I followed her into the house to see if she was all right.

I found her in the living room among the debris, talking urgently to the 911 operator. "Help me!" she cried. "Steve Allen just murdered my husband, and now he's trying to kill me!"

I was starting to suspect that this just wasn't my day.

chapter 17

In the next few hours, Cass and I discovered what it was like to be surrounded by a squad of police officers with their pistols drawn nervously and pointed in our direction. It wasn't fun. We were rudely made to stand against the side of a patrol car, patted down, handcuffed, and hauled to the police station. Here we were separated, each to our own grim, windowless room, and interrogated by Lieutenant Kripinsky. Time passes slowly when you're no longer master of your fate, and the questions seemed endless.

Kripinsky, as you may imagine, was not amused to have found me at the scene of a new murder. "My God! Another corpse!" he said. "Don't you ever take a holiday?" Then, just when I was starting to wonder if I'd spend the rest of my life behind bars, the lieutenant released me. I have no idea if he had decided I was innocent, or simply did not have enough evidence to book me yet, but I wasn't about to question his decision.

Perhaps he was still suspicious but felt that as an easily-recognized public figure I wasn't about to flee the area, although the O.J. Simpson case would argue to the contrary.

I found Cass and Jayne downstairs in a waiting room crowded with a sad assortment of humanity—some with anxious faces, others bored and resigned. Jayne's face lit up when she saw me.

"Thank God, Steve! I was about ready to bake you a cake with a file inside!"

I gave her a hug, and Cass, too—I was so glad to see them both. It turned out that Cass had been questioned only briefly and released hours earlier. He had managed to return to the

D'Amato house to get the limo, which was now waiting for us, parked outside the station.

"Home?" Cass asked when we were breathing free air.

"Not yet," I said. "Someone set us up to take the rap for this murder—and we're going to find out who!"

It was nearly five o'clock in the afternoon when we left the station. What I wanted to do most was to question Rosalie D'Amato—the redhead who had found me and Cass with her husband's corpse. I was curious to know precisely where she was when Billy was murdered. But I doubted she would be pleased to see me, and since I had gotten into enough trouble for one day, I thought I'd better give her a raincheck. I decided on a more oblique approach.

I made a few calls from the car phone, then Cass pointed the old Cadillac onto the Santa Monica Freeway, then north on the Pacific Coast Highway to Topanga. The canyon communities in West L.A.—Coldwater, Benedict, and Laurel—have their own separate identities. Topanga Canyon is the oddest of the lot, a rural community that is home to an interesting assortment of hippies, artists, actors, rock stars, dropouts, and eccentrics of all shapes and sizes. We were headed to the home of a retired police artist I knew, a woman named Alice Obrecht who had been employed by the LAPD for thirty years, and now was doing her own work, wonderfully impressionistic watercolors of the California landscape.

Alice lived in a converted barn on ten acres of rolling hills in a spot that seemed a thousand miles from busy Los Angeles— but was in fact a mere forty-five minutes away by car. I hated to tear her away from her watercolors and bring her back to the sordid realities of her old profession, but I needed a sketch of the man who had broken into our bedroom. Alice spent the next two hours working up a likeness, beginning with the basic shape of the head, then gradually filling in the details. She kept asking Jayne and me if the mouth was right, or the nose or hair. She was good at her craft, and worked patiently, step-by-step, until at last she had our intruder on paper with such accuracy that it gave me goosebumps—the long, greasy, dark hair, the sloppy mouth, unshaved chin, even his shifty eyes.

I tried to give Alice some money for her work, but I had helped her out of some trouble a long time ago and she wouldn't accept a penny. We took the sketch, left her to her rural idyll, and returned to town along the coast road, then Sunset Boulevard. We found a photocopy shop in Pacific Palisades and ran off thirty copies of the sketch, then continued along Sunset to Bel Air, making a left turn through the Bel Air gate onto Stone Canyon Drive. The road winds its way up past some of the most expensive homes in Los Angeles. At last we arrived at an impressively high brick wall and a wrought iron gate that was closed to traffic. The huge gate had decorative spikes on top to discourage intruders, and the high wall probably had some booby traps as well.

Cass spoke into a small speaker-box by the gate. "Mr. and Mrs. Allen are here to see Mr. Murano. We called earlier to make an appointment."

"You are expected," said a well-modulated male voice on the speaker. "Please drive on up to the house, Mr. Cassidy."

Darkness had fallen hours ago. Cass stepped cautiously on the gas and drove us up a long, winding driveway through a dark forest of trees toward the glowing windows of a large house beyond. Coming up its driveway was like stepping into the mouth of a lion; the few times I had occasion to be here before, I always wondered if I would be able to get out again.

We had come to see Pete Murano, the aging Mafia lord, a man who had more power than many top-level studio and network executives. To solve a murder, there are times you need to travel into the very jaws of death.

chapter 18

My association with the Murano family went back nearly fifteen years, and came about quite accidentally. I was working on a film when I met a pleasant young man with dark hair and expressive brown eyes named Jonathan Muir. He was in his early twenties and was working as an assistant director. We all called him Jonno—he was a bright young fellow, popular with the cast and crew, who loved to talk about the movies and hoped one day to be an important film director. I remember having conversations with Jonno about Fellini, Orson Welles, Goddard, Jean Renoir—all great directors. He was the sort of young man with whom it was fun to have such conversations. He became very passionate when he discussed film making, and I sensed that one day he might leave his mark on the world.

Then late one afternoon Cass picked me up at the studio, and as we were driving toward the main gate, I caught a glimpse of Jonno running down a narrow alley between two soundstages, pursued by two men. I thought it was probably a game. "Can you imagine having so much energy—to spend your free time running around like that?" I remember saying to Cass.

"It would be nice to be young again," Cass agreed.

But as we drove toward the main gate, my brain continued to process the picture I had seen—like photographic paper bringing an image into sharper focus as it sits in the chemical wash. I had only had the most fleeting glimpse of the scene from the car window, but there had been something unplayful about the body language. Jonno had not been running as a game; he had been running for his life.

"Turn around, Cass," I said. "I want to get a better look at that alley."

We returned to the alley and the scene was no longer even vaguely playful. The two strange men were crouching behind a metal garbage Dumpster with pistols in hand, firing at Jonno—who was doing his best to hide behind a parked pick-up truck. At first I couldn't understand why the men with guns didn't simply rush Jonno, but then I saw that Jonno was throwing spears at them to keep them at bay. Yes, that's what I said, *spears*—props for another movie that luckily were stacked in the rear of the parked truck. Jonno was making a valiant effort to defend himself, but I could see that his immediate future did not appear bright.

Cass and I didn't stop to think. Cass hit the horn to attract attention, gunned the old Cadillac limo, and we sped to the rescue—down the alley to the pick-up truck. A bullet shattered our right window and punctured the fender.

"Jump in!" I shouted to Jonno, throwing open a door as we came abreast of him. He dived into the back of the limo, and as we sped away I suddenly became aware of a pain in my right calf. One of the bullets had hit me—only a superficial flesh wound, it turned out, but the amount of blood was impressive.

There is precious little connection between consciousness and memory and the sudden awareness that I had been hit flashed me back to an incident that happened when I was about eleven. I was riding a bicycle along the sidewalk and on seeing that a man was approaching me with a rather large, threatening-looking mastiff on a leash, I stopped my progress and sat motionless to give the two an easy opportunity to pass.

As the dog strolled slowly past he paused, for just a moment, turned his enormous head slightly to the left, and calmly sank his teeth into my left leg just below the knee. What was most remarkable about the moment was that there was almost no pain. I felt that the dog had simply gripped me loosely in its jaws and then released me. It was only about two minutes later when I felt a faint tingling sensation in the leg. I looked down and saw that a small amount of blood had trickled down over my shoe. I have the scar to this day and it is available, as we say, for inspection.

The impact of the bullet fortunately did not encounter bone, which would have been dreadfully painful. Jonno had been hit as well, suffering a more serious wound to his left shoulder. Cass sped us immediately to the nearest hospital.

Such was the dramatic rescue. The hospital stitched us both up, and that would have been the end of the story—except Jonathan's real last name turned out not to be Muir but Murano. Apparently Cass and I had saved the life of Pete Murano's youngest and favorite son, who was trying to escape the sordid family business and work his way up the Hollywood ladder to become a film director. The attempted hit, I learned eventually, was part of an elaborate feud with another crime family, and had nothing really to do with Jonno—except that he was his father's son and thus an appropriate target. The next day a huge black limousine appeared at my house and I met Pete Murano for the first time. He let me know that he was deeply in my debt and that if there was ever anything I needed—*anything*—I only had to ask. I told him it wasn't really a big deal, and that he should forget about it. Frankly, I didn't want to encourage the friendship, and he seemed to understand. But every Christmas, Cass and I to this day both receive a case of extremely rare and expensive champagne that comes with no note attached but we know very well its source.

In the years that have passed, I have met with Pete Murano on exactly three separate occasions to ask small favors—information that has been helpful in solving some of the various mysteries that have occupied my attention from time to time. He has always treated me with grave, old-fashioned courtesy, and sometimes I have difficulty squaring the image I have of the man—an aristocratic, silver-haired gentleman—with that of the ruthless crime lord that he indeed is. But it's a complicated world, and nothing is quite black and white.

To the extent that I might be said to have a relationship with organized crime, it has been a rather curious one. Having grown up in Chicago, I was naturally familiar with the enormous power wielded in that great city by Al Capone and his associates in the twenties and thirties, but I was unfamiliar with finer-point details.

It was only when the CBS network brought me to New York the winter of 1950–51 that I saw what it means when life-long professional criminals have more authority than a community's elected representatives. They achieve this partly by deciding which representatives will be elected in the first place, and the simple fact of their reputation makes it unlikely that any young man with political ambitions will start out by taking a courageous position in opposition to the Mafia and other non-Sicilian organized crime leaders. The one area of exception, of course, concerned those who became Public Prosecutors, District Attorneys, States Attorneys, and Federal Prosecutors.

Tonight Jonno was waiting for us at the front door of the huge, Tudor-style mansion as we drove up the long drive. He has become heftier during the past fifteen years, and his brown eyes have grown colder and more cautious. He never did become the great movie director of his youthful dreams; after the attempted assassination, he settled into the family business, and now he is his father's right-hand man.

"Steve!" he said, opening the car door. "Jayne, so good to see you again! And Cass, my God, it's been a few years—I can't believe you still have this old burgundy-colored limo!"

"Oh, like the pink rabbit she keeps running and running," Cass said.

"Well, she ran good enough to save *my* hide that time . . . Come in, come in. We've been holding dinner for you."

"We wouldn't want to intrude on your dinner, Jonno," I objected.

"Nonsense! Anyway, it's just at-home night, nothing special."

Jonno was full of more charm and warmth than ever, but it seemed only a surface thing. His eyes gave him away. There was a great weariness that saddened me, and he looked prematurely old.

"Please come in—Pop's waiting."

Papa Pete Murano was waiting with his wife at a huge table in a dark, wood panelled dining room with a heavy chandelier overhead. There were also three young children around the table—grandchildren, I gathered. It had been a long day, and I was impatient to get home, but I knew it was not appropriate to discuss "business" during the meal, so I forced myself to be patient. The simple, nothing special "at-home night" dinner began with *insalata mista* followed by a pasta—spaghetti *carbonara.* The main course was a delicious *osso bucco,* a kind of veal shank stew, along with roast potatoes, spinach with a squeeze of lemon, then chocolate torte for dessert and strong espresso coffee.

You're probably wondering what one talks about with a notorious gangster at dinner. Pete Murano and I discussed art—an exhibit of nineteenth century Japanese woodcuts we had both seen in New York. On the surface he is one of the most elegant old gentlemen I have ever met, though you wouldn't want to find yourself on the wrong side of him. Jayne talked mostly with his wife, Rosemary, about grandchildren and such, while Cass and Jonno discussed automobiles—past, present, and future. At last, Jayne, Cass, Jonno, Pete, and I retired to the den where we seated ourselves in heavy leather chairs around a large fireplace. We were served more coffee, delicately flavored with *amaretto.*

"So what can I do for you, Steve?" Pete said finally.

"Cass, please give Mr. Murano the art work . . . this individual broke into our bedroom the other night," I explained to the old gangster as he studied the portrait.

Pete Murano sighed. "The human propensity for violence always amazes me. He certainly does look like a cheap thug . . . you want me to take care of this individual for you?"

"Do you know him?"

"I do not. But the chances are I can discover who he is. What do you want me to do with him when I find him?"

"Nothing, Mr. Murano. I simply want to find him and ask some questions. I want to know who hired him to break into our house."

"That should be easy enough," he agreed with a small smile. "Anything else?"

"I also wanted to ask you if you've heard anything about Terry Parker's murder a few days ago—any rumblings or rumors as to who might have done it?"

He shook his head. "Frankly, I don't have my ear to the ground anymore, not like I used to. I'm in a kind of semi-retirement. Jonno?" he asked. "Have you heard anything about this?"

I was chilled to realize that Jonno, my old friend, was now apparently the active boss of the family business.

"I've only seen the TV reports," the son replied. "Offhand, I doubt if it's anything connected with any of the families, or I would have heard. Probably a private feud of some kind. But I'll look into it."

"I'm also curious about Billy D'Amato's death today. He was stabbed in the same way," I mentioned. "I'm wondering if these could be professional hits."

Jonno gazed at me solemnly. "I understand the widow found you by their swimming pool with D'Amato's body."

"Good God! Is that on the TV news already?"

"No, I heard it from an LAPD cop who . . . well, who reports to me. As it happens, Billy D'Amato is a friend. I financed his last two films."

I smiled sourly. "So you got into the film business after all, Jonno!"

"Only indirectly," he said in a flat tone, without a smile. "I've already ordered some inquiries into Billy's death, and I will do the same regarding Terry Parker. It disturbs me that someone is killing such talented people."

As we were leaving, Jayne said, "Now, Jonno, listen to me. If you find out who the killer is, I want you to promise that you'll tell Steve or the police. I wouldn't want to think of you taking vengeance into your own hands."

Jonno's eyes became impenetrable slits. "I wouldn't think of it, Jayne," he said smoothly.

chapter 19

I wondered what I had let loose. I was grateful for the Murano family's help—for any help at all, in fact—but now I had a new worry: if I didn't solve these murders fast enough, Jonno might indeed take matters in his own hands.

"That was curious what Jonno told me last night—that he had financed Billy D'Amato's last two pictures," I said to Jayne over breakfast the following morning. "I wonder exactly how tight Billy was with the Murano family."

"You think it could have something to do with his death?"

"Possibly. Being friends with the Murano family is a bit like having a pet tiger—very exotic, but you always wonder if your tiger's going to gobble you up!"

"Yes, but if they had Billy killed for some reason, perhaps they were also responsible for Terry's death. Remember—they were both killed with kitchen knives from the same set."

"*Our* set!" I agreed with a sigh. "No, none of this makes any sense at all, and I have a bad feeling there's no time to lose. Here's what I suggest for today—a chat with the widows. Darling, why don't you tackle Gloria Hartman, since you're already such close friends. See if you can find out anything more about that burglary when the knives were stolen. Meanwhile, I'll pay a visit on Rosalie D'Amato. As far as I'm concerned, she has some questions to answer, starting with where she was at the time of her husband's murder."

"I have a better suggestion," Jayne said. "Let's exchange widows—you take Gloria—metaphorically speaking. But watch your step, sweetheart—she eats men like you for lunch. I'll go see Rosalie."

"Does this mean you trust me with blondes, but not red-heads?"

"I trust you with all hair colors, Steve, but that's not the point," said Jayne. "Rosalie D'Amato seems to think you murdered her husband, and she'll probably dial 911 at the sight of you. Frankly, I'm not anxious to see the inside of another police station."

And so our day's itinerary was settled.

Jayne spent nearly an hour in the morning trying to phone the D'Amato residence to set up an appointment. When no one answered the phone—not even an answering machine to take a message—Jayne decided she'd zip over to Brentwood on the chance that she might find Rosalie at home anyway.

She drove herself in an unpretentious, spiffy little red Plymouth. Later I told her she should take our driver, but she insisted that Cass remain with me—to protect me, I suppose, from any man-eating impulses on the part of the blond bombshell, Gloria Hartman. It was one of those perfect early-summer mornings, fresh and fragile with a scent of flowers and new-cut grass, a morning on which it was hard to believe in violent death and other wintry things. Jayne drove from the Valley on the San Diego Freeway, getting off at the Sunset Boulevard exit, then traveling west, toward the ocean, to Brentwood.

She wasn't certain what kind of reception she'd receive at the D'Amato house. There were three cars in the curving driveway before the grand colonial-style mansion: a yellow Jaguar and two late-model Fords, whose very unmarked plainness and drab off-white color suggested the word *police*. Jayne parked across the street and wondered how best to proceed. It didn't seem a good idea to disturb the police in their official duties at a crime scene, so she decided to simply wait a few minutes and hope for inspiration. Ten minutes later, just when she was ready to give up and go home, the front door opened and the large, unmistakable figure of Lieutenant Kripinsky appeared on the doorstep. In a moment he was joined by three other plainclothesmen. They conferred among themselves for several seconds and then got into the two Fords and drove away.

Jayne started up her engine and was about to pull into the D'Amato driveway when she saw Rosalie appear in the doorway. The widow, wearing huge dark glasses and a straw hat, seemed nervous. Almost furtive, Jayne thought. She moved quickly to her yellow Jaguar, hit the ignition, and drove toward Sunset Boulevard.

Jayne hesitated only for a heartbeat. It seemed a pity to waste the morning and come away with nothing.

"Well, why not?" she said to herself.

She pulled out of her parking spot and followed the yellow Jaguar, doing her best to remain several car lengths back. Rosalie D'Amato turned right on Sunset, drove a few blocks, and then— to Jayne's surprise—turned left into the driveway of a small motel, the Brentwood Motor Inn, five minutes away. Jayne, caught by surprise, drove past the entrance to the motel, swerved into a private driveway, backed up onto Sunset to the accompaniment of several angry drivers honking at her, and returned to the motel just in time to see the redheaded widow walking from the office toward a room.

Why, Jayne wondered, would someone with a huge mansion—some twenty rooms at her disposal—check into a small, inexpensive motel room? Jayne pulled up next to the curb and in a moment the answer was clear: As she watched, a brand new Volvo sedan arrived from Sunset and parked in front of the room Rosalie had entered. The man who stepped from the Volvo was wearing dark glasses and a large fedora which obscured the upper part of his face. Despite the summer heat, he wore a brown leather jacket with the collar turned up. He glanced about nervously before knocking on the door of the motel room.

This was a man who clearly did not wish to be recognized, but Jayne knew who he was immediately. It was Harvey Roth.

chapter 20

This just gets curiouser and curiouser, said Jayne to herself. I'm sure most amateur busybodies would have returned home at this point and allowed the matter to rest. Harvey was evidently cheating on his girlfriend, Melissa Courtney, which was his own business. But it seemed to Jayne a peculiar coincidence that Roth had been feuding with Terry Parker before his death, and was also apparently having an affair with Billy D'Amato's wife. To be connected in a suspicious fashion to two murder victims obviously went beyond the simple laws of probability.

Jayne debated with herself—what in the world should she do next? She was dying to know what Harvey and Rosalie were talking about inside the room, but it seemed impossible to find out. She drove her Laser into the motel driveway, found a free parking spot, and peered about for any signs of life from the office. It was a sleepy little motel and there was no one in sight. Jayne thought she might leave her car and walk casually to the room where Harvey and Rosalie had disappeared and perhaps put her ear to the door. It was doubtful she would hear anything, but you never could tell.

The number on the door was 103. Jayne stepped as close as she dared, then opened her handbag and pretended to be searching for a key, just in case anyone from the office happened to be looking. It was a flimsy pretense, she knew, but better than none at all.

Suddenly she heard Harvey's voice coming loudly through the closed door: ". . . I'm a nervous wreck, I tell you! I can't eat,

I can't sleep, I can't concentrate on the movie I'm trying to make! I can't live like this, Rosie . . .''

Rosalie said something which Jayne could not make out. Then she heard Harvey again. He was nearly shouting: "My God, Rosie! Do you know what they do to you in California? They still have the gas chamber in this state! Can you imagine what that's like—to be strapped in a chair in that horrible metal chamber? There you are, waiting for the pellet of cyanide to be released! You try your best not to breathe. Just one more second of life! But then your lungs seem to burst . . .''

"Harvey! Shut up!" Rosalie said. "I saw that old black and white movie, just like you did. *I Want To Live* with Virginia Graham from the early sixties . . .''

"Rosie!—I can't believe I'm having an affair with someone who's so utterly ignorant about movies! The picture was made in the late fifties, not the early sixties. And the star was Susan Hayward. It was about *Barbara* Graham. Virginia Graham, by the way, was a TV talk show host.''

"Harvey, listen to me. This is *not* a movie! This is real life, for a change!''

Jayne was so intrigued by the conversation that she moved closer to the closed door and placed her ear against the wood so as not to miss a word.

"Darling, we are *not* going to the gas chamber!" said Rosalie D'Amato. "Not if you keep your head and . . .''

"Can I *help* you?" came a stern voice from a few feet behind Jayne. She turned and found a slim, gray-haired woman on the path in front of the room. She was staring at Jayne sternly.

"I'm the manager," the woman announced. "Are you having some sort of problem?''

"This is very embarrassing," Jayne admitted, stepping back from the closed door.

"It certainly is," the woman agreed. "I suggest you leave these premises immediately, before I call the police.''

"It's my husband," Jayne said suddenly. It was the first excuse that came to mind. "He's in that room with another woman!''

"Your husband?" the manager repeated. "With another woman?''

Jayne nodded tragically—she's a very convincing actress, after all. "He's with my best friend!" she managed, with a slight break in her voice.

"*My* husband did that once," said the stern manager. "I threw him out."

"I'd like to," Jayne agreed. "Except for the children . . ."

The manager narrowed her eyes, stepped up to the door, and knocked loudly. When there was no answer, she knocked again. "Open up!" she cried. "This is a respectable motel and I won't tolerate these sort of goings-on!"

In a moment, Rosalie opened the door cautiously, just a crack, and stared in utter dismay at Jayne and the manager.

"Rosie, how could you!" Jayne cried, pushing the door open and charging inside. "I can handle this now," Jayne said to the manager, who had remained on the doorstep. "I think it's best we all sit down and have a frank discussion."

"There won't be any violence, will there?"

"Not at all."

"Well, you can phone me in the office if you need any help," the manager said.

Jayne smiled and closed the door on the woman. Then she turned to the astonished people in the room. Fortunately, they were fully dressed.

"Jayne!" Harvey cried. "My God, what are *you* doing here?"

"Jayne Meadows?" Rosalie said suspiciously. "You're the wife of the bastard who killed my husband!"

"You don't have to pretend innocence with me," Jayne said archly. "I overheard your conversation just now—how you're both so terrified of the gas chamber! The two of you killed Billy together, didn't you?"

"Oh, my God!" Harvey moaned, collapsing on the bed and hiding his head in his hands. "She's going to tell Melissa about this! I'm ruined!"

"Shut up, Harvey," Rosalie ordered. "This is insane, and as far as I'm concerned, I wish I'd never laid eyes on you. And as for Billy," Rosalie said, looking back toward Jayne, "the only thing I know about his death is that I discovered your husband and your chauffeur at the—"

"Steve had an appointment to see Billy. When he saw the state your house was in, he broke in and found your husband dead in the swimming pool . . . The question I have, is where were you while all this was going on, my dear?"

"Where was *I*? Not that it's any of your business, but I was doing an aerobics class at my health club in Westwood—along with a dozen other women, by the way, who will vouch for me. When I came home, I was shocked to see the living room was torn apart. I was calling for Billy when I happened to glance out a window to the swimming pool in the backyard."

"I see. And how about you, Harvey? What's *your* alibi?" Jayne asked with considerable sarcasm.

"Oh, this is terrible! Absolutely terrible!" he continued to moan.

"*Shut up,* you idiot!" Rosalie said to her lover with a considerable lack of warmth. "Tell her your alibi, stupid."

"My alibi?" Harvey seemed bewildered.

"Exactly where were you, Harvey, yesterday morning when Billy was killed?" Jayne asked.

"I was on the set, of course. Shooting *Flower in the City,* my new flick. At Paramount."

"And how many people can vouch for you there?" Rosalie prompted.

"Why, the entire cast and crew, I guess. About fifty people."

"I see. So you *hired* someone to kill your husband," Jayne suggested. "You didn't quite dare do it yourselves."

"Look, I'm not certain why I'm bothering to tell you this— but I did not kill my husband. *We* did not kill my husband," Rosalie said, indicating Harvey on the bed. "And neither did I *hire* anyone to kill my husband! As a matter of fact, I loved Billy very much."

"Then what exactly are you doing here?" Jayne asked.

"*That,*" said Rosalie, "is a very good question. Maybe things were going too smoothly with me and Billy and I was bored. We'd been married seven years, you know—so it was just the usual seven-year-itch that made me curious to—"

Up to that moment, Jayne had really believed she had caught

Billy's killers—and probably the killers of Terry Parker as well. Now she was starting to have her doubts.

"How long has this affair been going on?" she asked Rosalie.

"About two months, I suppose. And I write it off as the greatest mistake of my life. If I was going to stray, at least I should have found myself a real man—not this crybaby!"

"Jayne, promise me you won't say anything about this to Melissa! She'll kill me!" Harvey begged.

"You see?" Rosalie said with a shake of her head. "He's not exactly Romeo, is he? If you've gotten all the information you want, I'd appreciate some privacy to break up with this jerk."

"Just a moment—what was this bit about going to the gas chamber?"

Rosalie laughed unkindly. "That's only Harvey's paranoia and overactive imagination. He's afraid the cops will find out about us and think we planned Billy's murder."

"Well, it's classic, isn't it?" Harvey said. "What else are the cops going to think? You jumped to that conclusion yourself. It doesn't matter that we didn't do it."

"Any other questions?" Rosalie asked wearily.

"Sure, one thing more. Last night, I was told that Jonathan Murano financed Billy's last two films. How exactly did your husband get involved with the Murano family?"

"It's simple—Billy was approached by an intermediary, a company that called itself Star Productions that had a few scripts it was peddling that were very good. There was a big name ex-studio exec in charge, so it all seemed legit. And it was, in fact—except for the source of the money. But Billy didn't learn about that until recently."

"You're telling me he didn't *know* the two movies were financed by the Murano crime family?"

"That's what I'm saying. Star Productions seemed extremely respectable. Finally someone told him, and he was angry—he said he'd never do a movie for a bunch of gangsters again."

"Who told him?"

Rosalie nodded toward Harvey. "Him."

"Harvey? How did *you* find out!"

"Good Lord, it was common knowledge! Star Productions

had wanted to finance one of my projects a few years back, so I had my accountant look into them. I thought I should warn Billy—after all, he was my friend.''

"Your *friend!*" Rosalie said sarcastically.

Harvey shrugged. "I can't help it if I have complicated friendships,'' he said weakly.

"Anything else?'' Rosalie asked Jayne.

"Just this—how did you two get started?'' Jayne inquired, truly curious.

"It started when Harvey began coming over to the house last winter. He and Billy were talking about doing a play together. An updated version of Hamlet.''

"Hamlet!'' Jayne cried.

"I know it sounds weird,'' Rosalie admitted. "But Harvey and Billy had an idea of giving the play a new slant—turn it into a kind of black comedy. They were both looking for some project that was different from the usual movie job. Meanwhile, crazy as it seems, I found Harvey intriguing. At least for a short while . . .''

"Man, it would have been great, too! We were going to do the play as a comic farce,'' Harvey said with sudden enthusiasm, forgetting for a moment his present distress. "As far as I'm concerned, tragedy and comedy are almost the same thing. I'm certain Shakespeare would agree . . .''

But Jayne was hardly listening. *"Ham*let!'' she mused.

chapter 21

Gloria Hartman was very gushy over the telephone.

"Oh, Steve—*just* the person who's been on my mind! Yes, I'd *love* to see you! Why don't we have lunch together? I know an *adorable* little spot. It's *très* romantique."

I did my best to wiggle out of lunch. I suggested we keep it simple, and that I merely stop by her house for a chat. But Gloria wouldn't hear of it. She said her house was an absolute mess and she'd be embarrassed for me to see it. And anyway, she was starved, and she couldn't *think* of talking until she had eaten something. So I asked directions to the "adorable little spot" she had in mind, but she wouldn't hear of that either. She would swing by my house and pick me up. I told her this was quite a swing, since I lived in the Valley and she lived in Beverly Hills, but she assured me that there was no problem at all.

"I'm a swinger, Steve," she confided with a giggle. "Anyway, why waste gas with two cars when we could be so much more cozy in one?"

Gloria was a curious combination of coy, bubbly, and hard as nails. I saw there was no arguing with her so I gave in. About forty-five minutes later I heard a car honk in my driveway and I looked out the window to see a Jaguar convertible—not yellow, like Rosalie D'Amato's, but fire engine red. Jaguars, of course, are the trendy car at present for the rich folk of Los Angeles.

"I know a nice restaurant ten minutes away in Burbank," I suggested when I walked out into the driveway.

She laughed. "Come on, get in, Steve—said the spider to

the fly," she said cutely, lowering her voice dangerously. "I have something *very* special in mind for this afternoon!"

The lady was dressed for big game hunting in tight black toreador pants, a snug red pullover sweater, and a paisley scarf tied around her blond hair. I made my first mistake of the day: I thought I could handle her, and got in the car.

"Up or down?" she asked.

"I'm sorry?"

"The top."

"Up, please."

"Mmm . . . *much* more intimate!" she agreed, pushing down the button that raised the top. Her tone was mock flirtatious, halfway between high camp and the real thing. I couldn't quite believe she was serious, but she worried me nevertheless. I thought of reminding her that I was old enough to be her father, but after being married to Benny—who was old enough to be her grandfather—I realized this probably would only make me seem youthful in her eyes.

So I used another tactic. "I'm awfully sorry Jayne couldn't come along today. I'll know she'll be very disappointed to have missed you."

"No problem," Gloria said vaguely, steering her Jaguar onto the Ventura Freeway.

"Jayne mentioned she had an interesting chat with you in a Neiman Marcus dressing room the other day."

"Goodness, Steve! Let's not talk about Jayne, shall we? I mean, here we are together. Alone."

"But I like talking about Jayne. She's my wife, and I'm—by the way, where are you taking us?" Gloria had pointed us north on the Ventura Freeway and she showed no interest in any of the exits that were whizzing past.

She giggled naughtily. "Maybe I'm going to kidnap you."

"No, really," I said, "where are we going?"

"What if I told you . . . San Francisco!"

"I'd say you were crazy. And please turn around and take me home."

"Okay, then. Monterey! I know an *adorable* little inn, right on the water. We could spend a few days getting to know each other."

"I'm afraid Jayne would not be amused, my dear."

"Oh, Jayne, Jayne, *Jayne* . . . that's all I ever hear out of your mouth!" she pouted. "Anyway, I'm just kidding. We're not actually going all the way to Monterey."

"I'm glad to hear it."

She smiled impishly and seemed very pleased with herself. "We're going to Ojai!"

Ojai is a quaint, arty little town nestled in a sleepy valley about ninety minutes north of Los Angeles. I accepted the news that this was our destination with some equanimity. On one hand, this was a much longer journey than I had intended; but on the other, it was a great deal shorter than San Francisco or Monterey. The way Gloria presented it, it was a compromise—so how could I possibly object? To tell the truth, it was difficult to have a logical conversation with Gloria Hartman, and it seemed easier for the moment just to go along.

So I made my second mistake of the day: I said, all right, then. We'll have lunch in Ojai. And then immediately after lunch we'll drive back to Los Angeles. My wife, Jayne—I mentioned her name several times—was expecting to see me later in the afternoon.

With that out of the way, I tried to question Gloria about the set of kitchen knives which had been stolen from her house, but Gloria said we could talk about "all that boring stuff" at lunch. She promised—and I made her promise, too—that I could ask her any questions I liked then.

Meanwhile, Gloria insisted on telling me her Life Story. How she grew up in a middle class neighborhood in the Bronx, dreaming of exotic places and beautiful people . . . sunshine and palm trees swaying in the breeze. "Like Ft. Lauderdale at Spring Break," she sighed. "I went down there with a carload of my girlfriends when I was seventeen . . . It was totally awesome!"

Swell. Valley Girl talk from a woman in her late thirties.

Inspired with almost a mystical vision of Something Grand, little Gloria had enrolled in drama and dance classes back in New York. Trying to better herself. The only problem was that when

it came to dancing, she was a klutz—as she readily admitted—
and a lousy actress to boot. When she was nineteen she was married
briefly to a man who owned a nightclub in Brooklyn, but she left
him six months later because he beat her when he was drunk. As
a single woman once again, she needed to find a way to support
herself, so she took a computer class. She learned about spread
sheets and word processing, and armed with this knowledge—
and still clinging to a slightly tarnished dream—spent her last
hundred dollars on a bus ticket to Hollywood, confident that a
bright destiny awaited her in California.

It was a somewhat seedy tale, yet fascinating in its own way.
It boggles the mind how many young women like Gloria have
arrived at the Hollywood bus station over the years, hoping that
the most unrealistic dreams will come true. Gloria Wallenberg,
her maiden name, did significantly better, of course, than the
great majority of these girls: she did indeed marry a star, even if
it happened to be one who was more than fifty years her senior.
She had met Benny by answering an ad in the *Hollywood Reporter:*
"Sec'y with wordprocessing skills wanted." Benny had placed the
ad himself, she said; he was working on his autobiography and
needed someone to transcribe his spoken anecdotes from cassette
tapes onto a computer disk.

The rest, as they say, is history. Benny's second wife, Gladys,
had recently died. He and Gladys had spent thirty mostly happy
years together and he was lonely for female companionship. The
young woman who showed up five days a week at his Beverly Hills
mansion had a certain eagerness for life that he found attractive;
and besides, she laughed at his jokes. There was intimacy from
the start, I suppose, working together on his autobiography—
sharing the stories of his childhood and youth, and his long and
colorful career.

It is my opinion that she truly liked Benny and basked in his
attention—the way a favorite granddaughter might enjoy finding
herself pampered by a fun-loving old rogue of a grandfather.
Despite his age, Benny could be very child-like and well, cute, and
I think he and Gloria had a good time together, and made for
themselves an enjoyable world for two. It wasn't a sexual love,
certainly—at least not on her part—but I don't think that both-

ered either of them at first. An attractive blond creature like Gloria must get tired of younger men pawing at her, and probably it was a relief to be with someone like Benny who made few demands except just to be there and laugh it up.

But, of course, the difference of age was bound to be a problem eventually. Frankly, I was curious, from an investigative point of view, if she had had lovers while Benny was still alive. To get to the point, I simply asked her point-blank. In response, she became very coy, batted her eyelashes a little, then said: "No, of course not. I won't say I wasn't tempted every now and then. But I loved Benny too much to be unfaithful."

I'm not sure I believed her, but I had no way of knowing at the moment if she was telling the truth. Meanwhile, she made it clear enough by body language—and I do mean *body* language—that now that Benny was dead, she was eager to make up for lost time.

We had a late lunch at the old Ojai Valley Inn—a languid Spanish-style country club with a richly green golf course extending right up to the restaurant window.

"Now, Gloria," I said, "tell me about the burglary six months ago."

"Oh, that's all so boring! Can't we talk about us?"

I shook my head. "Remember, you promised."

"Well, all right then. There's not much to tell. Last year in mid-December, Benny and I flew to Switzerland for the Christmas holidays. A kind of special treat. We stayed at the lovely old Palace Hotel in St. Moritz—but we didn't tell anyone where we were. Not his children, not his agent—nobody. We just wanted to get off by ourselves, you know. I had a lovely time skiing every day. And ice skating on their big outdoor rink. We were gone about three weeks and when we got back to Beverly Hills, we found there had been a burglary while we were away. The private security company that guards the house was waiting with the news. Normally they would have phoned us, but they didn't know where we were. Said Benny's secretary refused to tell them!"

"You left the house empty?"

"Sure. We have a butler and a chauffeur who normally live on the grounds, but since it was Christmas and we were going to be gone, Benny gave them each a bonus and told them to spend the time with their families. The chauffeur went home to New Jersey, I think, and our butler took a trip to Hawaii."

"What was the exact date of the burglary?"

"December 24. According to the security people, it happened about eleven PM."

"Christmas Eve! And what exactly was stolen?"

"Well, those knives, of course—the ones with the nice teak handles. A mink coat Benny had given me for my birthday. A string of pearls. A small diamond brooch. And a lot of our electronics—all three of our TV sets, the VCR, the stereo system. They really cleaned us out."

"Was everything insured?"

"Naturally. But still, it's scary thinking of some stranger pawing through your personal things like that. Benny ended up changing security companies over it."

"And none of the stolen items were ever found?"

"Not a thing. We lost the works."

"You know, I'm surprised that ordinary thieves would try their luck at a Beverly Hills mansion these days, what with all the high-tech security devices people use."

Gloria shrugged. She made a show of being embarrassed, though I don't think she really was. "Actually—if you can believe it—Benny forgot to turn on the alarm before we left for Switzerland."

"He *forgot?*"

"Well, sure. It's just a matter of hitting some computer-code numbers as you go out the front door, but he *was* getting kind of forgetful the past few years."

"I don't want to cast undue suspicions on your domestic help, but the butler and chauffeur . . ."

"They were thousands of miles away when the burglary happened. Believe me, Steve, they were the first people the police questioned, and they went over their alibis carefully. Like I said, our butler was in Hawaii over Christmas, and the chauffeur was with his family in New Jersey. Anyway, they'd been with Benny for years—I can't believe they'd rip us off."

"Still, I'd like to speak with them, if you don't mind. It's very strange, to say the least, that these kitchen knives I gave Benny years ago keep ending up in people's backs!''

Gloria put her hand on top of mine. ''Poor Steve!'' she said. ''You must feel just a little guilty.''

I took my hand away.

''No, worried. There are two more knives in that set that are not yet accounted for.''

''You worry too much, darling. You should relax more,'' Gloria said, moving closer.

I moved back.

''You know what I did? I was a naughty girl!''

''What did you do, Gloria?'' I asked with a sigh.

''I phoned here earlier—I reserved us a room.''

Was I tempted? Why lie? Yes, I was. I'm no saint and the last time I thought it possible I might someday become one, I was twelve years old. Fortunately, despite Gloria's bubbly charm and physical attributes, she didn't really appeal to me.

The situation was rather complicated in that I really didn't want to hurt Gloria's feelings.

''Anyway,'' she said out of the blue, ''there is just one little teensy favor I'd like to ask of you.''

''Oh?'' I said, ''and what's that?''

She made an awfully cute face. ''You don't want to see me destitute, do you, darling?''

''Of course not, Gloria.''

''Then be my very good friend . . . there's a probate hearing in L.A. next week about Benny's will. Come to court with me, darling—tell that nasty ol' judge that Benny was getting awfully old and senile, and he really wasn't in his right mind when he left all that nasty ol' money to that dumb ol' awards show . . . you were Benny's *very* good friend. The judge will believe you . . . you want your little Gloria to have *lots* of lovely money, don't you? This way, maybe you and I . . .''

''Sorry, Gloria,'' I said, ''I can't.''

''But why?''

''Benny seemed very sane to me when I saw him in the hospital. He knew exactly what he wanted to do with his money. I'm not saying I'd do the same thing myself, but it was his money, after all—he earned it, and he should be able to dispose of it as he pleased.''

The decades returned to Gloria's face. ''You're not going to help me?''

''I wish I could, Gloria. But I can't.''

She stood up from the table. For a moment I thought she was going to throw her lunch at me. But she controlled herself.

''You son of a bitch! You can walk back to Los Angeles, for all I care!'' she said coldly.

Then she stormed out of the dining room, leaving me high and dry—and ninety miles from home.

chapter 22

"**W**ell," I said to Jayne, "this is quite a comedy of manners. As far as I can make out, Terry Parker was having an affair with Harvey's girlfriend, Melissa Courtney . . . Harvey, meanwhile, has been making it with Danny D'Amato's wife, Rosalie . . ."

"And Gloria Hartman nearly snagged you!"

"Not by a mile!" I objected. "Anyway, what other people do is their own business. But it *does* seem curious that both Terry and Danny, two of the three men in this pentangle, are dead . . . stabbed in the back with our knives!"

"Oh, I like that word, *pentangle!* It sounds much more decadent than a simple triangle! But do you really think these were crimes of passion?"

"I don't know *what* to think!" I admitted. At first I thought they were connected with the comedy awards in some way, but . . . who knows?"

Jayne, bless her heart, had driven to Ojai to rescue me. She had a good laugh at my expense; it seemed to tickle her funnybone to see me get dumped like that by a blond bombshell, but at least Jayne didn't leave me to hitchhike home.

Jayne does not like car phones, and she hadn't brought her portable phone, so I asked her to stop at a gas station near Streamline Realty in Oxnard. I used a pay phone to call a Beverly Hills cop I know, Det. Pat Harrington—Patricia, that is—a small dynamo of a woman who has helped me in the past. I reached her just at the end of her shift as she was about to leave the station and drive home. She agreed to take a quick peek at the file on the Hartman burglary of last December, and suggested we rendezvous at her apartment in Burbank in one hour's time where she would tell us what she had learned.

Detective Harrington lived on the second floor of a low, modern complex of apartments built around a swimming pool. Jayne and I found her about to devour a huge pizza she had picked up on her way home from Beverly Hills. The detective was a slim woman, about five-feet-two-inches tall, with large, expressive eyes—about the last person you'd expect to be a police officer. The pizza seemed bigger than she was. She said we had to help her out by taking a slice.

"So, Pat, about the burglary," I said, melted cheese dripping from my chin. "You saw the report?"

"Yes. And better yet, I ran into Tom Robinson in the parking lot—he's the detective who investigated the case at the time. I don't know what to tell you—it's like a zillion other unsolved burglaries in L.A. County. An officer goes to the scene, fills out a report, maybe checks with some of the local fences . . . and that's about it. Generally in Beverly Hills we take this kind of crime more seriously than in other parts of the city—after all, there's a lot of property there worth stealing. But still, with a B and E of this type, you pretty much gotta catch the perp in the act while he's climbing out the window with a TV set. Once he gets away, he's gone."

"Were there any suspects? Can you tell me anything at all?"

She shook her head. "Not really, I'm afraid. The crime has received new attention since some of the stolen items—the box of kitchen knives—have been involved with two murders. But Tom wasn't optimistic."

"I understand there's a live-in chauffeur and butler at the Hartman house. Were they ever considered possible suspects?"

She rolled her eyes at me. "Steve! Every crime of this sort, in a big house in Beverly Hills—that's the very *first* thought, that maybe it's an inside job. But they both had airtight alibis and checked out clean as a whistle. The butler, an old fellow named Patrick Larson, was taking the vacation of his dreams at the Royal Hawaiian Hotel in Waikiki. The chauffeur—his name is Bud

Albertson—was spending Christmas with about twenty of his relatives back East.''

"You had someone actually phone the Royal Hawaiian . . .''

"Do you think we're amateurs? Tom did better than that—he had someone from the Honolulu Police Department go to the hotel with a photograph of Patrick Larson and ask around a bit. Christmas Eve, when the burglary took place, the butler went with some other people from the hotel to a special event at the Hawaiian Cultural Center on the windward side of the island. As I say, an airtight alibi.''

"I know we're being very nosy," Jayne said, "and neither Steve nor I mean to imply that the Beverly Hills police didn't follow through with every possible lead . . . but by any chance did your Detective Robinson check the Hartmans' alibi—that *they* were indeed in Switzerland as they claimed?''

"You would have made a swell cop, Jayne—don't believe anybody, and take nothing for granted. But the answer is, yes. Tom spoke on the telephone to the manager of the Palace Hotel in St. Moritz where they were staying, and he was able to vouch for them.''

"So there it is!" I sighed. "I was sure hoping the butler did it. Or someone close to the Hartman family in some way. As it is, it's hard to believe that some anonymous thief broke into the house and the knives just happened to be used in two murders that were at least remotely connected with Benny Hartman.''

"Well, it's still possible, of course, that someone in the house arranged the burglary," Pat told us. "Benny, Gloria, even the chauffeur or butler—they could have set it up so that they were far away when some local accomplice broke into the mansion. It's just very difficult to prove, one way or the other. Frankly, a crime like this had low priority when it happened—after all, everything was insured and no one was hurt. Now there's a murder case, but the trail's awfully cold . . . by the way, where were you and Jayne last Christmas Eve?''

I blinked. The question came so suddenly and out of the blue that it caught me completely off-guard.

"I beg your pardon? Are you really asking for our alibi, Pat?''

"*I'm* not, Steve. Honest. But my boss is. Captain Molinari.

There's a Lieutenant Kripinsky from the LAPD who has a suspicious mind. So I thought I'd get it out of the way, just to clear any possible misunderstanding. So what about it?"

"We were in Los Angeles," Jayne said. "We had a quiet Christmas Eve last year—didn't we, dear?"

"I'm trying to remember. They all tend to run together after a while . . . but yes, I believe we had dinner with our old friends, the McDonalds. They have young children, so it was fun. Then we just went home."

"Well, there it is—certainly the McDonalds will vouch for us," Jayne said pleasantly.

"I'm sure they will," Detective Harrington agreed. "How late did your dinner last?"

"It was early, I recall."

"We must have left their house by ten o'clock, Steve—don't you remember?" Jayne added. "We came back here and opened a bottle of champagne, determined to stay awake to welcome in Christmas at midnight. But we were so sleepy we went to bed just after eleven . . . what time do you estimate the burglary happened?"

"We don't know for sure, but probably between ten PM and midnight . . . hey, have some pizza, you guys."

But my appetite was gone. Everybody seemed to have a great alibi except me and Jayne.

chapter 23

Some mysteries you just can't explain. Here's a good one:

After our informal pizza dinner with Detective Pat Harrington of the BHPD, Jayne and I got so busy with our respective careers, as well as with the demands of the Benny Hartman Memorial Comedy Awards—her judging and my organizing—that time literally flew by. Imagine one of those old-fashioned movies where the camera pans to a calendar on the wall; a wind comes up and starts blowing the days and months quickly by—well, that's pretty much what happened with us. Somehow the summer passed in the blink of an eye.

Where did the time go? I woke up one morning, glanced at my calendar, and was shocked to find that it was the last week of August, only seven short days away from September 2—the big Friday night extravaganza at the Dorothy Chandler Pavilion. I still count it a miracle that we got the show together at all in so little time. There had been hundreds of details, large and small, that needed to be worked out—from negotiating contracts to making certain the orchestra had the arrangements it required. Each day that passed was full of crises and triumphs. Key people dropped out at crucial moments and new talent had to be found. Two weeks before the show, it appeared as though an important union was going to go on strike, and we would be left with no technicians to run the lights. The strike never materialized, but a few days later, the stage manager had a small heart attack—not serious as heart attacks go, but enough to take him out of the show. He had the entire sequence of the evening in his head, and to bring in a new person at such a late date had all of us pulling our hair.

Anyway, such is Show Biz. At least during these passing months, there were no new murders to report, no one else broke into our bedroom, and there were no particular breakthroughs in the case. It's not that I lost interest in finding Terry and Billy's killer(s)—singular or plural, male or female. It's just that I became too busy to pursue the matter. Meanwhile, the case appeared stalled, caught in the doldrums of a stalemate. I saw Lieutenant Kripinsky a few times during the summer and he looked even gloomier. Detective Harrington told me that generally with murders, if you don't solve them fast in the first few days, you often don't solve them at all. Personally, I was not planning to accept defeat in the matter; I was simply waiting to get back to the case when I had more time.

Then, exactly one week before the show, something odd happened. Jayne and I had been invited for dinner at the home of a friend of ours—a screenwriter, Bob Disher, who lives with his wife, Sarah, in the Malibu Colony. Cass was taking a rare evening off that night, going out to dinner and a movie with a "young woman friend," as he called her. A young woman friend of fifty-three, in fact, who shared Cass's love of Westerns. So Jayne backed her little Red Laser out of the garage and drove us toward Malibu. We reached the Pacific Coast Highway just in time to catch the last rays of a glorious California sunset over the water. Then night fell, cool and salty and moist with ocean air.

We were driving in a companionable silence, each of us lost in our own thoughts. My brain was floating in a kind of serene free-fall when we pulled up to a red light on the Coast Highway near the Malibu Pier. It took me a moment to come out of my reverie and realize that the light had changed to green, but Jayne was not moving.

I turned to her and saw in a passing headlight that she was white as a ghost, speechless with shock.

"Jayne! What is it?" I cried.

"My God! Hold on!" she said.

Without warning, she executed a dangerous U-turn on the highway, narrowly missing an oncoming BMW. She pressed down hard on the gas and roared off back toward Santa Monica.

"I'll explain in a moment . . ." she muttered. I had no idea who we were chasing, or what—but our pursuit didn't last long. Within minutes, we heard a siren behind us and saw the bright pattern of revolving red and blue lights in our rear window.

"I'll outrun them!" Jayne said wildly.

"*Jayne!* You will do no such thing! Now behave yourself, darling, and pull to the side of the road."

With a sigh and a shake of her red hair, Jayne gave up the chase. She slowed and pulled off onto the shoulder of the road. While the Highway Patrolman called in our license over his radio, I tried to get out of her what phantom she had been racing.

"It's too crazy, Steve . . . I'll tell you in a moment."

Whatever it was, Jayne was shaken. Fortunately, she pulled herself together for the benefit of the cop—a handsome young African-American with a kind face. In a convincing voice, she explained that I had suddenly discovered that my wedding ring was missing. Panicked at the very thought of such a sentimental loss, Jayne had executed her wild U-turn in order to return to the restaurant in Santa Monica where we had eaten dinner. I had taken off the ring, she said, to wash my hands and perhaps had left it in the bathroom there. It was very clever of Jayne to come up with such a quick story, but meanwhile I had to keep my left hand out of sight because, in fact, my wedding band was still there.

The officer was sympathetic but not about to let us completely off the hook. He said it was a shame to lose a wedding ring, but a much greater shame to lose our lives if Jayne continued to drive like that. So he gave us a ticket for an illegal U-turn just so she'd be more cautious in the future. Personally, I thought he was the King Solomon of California Highway Patrolmen, and I was on his side completely. After all, he could have given Jayne a much more expensive citation for reckless driving.

"All right," I said to Jayne when the cop had left us. "Now what was that crazy U-turn all about?"

"You won't believe me. I'm not even certain I believe myself."

"Try me."

"When I was waiting at the red light, I happened to glance at a limousine that was passing in the opposite direction. It was a Lincoln Continental, I think. The rear window was open so I had a glance at the person inside. It was only a quick glance, of course . . . so I must be mistaken."

"Jayne! Who was it?"

"It was Benny Hartman. He was smoking a cigar, Steve, and laughing as if he had just heard the greatest joke of all time!"

chapter 24

Naturally, Jayne had to be mistaken. It was night and the phantom limousine had rushed past in the blink of an eye. Not only that, but we had attended Benny's funeral and had seen his casket lowered into the ground. Nevertheless, I wished the CHP patrolman hadn't stopped us. I would have liked to catch up with that Lincoln just to discard every possibility—wild and improbable as it might be.

There was nothing we could do now except continue on to our dinner date. Bob Disher is a hugely successful screenwriter, but in person he is a modest, lanky, vaguely-scholarly man. He and his wife Sarah live in an old-fashioned Cape Cod-style beach house in the Malibu Colony with their two young children and a shaggy dog. We showed up at the Dishers' doorstep around seven PM and had a noisy, casual meal—homemade chicken burritos—which we ate around their kitchen table.

"We had quite a shock driving here tonight," I told Bob while we were eating. "Jayne thought she saw Benny Hartman sitting in a passing limousine."

"He was smoking a cigar and laughing!" Jayne added.

"Is that so? You know who I saw a few months back? Spencer Tracy. He was in a shopping mall in Pacific Palisades."

"Bob, Spencer Tracy has been dead—what? Twenty-five years?"

"That's what I'm saying, Steve. It's remarkable how many look-alikes there are—people who resemble someone famous."

"I guess my sighting was the same sort of thing," Jayne admitted. "I certainly *thought* it was him. But the light was terrible and I only had the quickest look."

"Well, at least it wasn't Elvis," Bob grinned. "But look, if you think there's any chance it actually *was* Benny, I know how you can find out."

"How?" Jayne and I asked in unison.

"I know Benny's doctor, David Diehl. We play tennis together sometimes—he lives just down the beach a few hundred yards. I'm sure he would have been the guy who signed Benny's death certificate. So why don't you give him a call?"

"You know, I'd like to do that, Bob—crazy as it sounds."

Disher gave me the phone number and pointed me toward a den telephone where I could get away from the chatter and giggling of his two lovely children. I reached Dr. Diehl on the second ring. Now that I had him on the phone, I hardly knew how to begin.

"What can I do for you, Mr. Allen?" he asked while I stalled for time.

"My request is a little strange, doctor. I understand you were Benny Hartman's private physician. I wanted to ask you a few questions about his death."

"Of course. I'm glad to help you, if I can."

"Did you, by any chance, attend his final moments?"

"You're asking, was I present when he died? As a matter of fact, yes, I was. What precisely is your interest in this, Mr. Allen?"

"Well, as you may know, Benny was a fairly close friend of mine, and he left me in charge of the award ceremony that's going to be televised next week. What I want to know . . . I'm simply curious," I faltered, "to find out exactly how he died."

"It was congestive heart failure—that's what I put down on the death certificate, at least. But with someone of his age, of course, the body simply runs down—of its own accord, you might say. There comes a moment when things simply stop working."

"I understand. So you were the one who signed the death certificate?"

"Yes, I did. I was Mr. Hartman's doctor for . . . goodness, over thirty years! I was glad he went peacefully at the end."

"Then you actually *saw* his body?" I pressed.

There was a small pause on the other end of the phone. "Mr. Allen," he began, "I wouldn't have signed the death certificate if I hadn't *seen* the body. I'd like to help you, but I'm not exactly certain what you want to know."

I was starting to feel foolish about this conversation, so I simply told Dr. Diehl the truth. "Look, this is crazy, but my wife thought she might have seen Benny today riding in the back of a limousine."

"That's impossible," the doctor said. There was now a slight chill in his voice. I suppose he was not pleased to have me doubt his professional qualifications by implying he wouldn't know whether a patient of thirty years was living or dead. "Benny Hartman died at his home on May 17. There was a nurse present, as well as myself . . . I can give you her name and telephone number, if you wish further corroboration."

"No, no, that's not necessary. I guess it was just a silly mistake. But you say that Benny died at home? That surprises me. When I saw him last, he was in the hospital."

"Two days before his death—when he knew his situation was hopeless—he elected to leave the hospital and return home. It's not an uncommon wish, to spend your final moments in more intimate surroundings. Please let me give you the nurse's name— I've worked with her before and I happen to have her number handy . . . yes, here it is. Janet Dorfman. She lives somewhere in the Valley at 555-9213. Besides the nurse, his wife, Gloria, was there to look after him as well, so I was glad to give my approval to the arrangements."

I put down the phone feeling slightly embarrassed. Dr. Diehl seemed the sort of old-fashioned professional who is not happy to find his judgment questioned. I was about to return to the kitchen table when I thought, what the hell, since I had started with this line of inquiry, I might as well go all the way and make a complete ass of myself.

So I called Janet Dorfman, the nurse, and I was lucky to find her at home. I decided to handle her call in a more casual manner—to tell her from the start that my wife thought she saw Benny tonight, which was obviously crazy. But nevertheless, just so we could sleep easily tonight, I was checking every possibility.

Was there any chance at all that Benny Hartman had *not* died peacefully at his home on May 17?

At least Janet had a sense of humor about my question, and did not become uptight like Dr. Diehl. She laughed. "No, I don't think your wife saw Benny tonight—not unless you believe in ghosts. He died very quietly, really. Sometimes with someone that age, it's like their spirit just slips away. He was quite a sweetheart ... an hour before he died, he was telling jokes and making all of us laugh. I'm glad he didn't suffer."

"You were in the room when he died?"

"No, I had stepped out for a moment. I was downstairs conferring with Dr. Diehl, who had just stopped by for his daily visit."

"Really? I must have misunderstood—I thought Dr. Diehl was actually with Benny at the end."

"Well, for all practical purposes he was. As I say, we were downstairs, about thirty feet away. When Gloria cried out, we both ran up to the bedroom. We were there within seconds."

"Then Gloria was alone with Benny in his bedroom at the actual moment of his death? Is that what you're saying?"

"Yes ... is there anything wrong with that? She was very helpful, actually. She told me she used to be a nurse, years ago. Sometimes she gave her husband his medicine. Occasionally even injections."

"Really?"

I hung up the phone and stared for a long moment out the den window at a sliver of moon that was rising over the ocean. I wondered exactly when Gloria Hartman had found time in her short, busy life to be a nurse—and if any of the life story that she had told me in Ojai was true.

In the bedroom, with no one looking, alone with an aging husband who was ill but oddly clinging to life ... had she given death just the smallest helping hand?

chapter 25

didn't sleep very well that night, imagining Gloria Hartman alone in her husband's bedroom at the time of his death. It's true, I didn't like Gloria very much—particularly after she had driven me clear to Ojai and then left me stranded. So maybe I was prejudiced against her. Still, the more I reviewed the details, the more my suspicions grew.

In the morning, I glanced at my calendar and saw there were only six more days to the awards ceremony. I simply did not have time to go off detecting. So I said to Jayne:

"Darling, how would you like to do me a small favor? Your judging is done, so you have a bit more time on your hands than I do . . ."

I asked Jayne to telephone Janet Dorfman, and perhaps make an appointment for lunch—some nice intimate place where two women might be able to talk. What I wanted were Janet's impressions of the Hartman household. Were there any strange undercurrents between Gloria and Benny? Any men, by chance, calling for Gloria? Anything odd that she might have noticed?

What I had in mind was a fishing expedition, but it seemed worthwhile. As a private nurse living at the Hartman house even for a short while, Janet might have some relevant observations to pass on to us. Jayne agreed to take on the assignment. Then she went to her office downstairs in our house, and I went to mine—a small library where I keep a desk. A few hours later I was in the midst of yet one more production crisis: One of the stars I had signed to help present the awards—a big name indeed—had come upon his beautiful wife yesterday in the arms of another man. I was not surprised; the woman was your model G-47 bimbo but suddenly the actor's life was topsy-turvy, he was going to get a divorce, and he wanted out of the show. I ended up spending more than an hour on the telephone with the fellow, playing psychiatrist, trying to convince him that during such a moment of domestic crisis he would be foolish to cancel. What was he going to do? Sit around and mope? He should keep busy, I suggested. Perhaps the comedy show was just the thing to get him laughing again.

Jayne put her head in my office door just as I was hanging up.

"Strange," she said, "I kept trying that number you gave me for Janet Dorfman, but it was busy all morning. Finally I gave it one last try, and this time I got a recording saying the number had been disconnected. This seemed odd, so I phoned the operator and she checked the number out for me—and yes, it *has* been disconnected."

"That *is* odd," I agreed. "When I talked with her last night, she didn't give any indication that she was moving today. Not that I asked her, of course."

"You know what, Steve? I think I'll run over there—I looked up her address in the phone book and she lives in Tarzana, only about twenty minutes away. Perhaps I'll find a neighbor who can tell me something."

"Good idea," I said.

So Jayne left to find out what had happened to Janet Dorfman, and I remained at home. My next task of the morning: to telephone the star's unfaithful wife and urge her to make a reconciliation . . . at least until after September 2.

It was midafternoon when Jayne returned.

"You're smiling, dear," she remarked.

"You bet! I just spent two hours on the phone saving a marriage . . . and the show as well! I've got my star back! So how about you—did you discover what happened to the nurse?"

"Well, it just gets odder and odder, Steve. There was no one in her apartment, and it wasn't the sort of building where people seem to know much about their neighbors. So I gave up temporarily and wandered down to a coffee shop a block away and found a telephone. I must say, I was *awfully* clever. Guess what I did?"

"What?"

"I phoned Cedars Sinai Hospital and managed to track down one of the head nurses there. I asked her if she knew Janet Dorfman, and she said yes, Janet was a good friend of hers though Janet didn't actually work for the hospital itself these days, but was in fact a private nurse, the sort doctors occasionally bring in for one reason or another. According to the woman at the hospital, Janet worked for a company called Loving Care, Inc., which handles a network of private nurses and sends them out on jobs, etcetera. So when I was done with the hospital, I phoned Loving Care to see if *they* knew why Janet Dorfman's telephone has been disconnected."

"And?"

"They were even more mystified than I was. I spoke to the head of the outfit, a nice man by the name of Donald Tansey. Apparently Janet was supposed to start a new job today taking care of a very sick woman in Laurel Canyon, but she didn't show up."

"Has she ever been unreliable in the past?"

"No, never—at least according to Mr. Tansey. And Janet has worked for him for nearly four years. Incidentally, I asked about the Benny Hartman job last May—how she happened to land that particular assignment. He was kind enough to check his records. It turns out that in this case, Dr. Diehl asked for Janet specifically. Apparently this is a common practice. Doctors develop working relationships with various nurses they like, and they hire them for different jobs."

"Then maybe you should give Dr. Diehl a call. Perhaps he knows where Janet has gone."

"I'm ahead of you, dear—I've already done it. But it's quite curious—the receptionist at Dr. Diehl's office told me that the good doctor was called away this morning, out of town on an emergency case, and she didn't know precisely when he was due back."

"Interesting! So he's disappeared, too! I wonder how far out of town he was called?"

"Quite extraordinarily far, it seems. A small village some miles outside Lhasa."

"When you say Lhasa, I presume you mean the Lhasa in . . ."

". . . In Tibet, dear. According to the receptionist, it's quite a remarkable story—he's gone to take care of a sick monk who's supposed to be the reincarnation of someone very high up in the Buddhist hierarchy. I gather in the village where Dr. Diehl has gone there's no telephone, no fax, no e-mail. There *is* regular mail, though it takes a few weeks to get through—probably delivered by yak!"

Jayne and I sat thinking about this development for a few moments. I could accept that Janet Dorfman might disappear unexpectedly, but not Janet and Dr. Diehl both. Not after I had talked with each of them the previous night about Benny's death.

"You know, darling," Jayne said after a while, "Dr. Diehl lives in the Malibu Colony near the Dishers. Perhaps we should stop by his house and see who's home."

"You don't think he's really in Tibet?"

"Taking care of the reincarnation of some monk? It sounds sideways to me. Let's go investigate."

I shook my head. "Somehow I doubt if the good doctor will tell us much, even if we find him at home. He struck me as the cautious, closed type. We're going to have to arm ourselves with more information before we approach him."

"So what's our next move, Steve?"

"You're going to laugh, but I think it's time we have a heart-to-heart chat with Lieutenant Kripinsky."

chapter 26

On the telephone, Lieutenant Kripinsky let us know that he was a *very* busy guy. Apparently there had been other homicides the past few months in Los Angeles besides ours, and a host of other major crimes as well, so he couldn't simply come running over to our house just because we had some harebrained theory we wanted to discuss.

Fine, I said. We'll come to you. Just name a time and place. After a few long sighs, the lieutenant agreed that he would give us a few moments today if we would meet him at six PM at a gym on Santa Monica Boulevard near Fairfax where he volunteered his time helping some neighborhood kids. Even a busy cop had to eat, and he was planning to grab a bite at a little Chinese restaurant nearby before heading to the station at seven.

When the time came, Cass drove us on the freeway to Santa Monica Boulevard and then east past Beverly Hills. The address we had was in a dubious section of town, a squat cement building that was squeezed in between an adult movie theater, Triple-X rated, and a small Korean grocery store. We were a few moments early and when we entered the gym, we had a surprise in store for us. Lieutenant Kripinsky was dressed in white pajamas and teaching tai chi, the ancient Chinese martial arts skill, to a group of teenage boys. For a big man, the lieutenant moved with a cat-like grace I would never have suspected was in him. Not only that, but prancing about the floor of the gym, his usual gloominess had disappeared; he glowed with enthusiasm. The teenagers, fascinated, hung onto his every utterance.

Jayne, Cass, and I were impressed. But he was back to his usual glum self fifteen minutes later when we sat with him at a round table at a modest Chinese restaurant a few doors away.

We ordered and then Jayne told her tale—how she had seen Benny Hartman, or someone who looked very much like him, sitting in the back of a limousine on the Pacific Coast Highway. And how I had spoken with Dr. Diehl and later the private nurse, Janet Dorfman, who assured us we were mistaken. And then today how both the doctor and nurse had disappeared, which obviously was *very* suspicious.

The lieutenant listened without expression; I don't believe I've ever seen an individual before who could make his face such an absolute blank.

Finally he nodded. "I see. Now let me see if I have this right. At night, on a very busy highway, you glance over to a car in the next lane and you think you see an old gentleman who reminded you of Benny Hartman. Can you tell me the length of this visual contact, please."

"Perhaps three or four seconds."

"Now, Mrs. Allen, may I ask you something else—do you wear glasses?"

"Yes, to drive. And I had them on."

"Very good. And when's the last time you saw an optometrist to have your vision tested?"

"Well . . . five years. Perhaps six."

"Ah! So there's a good chance you need new glasses! No, don't interrupt, please. What I'm doing is giving you a preview of how this would go over in a court of law . . ."

"We're not *in* court, Lieutenant," I objected.

"Mr. Allen, let's leave the question of the glasses aside for a moment, as well as the fact it was night, etcetera. How many other people have you talked with who have seen Mr. Hartman back from the dead?"

"No one, as far as I know. But Jayne isn't the sort of person to imagine something like this. And what about Dr. Diehl and Nurse Dorfman disappearing like that?"

"Mr. Allen," he cried in frustration, "it is perfectly legal to fly to Tibet, or anywhere else in the world, to help some sick Buddhist monk. Perhaps the nurse went along."

"And left her phone to be disconnected?"

"Why not? Maybe she decided to stay in Asia for a year and do some traveling."

"And simply not show up at a nursing job today? Don't you think that's just a bit suspicious?"

He sighed. "Mr. Allen," he said ponderously, "Mrs. Allen . . . Mr. Cassidy—I'm sure you mean well, interfering in this matter. But if you were a cop, you would have seen all these scenarios and more—hundreds of possible reasons why someone might not show up at work one day, even if they've been absolutely reliable in the past. Janet Dorfman may have run off with her lover. Or decided to give away her worldly belongings and join some religious sect. A brick could have fallen on her head and she's in a hospital with amnesia. Human behavior is unpredictable and fate is fickle. Meanwhile, what—are you trying to tell me you truly think Benny Hartman is alive?"

"It's possible," I said. "Or maybe he's dead, but his death was not due to natural causes."

"Make up your mind."

"Well, I don't know," I admitted, "but there's one way to find out."

He stared at me a moment. "What exactly do you have in mind?"

"Exhume Benny's coffin," I said. "Pry off the lid and see who—if anyone—is inside. And if Benny's there, perform an autopsy."

For one wild moment, I thought Lieutenant Kripinsky was actually going to laugh. The sides of his mouth twitched in an involuntary manner. But then he merely smiled a smile that was world-weary and sad.

"Do you have *any* idea how difficult it is to get a court order to exhume a body. In normal cases, it's just about impossible. With someone famous like Benny Hartman, and the publicity such an exhumation would entail, *impossible* is optimistic."

"Okay, I can accept that," I told him. "What sort of evidence would the court accept?"

"That's hard to say—it depends on the judge. If you could find a dozen reliable witnesses who have seen Benny Hartman since his death, that might work. If not . . . well, I don't want to encourage you to do anything rash or illegal. And I certainly *don't* approve of amateur detectives . . ."

"But, what?" I asked, sensing a *but* in his argument.

"But . . . a judge might be impressed if you could get someone to talk. Like this Dr. Diehl, for instance. Get him to admit that he faked the death certificate. Or that he knows of some question concerning the cause of death."

"But he's not exactly a talker. And not only that, he's in Tibet!"

The lieutenant shrugged. "Well, we all have problems. And no one ever said cracking a homicide is easy. Anyway, I've got to go," he said, glancing at his watch. "This week we got a serial killer on the loose who's strangling old women with blue hair."

Lieutenant Kripinsky asked for his bill, but I fought him for it and managed to pay.

On the way out the door, he gave me a shrewd glance and said: "If I were you, I'd forget the doctor for the time being and concentrate on the nurse."

"You mean . . ."

"Find her," he said. "Women break easier than men."

"I beg your pardon!" objected Jayne.

"Sorry, but it happens to be true. Find out what happened to Janet Dorfman. If you get her to talk, I'll get a judge to dig up Benny Hartman's coffin."

chapter 27

Had Lieutenant Kripinsky actually given us a green light to go ahead with our investigation? Cass, Jayne, and I agreed that he had been encouraging. It was heady stuff. But what could we do next?

"Let's try Janet's apartment one more time," I suggested after we left the Chinese restaurant. "Maybe we can knock on some doors. Talk with the manager. We might be able to stir up some trace of her."

"It would be better if we could actually get inside her apartment," Jayne mused.

"No problem," said Cass. "I'm pretty good with locks, remember."

"And the lieutenant *did* give us permission . . . almost," Jayne added.

"Not *that* sort of permission," I said. "But let's go over there. Who knows . . ."

Not knowing exactly what we planned to do, Cass pointed our old limo back toward the Valley and to the apartment complex where Janet Dorfman had been living. The Valley Oasis was a three-story building, perhaps thirty or forty apartments with a swimming pool in the inner courtyard. In Southern California, there are thousands of apartment complexes like this, often catering to young unmarried professionals with busy lives. The Valley Oasis was the sort of place with palm trees that were lit up from underneath by orange or blue floodlights. Jayne, who had been there that afternoon, led us to the row of buzzers by the locked front door. Finding a small plaque for J. Dorfman, we rang the buzzer on the off chance that she had returned. There was no answer and after three rings, Cass and Jayne and I had a brief conversation to decide what to do next.

"I could open this door easy. A piece of cake," Cass said enthusiastically, studying the lock.

"Cass! I'm ashamed of you!"

"Well, it's for a good cause, Steve," said my wife.

"Let's behave ourselves. We'll try the manager," I suggested, pushing the appropriate buzzer.

"Yes?" came a female voice through a small box.

"Hello, this is . . ."

"Oh, hello!" she interrupted. "You must be the people here about the vacant apartment?"

"Okay," I said, taking advantage of the unexpected opportunity.

The manager buzzed us in and told us to walk through the hall to Apartment 1-D, all the way in back. She was waiting for us with her door open, a pudgy, middle-aged woman with blond frizzy hair and dressed in a blue jogging suit. A television set behind her was tuned loudly to a raucous game show where someone was apparently winning large sums of money.

As she looked at me, her eyes grew wider and wider.

"My God! I'm going to faint!" she cried. "It can't be! . . . You're Steve Allen!"

There are times when it's fun to be a celebrity. And times when it is a hindrance. I wasn't certain yet what sort of occasion this might be. The lady appeared overwhelmed, as if by magic her television set had come to life. I reached out to steady her.

"I can't believe it!" she said in a hoarse whisper. "I'm *touching* Steve Allen."

"Now, now," I chided, "it's not such a big deal."

But then she saw Jayne. *"Jayne!"* she gasped. *"Jayne Meadows!* . . . heaven help me! Are *you* someone famous, too?" she inquired of Cass. "Muffy! You'll never believe it—come look at who's here!"

Muffy turned out to be a small, vicious poodle who came running our way with teeth bared. Things got a little chaotic as Muffy took a bite of my trousers. The lady manager, of course, was mortified at her dog's behavior, but I assured her there was no harm done. Fortunately, by the time Muffy's jaws were pried open and the poodle placed into a back room, we were all better friends—and the lady was no longer quite so impressed by our celebrity status.

"Have you *really* come to rent an apartment at The Oasis?" she wondered.

No, we admitted now that we were such friends—we had not. I made up a story about a sick, elderly Aunt Mary, on Jayne's side of the family, and how we were looking for a good nurse. Someone had recommended Janet Dorfman, and since it was extremely important to us that we find just the right person for beloved Aunt Mary, we had been trying to reach Ms. Dorfman, without success, for the past day. Thus our presence here tonight.

"It's quite a mystery," Jayne added. "Her phone has been disconnected, and when we called the private nursing outfit— Loving Care—they said she didn't show up for a job today."

"Really!"

"Actually, we've become concerned," I mentioned. "From what we've heard of Ms. Dorfman, it's difficult to imagine she'd simply leave a patient dangling without a word of explanation."

"She always pays the rent on time," said the manager. "She seems *very* responsible to me."

"Perhaps she's sick or in trouble," suggested Jayne.

"Or maybe in a hospital somewhere with amnesia," added Cass. "Or kidnapped, or in a car wreck."

"Goodness!" said the manager, glancing from one of us to the other. "Well, we'd better find out!"

A few minutes later we stood together outside the door to Apartment 3-F. The manager—her name was Angie Smart—rang the buzzer. When there was no answer, she rapped with her knuckles on the door itself.

"Hello! Janet! This is Angie from downstairs!"

But there was no response.

"We don't really keep track of the tenants here," Angie told us. "Everyone comes and goes as they like. So I can't really say when I actually saw Janet last—it must be at least a week or two."

"I almost hate to suggest this," Jayne said delicately, "but by any chance, do you have a pass key?"

"Well, I do. But I hate to use it, of course. Janet, are you in there?" she called out loudly, rapping on the door with renewed vigor. "Guess what? Steve Allen and Jayne Meadows are here to see you!"

But still no answer.

"I'm starting to worry about foul play," I said.

"No telling *what* can happen to a single girl in this city," Cass added ominously.

At last, Angie slipped the pass key into the lock and let us in. The apartment was small but quite modern and comfortable. There was a kitchen with a counter and bar stools separating the cooking area from the living room. A bedroom, bath, a narrow balcony overlooking the turquoise waters of the brightly lit swimming pool below. There was no one at home. In the bedroom, the chest of drawers was half open, as though someone had packed quickly.

"It looks as though she's taken all her personal things," Jayne remarked, inspecting the empty hangers in the closet.

"She cleaned out her medicine cabinet, all right," Cass remarked from the bathroom.

There is a difference between a home which someone leaves for a week or two, and one which is abandoned forever. Janet Dorfman's apartment looked as if no one was ever coming back.

"But look—she left her stereo. And that's her rocking chair," Angie said from the living room.

"The apartment is furnished?" I asked.

"Basically. But most of the tenants add a few things of their own. I doubt if Janet would have left her CD player behind if she wasn't coming back. That's her answering machine, too."

"It looks to me as if she left in a hurry," I said. The answering machine gave me an idea. The device was plugged in and the message counter read "0"—no messages. However, answering machines often retain their last message unless they are deliberately erased. I pressed the "Play Message" button and turned up the volume.

I heard a male voice: "Sweetheart, I just called to say, don't bother to pack anything more than an overnight case. I'll buy everything you need. From now on, I'm going to look after both of us. All you've got to do is drive up to the cabin . . ."

Then a female voice, picking up the phone: "I'm here. I was in the shower . . ."

The machine cut off as Janet picked up. There was a "beep" and then an expressionless electronic voice: "Saturday, two-twelve AM."

This was the previous night, in fact. A number of hours after I had spoken with Janet from Bob Disher's house.

"Two o'clock in the morning sounds awfully late to be taking a shower!" Cass remarked.

"Not if you had just spent several hours frantically packing your car and were planning to skip town," Jayne told him.

This was the only message on the tape that had not been erased, and we listened to it several times. The male voice on the tape was familiar—I had spoken with this voice from Bob's house shortly before I had called Janet. It was Dr. Diehl, Benny's doctor who had signed the death certificate.

Somehow my phone calls last night to Dr. Diehl and Janet Dorfman had sent them both rushing out of town.

"Most curious!" I said, scratching my chin.

chapter 28

The red light of our answering machine in the kitchen was blinking when we returned home. Sometimes it's hard to remember the prehistoric days before answering machines, before My Machine might converse happily with Your Machine and a call to an empty house would result only in a lot of useless ringing in the dark.

Cass set about to make up a pot of tea while I listened to the messages. My domestically-troubled movie star had phoned to thank me for saving his marriage. He and his wife were more in love than ever, he said—they owed it all to me, would name their first child after me, boy or girl. And meanwhile, they were off to Rio de Janeiro for a second honeymoon, so he wouldn't be able to do the show after all.

"Remind me *never* to play Cupid again!" I swore. Fortunately, the next message brought some light at the end of the cliché: a *very* big star, an old friend of Jayne's and mine, who was just back in town after six months in India where he had been filming an expensive epic, was looking forward to getting together to celebrate his return to what he assumed was still civilization. I smiled fiendishly, knowing *exactly* how he was going to celebrate—onstage at the Dorothy Chandler Pavilion in front of all America.

There were more calls, of mostly minor interest. Then: "Hello, Steve—Jonathan Murano here. Sorry it took so long, but I've finally managed to get that information you requested a few months back. You can reach me on my cell phone any time up to midnight at . . ."

I scribbled down the number. To tell the truth, I had given

up on getting any help from the Murano family in identifying the sketch I had given them of the intruder who had broken into our bedroom last June—and my various other inquiries about that sleazy individual had also come to naught. Curious about what Jonno had managed to find, I dialed the number.

I was expecting to get some henchman, but Jonno himself answered on the second ring.

"I'm embarrassed this took so long," he said. "The problem was, Steve, your intruder isn't a professional—just a small-time hustler who picks up money any way he can. There are thousands of lowlife characters who fit this description in Los Angeles—mostly loners who live in the shadows and don't run with any particular crowd. So finding him wasn't easy. I wish I could tell you how clever we were, but basically we just got lucky. He came up in regard to another matter that interests us. A matter I don't think I'll tell you about."

"No, better not," I said quickly. It was bad enough dealing with the devil; I didn't want to know the details of his particular hell.

Jonno laughed slightly, reading me very well.

"Anyway, here's the bit," he said. "His name is Murray the Z, believe it or not . . . that's what he calls himself. God knows what 'Z' stands for. You probably remember the famous New York deejay, Murray the K, from some years back—I suppose our guy thinks he's being cool by appropriating the name. None of these small-time hoods are very smart or original. He lives in a rundown building near the beach in Venice—the Blue Moon Apartments. You'll be glad to know this upstanding citizen actually has a job—he works in a small store that rents surfboards and wetsuits. On the side, Murray the Z sells a little reefer. He's been busted for that a few times, as well as for breaking and entering and stealing cars. Not exactly a charming character. He has a few ex-wives, but his love life suffers from the fact that with a few beers in him, he likes to beat up on women. And that's about all I can tell you."

"Well, thanks, Jonno. I will definitely pay this Murray character a visit to find out who hired him to break into my house!"

"Look, Steve, I'd be careful if I were you. Generally you can trust professionals in this business to act rationally, and in their own best interest. But with these small-time sleazeballs, you never know what they're going to do. Half of them have mental problems. If Murray is high on something, or you catch him in the wrong mood, he could be dangerous."

"I appreciate the warning. I'll take Cass with me and tread cautiously."

"I got a better idea. This is my area of expertise, so why don't you let me take care of it. I have one of my people outside the Blue Moon Apartments right now keeping an eye on him—I'll just pop on over and get the information you want, and call you back in a few hours."

"Thanks, Jonno. I appreciate your help—but I'd like to go along," I told him. I had no tender feelings for Murray the Z, but nevertheless I worried that Jonno and his people would do some nasty things that I didn't want on my conscience.

Again I heard a slight, dark laugh from Jonno's end. He was extremely bright and I sometimes had the feeling he could almost read my mind.

"Are you sure you want to be a witness?" he asked with irony.

"Jonno, I know that deep in your heart, you don't want to be part of this either—I'll always think of you as that dreamy kid who wanted to make great movies."

"That kid doesn't exist anymore, Steve," he said. Then his voice hardened: "If you want to come, be ready in fifteen minutes. I'll pull by and pick you up. Not Jayne, not Cass—only you. This will not be a social occasion."

The line went dead.

Precisely fifteen minutes later I heard a car honk in my driveway. Glancing out the living room window, I saw a silver Rolls Royce. It was a vintage Rolls, probably from the late fifties. In the moonlight it looked like a phantom automobile, magnificent but somehow deadly.

"Are you sure you want to go through with this?" Jayne asked, looking out the window.

"Sure. It's only Jonno."

"Only Jonno!" she repeated with a shake of her head. "Well, be careful."

A very muscular chauffeur opened the back door of the Rolls

and I slipped in next to Jonno onto a seat of dark red leather. The car was full of highly polished wood and it smelled like an exclusive men's club—the kind that used to exist in London and New York. Jonno was dressed in an impeccable dark suit. He flashed me a pale smile.

"You know, I was just thinking, Steve, how most people in America go into a supermarket to buy their meat in very sanitized packages, all glossy and plastic. The way they wrap the meat, they do their best to disguise where it actually comes from."

"What are you trying to tell me?"

"Are you certain you really want to know where your meat comes from?"

"I can face reality. But look, I don't intend to harm this Murray the Z character—and I'm certainly not seeking revenge. All I want is some information."

"Exactly. But to get this information, we're going to have to frighten him. Do you understand me? We're going to appeal to his imagination—his worst nightmares, that is, of what will happen to him if he doesn't tell us what we wish to know."

I nodded. "I understand that. And it's fine with me . . . as long as we leave it in the realm of imagination. But I don't want to hurt him, Jonno."

He smiled. "What do you think I am—Attila the Hun? The *threat* of violence, properly applied, makes violence itself unnecessary. But once we're in the Blue Moon Apartments, I'm the one in charge, understand? As I said on the phone, small-time hoods like Murray the Z can be dangerous because they're unpredictable—and I don't want you to get hurt."

"Okay," I agreed. "We'll play by your rules."

Venice, just south of Santa Monica, has gone through a rebirth in the past dozen years—from a seedy, drug-infested neighborhood of beach bums and down-and-out hippies to chic and expensive. The Blue Moon Apartments, however, was on a narrow side street near a foul-smelling canal and had clearly not caught up with the new times. The building was a pre-war stucco, vaguely Spanish, a sickly green in color, and it looked more like a cheap motel than a place to call home. The name was spelled in blue neon rather grandly on the facade, but a few letters weren't working. So it looked like this: THE BLU MOO APA TMENTS. The muscular young chauffeur found a parking spot and then came around to open the rear door of the Rolls for us. As soon as we stepped out onto the street, another man came out from the shadows near an overflowing Dumpster and joined us.

"Is he still inside, Giorgio?" Jonno asked the newcomer.

"Yes. And he's alone."

"Good. Giorgio, meet my friend, Mr. Allen. Now it's time for the three of us to pay a social call on Murray."

Giorgio led the way up a flight of outside stairs that went to the second floor. The newcomer was older than the chauffeur, but he was bigger and nastier—with huge shoulders, the torso of a bull, and a face you might see in a bad dream. Jonno didn't need to tell me that this was The Muscle.

We stopped in front of the door to Apartment 204. Jonno and I stood to one side while Giorgio knocked.

"Who's there?" came a gruff voice from inside.

"Dave sent me," Giorgio called back.

I have no idea who "Dave" was, but the name seemed to do the trick. The door opened and Murray appeared. He was even seedier-looking than when I had seen him last—unshaved and disheveled, dressed in shorts and a T-shirt. When he saw me and Jonno, he tried to slam the door shut, but Giorgio was too quick for him. Jonno and I flowed into the apartment in Giorgio's wake, and closed the door behind us.

"Hey! What the hell is this?" Murray complained.

"We'll only disturb you for a moment. We have just a few questions to ask, Murray," Jonno said softly, "and then we'll be on our way."

"I don't know nothin'!" he said sullenly.

"How do you know? We haven't even asked you anything yet," Jonno said. "For example, how much is two and two?"

"What?"

"You heard me. It's an easy question, at least I think it is. How much is two and two?"

"Four, for Christ's sake," Murray said, beginning to look alarmed.

"There, you see?" Jonno said. "You *do* know something."

Murray looked at each of us with quick, furtive eyes. There was a smell of liquor in the room and I soon found the source—a half-finished bottle of tequila on a dresser table. The apartment was a mess. There were overflowing ashtrays and cigarette burns on the carpet. A television set was on softly to a rerun of "Charlie's Angels," but the reception was bad and all the girls had orange complexions.

"Murray," Murano said, "I saw you glance anxiously at Mr. Allen, so you know exactly what this visit is about. We want you to tell us, please, who hired you to break into Mr. Allen's house last June."

"I don't know what you're talkin' about. I never saw this guy before. And I didn't break into his bedroom, neither."

Jonno smiled dangerously. "Did I say *bedroom?*" He gave me a questioning look. "Is this the right guy, Steve?"

I nodded.

Jonno turned his attention back to Murray. "I'm sensing that we have a small communication problem, Murray. Do you know who I am?"

"Yeah. I recognize you. You're Jonathan Murano."

"Good! I'm glad you recognize me, because you know, Murray, friends are *very* important to me—and it's a lot better to be my friend than to be my enemy."

"I can't tell you nothin'," Murray said stubbornly. But his eyes were shifty and I caught a new scent in the room, the smell of fear.

"You . . . can't . . . tell . . . me . . . *nothing!*" Jonno repeated ominously. "Well, let's see. Can you tell me who's buried in Grant's tomb?"

"Yeah, Grant," Murray said.

"Beautiful. So it turns out you can tell me a few things. If you're smart you'll keep up the good work. You know, Giorgio, it's a terrible thing to come across an individual who doesn't speak English correctly. This man just used a double negative!"

"That means he *can* tell you somethin', boss. Two negatives cross each other out and make a positive."

"That's right! You see, Giorgio speaks English very well, even though he was born in Sicily," Jonno said, addressing Murray again.

So far Jonno and Giorgio had spoken only in the most commonplace terms—but Murray was streetwise enough to be terrified.

"Look, I'd love to tell ya anythin' ya wanna know, Mr. Murano . . . but this just isn't worth it to me. There's this guy who will come and kill me if I say anythin'."

"Interesting. A guy will come and kill you. But don't you think it's better, Murray, to deal with the danger you're facing now, rather than some future danger that might arrive at an unspecified date? You see what I'm saying, don't you? 'This guy,' as you call him, *may* come to kill you. But if you don't tell me who he is, *I* could kill you now."

"I can't tell ya! Honest!" Murray cried.

"Giorgio, it's time to show this man we're serious."

Giorgio stepped closer to the frightened, disheveled Murray the Z—a sad, second-rate crook if there ever was one. I thought it was time to get involved.

"Jonno, excuse me—I'd like to try my hand at asking a few questions."

"Steve, remember—you weren't going to interfere," Jonno reminded me with a thin smile.

"Look, I think I can do this the easy way. Without any rough stuff. Please."

Jonno shrugged. "Frankly, I doubt it. But if you're squeamish—go ahead and give it a try."

I stepped forward. "Look, no one wants to hurt you, but we need to know the truth, Murray. Who sent you to break into my house?"

He seemed relieved to face me, rather than Jonno or Giorgio. He appeared almost desperately eager to please me. "It wasn't personal, Mr. Allen—like I told ya at the time. I really needed the money."

"I understand. And you can keep the money, too. All I want to know . . ."

"I wish I could tell ya. God, I wish I could tell ya! . . . But you see, it was this guy who I never saw before, and I never saw him again. I don't know his name. Honest!"

Murray smiled eagerly, trying to show how forthcoming he was. But there was nothing even remotely honest about his face.

"Steve! Let me do this my way," Jonno urged behind my right shoulder.

But Jonno's "way" worried me, and I was certain I could do this in a more civilized fashion. "Let me have just one more minute," I said to Jonno. And then to Murray, in the most ominous voice I could summon: "As you see, Murray, you are just about out of time. So what's it going to be—are you going to tell me the truth? Or do we need to set Giorgio loose to work on you?"

"I'll tell ya the truth, Mr. Allen—please! Don't let those guys touch me."

"Okay, I won't let them, if you—tell me quick!"

Murray had inched himself backward while we were talking so that he was standing next to his television set. What came next happened so quickly that there was no time to react. While he was cringing and pleading for mercy, Murray managed to reach behind the TV and pull out a pistol. The first shot was so loud in my right ear that I thought for a moment I would certainly be deaf forever. Then someone pushed me aside—I think it was Giorgio trying to get me out of the way so that he could fire back. I fell onto the floor between a bed and a coffee table, and I stayed there. The noise continued to be horrendous as shots were fired in the enclosed room. I counted five or six blasts, but there may have been more; at each shot, I was certain I was a dead man. Smoke and the smell of cordite hung in the room. I heard the front door to the apartment open and close, and a moment later some shots were fired outside.

Then there was silence. And the silence, when it came, was nearly as ominous as the deafening explosions of gunfire. I was still crouching on the floor when someone shook my shoulder.

"We gotta get out of here! Hurry!" said a voice. It was Jonno's chauffeur, who I had last seen parking the Rolls; I have no idea when he had arrived at the battle, but he was standing now with his gun drawn. I stood up and saw a horrible sight. Jonno and Giorgio were dead, lying lifeless and broken about the room.

Jonno had been shot in the left eye, and I nearly got sick when I looked at him. I would probably have stood there until the cops arrived, unable to move, but the chauffeur hoisted Jonno's body up over his shoulder in one easy motion, leaving Giorgio on the floor. Then he hissed at me once again: "We gotta leave! Right this minute!"

"Where's Murray?" I asked.

"The son of a bitch got away—now let's split."

I followed him out the door and down the outside stairs to the street. With all the noise we had made, I expected faces to be peering out of every doorway—but apparently this was the sort of neighborhood where people minded their own business when there was trouble.

I was still shaken, hardly able to absorb what had happened. The chauffeur threw his boss's body in the back seat, and then pushed me inside as well.

We sped off into the dark and murderous night.

chapter 29

"Such a terrible waste!" I said to Jayne and Cass a few hours later. "I feel awful about this. I should have let Jonno get the information his own way—not only would he still be alive, but we'd know who hired that bastard Murray!"

"Steve, you couldn't just stand by while Giorgio did God-knows-what to that poor man!" Jayne objected.

"No, I was an amateur. I shouldn't have been there in the first place . . . Jonno warned me that Murray could be dangerous, but I didn't listen to him."

"You gotta stop blaming yourself, Steve," Cass said sternly.

"Cass is right," Jayne added. "Jonno and Giorgio both chose to live in a violent world where sudden death is always possible. It wasn't your fault."

I shook my head. "If I hadn't been standing between Murray and the others, Murray would never have managed to pull a gun. Sure, my intentions were good—but you know what they say about the road to hell."

It was two o'clock in the morning and Cass, Jayne, and I were sitting around the kitchen table going over and over the events of the night. Normally, I'm not much of a drinker, but I had a small shot of brandy in front of me. Jonno's chauffeur had dropped me off at home three hours earlier, but I was still in shock. I couldn't stop reliving the horrors of the gun battle.

Finally, about two-thirty AM I picked up the phone on the kitchen table.

"I'm calling the LAPD," I said grimly.

To my surprise, Cass put his finger down on the button, cutting my connection.

"Think about this a moment, boss. You went off in a Rolls Royce with a known Mafia kingpin in order to apply some serious pressure on a small-time hood. In the middle of all this, two people got killed."

"So what are you saying?"

"Don't go to the cops. Not yet, anyway. They'll eat you for breakfast . . . and what purpose will it serve?"

"I agree with Cass," Jayne said. "Find out who killed Terry and Billy first—*then* confess to the cops, if you feel you must."

"I don't believe you two! I was witness to a shooting in which two people were killed! I can't just keep quiet about it."

I still had the telephone receiver in hand, and Cass's finger remained on the button. Then the phone rang. It startled Cass so much that he let go.

"Hello?" I said warily.

"Don't worry about the son of a bitch who shot my son. I'll deal with him in my own way. But I do want you to worry about what has happened to my son—to me—to my family."

"I do feel awful about that, Mr. Murano," I said.

"Bullshit," he said. "Sure, you're sorry about it but sorry doesn't cut it. You have four sons yourself, I understand."

"That's right," I said.

"Have you any remote idea how you would feel if one of them was killed?"

"Well," I said, "I—"

"Bullshit," he repeated. "You can't ever feel a thing like this until it happens to you."

At that moment I had the impression that his voice was going to break. He sounded very near tears.

"That young man—that boy—who got killed trying to do you a favor—I don't care how old he was, he was still my baby. Do you know what I'm talking about?"

"I think I do, sir," I said.

"I hope so," he said.

"He was the hope for my family, do you understand that? He was a better human being than I'll ever be. Of course, we came from different worlds and to the extent that he eventually got into my business—that was my fault, not his."

"If there was anything I could do," I said, "I would—"

"Well, there ain't," he said. "Well, yeah, there is something you can do. For the rest of your life, stay away from me. I owed you one favor, and you called it. That's the end of that."

He continued and finally I put the phone down and sighed. "It was Pete Murano," I told Jayne and Cass. "The old man. He wanted me to know his debt to me is canceled. I saved a life, and I lost a life—so the balance sheet is clean. He also said that I'm not to call on him in the future, and that under no circumstances should I tell the authorities what happened tonight. He doesn't want a police investigation."

"You'd better do what he says, Steve," Cass advised solemnly. "Pete Murano is a serious man!"

"Yes, I'd better," I agreed. "At least for the time being. But I swear to God, I'm going to find out who hired Murray, and what these damned murders are all about!"

In my house, it didn't feel as if there was a comedy award show coming up in five days; after that night, Cass, Jayne, and I were about the grimmest group of people you might imagine. And we were absolutely determined to get to the bottom of the mysterious events that had led to two murders, and such wasteful violence.

In the morning, Jayne, Cass, and I gathered around our telephone answering machine in the kitchen and slipped in the small cassette tape that we had lifted earlier from Janet Dorfman's apartment. We listened to the single message over and over again, trying to divine subtle shades of meaning.

Dr. Diehl: "Sweetheart, I just called to say, don't bother to pack anything more than an overnight case. I'll buy everything you need. From now on, I'm going to look after both of us. All you've got to do is drive up to the cabin . . ."

Nurse Dorfman: "I'm here. I was in the shower . . ."

And then we heard the machine cutting off with a "beep" as Janet picked up, and the expressionless, robot voice marking the time of the call: "Saturday, two-twelve AM."

"The cabin!" I said. "But *what* cabin? Lake Arrowhead? Big Bear? Where do people have cabins in Los Angeles?"

"I have an idea," said Jayne with a smile. "Why don't you boys go off and do something useful and leave this to me. I'll find out where Dr. Diehl's cabin is."

It took Jayne a few hours. She simply opened a map of California and phoned directory assistance for all the likely communities that she spotted—various places where people who live in L.A. generally keep country houses. She began with the assumption that "cabin" implied a house in the mountains, rather than a place at the beach or in the desert, so she tried Lake Arrowhead, Big Bear, Idylwild, Mammoth, and a few other communities as well. She canvassed entire counties: Riverside, San Bernadino, Ventura, Santa Barbara . . . but none of the operators could find a listing for a Dr. David Diehl.

Next Jayne considered the possibility that the doctor was one of those people willing to travel far to escape city life. She tried San Luis Obispo, Big Sur, and all the pretty places up and down the coastal range toward northern California.

Then her eye fell upon a patch of blue on the California map.

"Of course!" she said aloud. "Exactly the sort of place an outdoorsy doctor would go!" She dialed 411 with the proper area code, and in a moment she had a phone number and address for Dr. David Diehl. The cabin was located at that prime California vacation spot, Lake Tahoe.

Within half an hour, Jayne and I and Cass had our tickets for a small commuter airline, and were on our way to the Burbank Airport.

chapter 30

The airplane seated twelve people and reminded me of a child's toy, one of those things with the propeller powered by a rubber band. We flew over the huge agricultural middle section of California, the San Joaquin Valley, and then into the Sierras, where the small plane pitched and bumped and skimmed along the mountaintops.

"If we flew any closer to these mountains, I could build a campfire," Cass observed, looking down nervously. Cass once told me that he would rather ride a bucking bronco than fly in a small plane—so he was being very brave.

"Look, if we crash, don't eat me," he said after a while.

I blinked. "I'm trying to catch your *non sequitur,* Cass, but it eludes me," I admitted.

"Wasn't there a crash some years back in the Sierras where the survivors ate the people who died?"

"You're confusing two separate incidents of cannibalism," I explained. "The plane crash you're thinking about occurred in the Andes. Of course, there was also the Donner party. *They* were in the Sierras, and ended up eating human flesh—but that was long before the days of airplanes."

"Would you two please stop talking about cannibalism!" Jayne murmured. She had her eyes closed and was actually relaxed enough in our tiny flying machine to attempt sleep.

Eventually the plane dove down into a bowl surrounded by mountains, flew close to the deep, ice-cold blue waters of Lake Tahoe, and then floated into the small airport. Cass almost kissed the ground when we were once again standing upon solid earth.

It was a beautiful day in the mountains, crisp and clear with the smell of pine in the air. I rented us a generic new American car; you can't tell if they're a Buick, Ford, or Chevrolet these days—not like the glory years when Detroit produced cars whose pedigree you could identify from a block away by the size and shape of the fins and taillights. Our rented machine was light gray in color. Cass said it was a Plymouth, but made partly in Japan and another part in Mexico—which probably accounts for its identity problem.

Cass got behind the wheel, Jayne sat in the passenger seat with a map of the Lake Tahoe area, and I settled into a back seat that was so cramped my legs hugged my chest. While we searched for Dr. Diehl's cabin, I used my cell phone to try to get some work done—Benny Hartman Memorial Comedy Awards work, that is. Riding about the narrow mountain highways, I managed to have a conference call with Jerry Williams and a VP from the network, and I also spoke to one of the writers who had spent the past few days reworking several intros and lead-ins. The writer was someplace on his ranch in New Mexico, with a cell phone of his own. Such is the new technology; you can travel to beautiful places and hardly see them, because you have a small plastic gizmo in your hand and someone yacking in your ear.

When I "hung up" the cell phone—pressed the "off" button, that is—I saw that we were climbing a steep, deeply shaded driveway to an A-Frame house that was built from redwood. Huge fir trees surrounded the house, cutting off the sky. There was a dusty Volvo station wagon by the garage door.

"This is it?" I asked.

Jayne looked up from the map. "I think so. By my calculations this should be 124 Woodpecker Terrace—which is the address I got from the phone book."

Cass parked alongside the Volvo and we stepped out in the fragrant mountain afternoon. The house was a modern design, built on several levels with a good deal of glass. The garage near where we were standing seemed to be a kind of basement level and the front door was not immediately apparent so we walked up a path to a sundeck, from where there was a scenic view of the lake through a break in the trees. Jayne rapped her knuckles against a sliding glass door.

"Hello! Anyone home?"

When there was no answer, we put our faces against the glass. Inside we could see a strangely-shaped living room and a combination kitchen-dining area, a large open space with a high ceiling. The interior of the house was attractive but lacking in human warmth.

"There's a bag of groceries on the kitchen counter," Cass observed.

"Look—there's a kettle on the stove with a gas burner going."

"Well, *someone* is at home . . . and not far away," I agreed. Meanwhile we kept peering in the glass, but didn't see a soul.

"Hello, hello, wherever you are!" Jayne cried.

"Dr. Diehl? Janet?" I shouted.

But there was no answer. I was starting to get a bad feeling. The last time Cass and I had peered inside a closed house, we found a dead body in the swimming pool in the backyard. But then I heard a car door slam and an engine start. We ran to the edge of the sundeck in time to see the Volvo station wagon turning recklessly in the narrow driveway. There was a woman at the wheel and she seemed desperate to avoid our company.

"Janet!" I shouted. "Wait! We just want to ask you a few questions!"

But apparently she wasn't in a mood to talk. She turned her wheel hard, but our rented car was in her way. She simply smashed it aside, bumping against the rear fender, and then continued at a great speed down the steep driveway.

Jayne, Cass, and I ran down the path toward our newly dented car, ready to rush off in pursuit. But just as we were piling in, we heard a terrible screech of brakes, and then the sound of a crash—metal against metal, the jangle of broken glass. Janet Dorfman had been in such a hurry to escape us that she had not stopped to look as she pulled out of the driveway onto the main highway; a bakery truck coming down the road had broadsided the Volvo.

Jayne ran back up to the house to find a phone and call for an ambulance while Cass and I jogged down the driveway toward the wreck. The bakery truck, smashed like an accordion, had spilled its load upon the highway—hundreds of donuts every-where, chocolate, glazed, frosted, and sugar-coated, up and down the road. Miraculously the driver—a middle-aged man—limped out of the wreckage, bloody but basically unhurt. Janet Dorfman had not been so lucky. She was pinned behind the wheel of her car, apparently alive but unconscious. The donut driver wanted to try to pull her out, but I stopped him.

"Better wait for the ambulance," I told him with a sigh.

It was starting to look like everything connected to Benny Hartman and his damned awards show was ill-fated in the extreme.

The Lake Tahoe hospital looked more like a nice hotel than a place for people to be born or die or get fixed up from their skiing accidents.

After about two hours of waiting, a doctor came out of the emergency room to where we were sitting. We had committed a small fib, I'm afraid: On our urging, Cass had told the hospital that the injured woman was his sister.

He was a young doctor with a well-groomed beard and glasses. "Well, Mr. Cassidy," he said, "there's some good news and some bad news about your sister—she's alive and her condition is stable. But she's in a coma. It's the sort of thing, she may come out five minutes from now . . . or in a week, a month . . . or she may never come out at all."

It was a tough break—for Janet, certainly, who had been so stupid as to run from us. And for us, too, since our questions were still unanswered.

We drove back to the A-Frame, hoping for any information at all. The house was open—an open invitation to nosy people like us—and we made a complete search, from the upper bedrooms to the garage below. There was nothing very much of a personal nature anywhere—few clothes, knickknacks, not even many paint-ings on the walls. Janet had unpacked a suitcase in one of the bedrooms upstairs, but her arrival had hardly made a dent in the basic sterility of the place. As far as the atmosphere went, the A-Frame could have been an expensive motel.

After a discouraging hour-long search, we discovered only

one item that interested us—a notepad by the phone in the kitchen. On the third page, not immediately apparent to view, there was a number written down for the Lhasa Holiday Inn in Tibet.

"Goodness! Do you think he's actually in Tibet after all?" Jayne asked.

"Let's find out," I suggested, picking up the phone.

"You're not going to call him, Steve! That's halfway around the world!" Cass objected. "Think about the phone bill."

"Tough," I said, dialing the international operator. "Doctors make tons of money."

In less than five minutes, I reached a very polite, English-speaking assistant manager at the Lhasa Holiday Inn. Yes, I learned, Dr. Diehl was indeed a guest at the hotel. But alas, he had left for several days on a tourist excursion to a remote region. I left my name and number and asked that Dr. Diehl phone me upon his return.

But I wasn't hopeful.

chapter 31

We flew back to Burbank in the twin-engine commuter plane, and found a message on our answering machine at home to call Lieutenant Kripinsky.

"Mr. Allen, I was wondering if you have any information about a body found shot to death at a small apartment complex in Venice—a sleazy little place called the Blue Moon? The blood of a second person was on the floor nearby. Were you there, by any chance?" he asked gruffly when I returned his call.

"I do my best to avoid sleazy places where people shoot each other," I assured him. "What's this place called? The Blue Spoon?"

"I think you heard me correctly, Mr. Allen. Strangely enough, someone answering your description was seen leaving the crime just after the shooting. Wearing glasses, about six-feet-three . . ."

"That could fit a few hundred thousand people here in L.A., Lieutenant."

"Yes, I suppose it could. But I'm starting to get superstitious about you, Mr. Allen. Somehow every time there's a body in this town, I blink and you're in the neighborhood."

"Well, I'm glad to be in your thoughts. You were certainly in mine today when we managed to locate Janet Dorfman."

"You found her, did you? Better tell me all about it . . ."

So I told him about our trip to Lake Tahoe in detail, glad to change the subject away from the Blue Moon Apartments. Kripinsky was particularly interested in the way Janet had run from us—fleeing with such blind haste that she had gotten into a serious car wreck. The lieutenant made me go over this part several times—his usual painstaking method of interrogation.

"You know, I think I will get a court order to have Benny Hartman's body exhumed," he said, almost to himself, when I came to a stop.

"I'm pleased, Lieutenant. But surprised. What made you change your mind? I was betting you'd find some excuse for Janet running off like that—like maybe she thought we were burglars!"

"No, it's not just Janet—though her running off is one more piece of the mystery."

"Then what is it?"

"There was another sighting of Benny Hartman last week. This time it was a maid who used to work for Mr. Hartman in his Beverly Hills home—like your wife, she only had a quick glimpse of him in a passing car, but she's positive it was him. None of this evidence is conclusive in itself, but it's starting to add up."

"Well, bravo, Lieutenant! I take back all the nasty things I've been thinking about city bureaucrats who are unwilling to make bold decisions."

"That's quite all right, Mr. Allen. If Benny's in his coffin, dead and peaceful, I'll figure out a way to blame it all on you."

Meanwhile, time was steadily ticking down, bringing us ever closer to the Friday night of the big show, just five days away.

On Monday we heard nothing from the lieutenant, and I passed the time by doing my best to forget the various mysteries and concentrate my energies on the show. I was starting to feel that our Friday entertainment at the Dorothy Chandler Pavilion might be a success—if no one new was discovered with a knife in his back, and if Benny Hartman, whose memory we were set to honor, was actually dead. These were some serious "if's," of course, but I was keeping my fingers crossed.

Then in the late morning on Tuesday, Lieutenant Kripinsky telephoned.

"I thought I should give you an update, Mr. Allen—we opened the coffin this morning."

"And?" I asked, holding my breath. "Was it empty?"

"There was a body inside . . . but it wasn't Benny Hartman. We just got a positive ID a few minutes ago by running a fingerprint

check on our computer. The body was that of an old street character who lived for years on various sidewalks downtown. The locals
called him Pussycat Charlie, because he always had four or five
cats with him in a cardboard box. The guy was a real eccentric,
but harmless. He drank Sterno and just about anything else he
could pour down his gullet, but he never gave the police any
trouble. But when I pulled up his fingerprints just now, I found
out a bit more about him. Are you ready, Mr. Allen?"

"What did you find?"

"Well, it turns out his real name was Charles Dougherty and
he was a comedian who did pretty well for a while during the
early years of television, the early fifties."

"A comedian!" I was filled with renewed worry about Friday's
show. "You know, I think I remember Charles Dougherty. He
used to play a very prissy butler with an English accent who was
always getting into absurd situations. He was in a sitcom in the
mid-fifties—I can't remember the name offhand. Dougherty had
only a bit part, but he was funny."

"Yeah, that's the guy, all right. On the show, he was always
the butt of other people's jokes. According to my information,
he did a few odd roles in the early sixties, but then he disappeared.
None of the other street-people had any idea that Pussycat Charlie
had once been a minor celebrity."

"It's certainly odd that he came to be found in Benny's coffin!
Have you determined the cause of his death?"

"Apparently natural causes—he was in his late seventies and
it's amazing he survived as long as he did, given his lifestyle.
However, the coroner is about to do an autopsy, so we should
know for certain later in the day if there was any foul play."

"What do they say at Forest Lawn about this switch?"

"They insist that this is the body they were given. Someone
cleaned old Charlie up a good deal—and actually, in death he
bore a considerable likeness to Benny Hartman. Since the widow
requested a closed-coffin service, they didn't try to do their usual
mortuary magic on him. So basically there was no reason for
Forest Lawn to question the identity of the body. Dr. Diehl had
it delivered to them, and they accepted what they were told."

"Diehl certainly has some explaining to do!"

"He does indeed. As far as we can tell, he actually is in China. He took a JAL flight to Beijing out of LAX on Saturday morning."

"So he ran after I called him on Friday night!"

"Yes and no, Mr. Allen. As you probably know, you need a visa to enter the People's Republic of China—you can get this from the Chinese Consulate in L.A., but it requires at least a full week. Dr. Diehl had his visa ready, so he had clearly made his travel plans before you spoke with him. However, he didn't actually have a plane ticket on Friday night. He got that Saturday morning, at the last minute. So perhaps you were partially the reason for his sudden departure. According to JAL, the doctor showed up at the airport Saturday morning asking for the next available seat to China—he claimed there was a medical emergency waiting for him there. He was lucky—there was a cancellation on their one o'clock flight, and they put him on. Apparently, as soon as he arrived in Beijing, he transferred to a domestic flight to Lhasa."

"You phoned the Lhasa Holiday Inn?"

"Yes—and got the same assistant manager you reached. It seems the doctor's off visiting some remote region where there's no telephone. Normally, we would ask the local police to investigate, but unfortunately the LAPD does not have much of a rapport with law enforcement in Red China."

"Can you send one of your people to Tibet?"

"Mr. Allen, please! The LAPD is a city agency, not a film studio! Our budget does not allow for sending officers halfway around the world, unless there is an extraordinary reason."

"So that leaves Janet Dorfman to tell us what happened to Benny. How's her condition?"

"Exactly the same. She's in a coma—she might wake up today. Or never at all."

"And what about Gloria, the grieving widow? In my one conversation with Janet Dorfman, she mentioned that Gloria was alone in the room with her husband when he died. *If* he died, that is. So *she* must have been in on this!"

"Perhaps," said Kripinsky with a sigh. "But Mrs. Hartman is telling a different story—that she was downstairs at the actual moment of her husband's death, and that she's such a coward about death, that she refused to take even a small peek at his body. According to her version, Dr. Diehl and Nurse Dorfman were alone with her husband at the final moment, and they managed to spirit the body out of the house without her laying eyes on it. She says she wanted to remember Benny as he was, full of life, rather than as a corpse."

"How convenient for her."

"Well, it's hard to say—it may be Janet Dorfman who's lying, or it may be Mrs. Hartman. However, the fact that Janet ran when she saw you does not speak well in her favor. And then there's the butler, Patrick, and the chauffeur, Bud. They're putting their money on Mrs. Hartman's version."

"Well, that's natural—she's their employer now."

"Perhaps. Anyway, they have both given convincing statements that Mrs. Hartman was in the living room when Dr. Diehl appeared on the stairs to announce her husband had passed away. According to the butler, the doctor asked if she would care to see the body, and she just about got hysterical. She said she was too young to think about dead people, and no one could make her—I'm quoting exactly."

"Hmm . . . that *does* sound like her," I had to admit. "Immature, egotistical, and utterly selfish."

"There's one more point in her favor," the lieutenant continued. "She's hired a lawyer to contest the will, claiming her husband was not in a sound mind when he left a million bucks prize money for the Funniest Person Alive thing. If she knew her husband was alive, would she really bother to contest the estate?"

"This gets more and more puzzling," I admitted. "And speaking of that million bucks, what the hell am I supposed to do about the show on Friday? If Benny is still alive, I can't really go ahead and hold a memorial awards ceremony in his honor!"

"Can't you? Maybe this is Benny Hartman's little joke on the world."

I thought about that for a moment. "You know, Lieutenant— that's not such a farfetched idea! I can almost imagine Benny pulling a stunt like that . . . I swear to God, if that clown *is* alive, I'll kill him!"

"I'll pretend I didn't hear that, Mr. Allen. Meanwhile, I have a suggestion to make."

"Yes?"

"Pay a social call on Gloria Hartman."

"What for?"

"She seems to like you. You might play up to her a little and find out some stuff she isn't telling the police. I'd certainly like to know exactly what's been going on in that household."

"But, Lieutenant—you haven't seen Gloria in action! She eats men alive!"

"What can I tell you, sir? Life is a risky proposition . . . and then you die."

chapter 32

I tried to get back to work after the lieutenant's call, but it was hopeless. The Benny Hartman Memorial Comedy Awards was a farce if Benny was still alive, and the only honest thing I could do now was to cancel the whole thing—unless I could discover what had really happened to him. There was a chance, of course, that he was dead and his body somehow misplaced. But I needed to know. The network could play a rerun or a film on Friday night, for all I cared. I wasn't going to be part of a deception.

So I put on my silkiest voice, swallowed my pride, and phoned an unlisted number in Beverly Hills.

"Hartman residence," sang a male voice into the receiver, with just a touch of an expensive English accent.

"May I speak to Mrs. Hartman, please?"

"I'm afraid, sir, that Mrs. Hartman is not home at present. However, if you will be so kind as to leave a message, I will make certain that she receives it upon her return."

"When do you expect her?"

"I do not precisely know, sir."

The man spoke in a stilted, almost absurdly formal manner.

"I presume this is Patrick?" I asked.

"Yes, indeed, sir. I am Patrick. The butler. And may I ask, sir—am I correct in assuming that you are Mr. Allen?"

"Yes, you may assume that, Patrick. At least *I* assume it—on good days, at least. Do you know where Mrs. Hartman is at the moment? It is important that I speak with her."

"I'm afraid I do not, sir. The madam does not inform me of all her movements."

"I see."

I was about to hang up when the butler surprised me.

"Sir, perhaps if Mr. Allen would care to meet me for a brief rendezvous, we might discuss some things of interest."

"Patrick, you may stop referring to me in the third person ... but yes, I'd like to discuss some things. What if I pop by the house right now?"

"Oh, no, sir! It would be *most* inappropriate indeed for me to receive personal guests at the Hartman residence. But if I can make a suggestion, sir. If Mr. Allen ... excuse me, if *you* will be so kind, I am about to take the Hartman canines on their morning constitutional. There is a small park directly across from the Beverly Hills Hotel, on the south side of Sunset Boulevard—by any chance, do you know it, sir?"

"Yes, I've passed it thousands of times."

"Very good, sir. I'll be there in exactly forty-five minutes near the fountain in the center, if you would care to stop by for a chat."

Cass drove me in the limo from the Valley into Beverly Hills. He let me out by the small triangle of greenery across from the Beverly Hills Hotel. There were a number of people in sight. I saw two nannies in crisp white uniforms, each pushing an expensive baby carriage—baby carriages that might have been made by Rolls Royce, by the solid look of them. A few neighborhood kids were roller-blading, and a woman jogger was doing stretching exercises on the lawn.

My eye came to rest upon an elderly gentleman in a dark blue suit sitting on a green park bench with three small shaggy dogs at his feet. At least, I assumed they were dogs—they looked more like fluffy dust mops in motion. As for the gentleman, he had white hair and a pink, well-scrubbed complexion. His blue suit seemed too formal for Southern California.

"Patrick, thank you for meeting me," I said, sitting down next to him on the park bench.

"My pleasure, sir ... Muffy, get down!" he said sternly to one of the dogs as it attempted to jump up into my lap. The dogs, I soon learned, were named Muffy, Missy, and Mopsy—though how anyone could tell them apart, I couldn't say. They were over-excited little things and our conversation was peppered with exclamations and commands for Missy or Mopsy to behave herself, or for Muffy to watch out lest she be sent to "the humane society"—as Patrick was wont to call the pound.

"I have a few questions for you, Patrick," I began, "but first I'd like to ask why you wanted to see me."

"It's a delicate matter, sir . . . Mopsy, stop that immediately, you dreadful creature! . . . As you may know, I've been in service with the Hartman family for over thirty years. I served Mr. Hartman loyally, and the first Mrs. Hartman, too. And, I must say, they have always treated me more like one of the family than a butler . . . so you can understand, sir, how painful it is for me to say anything unpleasant about the present Mrs. Hartman."

"Go on, Patrick."

"Missy! If you don't sit, I am absolutely going to feed you to a Great Dane! . . . now where was I? Yes, the present Mrs. Hartman—I hate to say this, sir, but I truly believe she sent Mr. Hartman to an early grave."

"Hardly *early,*" I said, "considering that he was eighty-five." I left aside, for the moment, the question of whether he was in any grave at all.

Patrick sighed with displeasure. "Oh, no, sir—Mr. Hartman was a man who planned to live at least until a hundred. He was a force of nature, sir. Unstoppable. I am certain he had another good decade in front of him if it hadn't been for that woman."

"What precisely did she do to him, Patrick?"

"She broke his heart."

He let that hang for a moment, then continued. "In short, sir, she was boffing the chauffeur."

"Boffing?" I questioned. This was a word I had not heard, in actual conversation, for at least forty years.

"Sexual intercourse, sir."

"I'm aware of the general meaning. You're talking about Bud Albertson, I presume."

"I am indeed. The chauffeur. *Bud.*" He said the name with acute disdain. "A newcomer in our midst, I'm afraid. He's only been with the family for six years."

"Bud actually lives on the premises?"

"Yes, in a small guest house behind the pool. Naturally, I live in the main house itself, in a lovely upstairs bedroom . . ."

"Please go on about Bud and Mrs. Hartman," I encouraged.

"This is very painful to relate, sir, as I'm certain you can understand. Late last fall—I believe it was the morning after Thanksgiving—Mr. Hartman walked back to the guest house to ask Bud something, and he found Mrs. Hartman there. They were *en flagrante*—I believe that's the proper expression. From that moment, Mr. Hartman went into a decline, and I don't believe he ever truly recovered from the shock. I'm certain it brought on his early death."

"We'll discuss this so-called early death in a moment, Patrick. But as for Benny's decline, as you put it—didn't the Hartmans go to Switzerland that Christmas? *That* doesn't sound as though he was in ill health?"

"Oh, but he was, sir. He only did it to try to keep up with her—to act as though he were young and jolly. You know, 'with it,' as the young people say."

"But what exactly was wrong with him?"

"It was like he just lost the spirit to live, sir. For a few months he was terribly depressed and quiet, as though the life had drained out of him. I think it was a real blow to his ego that his wife should cavort with the chauffeur—it made him feel his age, sir—yes, it did. This mood lasted, I would say, until April or so, and then he began to rally. But he often acted quite strange, even then. Sometimes I would come across him sitting in a room all by himself, just sitting there laughing for no apparent reason. I believe his mind was damaged. And it was all her fault!"

I was finding the conversation more and more interesting.

"So after April, when he began to rally, and laugh for no apparent reason . . . would you say that he had thought up some plan?"

"I'm not sure I follow you, sir."

"Well, is it possible that he had dreamed up some wild scheme for . . . revenge? To pay Gloria back, for instance, for sleeping with the chauffeur?"

Suddenly, to my surprise, Patrick began to laugh, starting with a chuckle and then for a moment behaving almost boisterously.

"What's so funny?" I said.

"For some reason or other that phrase *sleeping with* reminded me of something you said—it must have been two or three years ago—when I saw one of your comedy concerts. Do you remember?"

"No," I said. "My concerts are largely ad-libbed so it's pretty much a different show every night."

"Anyway," he said, "I remember that an elderly woman in the audience asked you if you thought it was good form for a young woman to *sleep* with a man on their first date, and you said—"He began to chuckle again. "You said that you definitely did *not* recommend that she sleep with the man. You said that she should stay awake all night because if she ever fell asleep there was no telling *what* he might do to her."

Patrick continued to chuckle for a moment, then suddenly became so thoughtful that he did not even chide Mopsy when she jumped up on his leg.

"You know, now that you mention it, sir, Mr. Hartman *was* like a man who was thinking about something . . . mulling over some joke that only he understood. There were times he was positively gleeful. I believe Mrs. Hartman was worried about his behavior. A few times I caught her looking at him in a very quizzical manner."

"Was she still . . . you know . . . with Bud?"

"Yes, sir! I believe she was—that wicked woman! On several occasions, I saw her leaving Bud's room in the guest cottage."

"Was Mr. Hartman aware of this?"

"I don't know for a fact that he was, sir, but, I imagine so."

"Tell me something, Patrick . . . Benny Hartman was quite a prankster in his day. Do you think there's any chance he faked his death to avenge himself upon Gloria in some elaborate way for being unfaithful?"

Patrick's mouth fell open in astonishment.

"My God, sir! If only it were true! But of course, Dr. Diehl pronounced Mr. Hartman dead, so he can't be alive, I'm afraid. And not only that, if it were part of some elaborate revenge, I don't quite see the point. I mean, now Mrs. Hartman is able to spend *all* her time with Bud—and I can tell you, sir, it's quite disgusting to see how openly they frolic together!"

"I agree—I don't quite see how the prank is supposed to work," I admitted. "But perhaps it's an ongoing joke, and we haven't seen the end of it yet. I'm afraid Benny may have a few more surprises in store for us all. But let's leave that aspect aside for the moment and discuss his supposed death. As you may be aware, there's some question of who precisely was in Benny's bedroom at the final moment—if indeed there *was* a final moment. Nurse Dorfman told me that Gloria was alone with her husband when he died. But I understand that both you and Bud have given statements to the police that Gloria was downstairs in the living room, and that in fact the nurse and Dr. Diehl were the only ones who saw the body."

"Yes, this is basically true," Patrick agreed.

"Basically?" I said, pouncing on his words. "But not completely?"

The old butler scowled. "Mrs. Hartman was *not* in the living room, as Bud and I said to the police. She was, in fact, alone with Bud in his guest cottage at the time."

"Was she? But why did you and Bud lie about this to the police?"

"This was my idea, I'm afraid. I coached Bud, and told him he had better get Mrs. Hartman to go along with my story—if she knew what was good for her! You see, it simply didn't sound respectable to me that she should be occupied in such a way at the time. I didn't want there to be any sort of cloud upon Mr. Hartman's death. I hope you understand, Mr. Allen. I wanted everything to be more—more dignified."

"Frankly, Patrick, I don't think it was wise to lie to Lieutenant Kripinsky. But I think I understand. Now what about Dr. Diehl and the nurse, Janet Dorfman. Where were they at the time of this supposed death?"

"Alone with Mr. Hartman in his bedroom upstairs. That part is just as we told the police. Dr. Diehl came downstairs to inform me of the death, and *I* went to the guest house to inform Mrs. Hartman. I'm sorry to report, sir, that neither she nor Bud was completely dressed!"

"What did she do then?"

"It took them a few minutes to dress. Then they both came into the house. Mrs. Hartman was hysterical—or at least pretending that she was. She refused to go upstairs to see the body of her husband. Perhaps she felt guilty—who knows? So she sent Bud upstairs to have a look."

"She did? You're sure about this, Patrick?"

"Absolutely. I heard her say, 'Bud, you go up there—I can't. I can't quite believe it yet. You have to tell me if he's really dead.'"

"So Bud saw the body! What did he say to Gloria afterwards?"

"'He's a goner, all right.' Those were his exact words, I'm afraid. Bud is not exactly what I would describe as the scholarly type. Mrs. Hartman heard the news and fainted dead away. Bud had to pick her up and carry her off . . . back to the guest house, I'm sorry to report."

"I see," I said, musing on all this information, trying to decipher its meaning. "I certainly want to have a good long talk with Bud Albertson. When do you think it might be a good time to find him?"

"If I could make a recommendation, sir—this afternoon might be perfect. Every Tuesday he takes the limousine down to a car wash on Santa Monica Boulevard. *Very* lazy of him, I've always said. Back in *my* day, chauffeurs were expected to wash the cars themselves! But be that as it may, the job takes about an hour since the car wash people do all the detailing work by hand. Bud generally just stands there staring off into space—I would bring along a good instructive book myself, sir, if it were me. But, as I say, it might be a good time to catch him alone. He generally goes about two in the afternoon."

The little dogs had become restless and Patrick stood up to continue his walk.

"If there isn't anything else, sir, I had better be on my way," he told me. Then he shook his head solemnly. "But if you don't mind me saying, sir, I think you're on the wrong track. Mr. Hartman is certainly dead."

"Why do you say that?"

"I feel it in my bones. I really do."

"Even though there have been several sightings of him?"

"People see what they want to see," the old butler said. "And anyway, if he was alive, he certainly would have come to me for help these past few months. He was incapable of managing a single day without me—he truly was, sir. No, if he was alive, I would be the first to know."

chapter 33

The Big Octopus Car Wash on Santa Monica was one of those drive-through places where a car can go through wind tunnels and rainstorms and a whole fun house of dangly blue things and automatic arms.

Cass and I arrived at the Big Octopus before Bud Albertson, so we decided to send the old limo to the cleaners, having noted that it was covered with a powdery yellow dust of unknown origin, too common to L.A. in recent years. We chose the $9.99 "Beverly Special," which included a cleaning of the floor mats, the undercarriage, the trunk, vacuuming the inside, one alleged coat of wax, and a choice of scents for the interior. Cass wanted Forest Pine but I chose Lemon Mist. Then we settled down on an outdoor bench and watched the traffic on Santa Monica Boulevard. It was a hot, muggy, smoggy afternoon.

The Hartman limousine was a black stretch Mercedes, and we saw it pull up about five minutes later. Bud Albertson delivered the car to the entrance of the car wash tunnel, paid the attendant, and then moved to a bench not far from ours to wait for the job to be finished. He was a dark-complexioned young man, deeply tanned, lanky, with short black hair. Women would call him attractive, I suppose, though there was something sullen about him and coarse. He was not dressed much like a chauffeur this morning— a loud Hawaiian shirt, cut-off jeans, and rubber sandals. He wore wraparound dark glasses that obscured his eyes. He sat down, stretched out his rather hairy legs, and opened a paperback mystery. Cass and I switched seats to join him, arranging ourselves so that Bud was between us.

"Good book?" I inquired.

He shrugged and continued reading.

"I always like a good mystery myself," I continued. "I'm reading one now, as a matter of fact. It's called, *What Does the Chauffeur Know?* It's all about a chauffeur, as you might suppose from the title—a guy who's having an affair with the mistress of the house and gets involved in a couple of murders and switching bodies around. Quite an interesting story, really. Though the chauffeur comes to a bad end—the gas chamber at San Quentin, I'm afraid."

I had Bud's attention. He scowled at me and sighed and closed his book. "I know who you are," he said sullenly. "You're Steve Allen. Big deal. Gloria told me all about you. How you dragged her up north with you to Ojai and tried to seduce her at some fancy hotel. A married guy like you—you should be ashamed of yourself!"

"That's what she told you? That *I* tried to seduce *her?*"

"Yeah. She tells me everything. She's my girl . . . and before you give me any jive about getting it on with the lady of the house, I'd like to remind you that this is America, and a guy has a right to take whatever is available."

"Yes, I suppose he does," I agreed. "Within the law, at least."

"Hey, I haven't broken any laws," he muttered. "So leave me alone. I'm minding my own business here, and I suggest you buzz off and do the same."

"I'll be glad to do some buzzing for you, Pops, if you'll be so kind as to answer just a few questions."

"Why should I?"

"Because you told a lie to Lieutenant Kripinsky—and if I tell the lieutenant on you, you're going to be in big trouble. That isn't the sort of LAPD cop you want to antagonize."

"What lie?" he grunted.

"You told him you never laid eyes on Benny Hartman's body. But in fact, Gloria asked you to go up to his bedroom and make certain he was really dead. You came back to the living room and told her he was a goner—as you so delicately put it. But that wasn't entirely true. Benny was still alive when you went up to that bedroom, wasn't he? You know, Bud, I think you may be guilty of criminal conspiracy."

"Wait, wait, *wait* just a damn minute here!" he exploded. "Okay, I guess I forgot Gloria asked me to take a look at her husband, but that doesn't mean I did anything wrong."

"Benny Hartman was dead?"

"Of course he was! What are you, crazy?"

"Then why didn't you tell Lieutenant Kripinsky that you saw him? And don't give me any more nonsense about how you *forgot*. No one forgets seeing a corpse!"

"Hey, I just didn't want to get involved," Bud said with a shrug, returning to his sullen mode.

"Are you aware that Benny's body was exhumed today?"

"What are you talkin' about?"

"I'm telling you they dug up the coffin, opened the lid— and guess what? Benny was not inside."

I felt the intensity of Bud's eyes upon me through his wrap-around sunglasses.

"Come on," he said. "That's crazy."

"Is it? You had to be in on this, Bud, with Dr. Diehl and Janet Dorfman. You helped them switch bodies, didn't you? The doctor wrote out a phony death certificate and then you sent to Forest Lawn the corpse of an old street character you had somehow managed to pick up off the sidewalk. It was a body that looked just enough like Benny that you were able to get away with it."

Bud stood up. "Leave me alone!" he whined. "You're totally nuts, man!"

Cass and I stood up as well. "You'd better start talking, Bud. Who arranged all this? It was Benny, wasn't it?"

"He's dead, I tell you!"

"Is he? Then where's his body?"

"I don't know. I swear to God, he *looked* dead when I went into the bedroom. I mean, his eyes were closed and everything. I only glanced at him a second—it's not like I *enjoy* looking at dead people, you dig? What was I supposed to do? Take his pulse? They told me he was dead, so I believed them."

"Who told you he was dead? Dr. Diehl?"

"That's right. And the nurse, too. I had like this bad feeling that maybe the old man was going to haunt me since I was making it with his wife. So I didn't hang around."

"And you never saw the body again?"

"No."

"How was the body taken out of the house?"

"I don't know nothin' about that. I guess the doctor called someone from the funeral home or the county to come get the thing. I missed all that because I was busy."

"Consoling the widow?"

"Actually, yeah."

Our burgundy-colored Cadillac was clean and ready, fresh from the Big Octopus, and Cass went to pick it up. My questioning of the driver had reached a dead end. I was certain he had not told me everything. If I was Lieutenant Kripinsky, I might haul Bud downtown and make him repeat his story a few times until some cracks appeared. But as it was, there wasn't much I could do to proceed.

"So you're satisfied? You've ruined my damn afternoon!" he sighed.

"Where's Gloria today? I need to speak with her and Patrick says she's not at home."

"I don't know where she is. Maybe at her attorney's. She has a lot of important stuff to do."

"Like busting Benny's will, I suppose."

He shrugged. "Well, it's her money, isn't it? I mean, she married him for it—a disgusting-looking old guy. It's not fair after everything she done for him that he should just give away a million bucks like that."

"And I suppose you'll help her spend it, won't you, Bud?"

"Sure," he said defensively. "And why not? We're in love!"

chapter 34

"**H**a! Ha! . . . God, you're funny, Steve! *You* should win the award!" Jerry Williams gushed over the telephone.

"No, I'm serious, Jerry. If we haven't found Benny's body by Friday afternoon, we have to cancel the show."

Cass and I were sitting in the front seat of our freshly cleaned limo eating fast-food tacos from a drive-in on Beverly Boulevard. I took a bite while Jerry digested what I had just told him.

Then he exploded: "You *are* serious! My God, I think I'm having a heart attack . . . *cancel* the show? The man says *cancel* the show! . . . I *am* having a heart attack, and a good thing, too—I might as well be dead since no one is *ever* going to hire me again for anything! . . . Steve, do you have any idea what we have riding on this show? Can you imagine the lawsuits we're going to have if this goddamn show doesn't air?"

Jerry went on in this vein for some time. I ate my taco while he let off some steam. He said we were finished in Hollywood, absolutely ruined if we canceled. We might as well just drive up north and jump off the Golden Gate Bridge. Why, our main sponsor, the fabulously successful fast-food restaurant, was naming one of its new items 'The Funniest Burger Alive'! How could we let them down?

Some minutes later, when he was winding down, I repeated what I told him at the start of our conversation. "Look, Jerry, I'm as sorry as you are about this. But the fact is, we can't have the Benny Hartman Memorial Comedy Awards if Benny is still alive— it's as simple as that."

"He *has* to be dead, Steve! My God, the guy was eighty-five. Why does he have to be such a jerk and live longer than that?"

"Well, maybe he is dead. Believe me, I plan to find out. Meanwhile, I want you to sit in your swivel chair, or wherever you happen to be. Take a few deep breaths and then repeat these two phrases ten times: 'It's only a show. It doesn't really matter.' You got that, Jerry? The network will have a fit, but they'll rerun *Dr. Zhivago* and in six weeks no one will care."

"It's only a show . . . it doesn't really matter." He tried it experimentally, but the words might as well have been Chinese. "No, man—I'm going to kill myself. I really am."

"Well, at least hold off until Friday afternoon," I told him. And hung up.

My next call was to Lieutenant Kripinsky, who I reached at his office downtown. I gave him the lowdown on everything I had been doing including my chats with the Hartman household domestic help, Patrick and Bud. Everything, including the fact that Gloria was having a fling with the chauffeur.

"By the way, I have the wildest thought about Gloria," I mentioned. "What if she and Benny were in this together?"

"Even though she's boffing the chauffeur, as you put it?"

"Well, Benny *was* old enough to be her grandfather, as he always said. Maybe they had some kind of liberal arrangement about their sex life. Who knows? I told you it was a wild thought."

"It's always wise to consider every possible angle," he said. "Incidentally, we've been aware for some time about the chauffeur and Mrs. Hartman—but I'm gratified at how cooperative and forthcoming you can be when the mood strikes you, Mr. Allen."

"Believe me, Lieutenant—I'm not looking to solve this mystery on my own!"

"I'm glad to hear that. And now that we're such close colleagues, why don't you tell me what happened the other night at the Blue Moon Apartments in Venice?"

" 'Blue Moon'?" I repeated innocently. "That was always one of my favorite songs."

He sighed. "We'll get to the bottom of *that* mystery eventually—and I hope you're clean, Mr. Allen. Meanwhile, I don't know why I'm such a nice guy, but here's a tidbit of information we've managed to unearth: a long time ago, in 1969 when Dr. Diehl was a young MD, he performed an illegal abortion on a Hollywood starlet, a very pretty girl who had gotten herself in the family way before Roe v. Wade. He botched it and the girl hemorrhaged and died. Now guess who the father was, the guy who sent this pretty starlet to Dr. Diehl in the first place?"

"In 1969? I can't imagine."

"Benny Hartman, that's who. I'm sure you can see what an interesting coincidence this is."

"But how in the world did you find out?"

"The police can be thorough when we want to. Believe me, we've been putting Dr. Diehl's life on the examining table. We came up with this little tidbit from the doctor's first wife, Katherine, who still feels bitter about the divorce. They married young and she worked two jobs to help put him through medical school, and then he left her as soon as he was successful. So she told us about the botched abortion. At the time the doctor was pretty freaked out, apparently, and believed his career was over. But Benny Hartman was the only other person who knew, besides Katherine, and he kept the secret safe all these years. Of course, Mr. Hartman was married at the time of the incident so he had his own reasons for secrecy . . ."

"But he could have ruined Dr. Diehl anytime he wanted! No wonder the doctor did what he wanted—Benny owned the guy!"

"That's right, Mr. Allen. Of course, we don't know for certain that it happened this way, but it's an interesting angle."

"It explains why a successful, elderly doctor would risk signing a fake death certificate! But what about Janet Dorfman? Why did she go along?"

"For the past seven years she's been the doctor's girlfriend. Not entirely a satisfactory relationship, since Dr. Diehl is married to his second wife and has children, but conceivably she would do what he told her—for love. Ms. Dorfman is still in a coma, by the way, so we can't ask her."

"And the doctor himself? Any word from Tibet?"

"You bet. The Chinese police have proved unexpectedly cooperative. They've picked him up and they're holding him.

The doctor isn't answering any questions yet, but the Chinese authorities will be sending him back to California within the next few days. We'll get the truth out of him eventually, I assure you."

"So now we just have to find Benny," I mused.

"Yes, we do," he agreed. "Dead or alive."

chapter 35

On Wednesday morning I attended an emergency meeting with the brass at the network. They were freaked out, to put it mildly, that it might be necessary to cancel the Benny Hartman Memorial Comedy Awards on Friday and they impressed upon me that there were millions of dollars at stake, as well as an assortment of careers and ulcers. One of the network executives tried to make it sound like the whole show had been my idea from the start, and if it didn't air, I should be the sacrificial lamb. No, I replied. It wasn't my fault that Benny wasn't safe and sound in his coffin, where a well-behaved corpse should be. I tried to put a good face on things by assuring them that there was still a chance we would clear up the mystery in time, discover Benny was truly dead, and proceed with the broadcast with no more problems.

"But you're saying we're not going to know until the last minute?" a particularly anxious VP inquired.

"Show biz is *supposed* to be exciting," I reminded him.

While I was thus engaged, Jayne carried on the search for the missing joker himself: Benny Hartman. Lieutenant Kripinsky had given us the name and address of Darlene Bronson, the maid who had worked in the Hartman house and had made the second Benny sighting. The lieutenant had only talked with Mrs. Bronson on the phone. Because of L.A.'s budget problems he was so stretched-thin in terms of manpower that he had not had a chance yet to send anyone around to interview her, so he was in fact grateful for Jayne's help and asked her to report in to him later about the meeting.

She drove her Plymouth to a residential street in Culver City not far from LAX. The house was small but attractive, surrounded by flowers and shrubs. Jayne was met at the front door by an elderly black woman who had a pleasantly round face.

"Come in, Mrs. Allen, please. I've made up a pitcher of iced tea for us," she said warmly. "I thought we might sit in the back garden where there's plenty of shade. I'm glad to answer any questions I can, though I don't know how much help I'll be."

It was a hot late-August morning and the garden seemed an oasis of green tranquility. Jayne—a green-thumb type herself—took a few moments to talk about flower beds, organic fertilizers, insects, and weeds and James Whitmore. Darlene Bronson insisted on filling a bag for Jayne with oranges from her tree.

Eventually, after these preliminaries, Jayne asked: "Now, Mrs. Bronson, where exactly did you see Benny Hartman?"

"Please call me Darlene, Mrs. Allen . . . I feel like we're old friends!"

"So do I, Darlene . . . now about seeing Benny . . ."

"It was in Santa Monica. Goodness, I don't even know the name of the street—up on the palisades, you know, just where the road goes down to the Coast Highway below."

"Near the beach! How curious—that's where I saw Benny, too, only further north at Malibu."

"Well, I was shocked, as you can imagine. I swear, my heart nearly stopped beating! There he was, grinning like always, smoking one of his cigars, sitting in the back of a limousine!"

"You had read of his death, I suppose?"

"Oh, my, yes! And seen all the reports on TV. I cried and cried. I was very fond of that man—I truly was."

"What time of day did you see him?"

"It was broad daylight, about two o'clock on a sunny afternoon. I had just taken my nephew shopping at the outdoor mall on Third Street and we were in the car. I was at a red light, about to drive down to the Coast Highway and get on the freeway. And that's when I saw him. He was in the next car over."

"And you were certain it was Benny Hartman?"

"There's not a doubt in my mind! Why, he recognized me as well—and actually waved."

"Did he? When exactly was this, Darlene?"

"Let's see . . . it was the weekend before the July Fourth holiday, back in the early summer. A Saturday, I believe."

"That long ago? Why didn't you report it sooner?"

She lowered her voice. "And have people think I was crazy? No, thank you! The next day, I started doubting it myself. I wouldn't have mentioned it at all, except a few days ago I started thinking, maybe I should say something after all. I was reading the *TV Guide*, you know, about the big comedy awards, and it just all felt like something wasn't quite right. So I called the police, and they put me through to that nice Lieutenant Kripinsky."

"Darlene, how long did you work for the Hartman family?"

"Oh, sixteen years. A long time. I started back when the first Mrs. Hartman was still alive. She was such a lovely person, you know, and I was terribly saddened by her death. I stayed on to look after Mr. Hartman. Until he got married again, to that young woman."

"From your tone, Darlene, I gather you didn't approve of 'that young woman.'"

"It wasn't up to me to approve or disapprove, Jayne. I just wanted Mr. Hartman to be happy, and I was fearful he was making a huge mistake."

"Because of the difference of age?"

"Yes, naturally. She was so very young and pretty—and he was so old. It seemed obvious to me that she would start missing people her own age. But perhaps I was wrong—as far as I could see, she adored him. They were like a honeymoon couple. Always cooing and gooing at each other."

Jayne was surprised to hear this. "Really? Was Bud working there at the time?"

"The new chauffeur? No, he was hired only a few weeks before I left. Up until that time Patrick had done all the driving. But you know, Patrick has gotten rather old himself, particularly with L.A. traffic such a nightmare these days, so Mr. Hartman decided he should hire a young chauffeur."

"How did he find Bud? Through an agency or the newspaper?"

"No. Mr. Hartman knew him from somewhere. I believe he said he was friends a long time ago with Bud's mother back East."

"Really?"

"That's what I remember, at least."

"Darlene, what is your personal opinion of Gloria Hartman?"

Darlene was quiet for a moment. Then she said, thoughtfully: "Why, I like her, Jayne. I think she's had a difficult life, and that she wanted to marry someone rich and important, thinking it would be a safe harbor. But I can understand that, can't you?"

"Yes, I can," Jayne answered, suddenly liking the old woman very much. "But I'm afraid Gloria was in for a disappointment if she thought fame and fortune in Hollywood was a safe harbor."

"Yes, I think she was in for some grief."

"Why, exactly, did you quit work at the Hartman house, Darlene?"

"Oh, honey! I was ready to retire to this garden years ago! I only stayed on, like I told you, 'cause I thought Mr. Hartman needed me after his first wife died. But when I saw he was happy with his new bride, I believed it was time for me to take my departure."

"Then in your opinion, this was a happy second marriage?"

"I hoped it would be, at least. As I say, I foresaw problems— but isn't that true with every marriage? I just hoped this time Mr. Hartman would behave himself better and not cheat on her like he had done in the past with his first wife."

"You were worried that *Benny* would be the one who was unfaithful?" Jayne asked.

"Oh, he was quite the ladies' man!" Darlene said with a fond smile. "I used to tell him to watch his step—I surely did. It's a mighty good thing the first Mrs. Hartman never found out about that secret house he always kept at the beach, where he and his men friends used to party something terrible!"

"A secret hideaway at the beach!" Jayne repeated in astonishment.

The old woman nodded.

"Darlene, I think you need to tell me all about this."

chapter 36

 "**Y**ou should check the answering machine," Cass told me when he picked me up at the network. "There's some guy named Dick Hamford trying to get you. It sounds urgent and kind of weird."

"Dick Hamford?" I wondered. "I know I've heard that name someplace, but I can't place it."

"Well, he seems to know you."

I was sitting in the front seat of the limo with Cass. He handed me the cell phone and I pressed the pre-set button to dial the answering machine back home. "You've reached the Allen residence. Sorry, nobody's free to answer . . ." I punched a code into the cell phone and the recorded voice back home—my own voice—stopped in mid-sentence. In a moment I was listening to all the recorded messages that had come in so far on Wednesday morning. The first two were about Friday's show; Dick Hamford was number three.

"Mr. Allen . . . Dick Hamford here. Look, this is the craziest thing, totally weird. I don't quite believe it myself, frankly . . . It's something I found going through Mr. Parker's things . . . I'll be home most of the day and I'd really appreciate it if you'd give me a call . . ."

A telephone number followed. The message was mysterious, but at least I had managed to place Dick Hamford in my scattered memory. He was Terry Parker's personal assistant, the preppie young man I had met a few months ago at Terry's penthouse suite at the Chateau Marmont Hotel. I dialed his number.

"Mr. Allen, thanks so much for returning my call," he said
once we had gone through a few hellos. "You're going to think
I'm nuts, but I found something very strange that Mr. Parker
scrawled in one of his notepads. You'll never guess who he had an
appointment to meet on the day he was killed at Benny Hartman's
funeral!"

"Let me guess," I said. "It was the dead man himself, wasn't
it? . . . Benny Hartman!"

Dick Hamford lived in a small apartment on a residential
street in Westwood near UCLA. He looked older than when I had
seen him at the start of the summer at the Chateau Marmont,
and he had grown a short, blond beard. But beyond that, he was
still a perfect specimen of young yuppie-dom, dressed in beige
slacks and a Ralph Lauren Polo shirt with the little horse and
rider on the pocket.

"Here, take a look," he said without preamble when Cass
and I walked in the door. He handed me a small spiral notebook
that was flipped open to a particular page.

"You're certain this is Terry's handwriting?"

"Oh, yes. No mistake about that."

The writing was neat, considering Terry Parker's somewhat
messy and flamboyant personality. The note read:

Dickie Boy,
Just in case I run into trouble tomorrow I want someone to
know the truth. Benny's planning to pull a Huck Finn at his
own funeral. That joker isn't dead at all! I ran into him by
accident and he's about as live as a guy of 85 can be, kind
of embarrassed when he saw me. We went back to an old
beach house where we used to party pretty wild in the old
days. (I'll tell you all about that house sometime, Dickie,
when you're older.) We talked for a while and came to an
agreement, but this joke of his worries me. If anything bad
happens tomorrow at Forest Lawn I want you to

"Want you to *what*?" I demanded, examining the pages of
the spiral notebook. Terry's note to "Dickie Boy" covered two

and a half pages in the notebook, but it ended abruptly and inconclusively.

"Where's the rest of it?" I asked.

Dick shook his head. "I don't know. It just stops. Maybe he was interrupted. The phone could have rung. Or he might have stopped to make himself a drink and he never got back to finishing it. Terry could be pretty scatterbrained."

"Maybe someone came along later and tore off the important part," Cass suggested.

"Maybe . . . but I doubt it," I told him, studying the notebook carefully. "The message breaks off in the middle of the third page, as if he simply stopped writing. And offhand it doesn't look to me as if any of the following pages are missing. Usually with a spiral notebook like this, if you tear off a page you leave a little strip of torn paper behind."

"Unless someone very carefully took the time to get rid of the little strip," Cass said.

"Yes, that's possible. *Anything's* possible," I sighed. It was extremely frustrating that Terry had thought to write a message, but hadn't finished his thought.

"What do you think he meant saying Benny planned 'to pull a Huck Finn at his own funeral'?" Cass asked, reading the message one more time.

"Don't you remember your Mark Twain? Everyone thinks Huck Finn has drowned, but he's still alive and he gets a kick going to his own funeral and watching everyone crying over him . . . I should have known this was just the sort of stunt Benny would pull! Where did you find this notebook, Dick?" I asked.

"It was in a box of papers that I packed up from Mr. Parker's hotel apartment—I'm not sure where the notebook was originally. It might have been on the desk in the living room, or on a bedside table."

"But Terry died all the way back at the end of May—and now it's almost September. How come this note only came to light now?"

Dick was embarrassed about the delay, and it took a few minutes to get the reason from him. Apparently back in May, Terry's attorney had pressured Dick to pack up all the belongings at the Chateau Marmont as quickly as possible to avoid paying an extra week's rent on the suite. There had been a great deal to do. Dick had managed to get nearly all the papers, clothes, and knickknacks packed and delivered to the attorney in Beverly Hills. When the time came to vacate the suite and return the key to the hotel manager, Dick had only two small boxes of stuff he had not sorted out properly—so he took them home to his apartment in Westwood, planning to finish going through them later. But the death of his employer had been so traumatic for the young man that he suffered a small emotional collapse. He went back home to Maryland for a two-week vacation to see his parents, and when he returned to California, he decided he would go to school. He enrolled in a summer program at UCLA with an eye on getting into graduate school in the fall. Somehow, with all these changes going on in his life, he had forgotten about the two small boxes in the rear of his closet.

"You know, it's like I couldn't bear to deal with them," Dick said. "Then about a week ago I was looking for some old tennis shoes at the back of my closet and I saw the boxes. Even then, I put off opening them for a few days. It was just too painful."

"Didn't the police want to see all of Terry's personal things?"

"Sure. There was a big, gloomy-looking lieutenant who came by the Chateau once or twice."

"But he missed this spiral notebook?"

"I guess so. There was a lot of stuff, Mr. Allen, and the lieutenant didn't do a real thorough search at the hotel. I think he said he'd have a few of his detectives go through the boxes *after* they were delivered to the attorney. I feel pretty awful about this, I really do."

"Feeling awful's not going to help matters any, Dick. Tell me about the old beach house where Benny and Terry used to have parties—what do you know about that?"

Dick shook his head. "Not a thing. Terry never mentioned it—I guess he was planning to, judging from the note he wrote. But he never got around to it."

"So you don't have any idea where this beach house might be?"

"Not the foggiest."

"Then let's go through these two boxes you have," I suggested. "Maybe, if we're lucky, Terry has left us a clue."

But he hadn't. There was no clue at all, at least not in the two boxes which had been stored and forgotten for three months in Dick Hamford's closet. I found movie scripts, Christmas cards, old love letters from girlfriends of many seasons past, as well as a few stray socks, eyeglasses, and even a half-finished bag of pretzels.

But not a hint as to the whereabouts of Benny Hartman's party-house at the beach.

chapter 37

I t was unfortunate, that Wednesday afternoon, that I had no idea what Jayne was up to. Nor did she have an inkling that I was following a series of clues from a different angle, which led to the same mysterious beach hideaway.

After Cass and I left Dick Hamford's apartment in Westwood, I used the cell phone to try to reach Jayne at home. But there was no answer. When I dialed again to replay the messages on our answering machine, I found only a quick call from Jayne:

"Hi, darling! I hope you're having a marvelous day. I've just been drinking iced tea with a wise and wonderful old woman who's given me a few interesting ideas to pursue. I don't know if they'll lead anywhere, but don't expect to see me until dinnertime. Love and kisses . . ."

I hung up and dialed the house again. This time I left a message for Jayne, should she call:

"Hello, darling, to you, too. Look, I'm really onto something. I'm so close to finding that old rascal, Benny Hartman, I can almost smell his cigar smoke! But we're running out of time, and I need your help. So if you call in and get this message, please *do* return home by dinnertime."

Such is modern marriage, I suppose: His and Hers messages on the answering machine. Meanwhile, Jayne was off in one end of L.A. County following her leads, and I was off with Cass in another following mine. And we didn't know until later that we were closing in, step-by-step, on the same elusive truth.

* * *

"My, what a pretty little car!" Darlene Bronson said as she slipped into Jayne's red Plymouth Laser.

"It's cute, isn't it? Would you like the radio on?"

"You bet!"

And so Jayne and Darlene drove from Culver City with the radio blasting—not looking very respectable, but having a good time. They were heading west once again toward the Pacific Coast Highway. Unfortunately, Darlene had only a vague idea where Benny Hartman's secret beach hideaway might be. She had been there exactly once, nearly twenty-five years earlier, to help clean up after a particularly wild party.

"Lord, there were champagne bottles everywhere!" she told Jayne. "And as if that wasn't bad enough, I found a pair of girl's underpants hanging from the chandelier! I gave Mr. Hartman a lecture, indeed I did—I told him it was a terrible shame behaving like some wild bachelor when he had such a lovely wife and family waiting for him at home. After that, I guess he figured it was best to keep me in the dark, 'cause he never asked me to come to that place again."

"That old satyr! I'm shocked, Darlene—I really am. His first wife, Gladys, was a good friend of mine!"

"Well, the way Mr. Hartman put it—he said, 'Darlene, I've worked hard to get to where I am today. And what use is it to *be* a star if I can't do exactly as I please?'"

"That's the reasoning of a spoiled ten-year-old child!" Jayne observed. "An actor has responsibilities, just like everyone else."

After twenty-five years, Darlene remembered exactly three things about the beach house: It was blue in color, the beach itself was wide and lonely, and it was located on a small road that was off the main highway. In twenty-five years, of course, the house could well have been painted a different color, and with all the development in Southern California, it was doubtful the beach was quite as wide and lonely as it had been in the past. This left only one substantial clue: a house on a small road off the main highway.

For the next three hours, Jayne and Darlene drove up and down every road to the north of Santa Monica that jutted off from the Pacific Coast Highway toward the beach. There were more of these than Jayne had realized, both public roads and small, private lanes to very exclusive beaches where only residents were allowed. Darlene had not driven this way in many years and she kept shaking her head in amazement.

"Lord, there never used to be so many houses! A person can hardly see the ocean anymore!"

With the recent spurt of building, there was now an unbroken wall of houses separating the highway from the beach, and the Malibu hills themselves—once so empty and wild—also were full of houses and even high-rise apartment complexes. To Darlene it all looked very different from her memories, and she could hardly find a single landmark she recognized.

"I'm awfully sorry, Jayne, to take you on such a wild-goose chase," she apologized. "I feel stupid not to remember better where that house was!"

"Darlene, I can hardly recognize Malibu, either," Jayne agreed. "There used to be such cute little weekend houses here— now we might just as well be in Beverly Hills!"

"I just feel sorry for the young people," Darlene murmured. "They'll never know how truly beautiful the coast used to be in California—and it's all changed in such a short time."

Jayne and Darlene were in perfect agreement that the beaches of Southern California had been much nicer with fewer houses and less people, but this did not help them find the particular house they sought.

"Maybe it was farther north," Darlene suggested. They drove to Paradise Cove and then to Zuma, a long public beach with a wide stretch of clean, white sand reaching toward the water. It was a clear, lovely day—warm but with enough breeze offshore to stir up whitecaps on the ocean. After Zuma Beach they came to a stoplight several miles north at Trancas, and an intersection leading to Broad Beach Road.

"Broad Beach Road!" Darlene cried. "This is it! I remember the name!"

"Are you certain you can remember the name after twenty-five years?"

"Yes, because Mr. Hartman once made a dumb joke about it. That man was incorrigible, I swear to God!"

"A pun on the two different meanings of 'broad,' I presume?" Jayne asked grimly.

"You got it, Jayne! He thought he was being very funny. I told him he ought to grow up."

Jayne and Darlene drove north on Broad Beach Road, past an assortment of posh homes. Jayne hadn't been to Trancas in several years, and it seemed grander than she remembered. As in Beverly Hills, very wealthy people had been buying up the smaller, older homes in Trancas, tearing them down and building in their place much larger and glamorous structures that covered almost every inch of ground space.

"Goodness! Some of these places look more like department stores than homes!" Jayne said.

Darlene was once again bewildered, since the neighborhood did not fit her memory. Broad Beach Road traveled north for several miles, and then began climbing back toward the Coast Highway. Jayne was just starting the climb when Darlene said, "Stop! I think I recognize those wooden stairs!"

Jayne and Darlene stepped from the Laser and examined a flight of wooden stairs that went down the face of a cliff toward a group of houses and the beach below. The wind was coming up more strongly now, and the sound of the surf was loud as it crashed against an out-jutting of rock. From where they stood, the ocean formed a wide, tranquil bay. Above Jayne's head, a seagull made its lonely cry.

"What a beautiful spot!" Jayne said. "Is this it?"

"I'm not sure anymore . . . I'm sorry."

"Let's go down and investigate."

Jayne and Darlene walked down the steps toward a modern house that seemed entirely made out of tinted glass. The house was very still and quiet and showed no sign of life. Darlene shook her head.

"No . . . I guess I was mistaken."

"Well, it's nice to get some sea air," Jayne told her. They were about to head back up the steps when Jayne felt Darlene tug her arm.

"There it is!" she said, pointing.

It was just on the other side of the all-glass house, almost hidden from view: a snug, old-fashioned clapboard house of the sort you might find at Cape Cod, painted a dark blue. Wood smoke was coming up from the brick fireplace. Jayne had expected something more like her idea of a Den of Iniquity. This particular beach hideaway looked positively cozy.

She studied the house for a moment, and then turned back to Darlene. She was about to say what a pretty little house it was, when the words died in her throat. To her astonishment there was a gun in Darlene's hand and it was pointed directly at Jayne's heart.

"What's the meaning of this, Darlene?" Jayne managed. "I can't quite believe I was so wrong about you."

"Behave yourself now, honey," the old woman replied, still in her very pleasant way. "You and I have reached the end of the road."

chapter 38

After Westwood, my next stop with Cass was to see Don Mulberry of Bernstein, Hughes, Mulberry, Mulberry, and Johnson—Benny Hartman's attorneys. They had an entire floor of an office building just off Little Santa Monica Boulevard near the Beverly Hilton. Lawyers do well in Beverly Hills, and this seemed a particularly prosperous firm. There were two Picassos on the wall in the reception area, and I sensed they were not reproductions.

I had Cass drop me off and then I sent him on another errand, which I will recount shortly. Meanwhile I cooled my heels on a very modern sofa of chrome and black leather in the reception area of the attorneys' office. I had phoned Don Mulberry from the car. At first he said he didn't have time to see me that day, but when I stressed it was important, he agreed to squeeze me in between appointments. So I studied the Picassos and read a copy of Gene Lees' *Jazzletter,* one of my favorite periodicals, for nearly half an hour as I waited on the ebb and flow of Beverly Hills law. At last a young woman from the inner office appeared and led me back into a corner suite. Don Mulberry was a distinguished-looking, silver-haired man in a pinstriped shirt and fancy suspenders. He had a tennis-court tan and despite his age, was one of those Ivy League sort of men who always retain a hint of the schoolboy they used to be. His hair was slightly long and shaggy, and in the most serious conversation he had a way of suddenly flashing a disarming grin.

He was on the phone when I came into his office, sitting behind a huge white desk in front of a tinted floor-to-ceiling window, looking every inch a Hollywood mover-and-shaker. He managed to greet me and keep a high-powered business deal going on the telephone at the same time.

"Have a seat, Steve. Be right with you . . . no, Larry, two-million-five is *not* adequate. We are absolutely unwilling to discuss anything less than three million dollars . . . Would you like a cup of coffee, Steve? Some sparkling water? . . . I tell you what, Larry. Let's have lunch next week at Spago and we'll see if we can kick these figures into shape. Give my love to Helen . . . Well, Steve, you certainly are looking well . . . Nancy, hold all my calls for a few minutes, my dear—unless it's Rupert Murdoch from London. I really *must* speak with him!''

Don Mulberry was a three-ring circus all by himself. At last he put down the phone and flashed his best little-boy grin as though to say, "Aren't I something?"

What he said, in words, was: "How's Jayne?"

"Very well, Don, thank you," I answered, ignorant at that moment of her true situation.

"Steve, I've been meaning to phone you, as a matter of fact, to say how much I appreciate you taking on Benny's award show. Before he died, Benny told me he could rest easier knowing you were doing this favor for him. It's truly a wonderful thing to honor the memory of a great comedian and a special friend to all of us."

"I'm canceling the show, Don."

". . . And I know wherever Benny is, he's looking down, smiling, smoking that big cigar of his in heaven . . ."

"Don! This is Planet Earth calling. I'm canceling the damn show on Friday—unless I get some satisfactory answers, and get them fast."

It took a moment, but I finally got through to him.

"What are you talking about?" he sputtered. *"Why?"*

"The why is the easy part—it's because I'm not convinced Benny is actually dead. I don't know what kind of crazy stunt that clown is trying to pull, but I'm not going to be part of it."

"Steve! Have you been drinking, or what? Benny died last May. We all went to his funeral! Remember?"

"As Benny's attorney, I can't believe you don't know this,

Don. Yesterday the police exhumed the coffin from Forest Lawn, and your client was not inside.''

Don sighed and looked momentarily exasperated.

"Well, the police told me, naturally—but Steve! It's obviously just a mixup at the mortuary. They just . . . misplaced the body.''

I leaned forward. "Don, places like Forest Lawn *don't* misplace bodies. Benny has disappeared, and the doctor who signed his death certificate is gone as well. Now, I'm not leaving this office until you tell me what this is all about.''

Don put on what passes among lawyers for a very sincere expression. He lowered his voice. "Look, he's dead, Steve. Honestly. He was my friend and I wish it weren't so. I'd love it if that crazy character was still alive, but he isn't. This thing about finding somebody else in his coffin—this is strange, I admit. I don't know exactly how it happened, but I've already got someone from my staff looking into it. And meanwhile, we're doing our best to keep it quiet. Until after the show on Friday, at least.''

"Sorry, Don. I told you—no body, no show.''

"Steve! Don't get difficult on me. This is just an unfortunate thing that Benny's body is missing. But I tell you, he's dead. Whatever's going on, *he* did not have any part of these undignified shenanigans, I can assure you.''

I studied the lawyer. I had known Don for quite a few years. He was tricky and smart, but not the kind of person who would go out on a limb and actually lie. It seemed to me that he believed what he was telling me.

"How do you know he's dead?'' I asked.

"Because I saw the body. That's how I know.''

"You *saw* the body? Where was it?''

"At his house, of course. Right after he died. The widow, Gloria, phoned me, so naturally I rushed right over. Benny had been my client for many years, Steve. I don't mind telling you, I shed a few tears that day.''

"You had a good look at his body?''

"Well, good enough! I mean, I didn't have a stethoscope handy—but the guy was lying there with his eyes closed looking awfully damned dead to me!''

"Don, I'd like to take a look at Benny's beach house hideaway, if you don't mind," I said, trying another tactic. "I want to make certain for myself that he hasn't been holing up there these past few months."

Don studied me for a moment. "I don't know what you're talking about," he said weakly. "I don't know anything about a beach house hideaway."

"Sure you do. You knew all of Benny's secrets, so don't get cute with me. I want to know where it is."

"Steve! I can't tell you. I would be divulging a professional confidence," he protested. "And not only that, if the media ever found out about this, his reputation would go down the drain. Those of us who loved Benny—we need to stand together to protect the posthumous reputation of this wonderful guy."

"Tell me about the house, Don."

Don Mulberry, at the moment, was a very unhappy attorney.

"Well, sure—there was a place Benny had. You wouldn't know by looking at him, but Benny liked the gals. He said it was what kept him young, and that if he ever lost interest in women, he'd probably turn into an old man overnight. I'm not condoning what he did—I'm a family man myself. But Benny had a consuming need to be loved, you know—women or audiences. It was just the way he was, a part of his great energy and talent. Personally, I don't have it in my heart to judge him. And I'm *certainly* not going to allow this to get out and let the media have a field day with the story."

"Well, that's your decision, Don. But again—I'm canceling the show. As I told you already, I'm not going to be part of anything that looks suspiciously like a hoax."

"Look, Steve—if there *is* a hoax, maybe it's the opposite of what you're thinking. Have you ever considered that?"

"I'm not sure I follow."

"I'm saying that maybe someone is trying to make us *believe* that Benny is still alive, when actually he's dead."

"That's an interesting possibility," I agreed. "But who would do such a thing? And why?"

"This is Hollywood, Steve! People do crazy things over famous people they love! Maybe it's some misguided fan. Or maybe," he suggested cagily, "it's the widow."

"Gloria? Why would she want people to believe Benny was alive?"

Don shrugged. "Maybe it's some imaginative way to challenge Benny's will—who knows? I'm not saying I can read that woman's mind. But I can assure you, for the record—my client Benny Hartman died last May."

"Sorry, Don, that just won't wash," I told him patiently. "People have actually *seen* Benny since then."

To my surprise, Don laughed. "Oh, so *that's* what's bothering you!"

"Yes, Don—*that's* what's bothering me! My wife, Jayne, happened to be one of the people who saw Benny, and she isn't the sort to imagine things."

He smiled.

"Come with me. I want to show you something."

I was puzzled, but I followed. We walked out of his office, down the hall, past the receptionist, and into a small conference room. I nearly had a heart attack when Don opened the door. Benny was sitting at the head of an oval conference table. He was dressed in a dark pinstriped suit, smiling at me in a knowing way, with an unlit cigar raised in his right hand.

"Benny! You have some explaining to do, you old bastard!" I said angrily.

I heard Don chuckle at my side. "It's pretty good, isn't it?"

I stepped closer and I saw that Benny was a fake—at least this particular Benny. It was only a clever mannequin, like the statue of Lincoln at Disneyland!

"Incredible!" I admitted. "It sure fooled me for a moment."

"It would fool anyone, Steve. Particularly if you only had a glimpse of it in the back of a passing limousine. The figure was stolen from Madame Tussaud's Wax Museum up at Fisherman's Wharf in San Francisco. It went missing back in early June."

"When did you get it, Don?"

"The day before yesterday. One of my secretaries spotted it sitting on a park bench in that narrow strip of greenery along Santa Monica Boulevard in Beverly Hills. It was just luck she turned her head and saw it—she nearly had an accident, poor thing. She stopped and picked it up, of course, and brought it down to the office. Someone from Madame Tussaud's is flying down from San Francisco to pick it up tomorrow.''

"Have you told the police?"

"Not yet. I suppose I should."

I examined the figure carefully. Up close, it was obviously a wax mannequin. But more than five or six feet away, it would be easy to mistake it for the real Benny Hartman.

"So, I guess that's one mystery solved," Don said. "Are you satisfied, Steve? Someone obviously has been playing a practical joke, using this figure to make people think Benny was still alive."

"Maybe so," I said, scratching my head. But for me, this mystery just kept getting deeper and deeper.

chapter 39

Cass was waiting by the curb when I walked out of Bernstein, Hughes, Mulberry, Mulberry, and whoever into the dazzling afternoon sunlight. Late August is generally a scorching time of year in Los Angeles, and this year was no exception. I ducked quickly into the front seat of the car next to Cass and was thankful for the air-conditioning.

I told him about the wax figure, and then he told me about his progress during the preceding hour and a half. I had sent Cass over to Benny Hartman's house hoping he might have better luck getting information from the domestic help than I had had. I thought he might be able to develop a kind of chauffeur-to-chauffeur camaraderie. But Cass had come up with nothing.

"Those bastards wouldn't talk to me, Steve. Particularly when I started asking about some secret hideaway at the beach. Patrick got real stiff and proper, like he wouldn't even listen to something unpleasant about his old boss. He cut me off real good. The same thing with Bud—only with him, I got the feeling that he just plain doesn't know about the beach house. He seemed surprised when I mentioned it, like it was news to him."

"But the butler—you think he knows about it?"

"Oh, yeah. That old guy must know everything about that family. He isn't talking, though."

"I'd sure like to find that house!" I said pensively.

"Even though it looks like Benny is dead after all?"

"You bet. Until I actually see that old geezer's body, I'm not taking anything for granted."

I tried to phone Jayne at home, but there was no answer, and no new message from her on the machine.

"Where to now, boss?" Cass asked. We were still parked at the curb in front of the attorney's office.

I thought and thought. I had a frustrating feeling that I was missing something, and that if I was only more clever I would have this case figured out by now. But I was stumped. At the moment, I couldn't even think of any new way to look for Benny's beach house. I decided I'd wait to hear from Jayne. Maybe by then I'd have some bright new ideas.

"Anyway, Terry Parker thought Benny was still alive," I mused, doing some sifting and sorting in my brain. "He thought he had an appointment to meet Benny at the funeral service at Forest Lawn. I only wonder who showed up for that rendezvous? It wasn't that wax dummy, that's for sure! And then we mustn't forget Billy D'Amato, stabbed with a knife from that same set. The question is, what did Terry and Billy have in common?"

"They were both comedians," Cass suggested.

"Yeah, but the same goes for a lot of people."

"Maybe Billy had an appointment to see Benny Hartman, too?"

I looked at Cass with appreciation. It wasn't such a farfetched idea.

"Let's find out," I suggested.

Forty-five minutes later I was sitting in the rear glassed-in porch of the D'Amato home in Brentwood, sipping cold Perrier water with Rosalie D'Amato. Over the past few months, she had forgotten how frightened she was of me and was now positively friendly. The back porch looked out over the swimming pool where I had found Billy's body, and both Rosalie and I did our best not to glance in that direction. She was wearing shorts and a T-shirt and no make-up. The way she looked this afternoon, she could have been a country girl, rather than a rich Hollywood widow.

"I'm embarrassed now—I thought at first that *you* were the killer, Steve," she said with a shy laugh. "You probably think I'm a terrible person, what with one thing or another . . . particularly after that horrible day when Jayne found me in that sleazy motel room with Harvey Roth.''

"I don't think anything of the sort. I'm not very judgmental, Rosalie.''

"Well, that romance is all over. I should have had my head examined—seeing a creep like Harvey in the first place. But I was all turned-around. The last year Billy was alive, we weren't getting on so well. I was susceptible to something new.''

"I'm interested in what you can tell me about Billy and Benny Hartman—were they friends?''

"Not particularly. They were friendly enough, I suppose, whenever they met at industry functions. Benny once said that he thought Billy was the best of the new young comics—it was flattering, but Billy didn't return the compliment. He thought Benny's sense of humor was, you know, old-fashioned.''

"Well, you have to appreciate vaudeville and the whole tradition of where Benny was coming from,'' I mentioned. "But what about the last year or so? Did Billy and Benny have any particular dealings together?''

"Not since *Flower in the City*—and that was a bit of a fiasco.''

"I don't quite follow. You're talking about Harvey Roth's new picture, aren't you—with Melissa Courtney and Terry Parker?''

"That's right. But originally Harvey wanted to make the movie with Billy playing the lead, and Benny playing the part that Terry eventually took. This was about a year ago, and the script was slightly different then—you know Harvey. He's always rewriting the plot. At first, Billy was interested. He had never been in a Harvey Roth movie and thought it might be prestigious and kind of arty. But when he found out Benny was going to co-star, he changed his mind. He told Harvey he couldn't see working with an old cornball like Benny Hartman. Harvey saw the point and dropped Benny from the project, but by this time Billy had lined up another movie. So Harvey ended up doing the male lead himself, and hiring Terry for the supporting part. Harvey's such an egomaniac, of course—the way he writes, directs, and stars in his own movies!''

"Do you think Benny knew he was dropped from the film because of Billy's objections?''

"Yes. I'm just remembering this—there was an unpleasant incident at a preview at the Screen Directors Guild about a month later. Benny came up to Billy in the lobby after the movie and he said, 'Hi! I'm the old-fashioned cornball. Want me to tell you a dumb joke, kid? You're the sort of star everyone's going to wonder what happened to three years from now. And you know why? It's because you don't got no class, and you don't got no heart. You're the sort of guy . . .' "

Rosalie stopped. All the blood went out of her face and she was deathly pale.

"What is it, Rosalie?"

"It's what he said, Steve! It's strange how I'd forgotten this conversation. He said, 'You're the sort of guy who would stab a friend in the back. But if you don't watch out, kid—maybe one day it'll happen to you!' "

Did it mean anything? Or was it only a figure of speech? Benny was such a huge star it was strange thinking of him getting upset about losing a part in a movie—but Hollywood egos are a funny thing, and often surprisingly fragile. As for Billy D'Amato, he was furious that Benny had spoken to him like that in public, and the two men—as far as Rosalie knew—never saw one another, or spoke, during the rest of their lives.

"So did you learn anything interesting, boss?" Cass wanted to know after he picked me up in the limo and we were cruising home.

"I'm not sure, Cass. Just another complication. Probably only a coincidence. But this case! I swear! It's like a ball of string that's all tangled up!"

We reached home at close to five o'clock. As I stepped out of the car I smelled something acrid in the air.

"Smells like smoke," Cass said. "It's far from here, though," he added when I looked momentarily anxious. This time of the year, in the late summer, everyone in Southern California worries a lot about fire—and with good reason, too. In past years, wild brushfires in the hills have burned thousands of acres and destroyed many homes.

Jayne was not home, and there was still no word from her. I was starting to get just a little worried, though I told myself I was being overprotective. I took a shower and then caught up on some letters I needed to write. But at six, Jayne had still not returned.

I decided I really *was* worried and I wasn't going to pretend otherwise. I went downstairs to the kitchen, where Cass was cooking dinner.

"Cass, do you remember the name of the maid that Jayne was going to visit?" I asked.

"Darlene, I think."

"That's right. Darlene Bronson," I said, remembering now. "Jayne said she was going to her home in Culver City."

I sat in the den and opened the huge L.A. County phone book. There was nearly three-quarters of a page of Bronsons, and perhaps sixteen or seventeen listings under "Bronson, D." But only one "Bronson, D." in Culver City.

I dialed the number.

"Hello?" said a friendly male voice.

"Is Darlene Bronson there, please."

There was a pause.

"Who is this?"

"This is Steve Allen. My wife, Jayne, had an appointment to meet Ms. Bronson this morning, and I'm wondering if she's still there."

"This *morning?*" asked the voice. "What kind of joke is this?"

"It's no joke, I assure you. Who am I speaking to?"

"This is Daniel Bronson. I'm Darlene's son."

"I'm glad to hear that. Did you see my wife by any chance earlier in the day?"

"No, I surely did not. I leave the house every morning by six-thirty—I work clear over in Riverside County and it's a long commute."

"Then perhaps you can let me talk with your mother . . ."

"Mr. Allen, someone's been pulling your leg. There's no one who lives in this house except me. My mother has been dead for nearly seven years."

I wandered, dazed, into the kitchen. It took me a moment to understand what Cass was telling me. He had the portable kitchen TV tuned to the local evening news and he was telling me about the lead story.

"That *was* smoke we smelled earlier, Steve. There's a few hundred acres burning in the hills just north of Malibu. Right now they're trying to keep the fire from jumping the Pacific Coast Highway and burning down that colony of expensive homes at Trancas. They're telling all the residents to evacuate . . ."

"Cass, please! At the moment I'm not interested in some damned fire! I'm worried sick about Jayne!"

chapter 40

It was nearly six-thirty on Wednesday night when I called Lieutenant Kripinsky to report that Jayne was missing after making an appointment that morning with a woman who had died seven years ago.

"I'm going to put every available detective on this immediately," the lieutenant said after he listened to my story. "Meanwhile, stay at home, Mr. Allen. I don't want you running about and getting yourself in more trouble. Leave this to the LAPD. I'll call as soon as I learn anything."

So I was left in a terrible limbo, pacing the living room floor, glancing at my watch every few minutes, waiting for the telephone to ring. About seven-thirty an old friend called to say hello, and I was so disappointed it wasn't either Jayne or the lieutenant with news of Jayne, that I shouted at the poor guy and hung up on him.

"Steve, you're not going to help Jayne any if you flip out," Cass said after a while. "Why don't you let me fix you up a plate of food, at least."

"I don't *want* a plate of food," I told him crossly.

I felt bad taking out my frustrations on Cass. Finally he convinced me to sit, at least, rather than wear out the carpet, and we watched some television together—a cop show whose plot totally eluded me. Throughout the evening, the show was interrupted by live reports from Malibu where the first fire of the season was raging out of control. They showed Shirley MacLaine evacuating her home, and a director who had won the Academy Award the year before arguing with a cop who wouldn't let him through a roadblock on the Pacific Coast Highway so he could check that his cat was okay.

"Why the hell does anyone still live in this horrible city?" I asked Cass gloomily. "Fires, earthquakes, floods, mud slides, riots, crime, pollution—what a swell place for a masochist!"

"I know," Cass said. "I remember your song."

"What song?"

At that he surprised me by half-speaking, half-singing a complete chorus as follows:

> *We got floods,*
> *We got fire,*
> *We got mud slides,*
> *With muck and mire.*
>
> *We got earthquakes*
> *And a million aftershocks*
> *And, when the tide comes in,*
> *Those old collapsing docks.*
>
> *We got riots,*
> *People sleepin' on the streets*
> *We've got drive-by gunplay*
> *UCLA and USC defeats.*
>
> *But hey,*
> *We can be forgiven*
> *'Cause we're livin' in L.A.*
> *And I think I see*
> *Some locusts on the way.*

> *II*
>
> *We got talk shows*
> *Where the guests are freaks*
> *We got strip joints*
> *Where you can meet a lotta geeks.*

We got cave-ins
And folks who want to close up schools,
And a lot of freaky cults
Takin' money from a lot of fools.

We once had a city
That was really kinda pretty
And the skies were always blue.
Life was smooth as butter,
Now we're livin' in Calcutta
And that's a kinda goofy thing to do.

We got poor folks,
Some livin' in their cars.
We got an awful lot of bimbos,
We call 'em movie stars.

But hey,
We can be forgiven
'Cause we're livin' in L.A.
And I think I see
Some locusts on the way.

When the TV show ended at nine o'clock, I couldn't stand my impatience another moment, so I tried to phone Lieutenant Kripinsky at the downtown station. The police operator told me he was not presently at the station, but I could leave a message. I left word for him to call me as soon as possible. For a few minutes after that, I was so frustrated I nearly started smashing furniture, just to let off some steam. But I realized Cass was right—I wasn't going to help Jayne any if I flipped out. So I spent some time just breathing deeply and doing my best to calm down.

"I wish I could think of something to do," I told Cass with a sigh, "but my mind's a blank. This case has gotten too weird—first Benny's dead, then it seems like he's alive, and now it looks like he actually *is* dead and someone is just using a dummy to make us believe otherwise. And now Jayne's off someplace with a woman who apparently *has* been dead for seven years . . . Talk about a mess!''

The front doorbell rang at close to ten o'clock, and Cass and I nearly jumped out of our skins. It was Kripinsky. He came into the living room with a tall, young black man in an elegant gray suit.

"This is Special Agent Bill Walker from the FBI," the lieutenant told me, introducing the man. "I thought it might be a good idea to get some help with this investigation."

"What have you found out?" I asked eagerly.

The two men sat on the sofa and Lieutenant Kripinsky told me where matters stood.

"We've just been in Culver City talking with the son, Daniel Bronson, but he doesn't know a thing. He left for work today early in the morning, and when he got home, he discovered that someone had drunk up a pitcher of iced tea and left two glasses in his sink. We're having the glasses checked for fingerprints, of course. But basically that's the sum total of Daniel's information. Someone obviously borrowed his house for a few hours today, but he doesn't have a clue."

"What about the neighbors?" I asked. "Did anyone see anything?"

"I'm just coming to that. Yes, here we got lucky. A woman across the street noticed your wife leave the house with an elderly African-American woman about eleven-thirty this morning. They drove away together in your wife's Plymouth. The car is what attracted the lady's eye, because of its bright red color."

"Good God! Why didn't she call the police?"

"Calm down, Mr. Allen. It's understandable that you're upset, but the neighbor had no way of knowing anything was amiss. She had only a slight acquaintance with Daniel Bronson, and there was nothing suspicious about two women leaving his house together. According to the lady, your wife and the older black woman were chatting in a very friendly manner and seemed to be on excellent terms."

"The old woman must have left a car behind!" I suggested, pouncing on the first constructive idea that came into my mind. "If she drove off in Jayne's Plymouth, and she didn't actually live at the Bronson house—then she must have driven there earlier in the morning."

"Perhaps—unless she was dropped off. But there's no extra car at the house, unfortunately, and no abandoned vehicles close by," the lieutenant told me.

"We're theorizing that she had an accomplice," the FBI man said, speaking for the first time. "Someone could indeed have dropped her off after Mr. Bronson left for work. We still have a team of investigators in the area going door to door, with the hope that someone noticed something. But so far, this is it. There's a police artist with the neighbor who saw your wife drive off, trying to get a likeness of the elderly black woman. But that doesn't seem too promising at the moment, because she was at least thirty yards away."

I could see that Lieutenant Kripinsky and Special Agent Walker, both skilled professionals, had done everything they could think of doing. Nevertheless, it was a bleak picture; I was not encouraged.

"Well, what do you plan to do next?" I asked in despair.

"Question you, of course," the FBI man said.

"*Me?* What for?"

"To find out exactly what you've been up to, Mr. Allen. If your wife has been kidnapped or some harm has befallen her, it very well may be connected to your amateur sleuthing, or whatever you call it—getting yourselves involved in something you should have left in the hands of people who do this sort of thing as a profession."

I was too demoralized to protest. "Please, if there's anything I can tell you that will help you find Jayne, just ask me," I said. "But I've already told everything to Lieutenant Kripinsky."

"Have you really?" the FBI man said with a grim smile. "I'm glad you are in a cooperative mood. Let's discuss, shall we, the Blue Moon Apartments in Venice Beach . . ."

I didn't hesitate. I told them everything about Jonno Murano and Giorgio's death that I had witnessed—or would have witnessed if I hadn't been crouching on the floor—and how Murray the Z had escaped. I wasn't sure how any of this would help Jayne, but if there was the smallest chance, I was willing to clutch at any straw.

chapter 41

Much later that night, the telephone woke me from an unrestful, shallow sleep. I woke not knowing at first why I wasn't in bed—for I was stretched out on a sofa in the living room, near the piano, at which I had been attempting to relax by writing a few songs. Then the bad memory of Jayne's puzzling disappearance returned.

Cass was on a nearby armchair. He sat up slowly, rubbing his eyes. A lamp was on, casting a warm glow. We both had been trying to stay awake, hoping for more news, but I guess we had dozed off. The digital clock on the end table said three-forty-three AM.

I picked up the phone. It was Jayne.

"Darling, it's me," she said simply.

"Jayne! Where are you?"

But her voice continued: "I've been asked to make this recording, Steve. I'm all right, and I'm told I will be released unharmed on Saturday morning if you will do three things. First, do not go to the police, or tell them about this call. Second, do not try to continue your investigation. Third, and most important, do *not* cancel the awards show on Friday night. I'm very much afraid I—I will be killed if the show is not broadcast. That's all I'm allowed to say, darling. I hope you're . . ."

Her voice cut off in the middle of the sentence.

"Jayne!" I cried. I knew it was a recording, but I couldn't help myself. "Are you there?"

But there was nothing, only a dial tone where her voice had been. I stood up with a sour feeling in my stomach.

"That was Jayne, huh?" Cass asked, watching me closely.

"A recording," I told him. I recounted the rest of the message, and the three points. I could understand the first two—not going to the cops, and dropping my own investigation—but the third request was trickier. I followed Cass into the kitchen where he began making a pot of coffee.

"You know, I'm going back to the theory that Benny *is* still alive. He's the one who's most gung-ho about this damned award show!"

"That's true, Steve. But now there are some folks hoping to win the million dollars. And what about that producer fellow—Jerry Williams. His career could take a tumble if you cancel the show. It seems to me there are a bunch of guys who have a possible interest in that broadcast proceeding as scheduled."

"I guess you're right," I conceded. "But how in the world did it get out that I was even considering canceling the thing?"

"Who did you tell?"

"Well, Jerry Williams, of course. He had a fit about it . . . and yesterday, I told Don Mulberry, Benny's attorney, who wasn't too happy either . . . Damn! damn! damn!" I said aimlessly.

While Cass was making the coffee, I stormed off into my office, turned on the light, and found my address book. Then I picked up the phone angrily and punched in the home number for Jerry Williams.

"Uh?" he said sleepily, picking up on the third ring.

"Jerry, this is Steve. Who did you tell that I was thinking of canceling Friday's show?"

"What—? You know what time it is? . . ."

"I don't care. Give me all the names of every person you told, and fast."

Jerry was not his usual plugged-in self at four-seventeen AM. He complained, yawned, and procrastinated for a few moments until I impressed upon him the urgency of my request.

"Well, let's see. I told my assistant, Susan, of course. And Slim Farrow at the network. Also Katie Lahr, Dick Crispin, Terry Matsu—a few other people at the network, too. I mean, Jesus, Steve—they gotta start thinking of how they're going to fill that time slot if we cancel. Meanwhile, Susan phoned a few of the sponsors, and Craig Wyman and Wendy Zimmerman at the Dorothy Chandler Pavilion. There were a few other people as well, but I'm too sleepy to think of them right now . . .''

"My God, Jerry—it sounds like you told half of Hollywood!"

"Well, I was upset, Steve. That reminds me, I told my psychiatrist, too. Does that count?"

"Go back to sleep, Jerry," I told him.

"Wait a second! Now that I'm awake, how do we stand? Is the show on or off?"

"It's on," I told him wearily.

Cass brought a big steaming mug of coffee into the den.

"So how many people knew?" Cass asked.

"Well, Jerry told about ten or fifteen people, and they probably each told another twenty or so apiece . . . a thing like this can grow exponentially. I was going to wake up Don Mulberry and ask who *he* told, but why bother? At this point, we're not going to learn who the kidnapper is by any process of elimination!"

Cass was giving me a funny look. "So, Steve—I guess you're not going to drop your investigation, huh?"

I sighed. "That's a hard call, Cass. There's no guarantee the kidnapper's going to keep his promise if I keep mine. I'm not sure what to do."

"Here's my advice, boss—keep looking for Jayne, and tell the cops, too. You can't trust a crook."

I thought this over, sipping the coffee.

"We'll proceed on our own, Cass, without the cops, at least for the time being. We'll move very cautiously. Maybe I'll even get some smart ideas for a change."

"That's the spirit! We're not going to give up! . . . So what do you have in mind?"

"I think the best way to find Jayne is to keep looking for Benny. And for that, we have to find that secret love nest of his. And as a matter of fact, this coffee must have given me a jolt of energy, because suddenly I have an idea!"

I reached Roger Morton at close to five on Thursday morning. At first I got his answering machine, but after I spoke a few words, he picked up the phone groggily.

"My dear boy! Do you have any sense of the hour?" he

demanded. "It always frightens me to death to get a phone call at such an odd time—I always think someone has died!"

Roger, you will recall, was Terry Parker's agent—the Brit whose British accent gets more pronounced each year of his long California exile. I had not seen Roger since earlier in the summer when he helped himself to our cheesecake extravaganza at Chasen's.

"Sorry to wake you, Roger, but I need an urgent favor. It's life or death," I told him, popping two vitamin C pills to get my brain cells in even higher gear.

I could tell he was getting interested. Roger Morton is one of Hollywood's greatest gossips, and he loves to be on the inside of things.

"You can tell me all about it, Steve. I'm all ears."

"That's the problem, Roger—I'm in a situation where if I say too much, someone could literally get killed. But if you can be an absolute friend and give me a hand finding something out, you'll be the first person I tell, as soon as I'm able."

"Really? You know how curious I am, dear boy! Does this by any chance have anything to do with the big award ceremony tomorrow night?"

"It does. And I'll be able to give you the full scoop first thing Saturday morning."

Like a sportsman feeling that first tug on the line, I knew I had my fish.

"All the details? Well, how can I resist? What can I do for you?"

"You know everything that happens in this town, Roger. I'm curious if you knew that Benny Hartman kept a little house, a sort of secret hideaway where he entertained guests of the opposite sex without his wife knowing."

"Yes, I've heard about that, Steve. It was quite a few years ago, back in the seventies when Hollywood was more of a party town than it is today. I believe the house was at the beach."

Bullseye! I thought.

"Which beach? I'm looking for the exact address."

"This is what you want to know?" he asked. He sounded surprised.

"That's it, Roger. And I can't stress how important it is that I find out as soon as possible."

"Hmm . . . the problem, dear boy, is that I never attended any of Benny's special little bashes myself. I've always found it a bit unappetizing, really, for people to be running about starkers in a social situation. Terry used to go, of course."

"Yes, I'm aware of that," I told him, remembering the note Dick Hamford had found. "Did Terry talk about the parties?"

"You bet. Terry was the original party animal and he loved to blab about indelicate things that would make the rest of us blush. Threesomes, foursomes, scenes in the hot tub—you can imagine. Unfortunately, Terry can't very well tell us the address, can he?"

"Don't you know the address yourself, Roger?"

"No. Believe it or not, there *are* some blank areas in my knowledge of this town. But I know who to ask. There's a girl I know who used to attend these little events. A very pretty model. Only she's married now to a rich banker and probably would not be pleased to be reminded of her wild youth. I'll have to handle this delicately and call you back later this evening."

"Roger, this evening's too late. Can't we speed this up?"

He started to tell me all the many reasons why gathering this particular information might take a day. I decided to take a big chance.

"Roger, this has to do with Jayne," I said. "She's been kidnapped and I think they may be keeping her in this secret hideaway. The police don't know anything about this yet. I'm going crazy, as you might imagine—and you've got to help me out."

I have to hand it to Roger Morton; he's the sort of Englishman who *likes* a good crisis, and often rises to his finest moment when bombs are falling all around.

"Leave this to me, Steve," he said crisply. And rang off.

It was nearly nine in the morning when Roger called back.

"This took a bit of doing, Steve, but here it is—3714 Broad Beach Road. That's at Trancas, you know—the private part of Zuma Beach."

"I know where it is," I told him gratefully, scribbling down the address. "Thanks, Roger. I'm heading there right away."

"Steve, are you crazy? Haven't you been watching the TV?"

"What do you mean?"

He laughed. "This is really quite absurd. You come to me asking for some *very* private information, but you don't even know what all of Los Angeles is talking about this morning!"

"And it's on television?" I repeated dumbly. And then some connections made a few sparks in my stressed-out brain. "Oh, my God! The fire!"

"That's right, dear boy! As usual, like clockwork once a year, the hills around Malibu are in flames. Three multi-million-dollar homes at Trancas have already burned to the ground. That whole area of the coastline was evacuated last night and they're not letting anyone through."

"I'll get through," I told him grimly. And added to myself, more thoughtfully, "Somehow."

chapter 42

After leaving the Malibu Colony, the Pacific Coast Highway meanders inland for a few miles, climbs briefly into the hills as it crosses a small peninsula, and then rejoins the ocean at Zuma Beach. It was about halfway across this peninsula, near the intersection to Paradise Cove, that Cass and I came to a police roadblock where they were turning back all northbound traffic.

The sky to the north was black with smoke and there was a sharp smell of burnt wood in the air. The highway looked like a battle scene, clogged with emergency vehicles and truckloads of men on their way to fight the fire. There were a few civilian cars as well, besides ourselves—mostly residents trying unsuccessfully to return to their homes. Cass and I came to a halt with about a dozen cars between us and the roadblock. Ahead of us, I saw a woman weeping and pleading with one of the cops, saying she had to get into her house to rescue some letters her husband had written shortly before his death in the Persian Gulf War. It was a painful scene to watch. But the cop was unmoved. He kept saying, politely but very firm, "I'm sorry, ma'am. This area's been evacuated. It's too dangerous, and we're not letting anyone through . . . No ma'am, not even if you're a resident . . . I'm sorry, ma'am . . ."

While Cass and I sat in the limo, another cop came up to us and pounded angrily on the roof of the car.

"Get this thing out of here!" he shouted without ceremony. "You're blocking traffic and there's an emergency convoy trying to get through!"

Cass was about to argue, but I restrained him.

"Do what he says," I told him. "Turn around and head south."

"But Steve . . ."

"Just do it. We're not going to talk our way past this roadblock. Anyway, I have an idea."

Shaking his head, Cass did a U-turn on the highway.

"Slow down," I said. "There's a small road coming up on the west side of the highway. I used to have a friend, a screenwriter, who lived here. Unless they've changed things, there's a series of back roads we can take that wind their way north—I think we can detour around the roadblock and rejoin the highway a few miles up the road."

It had been a number of years since I had been this way, but the road was where I remembered. Cass headed west for several hundred yards, and then I had him turn north onto a small gravel road that didn't even have a name. My screenwriter friend was quite taken with this particular part of the coast and had showed me around one Sunday afternoon. After we drove about five minutes, the gravel ended and the road turned to dirt. Cass looked at me questioningly, but I nodded for him to continue. Most people think of L.A. County as one of the most developed places in the modern world, but in fact there are still a few country roads left where you suddenly feel you have gone backward in time.

We passed an old barn and a huge estate, and then came to the rear of a new condominium development. The road we were on forked and went off in various directions. I no longer had any clear idea where we were, but whenever there was a choice to be made, I told Cass to keep heading north. Finally there was hardly even a road under our wheels—just parallel track marks through a field of wild mustard. The brush made a horrible noise as it scraped against the bottom of the Cadillac, but I told Cass to keep going. After a while, I caught sight of a convoy of heavy trucks traveling parallel to us on the main highway about a quarter mile away. I was fairly certain we must be past the roadblock now, but just when I was starting to feel optimistic, we came to a stream and a definite dead end.

Cass stopped and we sat in the car for a moment with the

engine idling, both of us feeling discouraged. It was hard to come this far and then be stopped by a small stream.

"What do you think, Cass?" I asked finally. "Do you think this old Cadillac could pretend it was a Jeep for a little while?"

"You're thinking we might just head off cross-country?" Cass's face lit up with a kind of wary pleasure. "Yeah! Ride 'em, cowboy!"

We plowed through the stream and up the far bank, and kept going through a field of tall brown grass. We bumped, we jolted, we skidded, we almost turned over in a ditch . . . but we didn't stop for a moment, not until we were back on the highway again heading north into an angry, blackened sky.

It's amazing what you can get away with if you have enough nerve. Cass and I sailed past various groups of emergency vehicles, men, and heavy equipment. Everyone seemed to assume that we must have some special clearance to be in a restricted area. Probably it was impossible to imagine how else we could be here—a vintage burgundy-colored Cadillac limousine speeding directly toward the fire.

It was early afternoon by the time we reached the entrance to Broad Beach Road. It was the strangest afternoon I have ever seen, with a shroud of dark smoke obscuring the sun, making it look as if all the color had been drained out of the landscape and we were caught in some old black-and-white movie. I couldn't see any actual flames yet, but I heard a distant roar that might have been either the nearby surf or the fire. As far as I could tell, all the houses on Broad Beach Road were unharmed, and this gave me some hope.

Cass drove along Broad Beach Road slowly enough to read the numbers on the mailboxes. As we drove north, however, the road became more and more congested with fire trucks. When we arrived at 3682 Broad Beach Road, still short of our destination, Cass shook his head and told me we couldn't go any further. There were two fire engines completely blocking the road.

"We'll leave the car and walk along the beach," I told him.

"Yeah, but how will we know when we've reached number 3714?"

"We'll count houses as we walk. Look—if you subtract 3682 from 3714, you get 32. Right? And we've noticed all the houses on the beach side of the road have even numbers—no odds. So half of 32 is 16. We're almost there! All we gotta do is count 16 houses up the beach, and we've found it.''

Cass was trying to follow my math when we saw a policeman appear from between the two fire engines. He did a double take when he saw us and started walking our way. Apparently he was a cop of a more skeptical temperament than the rest.

"Come on, Cass! No time for arithmetic," I said.

We ducked out of the Cadillac and began jogging down a narrow walkway between two houses toward the sand.

"Hey! Stop, you two!" the cop called after us. "This area is closed!"

Cass and I ran onto the beach and all the way down to the wet sand. When I dared glance behind me, the cop was nowhere in sight. I guessed he had more important things to deal with.

"My God! Look at that!" Cass said, pointing toward the hills to the north above the line of beach houses. It seemed to me that the hills had suddenly burst into flames—huge flames, a hundred feet high. It was a tall eucalyptus tree that had caught fire. From where we stood on the wet sand, it looked almost Biblical—an omen, or a warning to turn back. As I watched, I saw sparks blow onto the roof of a nearby house and it seemed only a matter of minutes before this entire colony of houses would turn into a firestorm.

"Quick, Cass! There's no time to waste."

We jogged as fast as we were able along the wide swath of hard, wet sand alongside the surf. It was low tide, which made our progress easier, but a few times the surf caught us unawares and we found ourselves knee-deep in foam. I was so busy counting houses I hardly noticed.

"... Twelve ... thirteen ... fourteen ... There it is, that little blue one there!"

Number 3714 Broad Beach Road, if I had counted correctly, was an old-fashioned wooden Cape Cod cottage with dormer windows that looked out of place amongst the newer mansions of tinted glass, marble, and steel that surrounded it.

"Oh-oh!" Cass shouted.

As we watched, the house next to the blue cottage caught

fire with a whoosh of flame. Orange tongues seemed to lick at the roof and the whole thing was steaming with black smoke, like a pot on the stove when the lid was loose.

Oddly enough, my mind flashed back to the night—a few years earlier—when our own home had been burned by fire so badly that we had had to move out of it for over a year. An inept electrician—he was actually a former officer in the Egyptian Army—had put a box of some kind over the ceiling of our kitchen and eventually the moment came when we paid the price. By coincidence I was having a bite of dinner while watching, on television, a motion picture about the World War II bombing of Dresden, Germany. Suddenly I smelled smoke. Within ten minutes I was standing in front of the house pathetically trying, with two garden hoses, to wet down the roof, another part of which was already in flames. There are few things that can make you feel as helpless as watching your own dwelling burn. There were even semi-comic aspects to such a tragedy in that the news-media cameras arrived at about the same time the fire department truck did.

But now there was no more time for flashbacks. Time was running out quickly. Cass and I sprinted up from the hard tideline onto the soft, white sand where the going was not so easy. We made our way toward a sand dune and over the other side toward the blue cottage. There was a patio and a glass windbreak at the front of the house, and large sliding glass doors looking in upon a darkened living room. Cass didn't waste time with subtleties. He picked up a loose brick from a barbecue pit in front of the house and smashed it through one of the windows.

And then I heard a familiar voice: "Help! . . . Help! I'm upstairs!"

Relief flowed through my veins like a warm elixir.

It was Jayne.

chapter 43

Jayne was in an upstairs bedroom tied securely to a heavy wooden chair. Someone had wanted to make certain she did not escape. It took Cass and me a few minutes to get her free. Finally, frustrated with the knots, Cass dashed downstairs and managed to find a knife in the kitchen, and used it to cut the final cords.

"Well, darling, I was wondering when you would get here," Jayne said chattily as we worked.

"Wait till I get my hands on whoever did this!" I said angrily. "And by the way, who was it?"

"A very charming woman. She called herself Darlene Bronson, but she wasn't, of course. We became quite good friends, really."

"I'd hate to meet your enemies!"

"Well, I don't think it was anything personal. She was hired to do it—she apologized, actually. Said she was trying to put her grandson through college back East. My God, Steve—are you aware what tuition is these days at a private school? Darlene told me it's twenty-five thousand a year!"

"Jayne! I can't believe you're discussing college tuition at a time like this!"

"Now, darling, it was bad enough to be tied here all day—it seemed silly to waste energy being angry as well."

"So did this charming woman happen to mention who was paying her?"

"No. I asked, of course. But she said she couldn't tell me—that it would be bad form to accept money to do a job, and then turn against her employer."

"Bad form!" I repeated grumpily. "When did she leave?"

"Early this morning. She said that the fire was an unexpected complication, and that she needed to find a working telephone to request further instructions. That was when she tied me up. But she never came back."

Jayne stood up, rubbing her wrists to get the circulation working.

"Hey, you guys—why don't you hold off your conversation until we get out of here," Cass said. "I hate to mention it, but this house could go at any time."

"I'll just use the ladies' room," Jayne said.

While Jayne ducked into the upstairs bathroom, I took a moment to look around the house. The decor was a kind of California Art Nouveau—rounded furniture, couches and divans of a sort that had been fashionably "modern" in Hollywood in the late thirties. An ornate old radio console stood against one wall. As I looked about the bedroom, I saw that every available inch of wall space was filled with photographs and framed newspaper clippings that documented Benny Hartman's long career. A photograph in a silver frame on the dresser showed Benny playing golf with President Dwight Eisenhower.

"My God, this house is a museum!" I said, wandering out into the hall and finding more photographs. On the wall near the stairs, I saw a series of old posters, carefully framed under glass, announcing "The New Young Comic Sensation—Ben Hartman" at different vaudeville theaters, in America and abroad. One poster had Benny appearing at London's Palace Theater, three weeks only, starting October 14, 1924. For me, even the names of some of these long-gone theaters summoned a glow of times past.

I poked my head into a second upstairs bedroom and saw more memorabilia. There were rare photographs of Benny standing with Al Jolson, a youthful Burns and Allen, and some old performers whose existence I had forgotten about.

"This is incredible!" I said to Jayne as she joined me from the hall.

"Hey, you guys! Hurry up," Cass warned.

"Just a minute longer, Cass."

There was an entire history of early twentieth century show business on these walls, and it was hard to tear myself away.

"Look at this!" I said to Jayne. "Here's Benny doing his old radio show. My God—look at that huge microphone!"

"What year do you think this was?"

"Must be the late thirties. Or very early forties."

Jayne and I wandered from room to room, fascinated, while Cass urged us to hurry up. Benny's collection was priceless—old *Playbills,* letters, drawings, photographs that spanned the history of comedy—vaudeville, radio, television, nightclubs, and the movies. In the dining room downstairs, I was struck by a photograph of a very young Benny, with all his hair, sitting in a vintage automobile with another young man whose face was oddly familiar. The date on the bottom of the picture said 1927.

"Who is this, Jayne? The young man next to Benny," I asked her.

She peered at the photograph. "William S. Hart?"

"No, I don't think so . . . Cass, come here a moment. Do you recognize this face?"

"Steve, are you crazy? We got to get out of this house. Like, pronto!"

"This will only take a moment."

Cass obliged me by glancing at the old photograph for half a second.

"No," he said, "I don't know who it is."

To my surprise, I heard the sound of hard rain against the roof.

"Listen to that! I guess we don't have to worry about the fire now," I told Cass, burying my nose back in the 1927 photograph.

"That ain't rain, Steve. It's the firemen spraying the roof with their hoses! Look, there's smoke coming in from the living room . . . we gotta split!"

I was starting to see his point. But it's frustrating to almost recognize a face, but not quite, so I lifted the old photograph from the wall and took it with me.

"Any more souvenirs you want, Steve?" Cass asked sarcastically.

"This one will have to do, Cass."

"Oh-oh . . . we can't get out the way we came in!"

The entire front of the house had burst into flames. Cass led us quickly to a side window by the kitchen and helped Jayne and me crawl through.

"Quick!" he said. "There's a propane tank up there, and it looks about ready to blow!"

We ran as fast as our legs would carry us toward the ocean. We had just cleared the sand dunes about fifty feet in front of the house when a percussive shock of air almost knocked us down. A millisecond later we heard the deafening explosion of a propane tank exploding like a bomb.

"Everybody all right?" Cass asked anxiously as we lay in the sand.

"I'm fine," Jayne answered.

"Steve?"

"Sure," I told him distractedly. The framed photograph I had taken from the house had slipped from my grasp when I fell. I picked it up from the sand and found myself staring once again at the young man in the ancient automobile sitting next to Benny Hartman.

It was really starting to bug me. *Why did that face look so familiar?*

chapter 44

We made our way southward along the beach, counting off sixteen houses, and then walked back up from the sand to Broad Beach Road. The old limo was just where Cass had parked it and we managed to drive against the flow of traffic—more men and machines coming to fight the fire—until we came to the intersection where Broad Beach Road meets the Pacific Coast Highway.

We were about to drive away when a Highway Patrolman came up to us angrily.

"Hey! What the hell are you people doing here?" he demanded. "This whole area's supposed to be evacuated!"

Jayne spoke up from the back seat, batting her eyes a little. "I'm so sorry, officer! I know it's terrible of us, but we came back to see if we could find my dog."

"And who let you through?"

"I convinced one of the officers at the roadblock near Paradise Cove to let us pass . . . you won't tell on him, will you? He was awfully sweet when I explained about my dog . . ."

"Just don't do this again, ma'am. This is a dangerous place right now . . . Did you find your pet, by the way?"

Jayne shook her head with a proper show of grief.

"Damn fire!" the patrolman muttered. "Well, you'd better get going—the blaze could start moving this way at any moment. And please don't stop until you're well south of the block."

Cass stepped on the gas and we got out of there. When we reached the roadblock at Paradise Cove, another CHP officer waved us through—apparently he assumed we were only just now evacuating. I felt pretty good about rescuing Jayne and getting in and out of the fire zone, and it wasn't until we were driving inland along Sunset Boulevard that I realized we were still a long way from being in a satisfactory situation. Ever since I had learned about Benny's secret beach hideaway, I had put my hopes on either finding Benny himself there, or at least discovering some surprise evidence that would explain everything. But with less than twenty-four hours left until the broadcast, we still didn't even know if Hartman was alive or dead.

"You're looking awfully thoughtful," Cass remarked as we waited for a red light to change in Pacific Palisades.

"I sure wish we'd had more time to search through that beach house!" I told him. "Who knows what we might have found out. As it is, we're back to square one—we don't have a clue who killed Terry or Billy and hired someone to impersonate Darlene Bronson. This is all as much of a mystery as ever!"

"I thought you liked mysteries, Steve."

I gazed at Cass in astonishment. "I *hate* mysteries, Cass. That's why I go out of my way to solve 'em—so that they're not mysteries anymore."

"I guess that makes sense," Cass admitted. "So what's our next move?"

I thought this over for a few blocks.

"Gloria Hartman," I said finally. "I'll bet she knows more than she's told us!"

It seemed to me that a wife who has been kidnapped, has spent a night in an uncertain situation, and the morning tied to a chair—should go home, take a long bath and a nap, and leave the detecting to the men.

"Nonsense!" said Jayne. "I'm feeling perfectly fine. Anyway, I don't think either of you is a match for Gloria. So you'd better leave her to me."

We had a domestic squabble in which I asserted my masculine independence, insisted that I was more than a match for any Gloria Hartman, and ordered Jayne home to bed—but she prevailed, naturally. We stopped at the house for a moment so that Cass and Jayne could drop me off. Jayne changed clothes quickly, freshened up, and then Cass drove her in the limo to the Hartman house in Beverly Hills. I was glad that Cass was there to keep an eye on her. Having found my wife so recently, I did not relish the idea of losing her again.

Alone in the house, I took a shower to wash off a combination of soot and sand and then telephoned the police to report the theft of Jayne's Plymouth, which had gone missing along with the "nice" old woman who was impersonating Darlene Bronson. I reported the theft to a sergeant I know at the local Encino police station, deliberately avoiding any mention of kidnapping and more serious matters that would embroil us in time-consuming interviews and official statements.

When this was done, I was of two minds about whether to phone Lieutenant Kripinsky. There were things I needed to do, and explanations to the police generally took too much time. In the end, however, I decided that he had been playing fair with me, and I couldn't very well leave him and his FBI helper searching for a kidnapped wife who had now been found.

I dialed the lieutenant's private number downtown, and I was delighted to get an answering machine:

"Lieutenant, Steve Allen here . . . I just wanted to tell you that I found Jayne and she's fine and dandy. It's a bit of a story, and I'll give you all the details as soon as I can. Meanwhile, I wanted to let you know so you can call off your search."

Then I phoned for a taxi, since I had a few ideas about how to track down the identity of the young man in the 1927 photograph with Benny. It was probably an inconsequential matter, but the feeling that I *almost* knew who it was, but couldn't quite come up with the name, bugged me so much that it was impossible to let it rest. I figured, what the hell—I'd spend an hour on the matter, and then at least I'd be able to concentrate on other things.

I put the photograph in a manila envelope and was waiting for the taxi to arrive when I glanced out the kitchen window to the backyard. I was so startled that I actually jumped in surprise. There was someone sitting at our patio table next to the pool. I walked out the back door to investigate, and I had another surprise: It was Benny Hartman, cigar in hand.

I laughed. "Now how the hell did this wax dummy get from Don Mulberry's office into my backyard?" I said to myself aloud.

It really was a good likeness. I walked closer to inspect the craftsmanship, and experienced a shock that nearly made my heart stop.

It wasn't a wax figure at all. It really *was* Benny Hartman.

chapter 45

The Hartman house was a languid, Spanish-style home on Alpine Drive in the "flats" of Beverly Hills—that is to say, in the expensive residential grid that lies between Santa Monica Boulevard and Sunset. The house was faded yellow in color with a red Spanish tile roof. There were bougainvillea vines climbing the walls, giving the place a sensual, Mediterranean feel.

Cass parked in the driveway behind a new silver BMW sedan. Jayne walked up a stone path to the front door. She was about to ring the bell, but before she had a chance—as if by magic—the door swung open and she found herself facing Gloria Hartman. Gloria appeared to be equally surprised to find herself confronting Jayne. She was wearing huge dark glasses, a silk scarf around her blond hair, a belted raincoat, and there was a small green suitcase in her hand.

"Going someplace, Gloria?" Jayne asked.

"Why, it's Jayne Meadows! What a lovely surprise," Gloria managed. "Whatever are you doing on my doorstep?"

"We need to talk, Gloria. I have a feeling that you're in big trouble, and I may be the best friend you have at the moment."

"I can't imagine what you're talking about!"

"I'm talking about your husband, who may not really be dead. And a coffin that had someone else's body in it. And a set of knives that were supposedly stolen from this house last Christmas, but have a nasty way of ending up in people's backs."

Gloria took a deep breath. "I'll tell you one thing—if Benny *isn't* dead, he's going to wish he were! After what he's put me through, I'm going to get a divorce settlement from that son of a bitch that'll leave him in the poorhouse.''

"Where is he?''

"I have no idea. Look, Jayne, maybe we can talk another time . . . at the moment, I really have someplace I must be.''

"Sorry, Gloria—you have a way of disappearing and I think I'd better hang onto you while I've got you.''

Gloria gave Jayne a withering look and then simply walked past her toward the silver BMW. She would probably have driven away without another word if Cass hadn't been blocking her exit with the limo in the driveway behind her.

"Would you please move,'' she told Cass.

Cass looked questioningly to Jayne, who shook her head.

"It would be easier to give me ten minutes of your time,'' Jayne told her, ''than to stand in the driveway all afternoon arguing about it. Frankly, Gloria, I'm not letting you go until you answer my questions.''

Apparently Gloria decided it was to her advantage to talk with Jayne, for she suddenly changed her manner. She smiled very sweetly.

"All right. I'd be glad to tell you anything at all.''

"How about the truth?'' Jayne said.

Gloria invited Jayne back into the house, but only as far as the foyer. She sat down on the edge of a decorative wrought iron chair by the front door, where no one had probably ever actually sat before. She kept her scarf around her head, her dark glasses perched on her nose, her raincoat tightly belted, and the small green suitcase by her feet—looking more like a person about to catch a train than someone relaxing at home. Jayne wondered what Gloria was so nervous about. She sat down next to her on a matching wrought iron chair with a huge ceramic Moorish pot between them.

"So what can I tell you?'' Gloria asked, glancing anxiously at her watch.

"Why are you in such a hurry?''

"Hurry? I don't know what you mean—I just have a full schedule, that's all.''

"And the suitcase?''

"Look, Jayne, I'm willing to give you a few minutes, but that doesn't mean I'm going to answer all sorts of personal questions that aren't any of your business."

"All right, Gloria. Let's get down to business. Why don't you tell me, first of all, what you know about the house on Broad Beach Road."

Jayne threw out this question as the wildest possible shot, an opening gambit, expecting only a blank stare in return, or a protestation of ignorance. But to Jayne's surprise, Gloria smiled knowingly.

"Benny's little party house? That was one of the best-kept secrets in Hollywood. How did you find out about it?"

"I've just come from there," Jayne answered, trying to imply that she knew a great deal more than she actually did.

Gloria shrugged. "So Benny was an old swinger. He used to say it kept him young, and that comedians could get a girl every time over a leading man. Benny's theory was that if you could get a girl to laugh, you were three-quarters of the way to getting her into bed . . . I guess it worked pretty well."

"So you didn't mind his little beach parties?"

"*Mind* it? That's where I met Benny. I was one of the party girls!"

"But you were his secretary, I thought."

"That came later. When he fell in love with me, he wanted to make things look more respectable."

"But you told Steve you answered an ad in the *Hollywood Reporter.*"

She shrugged. "Sure, that's what we told people. For his career, Benny was anxious to keep his personal life private. But as a matter of fact, the parties ended some years ago, soon after we first got together. He really *did* get too old after a while. Believe me, I was about all the woman he could handle at the end!"

"I do believe you, Gloria. You know, I was surprised—I heard so much about the private parties, I was expecting a different sort of house. A real swinger pad. Actually, it looked more like a museum."

"He remodeled after the parties ended. He was so full of himself, you know. Toward the end of his life, he wanted a place to go where he could admire himself and look at all the old souvenirs of his career. So yeah, the house *did* become a sort of museum. Kinda creepy, if you ask me."

"And the parties ended . . ."

"Five, six years ago. Anyway, Benny always said it wasn't so much fun being a swinger in the age of AIDS. They pretty much just ran out of steam on their own accord. Most of the guys, you know—Benny's cronies—they were getting kinda old for that sort of thing."

"And these cronies. Who were they?"

A cunning smile came to Gloria's lips. "Oh, no, Jayne—I'm not going to tell you *that!* There were some respectable names among that group, people you wouldn't expect to be leading a double life. They'd kill me if I gave 'em away!"

"Well, I already know who some of them are," Jayne fibbed.

"I don't believe it!"

"Terry Parker, for instance," Jayne said, supplying the one name we had already discovered.

Gloria shrugged. "Sure, everyone knew Terry would do just about *anything*—but he wasn't one of the heavy-duty family men with a reputation to protect. Anyway, Terry was never a regular. He only went once or twice."

"And the other—"

"Jayne, I'm not going to tell you."

She really wasn't terribly bright, Jayne thought. She studied Gloria for a moment, wondering about her, then decided to try another tack.

"Let's talk about the girls then," Jayne suggested. "I presume some of them were high-priced call girls—like yourself."

"Sure," Gloria admitted. "So what? But there were others girls, too—some who had respectable lives, just like the men. But I'm not telling about them either, and there's nothing you can do to make me so don't waste your time."

"Okay. But just tell me one thing. How did you get involved with his beach house crowd?"

"Through Don, of course. He was the one who found all the girls—the talent, as he called us."

"Don? You mean . . ."

"Don Mulberry. Benny's son of a bitch attorney. Now that's one rat I *won't* protect. If he keeps trying to screw me out of my inheritance, he's going to get a big surprise, I promise you."

Jayne felt she had struck an intriguing vein, and she was bursting with more questions, but just at this moment a black Mercedes limousine pulled up into the driveway behind Cass. Gloria saw the car arrive through the foyer window and became quite pale. The chauffeur, Bud, stepped out of the Mercedes and jogged quickly up to the front door. He did not ring, just walked in.

"There you are!" he said unpleasantly to Gloria, standing in the open doorway. Then he saw her suitcase. "Going someplace?"

"No. No place at all, hon," Gloria told him, putting on her sweet little-girl voice that she seemed to believe could smooth over any difficulty.

"Then what's this suitcase?"

"Oh, that! . . . That's Jayne's suitcase. Isn't it?" she asked, turning to Jayne.

Even though Gloria was wearing her huge dark glasses, Jayne felt the desperation in her eyes.

"Why, yes," Jayne said smoothly.

"Yeah? You always make social calls with a suitcase ready? What are you planning to do, move in here or something?"

"Bud! Don't be rude!" Gloria chided. "It's her make-up case."

"I *do* carry quite a lot of make-up," Jayne confided. She rose from the uncomfortable wrought iron chair and picked up the suitcase, sensing she had just gotten very lucky.

"Well, I'd better be getting on. Thanks for the lovely chat, Gloria." But Bud still stood in the open doorway, blocking her exit. "Oh, Cass!" Jayne called past him out into the driveway. "Cass! I believe we need to get moving. We don't want to be late for our appointment with Lieutenant Kripinsky. Oh, by the way, the lieutenant asked me to give you both his regards," Jayne added pointedly to Gloria and Bud, "when I told him I would be stopping off here on my way to see him downtown. Cass, would you mind carrying my make-up case, please."

Jayne was ad-libbing like mad, throwing off smoke in every

direction, hoping Bud would stand aside and let her leave. The chauffeur seemed uncertain. Fortunately, Cass had been paying attention and he moved quickly to Jayne's aid. The presence of an additional person, a man, seemed to turn the tide. Bud stepped aside, allowing Jayne to hand Cass the suitcase.

"But Jayne, darling! When am I going to see you again?" Gloria asked, her voice full of distress, following Jayne and Cass to the Cadillac.

"Call me anytime," Jayne told her.

"But I don't have your number!" Gloria hissed, watching in dismay as Cass carried her suitcase to the limo.

"Here, let me give you my card," Jayne said, opening her handbag. "Here's our home number, and cell phone as well. Let's talk soon, why don't we?"

"Better move the Mercedes," Cass said to Bud as he opened the car door for Jayne.

Bud seemed to sense that something was wrong, but he was too bewildered to do anything about it. He did what Cass told him; he moved the Mercedes so that Cass and Jayne could depart.

As soon as Cass pulled safely out of the driveway into the street, Jayne indulged her curiosity and opened Gloria's small suitcase.

"So what's inside?" Cass asked.

It took Jayne a moment to reply, so engrossed was she in the contents of the case.

Finally she said, "I'm not sure. But some answers, I think . . . at long last!"

chapter 46

The scene had become too familiar: police cars with their blue and red emergency lights revolving and Lieutenant Kripinsky staring at me with gloomy disbelief.

"You're a one-man disaster area, Mr. Allen. Do you know that?"

"Lieutenant, I can assure you I had absolutely nothing to do with this!" I assured him. "I was gone all morning, and when I got back, Benny was here—sitting at my patio table by the pool. Dead."

"Dead!" the lieutenant repeated with a ferocious scowl. "Well, at least the body has turned up. I suppose that's *some* progress, isn't it?"

Lieutenant Kripinsky was in such a bad mood that I was almost afraid to ask a question. But curiosity got the better of me, so I asked anyway.

"Er, Lieutenant . . . how long do you suppose Benny has been dead?"

He glared at me. *"That,* you might say, is the million-dollar question!"

"I realize the medical examiner will need to do an autopsy to get an accurate time of death. But meanwhile, surely you have lots of experience in this sort of thing, Lieutenant. Can't you give me an estimate? One hour? Three hours? What?"

It didn't seem possible, but Kripinsky's scowl deepened. "Longer than that," he told me. "Forty-eight hours ago, I would say, would be the earliest he died. Or it could be anything—as long at three and a half months ago, May 17, the date on his death certificate."

"Come on! Surely there would be more decomposition! When I first saw Benny at my patio table, he looked untouched—as though he might still be alive."

"That's because someone has stored him in a freezer," the lieutenant said crisply. "Didn't you notice, Mr. Allen? He's frozen solid—a damn block of ice! Just starting to melt a little in the sun. We'll probably never know the exact time of death!"

"I thought he seemed rather cold," I admitted. "But I didn't actually touch him."

"This offends me," he said, more to himself than to me. "I don't appreciate the fact that someone is playing with us! Bodies that disappear and then turn up frozen! And now, sir, if you don't mind, you have some explaining to do. I want to know exactly how you spent your morning. And don't leave out a single pertinent fact, because I am *not* in a good mood. I want to know precisely when, where, and how you found your wife. And then I will want to talk with Mrs. Allen as well, of course. Kidnapping is a serious matter."

I could see that the lieutenant was not to be trifled with, so I told him the entire account of how Cass and I arrived at the beach house at Trancas and rescued Jayne, every detail, start to finish. He was annoyed that Jayne and Cass weren't present to tell their part of the story, nor was he pleased that I had crossed a police roadblock to get to the scene of a dangerous fire.

"Mr. Allen!" he complained finally, "when you learned the address of the Trancas beach house, why didn't you simply get in touch with me? I could have radioed the fire department, who would have sent a rescue team to the house immediately!"

"That certainly *sounds* quick," I told him. "But with all due respect, Lieutenant—my experience with the police is that things go slow. How long, for instance, have you been cross-examining me just now? At least two hours. I had no idea how long it would take to convince you that Jayne was in that house. The second reason I didn't call you, of course, was that I was warned against going to the cops in Jayne's recorded message—and with her life possibly at stake, I wasn't in a mood to take chances. It seemed better to do it myself.''

"Mr. Allen," he said with strained patience, "the police *can* be discreet. And believe it or not, we can move very quickly, too, when occasion demands.''

As if to prove my point about speed, Special Agent Bill Walker arrived at just this moment and demanded that I go over the same story, from start to finish, that I had just been telling Lieutenant Kripinsky. Then he fetched a tape recorder from his car and had me do it all over again, an official statement. It was late afternoon before the authorities were done with me and when Lieutenant Kripinsky, Special Agent Walker, and the last county vehicle drove away.

I called Jerry Williams to tell him the news—that Benny Hartman's body had finally turned up.

"That's great, Steve! Now we can go ahead and do the memorial show, huh? No more problems?''

"You're all heart, Jerry.''

"Steve! I mourned Benny's passing last spring! Cried my eyes out. But my feeling is that once a guy is dead, and you go to his funeral and everything, he should have the courtesy to stay dead. Now listen, we've run into a few final glitches. You know Nina McConnie, the lead dancer in that Tribute to Vaudeville number? Well, she broke her ankle . . .''

Jerry and I spoke for nearly half an hour, discussing some last minute problems concerning the show the following night. The production meant everything to him, and he was like a horse coming into the final stretch, running high on adrenaline. I think World War Three could have broken out and he would not have noticed—as long as it didn't interfere with the broadcast.

"We're going to blow 'em away tomorrow night, Steve!'' he assured me just before saying goodbye.

My own hopes were less ambitious—that we simply get through the evening without any new disasters.

chapter 47

Jayne walked into the Beverly Hills offices of Bernstein, Hughes, Mulberry, Mulberry, and Johnson a few minutes after two in the afternoon with Gloria Hartman's small green suitcase in one hand. She asked the receptionist if she could see Don Mulberry.

The receptionist was a slim, pretty brunette who looked aghast at the very thought that someone should see her employer without an appointment.

"Oh, that's impossible. Mr. Mulberry has appointments until seven this evening. Let me check my computer, Mrs. Allen . . . I could squeeze you in next Friday at four o'clock . . ."

"Is Mr. Mulberry here in the building?"

"Yes, Mrs. Allen, but he's in a meeting with the senior partners until three. There's simply no way . . ."

"Do you have a small manila envelope, my dear?"

"Yes, of course."

The girl gave Jayne an envelope from a desk drawer. Jayne sat down for a moment on the black leather sofa near the two Picassos, where I had sat the other day. She opened the suitcase and searched briefly before finding a five-by-seven color photograph. Then she put the photograph into the envelope, sealed it shut, and wrote on the outside: *Don, I am waiting outside in the reception area. You have exactly five minutes before I take the rest of these photographs to the newspapers and the police.*

Jayne handed the closed envelope to the girl and assured her it was worth her job to get it to Don Mulberry immediately. The girl seemed dubious, but left her desk and took the envelope down the hall. Jayne sat down once again on the black leather sofa and looked at her watch. Two and a half minutes later, Mulberry came storming her way. He was in his shirtsleeves and his face was beet red.

"*Where* did you get this photograph?" he demanded.

"From Gloria Hartman. I must say, Don, you aren't the sort of person who looks particularly good without your clothes. But the two blond girls are certainly attractive. Are they hookers, or merely starlets hoping to get ahead in Hollywood by being nice to important people?"

Don looked nervously at the receptionist, who lowered her eyes and made a show of returning to work.

"Come into my office," he said gruffly. He led Jayne to his corner suite. "What is this? Are you trying to blackmail me?"

"Not at all," Jayne told him. "I simply want an explanation."

"The picture is self-explanatory, I should think. Benny used to throw some pretty wild parties at his beach house in the old days, but it's all past history now. This photo of me is nearly twenty years old. It's part of another time zone, Jayne—before AIDS, back in the days of the sexual revolution. We thought we were being free spirits."

"Don't give me that, Don—it wasn't that long ago. Gloria met Benny at one of these parties, and that couldn't have been more than six or seven eyes ago."

"Seven," he said flatly. "But I wasn't there. I stopped going to those little bashes in the early eighties. I told Benny I was getting too old for this sort of kid stuff. It's undignified after a certain age. But you remember Benny—he refused to grow up."

"Even if you're telling me the truth, Don, you certainly continued to help organize the parties. You were the procurer, weren't you? The one who found the willing girls?"

He sighed. "Well, yeah. I guess I was. Not because I wanted to, though. Benny didn't give me any other choice."

"This isn't your usual attorney-client relationship, Don."

"It had nothing to do with being his lawyer, Jayne. It was these damned old photographs. Benny said he'd show them to my wife if I didn't continue finding girls."

"He was blackmailing you?"

"You could call it that. It was a funny thing about Benny—he could be the nicest person you'd ever imagine, as long as you were doing everything his way. But the moment you crossed him, he could be a real son of a bitch."

Mulberry was referring to a behavioral phenomenon that on a more rational planet would be widely recognized, but on our pathetic sphere it fails to occur to most of us that people with charm or talent, particularly the former, can be near-monsters and get away with it. I would not be in the least surprised were biologists to discover that there is a gene for charm, just as it has already been established that there is one for physical aggressiveness and another for shyness. People with that quality, gravitate for obvious reasons toward entertainment or politics. And in the minority of cases where actual talent is also involved, then the situation is almost hopeless so far as the public perception of the individual is concerned. Perhaps in time it will be more widely recognized that it is possible to be a sensational trombone player, singer, dancer, or actor and yet leave a great deal to be desired as a human being.

"So yes," Mulberry continued, "the photographs put me in his pocket. And I guess Gloria was going to use them to try to blackmail me as well—probably to get a court order to stop the show tomorrow."

"Stop the show! Good God, why?"

"For the million-dollar prize money that Benny wanted to give away—why else? She's been trying to contest the will and get that show stopped ever since last May. Only Benny's will was tight as a safe—I should know, I drew it up myself. There was no way she could contest the thing, so she's trying other means. Frankly, I wish she *could* stop the damned broadcast—I sure as hell don't want to see any glowing tribute to Benny Hartman! I came to hate the guy!"

"So what about the mixup with Benny's body?" Jayne asked, unaware at that moment that Benny had turned up, frozen solid, at our swimming pool. "Is he alive, or is he dead, Don? And either way, where is he?"

Don Mulberry shook his head. "I don't know anything about that, Jayne. I swear to God. I *thought* he was dead—frankly, I think so still. But there's a lot of stuff that's gone on that's a mystery to me."

"Steve believes Benny was pulling a Huck Finn—you know, come back from the dead, show up at his funeral and surprise everyone. Perhaps he's even planning to attend his memorial awards show tomorrow night."

Again Don shook his head. "It may be, Jayne, but I don't know anything about it. Frankly, Benny knew I would never actually do anything illegal. It was one thing getting women, consenting adults, to come to his swinger parties. Sure, arranging for the expensive call girls, like Gloria, was not strictly legal, but personally I don't have a big ethical problem with the world's oldest profession, who in this case were paid extremely well. And even the hookers—they came late in the game, when Benny was starting to be an *awfully* old man and none of the amateur talent was interested anymore. As I told you, I didn't want to be involved even in that, but Benny forced me to."

"So you're telling me you don't know anything about Terry Parker's death, or Billy D'Amato getting stabbed, or the corpse of an old street character ending up in Benny's coffin?"

"None of the above," Don said firmly. "If Benny was planning anything dicey, he would never have confided in me. As I say, a little sex is one thing—I'm not a prude. But I'm an officer of the court, and I take the law seriously."

Jayne studied Don Mulberry and concluded that he was probably telling the truth. Being a shrewd lawyer, he saw her softening and immediately pressed his advantage. "So what about giving me that suitcase of photos, Jayne. I don't know how many other people he immortalized on film, but I know I've paid plenty for unwise behavior many years ago."

"I'll tell you what, Don. I'm going to keep this suitcase for the time being, until Steve and I know exactly what's going on. But if you're telling me the truth, as soon as the mystery is solved, I promise I will let you have all the photographs that pertain to you."

Don eyed the suitcase warily, and for a moment Jayne thought he might grab it from her by force. In fact, as a kind of insurance policy she had left the majority of the pictures in the trunk of the limo with Cass. Don seemed to struggle with himself. But then he visibly relaxed.

"Well, take good care of those things," he told her with a sigh. "I'd sure hate to see them fall into the wrong hands."

"Is there anything more you can think of to tell me, Don?" Jayne asked. "You probably know more about Benny Hartman's private affairs than anyone. The faster we solve the mystery, the sooner you'll get your photographs back."

"Well, there's one thing," he said slowly. "As Benny's lawyer, I shouldn't tell you this, but he was such a lousy client that I think I will anyway. You might ask his son a few questions. If Benny was plotting some crazy prank, the kid might know about it."

"His son? Benny had two children with his first wife, Gladys, if I remember correctly, but I haven't seen them since they were small."

"I'm not talking about Jonathan and Jennifer. I'm talking about the *illegitimate* son that Benny had with a showgirl who called herself Dawn Rose—a pretty girl, actually. But the kid, he turned out really to be a bastard. Benny knew about him, of course, from the beginning, and had me send money to the mother from time to time. But the boy grew up back East and Benny never actually met him until he showed up in California about six years ago . . ."

"Bud Albertson!" Jayne cried. "The chauffeur!"

Don nodded.

chapter 48

Jayne phoned home after leaving Don Mulberry. I told her my news and she told me hers.

"My God! So Bud is Benny's son!" I exclaimed, shaking my head in amazement. The full nastiness of the situation hit me in stages as I absorbed its implications. "When Bud started having an affair with Gloria, Benny must have been furious!"

"It's like something out of an old myth," Jayne remarked. "Or a tragedy like *Desire Under the Elms.* Or *Phaedra.*"

An aging husband, a young stepmother—it was a classic melodrama.

"I wonder if Gloria knew who Bud really was when she started up with him?"

"It seems like she must have known," Jayne said. "Though, according to Don Mulberry, Bud wasn't supposed to tell a soul that he was the boss's son, on pain of being shipped back to New Jersey and being disinherited. That was part of the arrangement."

I wasn't crazy about Bud, but this arrangement seemed a little harsh to me on Benny's part. After all, the kid apparently *was* the true flesh and blood offspring of Benny Hartman, and it certainly wasn't the child's fault that he was illegitimate.

"I wonder if Bud seduced Gloria to punish his dad in some way?" I said, thinking aloud. "You know, dear, I think it's time to pay another call on the Hartman house and find out."

Cass drove Jayne home, then she took a shower while I made up a few low-fat turkey sandwiches since we were all hungry. While I was busy in the kitchen, Cass went briefly to his apartment above the garage and when he returned he was carrying his gun—a huge, long-barrelled Colt .45 with a pearl handle that looked like something Wyatt Earp might have owned.

"I don't mean to worry you, Steve, but that chauffeur looks to me like a guy who could cause trouble. I think one of us should be armed," Cass said.

"All right, bring the Colt," I told him. "But don't you have a holster? You can't walk around Beverly Hills with that monster in your hand."

"Hey, sure I got a holster," he said enthusiastically. "Hand-tooled leather, silver buckles—the works."

"Hmm . . . sounds a little fancy. Let's just make sure we don't get stopped for a speeding ticket, shall we?"

We took the sandwiches along in the car and Jayne and I munched in the back seat, while Cass ate as he drove. He was wearing a light tan rain jacket even though the night was warm; the jacket did not do a very good job of hiding the bulge of the pistol in the holster around his waist, but it was better than nothing.

We arrived at the old Spanish-style house on Alpine Drive at close to eight o'clock. Gloria's silver BMW was nowhere to be seen. There was only one car in the driveway—an inexpensive car for Beverly Hills, a late-model Honda. But the house itself seemed to be blazing with light. Every window was glowing, on both the first and second floor. Except for the fact that there was only one car in the driveway, I would have thought there was a party going on. We parked behind the Honda and then the three of us walked up the path to the front door. As we approached the house, we could hear music blaring from a stereo system inside—grand opera. I recognized the piece as Puccini's *Tosca*. The music was working its way heroically toward a loud and frenzied crescendo as I rang the doorbell.

"Sounds like quite a bash going on inside!" Cass remarked.

"Strange. I wouldn't have taken Gloria for the opera type," Jayne added.

"Or Bud either," I said.

After a moment, I rang the doorbell again. I doubt if the chimes would have been heard over the stereo had the music not reached a sudden dramatic pause. The front door opened revealing Patrick, the butler. He had a glass of red wine in one hand and his face was flushed.

"Patrick! Goodness! You look like you're celebrating a bit," I remarked.

"I am indeed, sir," he replied. "I am being terminated . . . let go . . . in brief, sir, fired."

"Mrs. Hartman fired you?" I asked in astonishment.

"She did indeed, sir. Yesterday afternoon. She said I was no longer necessary, and that butlers are no longer the fashion in Beverly Hills. I seem to find myself an anachronism, sir."

"That's too bad."

"I just returned for my belongings and since the young madam is not at home, nor her young boyfriend, the chauffeur— I thought I might avail myself briefly of the joys of the wine cellar. At present, I'm enjoying a rather nice Bordeaux. Would you care for a small splash?"

He bowed in an absurd melodramatic fashion, not entirely sober, and ushered us inside, his behavior so overblown it was difficult not to laugh.

"So you're saying goodbye to the house, Patrick?" I asked.

"I certainly am, sir. I have spent a good part of my life in service here, and it didn't seem fitting to leave without some ceremony."

Patrick clearly had made himself at home in the living room. There was an empty chianti bottle on the coffee table in front of a large stone fireplace, and a second bottle of French Bordeaux, newly opened, standing beside that. He had been smoking as well; a cloud of tobacco hung in the room and an ashtray by the wine bottles was half-full. Meanwhile, the opera on the stereo system was once again soaring to a dramatic climax.

Patrick said something I couldn't hear over the music. Thankfully, he walked over to the cabinet where the stereo was housed and turned it down.

"I was saying, I was letting my socks down a bit, sir, as the saying goes. You know, in all these years, I've never actually sat in this living room."

"I would say it's about time," I told him.

"A glass of wine for the company?" he asked.

"That would be fine," I agreed. "We'd like that very much."

"Allow me to get the best glasses," he insisted, navigating unsteadily toward the dining room.

"Steve—wine is going to put me to sleep," Jayne whispered when he was gone.

"Just sip on it. You too, Cass. Patrick might have some very interesting things to say if we get him to let his guard down . . ."

The butler came tottering back, holding three crystal glasses by their long stems. He poured us each a generous glass and then proposed a toast.

"To freedom from servitude!" he declared grandly.

"Free at last!" I agreed as we raised our glasses.

He sank into an armchair and we gathered round.

"Well, Patrick, what are you going to do with yourself now?" Jayne asked.

"Oh, I've put aside a bit of money after thirty years. I shan't want for much. I was thinking of a sea cruise, perhaps. And then, who knows? Up until today, I owned a small cottage at the beach, but I'm afraid it burned to the ground in the fire. Seems I lost everything today—job and home. But the house is insured, so perhaps I'll build again."

"Wait a second, Patrick—are you talking about a blue cottage on Broad Beach Road in Trancas?" I asked.

"I am indeed, sir."

"The house belonged to *you?*"

"You seem surprised, sir. Mr. Hartman gave it to me many years ago. Of course, it wasn't really worth a great deal of money at the time. Real estate prices at the beach were not so extravagant as they are today."

"But Benny . . . Mr. Hartman . . . he continued to use the house for his private parties, didn't he?"

"Yes, sir, that he did. It was our arrangement when he gave me the deed many years ago. During his lifetime, he was to have use of the house completely. It only became entirely mine after his death."

"I'm not certain I understand, Patrick. This seems like a strange arrangement."

"It was a way to use the house, but not have it be in his name."

"I see. But was he really that worried about being found out?"

"You mean because of his sexual proclivities, sir? Not really, though naturally he was concerned to avoid a scandal. Nor was it entirely a matter of sentiment either—or gratitude for my service, I might add. It was in large part a tax dodge. A bit complicated, but as I understand it, the year he made the gift to me, he was able to put himself into a lower tax bracket."

"To get back to his proclivities, as you call them," I said delicately, "did you by chance attend any of these parties yourself, Patrick?"

"Only in a serving capacity, sir," Patrick answered stiffly. "They weren't my cup of tea, if you don't mind me saying so."

"I don't mind at all, Patrick, but I'm surprised you put up with it and didn't try to find a job in a more respectable household."

The old butler took a sip of his wine. A long sip. He drained his glass and poured himself another one.

"Well, we all have our foibles," he said philosophically. "And mine, I suppose, was that I was the last of the loyal household servants. I thought there was something noble about being in service, sir—I truly did. But I was mistaken."

"Mistaken? Why? Did Mr. Hartman let you down, Patrick?"

"Yes, he did . . . he truly did, sir. When he married that woman. She was—if I may be blunt—a woman of the streets."

"Why do you think he married her?"

"Oh, he was old . . . and she was young and laughed at his jokes. He was quite taken with her for a while."

"Until she became involved with Bud the chauffeur?"

Patrick nodded moodily. "Yes, things became rather a bit darker in this house when that started. Dark as sin, I can tell you, sir."

"Patrick, you must know everything that goes on in this house," Jayne said. "Are you aware who Bud Albertson really is?"

"An uncouth barbarian," he replied with disdain. "From New Jersey!" he added, as though that quite decided the matter.

Jayne glanced at me. Was it possible that Patrick didn't know about the relationship? I thought it best to wade into these complex waters slowly.

"Bud appeared, what, six years ago? Do you know how he got hired as chauffeur?"

"*She* wanted a chauffeur. She thought it was very posh, you know. She went on about it for weeks—how this person had a chauffeur, or that person, and why couldn't *she* have a chauffeur if she was married to a big star? Finally, Mr. Hartman gave in and he hired Bud."

"Do you know where he found Bud exactly?"

"No, I don't, sir. He just seemed to appear one day . . . like a plague!"

"Would it surprise you to know, Patrick, that Bud Albertson is Benny Hartman's illegitimate son?"

"No!" he said. "That isn't possible!"

For a moment I thought the old butler was going to have a heart attack. He stared at us without speaking, his eyes bulging out. Then his startled expression turned into a smile, and the smile broke into a laugh—a wild, frolicking laugh.

"Ha! Oh, that's rich . . . oh . . . ha! ha! My God, that's funny!"

"Is it really so very funny?" Jayne asked after he had calmed down somewhat.

This sent Patrick off into new peals of laughter. "Oh, ho! The seeds you sow come back to haunt you . . . ha! ha! . . . and the sins of the father visit the son! Oh, my word! There *is* poetic justice in this life after all!"

"I don't quite follow."

"Oh, ha! . . . I think it is a very good thing I'm ready to retire, sir," Patrick said with a sigh, becoming serious again. "Working in this house, I believe I have seen too much!"

That was exactly what Jayne and I and Cass were hoping to hear, of course. The precise details of this "too much-ness" that the butler had seen over the years in the Hartman residence. I was all set for a revealing chat when headlights appeared. They pulled up quickly, sending beams of light into the driveway. I heard a car door slam.

Cass peeked through the drapes into the front yard.

"It's Bud," he told us. "He's just pulled up in the BMW, but he seems to be alone—I don't see any sign of Mrs. Hartman . . . he's storming up the path to the front door like he's really bugged about something."

"Well, bully for him . . . the little bastard!" Patrick said, refilling his wine glass. He started to giggle again. Then he said, very nastily, "Screwing his stepmother! Not very pleasant, is it?"

Just then the front door was thrown open and Bud came in. He was disheveled. His hair was messed up, his tie was crooked.

"What are *you* doing here?" he demanded unpleasantly of Patrick. "You got the axe, remember? You've been fired, Pops."

"Just came back for my belongings, sonny boy," the butler said cheerfully, rising to his feet. "But I do believe I will toot along now . . . and leave you to rot in hell!"

Bud walked angrily to the old butler and for a moment I thought there was going to be violence. But then he said, "I'd beat the crap out of you, old man. But you're drunk and not worth the trouble. Now get out of here. If you ever come back, you'll regret it."

Patrick bowed slightly but formally to Jayne. "Mrs. Allen," he said, "it's been a pleasure . . . Mr. Allen, you are a gentleman, sir . . . Mr. Cassidy, *adieu!*"

The old butler walked uncertainly to the front door and out into the night. When he was gone, Bud looked at me and Jayne warily, but his eyes came to rest on Cass.

"Hey, what's this all about? You got a gun under that coat!"

I answered for Cass. "The way people have been dying, and coming to life, and dying again—it seemed a good idea. Perhaps you can tell us, Bud, how your father, Benny Hartman, came to end up frozen solid beside my swimming pool?"

He grinned. "So you know about my old man, huh? That was supposed to be a big family secret—I mean, I wouldn't want to be an embarrassment for him or nothing!" he said with crude irony.

"Tell me about his death," I insisted.

"Sorry, I don't know a thing about it. So maybe you'd better leave."

"That won't do, Bud. You know, I think I know why Benny's body disappeared. You want to hear my theory?"

"Not particularly."

I went on anyway. "I think perhaps Benny died after all back on May 17. But it wasn't a natural death, was it? He kept hanging on and hanging on, and it must have been very frustrating for you and your stepmother. So you killed him, and then you got rid of the body so there would never be a chance the police would do an autopsy on him . . ."

"That's crazy. It doesn't make sense," he said flatly. "Now get out."

"Oh, I don't know everything yet, I'll admit that. But I bet we'll know a lot more as soon as the autopsy is done."

He shook his head warily. "Man, sometimes I think I should have stayed in Jersey! People in California are nuts—you included."

"Tell me something, Bud," Jayne asked. "About Gloria. Did she know you were Benny's son?"

He grinned suddenly. "No, not at first anyway. I saved that for an extra-special surprise. As far as she knew, I was just the hunk who lived in the guest house a hundred feet away, while she lay in bed night after night with a scarecrow next to her who could have been her grandfather."

"You really hated your father, didn't you?" I said gently. "You came here from back East to get revenge. Seducing Gloria was just a way to cause Benny some anguish."

He shrugged. "Hey, I didn't grow up in Beverly Hills like Benny's other children. I grew up in a little house in a tough neighborhood by the railroad tracks. So I figured he owed me something . . . maybe even he owed me a lot. I took what I wanted, including the young wife. Now I think it's time you people leave."

I was set to ask more questions, but Bud suddenly had a small revolver in his hand. I'm not sure where he had it hidden, but it came out fast. The barrel was pointing at Cass's stomach.

"Reach for your gun and you'll be sorry," Bud told him.

Cass gave me an inquiring glance, but I shook my head.

"You people are trespassing," Bud said. "Now I'm through playing games with you—get the hell out!"

To make his point more emphatically, Bud pointed to the ceiling and fired. The noise was deafening in the small space and a trickle of plaster drifted to the floor. He really was a very angry young man.

We got out.

chapter 49

Friday morning. The day had arrived at last for the Benny Hartman Memorial Comedy Awards, but I woke feeling curiously bland about facing a coast-to-coast audience on live television tonight. I had done my work preparing for the show as well as I was able.

Oddly enough, I never experience stage fright when I'm going to perform. In fact, I'm often more ill at ease with six or seven people I've never met before than with a thousand gathered in the theater or the twenty million who might be watching on television.

"You're looking pensive, Steve," Jayne said, bringing me a cup of tea in bed.

"Flat," I told her.

"I beg your pardon?"

"I'm feeling flat. Down here it's showtime . . . but all I can think about is this damned mystery!"

"We've learned a great deal in the past few days, darling. You shouldn't be so hard on yourself."

"Sure! We know tons of stuff—too much, really. But the question remains, are we any closer to knowing who killed Terry Parker and Billy D'Amato? And possibly Benny as well, if it turns out that he didn't die from natural causes. I'm not sure we are."

"Perhaps it's like an anagram, Steve. You could have all the letters of the word spread out on the table, but they're all jumbled up, so they look like nonsense."

"So, we only need to arrange the letters properly," I mused as Jayne left me to sip my tea. But try as I might, I could not rearrange my particular "letters"—the information we had gathered so far—into any coherent order.

When Jayne came back to the bedroom a few minutes later, I was laughing.

"I just thought of an interesting suspect—Patrick," I told her. "He had a motive for killing Benny, at least."

"That ridiculous old man?"

"You bet! You heard him—Benny had given him the beach house, but it would only be truly his after Benny was dead. Now that cute little cottage on Broad Beach Road was probably only worth thirty or forty thousand dollars back when Benny gave it to him—but there's not a house on that beach today that's worth a penny under a million dollars!"

"Even though it's burned to the ground?"

"*Especially* burned to the ground . . . if the insurance is in order, that is. As far as I can see, a million dollars is a pretty fair motive for murder!"

Jayne shook her head. "No. I can see Don Mulberry as a killer—in the right situation, at least. Or Gloria, or Bud . . . or perhaps someone we don't even know about yet. But not Patrick."

"No?"

Jayne was probably right. But the butler seemed to me as good a suspect as any. And a further complication, just in case things weren't complicated enough.

There were still a number of things that needed doing to prepare for the show that night, but I decided to satisfy a small item of curiosity that had been puzzling me for the past twenty-four hours: the identity of the young man in the 1927 photograph with Benny Hartman. I had been on my way out of the house to investigate the matter when the discovery of Benny's corpse beside my swimming pool put everything else out of mind. It's impossible to say why I had this odd fixation about an unknown youth in a grainy black and white snapshot from long ago. His face simply haunted me, and his name was so close to my consciousness, on the tip of my tongue, that I felt I'd go crazy if I couldn't put this one small mystery to rest.

About ten o'clock, Cass drove me to Highland Avenue and then a few blocks over to Hollywood Boulevard—that depressing street of broken dreams.

My own mother, a once-successful vaudevillian of the twenties named Belle Montrose, had spent the last few years of her life in a somewhat rundown apartment building in the heart of the area which had, of course, been glamorous in the twenties and thirties.

A few tour buses were out this time of the morning, cruising in a misguided search for glamour, but finding only junkies, winos, the poor, and the desperate homeless. In front of the old Grauman's Chinese Theater, a group of Japanese tourists were looking at the famous foot- and handprints, but other than that, there is very little left on Hollywood Boulevard worth seeing.

Curiously enough, a few good bookstores remain from the old days, though they are almost lost amongst the Triple-X rated videos and peepshows. Cass and I were headed that morning to Old Hollywood Books, a musty store near the Pantages Theater where old editions are stacked chaotically up to the ceiling and you can find just about anything that has ever been written about Hollywood.

The proprietor, a white-haired man named Theodore Walinsky, was nearly as old and musty as his many books. He was on a tall stepladder searching through some of his old volumes when Cass and I walked into the store.

"Well, goodness gracious! It's Steve Allen!" he exclaimed, peering down at us through bifocal glasses. "Why, I don't believe I've seen you here for . . . let me see, it must be three and a half years now!"

He was exactly right. And that's what I liked about Theodore Walinsky—he knew his stuff. He climbed creakily down from the ladder. He was wearing a vest, a rumpled shirt with a polka-dot bow tie, and trousers that were shiny with age. With his unkempt white hair, he reminded me of Albert Einstein—and, like Einstein, I suspect that Mr. Walinsky lived more in his imagination than in the "real" world.

There are rituals that one must honor at Mr. Walinsky's bookstore. First, it was obligatory to have a cup of cappuccino with him, which he made for us on an ancient stove in a rear closet of the store. Then we needed to talk about the old days for a while, and some of the old-timers in Hollywood who had died recently—including, alas, Benny Hartman and Terry Parker. Mr. Walinsky did not mention Billy D'Amato's death—Billy had been part of a new Hollywood that held no interest for him. Only when these ceremonies had been carried out was it possible to mention business.

"So, what can I do for you today, Mr. Allen? Are you interested in a nice first edition perhaps? I came across a very interesting biography of the Boy Genius that was written in 1941—quite a find, if you're interested."

The "Boy Genius" to whom Mr. Walinsky referred was Irving Thalberg, once the young crown prince of Hollywood, though he died at an early age in the mid-thirties. To Theodore Walinsky, that probably seemed only yesterday.

"Actually, I was hoping you might be able to tell me the identity of someone in a photograph," I said, handing him the framed photo from a manila envelope.

"Ah, yes! That's Benny Hartman, of course! Doesn't he look young there?"

"It's the man sitting next to Benny in the car—he's the one I want to identify."

Mr. Walinsky studied the photograph with great seriousness. After a moment, he took it over to a messy wooden desk near the front window, where he brought out a magnifying glass from a drawer and continued his inspection. "Hmm!" he said from time to time.

"Any ideas?" I asked.

"Hmm . . . maybe. I'm not sure. Would you mind holding onto the ladder a moment, Mr. Allen? They don't make stepladders as sturdily as they used to . . ."

As Cass and I held onto the ladder, the old proprietor climbed up to the top of one of his many tall stacks and brought down a very thick, musty volume. At last he smiled triumphantly.

"Aha! I thought so. This is none other than P. Ellsworth Dodd, the theatrical agent."

"I never heard of him," I admitted.

"I'm surprised, Mr. Allen. Dodd enjoyed considerable success for a few years booking various vaudeville acts. His offices were in New York.''

It still didn't ring a bell. "I wonder why his face is so familiar. Was he by any chance Benny Hartman's agent?''

"Let me check . . .''

Theodore Walinsky located another musty volume, thumbed through it for a few moments, and then announced:

"Yes, he *was* Hartman's agent. Only until 1929, however. At that point, Benny Hartman switched to Dipsy Swann, who you probably haven't heard of either—but Dipsy was quite important until he died in a car accident in 1932. Probably Benny went to him from Dodd hoping to further his career.''

"Can you tell me what happened to Dodd? If he's alive or dead?''

"Sorry. He's one of a great multitude of people in the entertainment business who make a mark for themselves for a few years, and then just disappear. Maybe he was ruined by the stock market crash of '29, or perhaps he got into another line of work with the demise of vaudeville. If you like, I can check further . . . it might take me a few days, however.''

"No, that's all right, Mr. Walinsky. Thank you for your help— but I don't think it's important enough to spend any more time over it.''

I can never browse through a bookstore without buying a volume or two, though I'll never live long enough to read the books I already own. So Cass and I spent some time going through the stacks. I bought a history of the Garden of Allah, the legendary hotel where stars and writers used to live, and Cass bought a biography of Randolph Scott.

"So, the mysterious young man was only one of Benny's early agents!'' I mused, walking back toward the car, putting the photograph of P. Ellsworth Dodd back into the manila envelope. It didn't seem so terribly interesting after all.

But then, before I reached the limo—standing on Hollywood Boulevard—I brought out the photograph and inspected it one more time.

"My God! Of course!'' I said. "It was there in front of me all the time!''

chapter 50

About the same moment that I was standing on Hollywood Boulevard thunderstruck with recognition, Jayne was standing in our kitchen looking for a snack. She was peering into the refrigerator, trying to decide between peeling an orange or giving in to temptation and eating a piece of toast with the delicious homemade blackberry jam that my cousin "Doodle" Lowery had sent from North Carolina.

The balance tilted decisively toward the homemade jam. Jayne picked up the jar from the refrigerator shelf, and just at that moment someone rapped loudly on the kitchen window. Jayne was so startled that the glass jar slipped from her hand and shattered on the floor.

"Damn!" she cried. There was broken glass and jam everywhere, a nasty mess. Jayne turned to the kitchen window ready to shout a few unpleasantries at the person who had startled her and was further surprised to see who it was: Gloria Hartman. She was wearing dark glasses, the same scarf around her blond hair that Jayne had seen the day before, and was dressed in a floor-length mink coat—which was not only politically incorrect these days, but out of season in the warm California fall. Gloria was gesturing frantically to be let in.

Jayne opened the back door.

"Gloria! Look what you made me do! There's homemade jam all over my kitchen floor!"

"Let me in, Jayne . . . please!" she said in a squeaky little voice.

Jayne softened when she saw that Gloria had been crying. There was a bruise around her left eye, as if someone had hit her. She really was a mess.

"Come in, Gloria. Did Bud do that to you?"

She nodded. "I thought he was going to kill me. Jayne, I need that suitcase—I don't have any time to explain . . ."

"Whoa! Sit down, Gloria. I'll clean up the floor and make us a cup of tea, and you can tell me everything."

"I *gotta* have the suitcase, Jayne—it's my only chance!"

"All right, we'll talk about that. But first, sit down at the kitchen table and pull yourself together . . . What happened to your shoes?"

Gloria was barefoot. She sat at the table and promptly burst into tears. As she cried, the mink coat opened and Jayne noticed that she was wearing only her underwear underneath. Wherever Gloria had come from, she had obviously made a quick escape. Jayne got a mop and a broom and dustpan and took care of the broken glass first, so Gloria wouldn't cut herself. Then she put on a kettle and joined the unhappy widow at the table. Gloria had managed to pull herself together a bit.

"We were at a motel on La Cienega. I just took my mink coat and ran for it . . . I didn't have any money to take a taxi, so . . . well, I found a car on a side street and I stole it."

"You *what?*"

She shrugged. "I used to steal cars when I was a kid, so I know how. I mean, it's no big deal or nothin' to hot-wire a car— it was pretty old and it didn't even have an alarm on it . . ."

"Let's back up, Gloria. You were with Bud at a motel. Why were you there?"

"Bud thought like maybe it was time to drop out of sight for a while. Just until we figured out what to do next, you know."

"But who were you running from?"

Gloria looked uncomfortable. "It's kind of hard to explain. It has to do with what was in that green suitcase."

"Compromising photographs. I know—I looked inside, of course. You two were blackmailing someone, weren't you?"

She nodded. "It was Bud's idea. I didn't want to have anything to do with it, but he made me."

"Who were you blackmailing?"

"Well, a whole bunch of people . . . or Bud was planning to, anyway. I don't know how far he got. He said those photographs were worth a mint, if he handled it right. Personally, I only wanted to use them against one guy—Don Mulberry."

"You threatened to give the pictures of him to his wife unless he did as you said and overturned Benny's will?"

"Well, yeah—that's what I was *planning* to do. But I never got around to it."

"But, why, Gloria? Benny left you the house in Beverly Hills and quite a lot of money! It's not as though you were going to be destitute without the million dollars he was giving for the memorial comedy awards tonight."

She shook her head. "No, that's what I thought at first, too, that I was going to be pretty well off regardless. But there was a—a codicil I didn't know about. Because I was unfaithful to him when he was alive, he was canceling all his previous bequests to me and leaving me exactly one dollar . . . *one dollar,* Jayne!"

"When did you find out about this codicil?"

"Last spring. You know, right after Benny died."

Jayne frowned, trying to get this new information straight in her mind.

"But when you came into my dressing room at Neiman Marcus that time, I distinctly remember you telling me that Benny had left you the house in Beverly Hills and over a million dollars in stock . . ."

"I didn't want anyone to know how broke I was!" Gloria wailed, interrupting. "I owed money all over town! So I pretended to everyone that I would have cash to pay back my loans as soon as I sold the house and got the stock transferred to my name once probate was over. I thought if I had time, I could figure something out—maybe get Don to help me reverse the will. But he turned out to be a real bastard—he wouldn't help at all. That's when I got the idea to blackmail him with the photographs."

"And Bud . . ."

"He didn't know I was broke, either. Not until two days ago when I finally told him."

"But why, Gloria? Why didn't you tell Bud?"

She sighed. "I thought he'd leave me if I was poor."

Jayne shook her head at the folly of it all. The water was boiling on the stove and she stood up to make some tea.

"When did you discover that Bud was Benny's son?" Jayne asked as she brought the pot of tea to the table.

"Not until after Benny died," Gloria replied. Her voice seemed suddenly drained of energy. "Honest, I didn't know. Then Bud told me finally. He thought it was a big joke."

"I'm surprised you didn't dump him immediately!"

Gloria sighed. "It's kinda hard to explain. Bud had got under my skin somehow. I was broke and scared about the future, and I guess I'm not as tough as I like to pretend. Bud seemed my only friend."

"Did he talk about his relationship with his father?"

"*Relationship?* You gotta be kidding! Bud never even saw his father once until he was twenty-three. And then, big deal—Benny brings him to California and gives him a job . . . as his chauffeur!"

"So it would be safe to say that Bud did not like his father?"

She laughed nastily. "He hated the old jerk! Bud only stayed on thinking Benny had to die soon, and that there would be some money for him in the will. But that was a joke! There turned out to be something in the will about Bud as well—that he was originally to receive half a million dollars, but since Bud was screwing his stepmother and had showed himself to be a 'moral degenerate'—I'm quoting exactly—he too was to receive one dollar. Bud just about flipped out, I tell you! He only stayed around because of me, thinking I'd inherit a bundle for both of us. He only found out the truth a couple of days ago—that I was broke just like he was. And that's when I dug up all those old photographs . . . I had to think of *something*, Jayne!"

"But how did Bud find out you were broke? Did you tell him?"

"No, of course not. Someone told him, I don't know who—but it seems to me it has to be Don Mulberry, the creep! He's the only one in Hollywood who knows how broke I am! And speaking of money, where's my green suitcase?"

"I can't give it to you, Gloria."

"Come on! You *gotta* give it to me! Ain't I getting through to you? Bud will kill me otherwise—he's wasted six years waiting to be rich, and this is absolutely his last chance!''

"I don't have it. I gave the suitcase to my lawyer in Beverly Hills to hold—once I saw what was inside, I didn't want the responsibility of keeping it in the house. I'm not sure if you realize it, but there are quite a few lives and marriages at stake in that small suitcase, Gloria. It's not just a question of money.''

"I don't care. They probably grew up with all sorts of swell houses and swimming pools—I grew up with nothing. And now I want what's mine!''

Jayne shook her head. "No,'' she said softly.

"You really won't get that suitcase for me?''

Again Jayne shook her head.

They had arrived at an impasse. Gloria studied Jayne, and Jayne watched Gloria, wondering what was next.

"I tell you what,'' Gloria said finally. "Let's make a deal.''

chapter 51

Cass and I were driving home in the limo when Jayne reached me on the cell phone. "A deal!" I said skeptically as Jayne told her story. "But does Gloria actually know anything about the two murders—or even the true circumstances of Benny's death?"

"She says *she* doesn't—but Bud *does*. She could be lying, of course. Or exaggerating. She's like a child in many ways, Steve. She's not terribly mature. And of course she's desperate to get her hands on the suitcase of photographs."

"Speaking about the pictures—what's this about leaving them with your lawyer in Beverly Hills? I hate to tell you this, Jayne, but you don't *have* a lawyer in Beverly Hills!"

"It was a small fib, my dear. The suitcase is actually with you . . ."

"Me?"

"Darling, relax—it's in the trunk of the limo. Here's the deal, Steve. Gloria says you're to meet her inside the Griffith Park planetarium at exactly two o'clock this afternoon. You're supposed to come alone with the suitcase and sit and watch the show."

"That sounds a little melodramatic, don't you think?"

"Well, she *likes* the Griffith Park planetarium—she told me she always gets a thrill remembering that old scene in *Rebel Without A Cause* that was filmed there. She says she'll find you in the dark and tell you who the killer is. I mentioned we'll need proof, of course, but she says that won't be a problem."

"Jayne! This is unreal! For all we know, she'll whisper, 'James Dean did it,' in my ear, hand me a rubber dagger and say it's proof, and then disappear with the suitcase! This is a woman who has lied about nearly everything. Why should we trust her now?''

"Well, darling, I thought you'd be interested at least in listening to her. What do you have to lose?''

"The photographs, for one. Do you really think it's a wise idea to hand that suitcase over to her—and let her use those pictures to blackmail a lot of people?''

"I've thought about that, Steve. And I have an idea . . . it's a little sneaky, I'm afraid.''

"Lay it on me, sweetheart.''

And so at the appointed hour, Cass and I made our way to the planetarium in Griffith Park. The planetarium, of course, has been used as a location for countless movies and TV shows, including *Rebel Without A Cause,* and it's generally crowded with kids on school outings. Today when Cass and I arrived, there were several school buses and a few hundred young children milling about in the parking lot, chasing each other and being rowdy. In the presence of such innocence I felt out of place with my dark glasses and a green suitcase in my hand that was full of depravity.

"Well, Cass—have we got our plan straight?''

"Sure,'' he said. "It's as straight as a plan can be.''

I left him with the limo in the parking lot and walked up the path to the planetarium, joining a flood of fifth or sixth graders who were moving in the same direction. The planetarium is high on a hill and when I looked back at the parking lot, Cass was nowhere to be seen.

I paid my money for the two-fifteen show and walked out of the bright sunlight into the false twilight beneath the planetarium dome. I walked around the circumference to the far side, to a place where I could keep an eye on the main entrance. Then I settled into a low seat that was tilted backward so I would have a view of the "heavens." In the center of the room stood the complex projector that would cast a simulation of the night sky onto the domed ceiling. Some soft electronic music was playing, a synthesized space melody to get us into the mood. There's something fascinating about a planetarium, all the gadgetry and the sense of taking a leap into the universe.

I watched as the school children began piling into the room,

joking and laughing and pushing among themselves—but nevertheless glancing up at the dome occasionally with a certain awe.
It's hard not to feel the magic of this place. Eventually I saw an
especially large kid enter the planetarium—it was Cass, and he
found a seat directly by the exit. But I didn't see Gloria.

The kids filled about half of the room, and then there were
a few dozen stray adults like myself who had come for the show.
I took a seat in the second-to-last row, figuring that if I were lost
in the crowd Gloria might have trouble finding me. We all sat
expectantly until the music grew louder and the lights faded. All
of a sudden it was as if the roof had disappeared and we were looking
up at the night sky. In the dark, a man's voice began speaking.
He had one of those well-modulated voices that you often hear in
travelogues and documentaries, but even more relaxing and full-
bodied. It was a voice that was almost hypnotically tranquil.

The narrator introduced an early-evening sky that we might
see shortly after sunset on a late-summer's evening in Los Angeles,
if there was no smog. The Evening Star appeared like a twinkling
diamond low on the horizon; it seemed so real I almost made a
wish upon it. Then, bit by bit, we saw the Big Dipper, the North
Star, the constellations, and the Milky Way.

The simple combination of looking at the Milky Way and knowing the speed of light led me to marvel how some people—my friend
Pat Robertson, for example—can honestly believe that the entire
unimaginably vast physical universe is only about 7,000 years old.

It was all so fascinating that I had to concentrate on *not*
listening—for I had not come here today for a science lesson. I
hugged the small green suitcase in my lap and did my best to
keep my wits about me.

I must have drifted. The soft electronic music, the night sky,
the droning male voice . . . it all put me in a mood that was like
that moment right before a particularly welcome sleep when you
are entirely relaxed.

Then I heard a voice whisper in my right ear: "Is that the
suitcase?"

It was Gloria, though I had not seen her come up behind
me. "I have it," I whispered back.

"Let me see!"

"No way. I'm not letting this out of my hand until you tell me what I want to know."

"Bud told me everything, and I'll tell it all to you. But first I want to make certain you're not trying to trick me. I want those photographs, Steve."

"You know, Gloria—we've had a difficult relationship in the short time we've known one another. We always seem to come to an impasse. But I have a suggestion—why don't we do this in stages? You tell me who the killer is, and then I'll let you have a peek inside the suitcase while I still hold it. Then you tell me the motive, and give me a few details like when precisely your husband died—and perhaps a bit of proof so I know you're not just making up a lot of nonsense—and *then* I'll let you have the suitcase . . . Gloria?"

Probably it wasn't the most brilliant speech I had ever given, but still, I expected an answer. When she remained quiet, I turned in my seat to get a better look. Gloria was directly behind me, but there was a strange expression on her face. Her mouth was hanging open. She seemed dazed and confused. As I watched, she slumped forward and I soon saw what her problem was: she was dead. Exactly how this had happened, I wasn't certain in the darkness, but I wouldn't be entirely surprised if she had been stabbed with a teak-handled kitchen knife.

My shock at the turn of events made me stunned and slow. As I sat watching Gloria slump to the floor, a pair of strong hands grabbed the suitcase from my lap and tore it away from me.

"Hey!" I called.

I watched a shadow figure run from me down the aisle. I leaped after him, as fast as my legs would carry me. Unfortunately, there seemed to be a total lunar eclipse occurring on the planetarium ceiling, and things got very dark for a few moments. I collided with a woman who seemed to be an elementary school teacher.

"Would you please sit down and behave yourself!" she hissed.

I danced around her and kept moving toward the exit, where I saw Cass.

"Cass! Where is he?" I cried.

But Cass was clutching his stomach, doubled up in pain.

"Cass, are you okay?"

"Yeah," he said. "Just got the wind knocked out of me—I tried to stop him, but he hit me pretty hard."

"You see who it was?

He shook his head. "I feel awful about this, Steve. I was supposed to stop him!"

"You were supposed to stop *her*, Cass, not a strong guy—but Gloria's dead. I'm going to see if I can catch him."

"I'm coming, too . . . I'm okay, honest."

"Will you two *please* be quiet!" another teacher whispered hoarsely in our direction.

Cass and I ran out the exit to the lobby, and then outside into the dazzling sunshine. We stood on the stone balcony looking down upon the parking lot below—in nearly the exact place where James Dean and Natalie Wood had their first talk in *Rebel Without A Cause*. It was a nostalgic spot, I suppose, but it didn't help us see who had killed Gloria and run with the suitcase. Unfortunately, the photographs were in fact in the suitcase—now the property of whoever had run from the planetarium. We had known that Gloria would insist on checking that they were there before telling any interesting stories of violence, intrigue, and passion. We were not planning to let her get away with the suitcase, frankly—thus Cass's presence at the exit, in case she managed to elude me. But it was one thing to deal with a nervous widow, and quite another to stop a strong and desperate man. None of this had worked out according to our ill-conceived plan.

As we stood watching, we saw a man in dark clothes run out from the foot of the path into the parking lot below. Cass and I took off after him.

"Hey!" I called. "Stop!"

My shout caught his attention. He turned for a moment and looked up to where we were standing. It was a young man with long blond hair, a dark straw color, that was tied back in a ponytail. I was virtually certain that we must be chasing Bud Albertson, chauffeur and bastard son. But it was not Bud—it was an absolute stranger.

My heart sank a little to find myself facing an absolute question mark at this late stage. An unknown joker in our unruly deck of cards.

Who in the world could he be?

chapter 52

We had some luck—good luck, and bad. The good luck was that our unknown killer with his blond ponytail had unwisely parked quite far up the parking lot, while Cass had managed to find a spot for the Cadillac almost at the foot of the path. The planetarium parking lot at Griffith Park is a huge place, designed for school buses and big crowds, so this meant that even though the bastard had a good start on us, we got to the limo about the same time he reached his own machine—a sharp-looking red Corvette.

Cass and I jumped into the front seat, and he started the ignition before we even had the doors closed. With a squeal of rubber, Cass backed up, changed gears, and took off toward the Corvette at the top of the parking lot, hoping to block the car's exit. Meanwhile, Mr. Ponytail had fired up his sports car and was heading down toward us. There is a famous scene in *Rebel Without A Cause* where James Dean plays chicken with Natalie Wood's bad boyfriend—a rebel with even *less* of a cause than Dean, who kills himself driving off a cliff. There was no cliff in our immediate vicinity, but our game of chicken was very much for real: the Corvette and our stately old limousine were on a collision course, and it was going to be interesting to see which of us would give way.

"Careful, Cass!" I murmured. "No sense getting killed over this!"

"I got it under control, Steve. Just hang on tight!"

We met in approximately the middle of the parking lot. For

a second it looked as if we were going to have a head-on collision, but Cass chickened out, I'm happy to say, and swerved at the last moment. Mr. Ponytail also swerved, however, at the same instant and in the same direction. This meant that we collided sidewise with a terrible crash of metal against metal, like two bumper cars. It was bone-jarring and frightening, but Cass and I survived it without any injury. I'm glad to report that they made Cadillac limos pretty sturdy in the old days, and, of course, our machine was a good deal heavier than the Corvette, which gave us the advantage. My glasses had fallen loose in the collision, but when I got them perched once again on my nose, I saw that we had knocked the Corvette off its course and sent it careening into an unfortunate VW Bug parked nearby. Both the Volkswagen and the Corvette appeared ready for the wrecking yard.

Cass reached into the glove compartment and pulled out his huge Colt. 45. Then we both staggered out of the limo—unhurt but shook up. The man with the ponytail was emerging at the same time from the wreckage of his sports car, and he seemed to be moving slowly as well. He had the green suitcase in one hand.

"Goddamn it! Look what you did to my 'Vette!" he complained. "And I've only had these wheels three weeks!"

There was something oddly familiar about his voice, though nothing else about him was familiar at all. We were standing among the ruins of our automobiles about a dozen feet from one another. Up close I could see that he was wearing dirty black jeans and a black Harley-Davidson T-shirt. The jeans were torn at one knee and I could see that he was bleeding. He was deeply suntanned and had that salty look of one who spends a good deal of time at the beach but doesn't often take a shower. All in all, he looked like a thousand and one other unwashed, semi-literate, tough-guy hipsters.

"Who are you?" I demanded. "And why did you kill Gloria?"

"Man! You're going to be sorry you made me smash my car!" he whined.

Cass raised the barrel of his Colt and pointed it at Mr. Ponytail's stomach.

"Put your hands on your head," Cass told him.

"You must be joking, dude!"

"Better do what he says," I grunted, hoping to imply that Jimmy Cassidy was a mad killer I restrained from bloodshed only with great effort.

That's when Mr. Ponytail did something really unforgivable—he laughed at us, right in our faces. Then, with a quick weasel-like motion, he made a dash for it—ducking behind the ruins of his Corvette, continuing quickly past the remains of the VW, and darting away through the parked cars. There was something about his quick, furtive movements that rang a bell; I hadn't recognized his face, but I had seen this particular weasel run from me before.

"Come on, Cass!" I said grimly. "This time he's not going to get away!"

Cass was standing frozen in place with his huge pistol pointed toward the retreating figure.

"I'm trying to get a clear shot, Steve—I don't want to wreck any more cars!"

Dear old Cass. I knew it wasn't wrecking cars that worried him; he could have had a clear shot at the man with the ponytail, but was simply unable to put a bullet in someone's back.

"We want him alive," I suggested. "He's limping pretty badly—let's see if we can get him in a more civilized manner."

So Cass and I took off after him through the cars. The man with the ponytail was quite a few decades younger than either Cass or me, and normally we wouldn't have had a chance of catching him. But he had clearly banged up his knee in the collision and was not moving as quickly as I had seen him do in the past. We played tag in and out of the cars for a few moments, and then he broke free and made his way to a footpath at the far side of the parking lot and disappeared down the slope of a hill into Griffith Park itself. Cass and I arrived at the head of the path just in time to see him duck off the trail and disappear into the trees. We ran after him, but by the time we arrived at the spot on the trail, he was nowhere in sight.

"Damn! I should have shot him when I had the chance!" Cass swore.

"Cass, don't blame yourself for being decent. We'll find this son of a bitch yet . . ."

We were standing in a dry and dusty forest of elm and eucalyptus and scruffy brush. I led the way around a large boulder, hoping to get a glimpse of blond hair. But there were a thousand places he might be hiding in the park. We might have lost him completely at this moment, but then I heard a woman scream.

Cass and I continued past the boulder and found ourselves once again on the path. We jogged over a small wooden footbridge to a picnic table where a young mother was hugging a little boy who was crying.

"A guy with a blond ponytail," I panted. "Where did he go?"

She pointed down the path. "He stole his skateboard!" she said with breathless outrage. Then she saw the gun in Cass's hand and she hugged her child closer.

The path was gravel and uneven, so it was hard to imagine a skateboard would be of much use to our limping fugitive. We followed the path for several hundred yards as it wound its way through the dusty Southern California forest, arriving at last at a two-lane road that traversed the park. I looked up and down the road but didn't see him at first.

"There he is!" Cass said.

He was on an asphalt path that diverged from the main road, about twenty yards away from us. He made an odd sight, limping and struggling to use the skateboard, still clutching the small green suitcase in one hand. Cass and I caught our breath for just a second and then we ran after him. At the head of the path he had taken, I noticed a small sign with an arrow pointing TO ZOO. I didn't like the idea of our ponytail losing himself in the crowds at the Griffith Park Zoo, so I urged Cass to run faster. But it was no use. Even with a bad limp, a young man with a skateboard could easily outdistance two old-timers. We jogged all-out for perhaps another five minutes before we simply ran out of steam. We slowed to a walk, both of us wheezing and gasping for breath. Two young women on bicycles screamed when they saw us and took off quickly down the path. I couldn't imagine at first what they were afraid of. Then I remembered what was in Cass's hand.

"Better . . . put that gun . . . away!" I managed, breathing hard.

Cass stuffed the pistol into the waistband of his pants beneath his shirt, which made us slightly more respectable. Then we continued at a walking pace in the direction of the zoo.

"Well, we've lost him!" Cass complained. "What now?"

"I think the best we can do is continue to the zoo and find a telephone. We'll let the police take over . . . we're getting too old for this sort of stuff!"

Griffith Park covers a large area and I had no clear idea of where we were. We walked at a more leisurely pace for another ten minutes without finding any sign of the zoo—or our young man, either. The landscape changed. We found ourselves walking alongside a brick wall covered with vines and old growth. There must have been ground water nearby, for the woods in this section of the park were dense and green and the path was choked with weeds.

"Cass, I'm starting to think we're lost!"

"How lost can we get in a city park, Steve?"

"Lost enough," I assured him. "What do you think is on the other side of this high brick wall?"

We walked on uncertainly. I was starting to wonder if we would ever find our way out of the maze of paths back to civilization when I noticed an abandoned skateboard by the wall. The weeds nearby were trampled.

"Looks to me like our guy left his stolen transportation and escaped over the wall. What do you think, Cass?"

Cass studied the situation. There was a gnarly old tree, some sort of elm or maple, growing alongside the wall. Cass pulled experimentally on the lowest branch.

"It's strong enough," Cass said. "It seems to me he could have climbed up this tree and jumped down the other side and gotten away. Want me to climb up and see what's over there, Steve?"

"I don't want you to get hurt, Cass."

"This tree's no problem. Look at the way the branches are arranged—it's almost like a flight of stairs!"

I was more dubious. The tree did not look like a flight of stairs to me, not even with a generous amount of imagination, and neither Cass nor I was of an age for scrambling up branches.

Still, I was curious what was on the other side of the high wall, and where exactly the killer had escaped to.

"Well, give it a try then," I told Cass. "But take it easy. If the going gets tough, don't be foolish—just give up and come back down."

Cass handed me the Colt. 45 and then reached up and got a firm hold on the lowest branch. I didn't like the look of boyish resolve on his face. With a grunt of effort he swung his legs upward and tried to get his left leg hooked over the branch. He couldn't quite make it.

"Give me a push, Steve!"

"No, I think we should forget this."

"Boss, all I need is just a little help and I'll get to the first branch. And the rest of it's easy."

So Cass tried again, and this time I pushed upward on his back while he swung his leg toward the branch. Cass grunted and gasped and grunted some more . . . and then at last managed to get one leg hooked over the branch and swing himself up into the greenery.

"Man! Trees were different in the old days! A lot easier!" he muttered.

Cass rested a moment and then continued upward into the higher branches. He had a bad moment about halfway up where he lost his footing, slipped, and nearly fell. He managed to cling to the branch above him, and in a moment his feet found a new place to stand. He kept climbing steadily until at last he was high enough to peer over the wall.

"What do you see?" I called upward.

"Mmm . . . hard to say. Just more forest. It looks like a kind of enclosure . . . oh-oh!"

"Oh-oh, what?"

"Oh-oh, a dirty white tennis shoe sticking out of a clump of weeds."

"Maybe some kid threw some other kid's shoe over the wall, Cass. You know how kids are. Now if you don't see anything . . ."

"I'm going down to investigate. I can sort of swing down this long tree limb that falls over the wall to the other side . . ."

"Cass!"

". . . Piece of cake, Steve!"

Before I could stop him, Cass disappeared over the wall. I could hear him struggling for a moment and then there was a small cry and the sound of a body falling with a whoosh through branches and brush. A few birds were disturbed and flew into the air with a cry of outrage.

"Cass!" I cried. "Are you okay? . . . Cass!"

I called and called. But there was no answer from the other side. Not a word.

chapter 53

There seemed nothing to do but follow after Cass. I stuck the barrel of the huge Colt .45 in my belt, grabbed hold of the first branch as Cass had done, and swung upward. I am considerably taller than Cass—six-feet-three, to be precise—and this was helpful. I succeeded on the second try, though the pistol fell from my belt and clattered onto the ground while I was briefly hanging upside down. I did not try to retrieve the thing, but let it remain where it had fallen.

My hands were scraped and I had banged a knee. There is a certain lack of dignity in climbing a tree when one has reached a particular age in life, no matter how child-like one remains inside.

"Cass!" I called again. "Can you hear me?"

There was still no answer so I continued upward into the higher branches, some of which bent crazily beneath my weight. I tried not to look down—it was not a great distance to the ground below, but enough so that one could break a leg, or a neck, by making a wrong move. It took me several minutes to reach the top of the wall where I was able to peer down to the other side. I saw Cass immediately. He was sitting on the ground in the brush below, rubbing the back of his head.

"Cass! Thank God you're okay! Why the hell didn't you answer when I called?"

"I must have been out for a few minutes," he said thickly. "I banged my head against something kinda hard."

"Do you feel sick to your stomach?" I asked, trying to remember everything I knew about concussions.

"I'm okay," he told me—though he didn't sound okay. "Anyway, I'm in better shape than this guy."

I had been so concerned about Cass that I had not noticed until now the leg that protruded from the brush a few feet from where Cass was sitting. There was a dirty white tennis shoe attached to the gam, and a few inches away another tennis shoe as well.

"I'm coming down," I told Cass.

"Better not, Steve . . . damn!" he cried out in pain, trying to stand, but collapsing immediately upon the ground once more. "I think maybe I've broken something . . ."

That decided it. One of the large limbs of my tree had half-broken off from the main trunk, and fallen over at a steep angle to the other side of the wall nearly to the ground below. It made a sort of highway to Cass and the side of the wall where I wished to be. It seemed that I might do better than Cass had done if I was very careful and went slowly.

I decided to cinch down feet-first and turned over onto my stomach, wrapping my legs around the fallen tree limb and letting myself down in un-macho increments. It would have been a lot easier if the limb had been smooth and stripped of its tributary branches. As it was, I had to get around several awkward places and there were a few times I nearly lost my grip and fell. Cass had been too eager to get down quickly; I was determined to avoid his mistake and move methodically down the limb. It took me more than fifteen minutes. I tore my pants and skinned my knee. My right hand was bleeding, my left sticky with sap. It was not an experience I wish to repeat, but thanks in part to the help of gravity, I made it at last to the other side.

First I checked that Cass was all right. His left ankle was swollen badly, but I didn't think it was actually broken.

"Does it hurt a lot?"

" 'S'all right," he said thickly. "I'll just take a small nap . . ."

"No!" I insisted loudly. I recalled reading somewhere that a person with a concussion must not be allowed to sleep. "Wake up, Cass! Can't go to sleep now, pal!"

I left him for a moment to investigate the dirty tennis shoes sticking out of the brush a few feet away. As my gaze moved upward, I could see that the tennis shoes were indeed attached to legs in dirty jeans, a black Harley Davidson T-shirt, bare arms, shoulders, and head. The works, the entire human comedy. It was Mr. Blond Ponytail—except his blond hair was a wig and it had been knocked loose by his fall, revealing closely cropped dark hair underneath. The green suitcase lay beside him on the ground.

Up close, I could see the dead man was my old acquaintance, Murray the Z, who I had not seen since that awful night at the Blue Moon Apartments. This time he had run out of fancy tricks. Apparently he had been moving too fast and had fallen from the same limb as Cass as he had tried to escape over the high brick wall—but he had done a good deal worse for himself than a concussion and a sprained ankle. It was hard to say exactly how it happened, but he had managed to fall upon a knife he was carrying as he tumbled out of the tree, a kitchen knife with a smooth teak handle—part of a set I had come to know too well.

"Hmm . . . wake me when this is over," Cass said with a yawn, stretching out on the ground.

"No, you don't," I told him, leaving Murray and returning to his side. "You have to stay awake!"

"I can't, Steve . . . I've never been this sleepy in my life."

"Try singing a song."

"A *song?* Look, I'm a big music fan, but . . ."

"Let's do something up-tempo—how about 'Gravy Waltz'? *Pretty Mama's in the kitchen this glorious day . . .*"

Cass gave it a valiant effort. We were singing with near-gusto when I happened to look up and notice a large pussycat a few feet away, watching us with a curious expression on his face. It was a very large pussycat indeed—a full-grown African lion. It seems we had found the Griffith Park Zoo after all—or at least a back section of the park where they kept some of the animals that were not on display.

As Cass and I watched, the lion did a pretty good imitation of his famous MGM relative. For a moment, it seemed as if he were about to yawn. But then the yawn turned into a mighty roar.

chapter 54

It was a glittering crowd that drifted into the Dorothy Chandler Pavilion in downtown Los Angeles Friday night. On the street itself, searchlights scanned the sky, sending beams of light many hundreds of feet into the polluted heavens for all to see. The smog was so heavy that an old line from one of my TV scripts flew through my mind: *"I shot an arrow into air—it stuck there."* Huge crowds lined up along the sidewalks, held back by police barricades, as one limousine after another pulled up in front of the theater and deposited women in glittering gowns and men in new-fashioned tuxedos.

I draw a distinction between these soon-to-fade—God willing—goofy fad tuxedos and the traditional classic tux worn by Cary Grant, Henry Fonda, and other gentlemen with natural style. I don't fault designers for deliberately foisting bizarre accoutrement on a generation of young would-be hipsters. I'm all for change. But the new is supposed to be, at least in some regard, better than the old. Change for its own sake is dumb-o-rino. Hasn't it occurred to anybody that there's something essentially stupid about wearing a *black* shirt with a black tux? Incidentally, I exempt anyone connected with the rock music business from my judgment. Rock people, for reasons we don't have time to go into at the moment, *want* to look bizarre, so the fact that they do can hardly be held against them. But why young actors and studio executives—who one would assume might know better—consciously want to look like freaks is a question that I'm sure will fascinate cultural historians of the future.

The crowds cheered and sometimes even swooned when they

saw a famous face step from a limousine. And they groaned with angry impatience, and sometimes even booed, when it was a mere mortal, someone they did not know—a writer, producer, agent not familiar to them. Occasionally, when they saw a *very* famous face, a few from the crowd would idiotically try to lunge forward from behind the barricade to actually touch their beloved god. Most of the time the security force was successful in keeping the celebrities safe from their presumptive fans, but in one case—the arrival of a young man who had just been voted Sexiest Man Alive, God help us, by *People* magazine—a determined teenage girl who looked more than slightly deranged managed to get past security. Sobbing with passion, she clung to her idol's leg before a small platoon of human-stuffed uniforms managed to drag her away.

The invited guests made their grand entrance from the sidewalk into the Pavilion itself, where they lingered for a few moments in the huge, glittering lobby, talking among themselves and exchanging excited hugs and pecks on the cheek. Those who were inclined to advance their careers every hour of the day managed to arrange meetings and whisper quick messages about scripts and exchange rumors of executive positions up for grabs at Fox, Paramount, and Warners due to the constant reshuffling of talent.

When actors or entertainers are out of work, they're out of work, but executives have this cute habit of hiring each other. Of course, if you hire a man there's always the chance that in a few years he might be in a position to hire you.

At seven-fifteen exactly, the doors to the auditorium were opened and the ushers encouraged the guests to take their assigned seats. The question of time is always of utmost importance in any live broadcast and so people filed in obediently and took their places. At seven-forty-five the doors were closed and no one further was admitted—unless, of course, they were famous or important enough, and then the rule was bent.

The show began off-camera for the guests inside Dorothy Chandler Pavilion at precisely seven-fifty. The lights dimmed, the orchestra played, and a well-known TV sitcom star strode out onto the stage. For eight minutes, he told jokes and got the crowd warmed up and in the right mood. Meanwhile, the seconds ticked down toward airtime. The technical people stood by, tense and ready. There were five cameras—three in front of the stage, and two far back in the upper balcony. In the control booth, far in the rear of the upper balcony, men and women sat with earphones watching their monitor screens, while Jerry Williams, the producer, paced back and forth in the enclosed space, making everyone nervous. At fifteen seconds to airtime, the floor manager onstage, a young man with headphones, began his final countdown: "Fifteen . . . fourteen . . . thirteen . . . twelve . . . eleven . . ." The final five seconds were counted silently, on his fingers, and then at last—after all these months of planning—the music swelled, the applause burst forth, and the Benny Hartman Memorial Comedy Awards was on the air.

An announcer with one of those immaculate TV voices announced a Very Famous Late-Night TV Talk Show Host—a man who had retired in glory some years back, but was now returning in front of the cameras for this special broadcast. He was greeted by thunderous applause. His presence tonight, if I may be allowed to brag a moment, was one of my greatest coups—and not so easy to arrange. The Very Famous Talk Show Host delighted everybody by doing one of his trademark monologues for precisely four and a half minutes, leading to the first commercial break.

After the break, the famous comedian spent a few moments clowning, and then, going for the overworked cliché—and aren't they all?—introduced the "Renaissance man himself and old buddy of mine . . . our emcee, STEVE ALLEN!"

The band struck up my theme song, "This Could Be the Start of Something Big." And then, from stage right, followed by a roving spotlight, walked . . . not me at all, I'm afraid, but my dear wife, Jayne Meadows.

The Very Famous Talk Show Host wasn't quite as fast as he used to be.

"Hey, Steverino!" he began, facing the audience rather than Jayne. Then he saw it was not Mr., but Mrs. Allen onstage with him and did a double take.

"Hey . . . what the . . . you're not Steve Allen!" he managed.

"How sweet of you to notice," said Jayne.

The audience thought it was all planned and laughed, but

the host was not pleased. He peered at the TelePrompTer seeking some clue as to what to do next, but there was no help in that direction either. Fortunately, Jayne managed to take the ball.

"I know you were expecting Steve," she began, "but he's hoping to make an appearance later. Meanwhile, we have some awards to give away. So without further ado, let's get down to business . . ."

Jayne introduced the first celebrity couple—he, a romantic star of the movies, she, a queen of the sitcoms—to give away the first "Benny" for Best Female Stand-Up Comedian. From there the show truly got underway. Best Male Stand-Up Comedian . . . Best Comedy Screenwriter . . . Best Producer of a Comic Television Series . . . and more. Some of the recipients were long dead and the award of an honorary nature; others were very much alive and came bounding onstage to accept their bronze statuette. It was turning into a successful evening. There were film clips of Buster Keaton, and my favorites, Laurel and Hardy, Charlie Chaplin, and some truly rare archival footage of Benny Hartman himself doing vaudeville. The people who make up the entertainment industry are their own biggest fans, and with every eye focused upon the stage, few of the spectators in the audience—and certainly no one sitting at home—noticed the discreet police presence, the dozen plainclothesmen who took up positions at every exit. Nor did they observe a particularly tall and gloomy policeman standing at the top of the central aisle, a man who looked absurdly like Bela Lugosi and who refused to laugh at a single joke coming from the stage. Not so much as the smallest smile illuminated this glum individual's world-weary face; instead, the comedy only seemed to make him look as if he could not understand how anyone might be so shallow as to laugh in such a grim world of sorrow.

There were vocals, dance routines, and, despite Lieutenant Kripinsky, lots of laughs. If you missed the show, you truly missed a real extravaganza. And then, at almost exactly one hour and forty-five minutes into the broadcast, Jayne once again took up her duties.

"And now at last we have come to the moment you have all been waiting for . . . the grand one-million-dollar prize for the

Funniest Person Alive. And to present this award, I would like to welcome at this time your friend and mine . . . Steve Allen!''

The band hastily struck up my theme song for a second time and I walked from the wings of the theater out onto the stage, saluted, faced the bright lights and cameras, and began:

"Ladies and gentlemen, I'm glad I could make it tonight. And just to show *how* glad I am, I'm going to put you all out of your misery right away, cut through the suspense, and without any preamble whatsoever, I will tell you the winner of the Benny Hartman Memorial Comedy Award grand prize for the Funniest Person Alive . . . the envelope, please.''

I had departed wildly from the script. The floor manager was gesturing wildly to me, the TelePrompTer had nearly short-circuited in electronic confusion, and it took a few seconds of dead air before a pretty young actress trotted dutifully on stage to give me the proper envelope.

I opened it with a flourish—though it was clearly not the job of the emcee to perform this particular task.

"The winner of the million-dollar Benny Hartman Memorial Comedy Award prize for the Funniest Person Alive . . . let's see! My goodness! The winner is . . . Benny Hartman!''

There were some chuckles from the audience from a few people who thought I must be doing something funny, even though they couldn't understand it. But mostly there was a feeling of embarrassed uncertainty, and a sense that I had gone beyond good taste or judgment.

I faced the audience with an apologetic smile.

"At this point,'' I explained, "Benny was supposed to make a grand reappearance from the dead, and walk, mosey, amble, sidle, or trip up here on stage and collect his own money and his own reward. Benny, you see, had planned to play a joke upon us all, but murder intervened. And so we are forced to end this show on a serious note—the human comedy, alas, rather than the kind we had gathered to celebrate tonight. Murder is no joke—and since there are in fact four murders to explain—those of Terry Parker, Billy D'Amato, Gloria Hartman, and Benny himself—I want to take the few minutes that are left to us tonight to narrate a very sad tale: how a joke, not a very good joke to begin with, got out of hand and turned desperately bad.''

Now there was definitely a stunned silence in the auditorium. The floor manager took off his earphones in dismay, probably to escape the frantic shouts of Jerry Williams having a nervous breakdown in the control booth.

"Let me begin with the joke itself that turned out not to be so funny: Sometime, probably last Christmas when he was vacationing in Switzerland with his wife, Benny came up with the idea that it might be fun to pull off a grand hoax, make a big splash in the media, and have himself a little fun. Why he decided to do such a thing, we can only guess. He was eighty-five years old, but he felt in top form and was planning to live at least to one hundred—our dear friend George Burns did. But maybe he craved some excitement, as well as a chance to punish his wife, Gloria. We'll get to her part in this story shortly.

"Anyway, whatever the reasons, Benny decided he would fake his death, attend his own funeral, and eventually show up here tonight and blow everybody's mind by walking on stage to accept the million-dollar prize—his own million. He was the ultimate ham, you might say, if you'll pardon the use of an old expression— one we'll return to shortly. As for the award itself for funniest person alive, I'm sorry to report that this was rigged from the start for Benny's name to be in the envelope as you just heard me read it, despite the judges and a bunch of us wasting our time under the assumption that this was an honest show. Exactly how this was rigged, and by whom, is a subject we'll return to as well.

"First of all, to set his joke in motion, Benny needed to get sick and fake his death in a convincing manner. For this, he needed the service of a reputable doctor, and it just so happened that he had such a doctor in his pocket, a certain Dr. David Diehl—who is in Hong Kong at the moment, incidentally, and has just made a lengthy statement to the police. A good number of years ago, before Roe v. Wade, young Dr. Diehl performed abortions without the blessings of the law from time to time in his office. Unfortunately for the doctor, a pretty young woman died in his office one afternoon, and the father of the aborted fetus was none other than our Benny Hartman, who had sent the girl to Dr. Diehl. And so several decades later, when Benny needed an obliging doctor, he knew exactly where to go. He approached Dr. Diehl—who was now a successful and conservative gentleman of late middle-age—and threatened to reveal his long-hidden secret if he did not do exactly what Benny told him.

"Dr. Diehl believed he had no choice but to go along. He had a relationship with a nurse by the name of Janet Dorfman, who was very loyal to him, and together the nurse and the doctor helped create the fiction that Benny was sick and dying. Eventually they faked the death itself, providing a false death certificate. Naturally, Forest Lawn required a body for there to be a funeral, and here also the doctor used his medical contacts to find a suitable corpse—a street character known as Pussycat Charlie with no relatives who was lying in the county morgue.

"So now all the elements of the hoax were in place. But there is a Greek word, *hubris,* which refers to a person like Benny who tempts the gods with his pride and arrogance. At least one person who knew about this hoax thought it might be tempting to transform Benny Hartman's make-believe death into the real thing. Let's leave the name a blank for now and go on to some new complications that were about to occur.

"Benny, as everyone knows, died *officially* on May 17. In truth, he disappeared on that date to a convenient hideaway he had kept for years at Trancas Beach north of Malibu, a place few people knew about. He set about to enjoy himself greatly—all the fuss the media made about his passing, the film clips covering his long career, even a statement from the President of the United States. For a guy with an ego like Benny's, this was like Christmas. There was a cruel element to this hoax as well—his wife Gloria's reaction when she discovered she had been left penniless in his supposed will, which was meant to teach her a lesson for being unfaithful with their chauffeur, a young man named Bud Albertson. More about him shortly.

"Benny enjoyed all this so much that he became incautious. He should have stayed put in his beach house hideaway, but he decided to make a few trips about town in order to observe the national grieving firsthand. He had a limousine at his service, and a driver—not his own chauffeur and limo, by the way, but hired from a local company that guarantees complete discretion as part of their service. It was during one of these jaunts about town— to the Chateau Marmont Hotel on Sunset Boulevard—that he had the misfortune to be seen, quite accidentally, by an old friend, Terry Parker, who had a penthouse there.

"Now Terry, as most of you know, had his own odd sense of humor, and I doubt if he was too shocked at the hoax. He was quite willing to stay quiet about it—but at a price. By this time, of course, everybody in Hollywood knew about the award show that was planned for tonight, along with the million-dollar prize. Terry's price for staying quiet was simply to have Benny arrange for *him* to win the grand prize. This was quite awkward, of course, since Benny planned to receive the award himself. Nevertheless, the two men apparently made an appointment to meet at the mock-funeral at Forest Lawn to discuss the issue further, naturally with Benny in disguise. Unfortunately, this rendezvous turned out very differently than either of them imagined.

"We need to pause for a moment to ask a question that some of you have probably wondered about as well—namely, how did Benny manage to rent a limousine, take care of himself in a beach house, get around town, and arrange various meetings all by himself? He wasn't ill and dying as he had pretended, but he *couldn't* manage all these things by himself. Benny had to have an accomplice.

"So who could that be? Who could help set up such an elaborate deception—and also assure, incidentally, that at the end of this very grand production you're watching tonight, the winning name in the envelope for the grand prize would be that of Benny Hartman, no matter what the judges had decided? A deception such as this required the help of a clever attorney who was accustomed to arranging intricate details of important deals. Or better yet, an accomplished showman who had experience in making the public believe the illusions of Hollywood . . . a first-rate producer, perhaps. After all, what was this hoax anyway but a very well-produced show?

"As it happened, Benny had both a good attorney and a good producer in his pocket, due to some more of his blackmailing ways. For his accomplice, he chose the producer. And this was the person he had gone to see at the Chateau Marmont when he ran into Terry Parker in the hallway.

"We are talking, ladies and gentleman, of the producer of this very show, and co-conspirator of this most unscrupulous hoax—Jerry Williams."

I was watching the floor manager as I said this—the young man with earphones on who was standing close to camera number two and was in constant contact with the control booth upstairs. His face contorted with the blast of swear words and abuse that Jerry was doubtlessly shouting in his ear.

Then the plug was pulled. Literally. The lights went out in Dorothy Chandler Pavilion and we were off the air.

chapter 55

We were left in relative darkness for only a few seconds, but it seemed longer at the time. Long enough to cause a small panic and shouts of surprise from the audience. The dark brings out our most primitive fears—and some very real fears, as well, when one is trapped in a large public building with several hundred other humans. Fortunately, just when the panic was about to ignite, the emergency lights came on—harsh, white floodlights that cast strange shadows but were welcomed nonetheless.

"Take it easy, everybody!" a figure shouted, walking down the main aisle toward the stage carrying a bullhorn. "This is the LAPD. Everything's under control—please remain in your seats. That's right, sit down, please," he urged to some who had half-risen and were looking about with anxious expressions. "The LAPD has everything under control . . . are you okay, Mr. Allen?"

It was, of course, Lieutenant Kripinsky.

"I'm fine. But what happened with the lights?"

"Mr. Williams managed to pull a few master switches, hoping to escape in the dark. But we have him."

As if on cue, two detectives appeared at the top of the aisle with the producer between them. He did not look happy.

"Bring him down to the front," the lieutenant commanded, "and see if you can find some folding chairs to put in the aisle so we can sit down. Now why don't you continue, Mr. Allen. We may no longer be on the air, but I'm certain there are quite a few people here who would like to hear the end of your account."

"Steve, I'm innocent!" Jerry called to me from the aisle. He made a pitiful attempt to laugh. "You know me—I wouldn't kill anybody!"

"I never accused you of murder, Jerry. I accused you of complicity in an elaborate fraud. You and Benny planned this entire hoax . . ."

"I had to do it!" he interrupted. "Benny made me. He had, well, some stuff on me that I didn't want to become public knowledge."

"Yes, I can imagine what he had on you. And maybe that's why you got involved in this deception, but you continued with it even after you knew that Benny was dead. Why?"

He shrugged. "Well, it seemed like one hell of a show, Steve. And after all, that's what I am—a showman."

"When did you know that Benny was dead?"

"I never actually knew for certain. I just suspected it when he never answered my phone calls. The last time I saw him was the day before his funeral—when he came to the Chateau Marmont, like you said. I'd been living there for about a month, after my wife threw me out of the house . . . but that's another story. Terry and I used to pal around a little during that time—he was only one floor above me at the hotel. And that's how he saw Benny. Terry dropped by without phoning just as Benny was leaving. I told Benny it was nuts him coming over to visit me when he was supposed to be dead. But it was like Benny thought he was some sort of god who could get away with anything, just by wearing dark glasses and an old, you know, Rex Harrison hat. He wanted to gloat with someone about how clever he was, and I was the only person who knew about the hoax, so I was it."

"Careful, Jerry!" I warned. "If you were the *only* person who knew, that makes you the killer . . . but fortunately for you, there was someone else following these developments with enormous interest. Someone who had been wishing for an opportunity such as this to get away with the perfect murder—for after all, how can you get caught when the world believes the victim has already died of natural causes?"

Needless to say we had the attention of the audience. As I spoke, the regular lights came back on. I was glad we remained

off the air, for there was no reason to clean house in such a public
way.

I continued:

"This would have been a much simpler affair had Terry
Parker not stumbled into it, catching a glimpse of Benny as he
was leaving the Chateau Marmont. With Terry's knowledge of the
hoax, this could no longer be the perfect crime—and so poor
Terry had to die."

"Wait a second, Steve," someone objected from the third
row. I saw it was Harvey Roth. "Is it okay to ask a question?"

"Sure."

"Well, Terry wasn't the only one who knew Benny was alive—
you've just told us that Dr. Diehl knew about the hoax, as well as
his nurse friend, and Jerry Williams, too. Why didn't they have
to die also?"

"Because they were part of the plot and weren't about to
blab about it. After all, they were all breaking the law in one way
or another, they had their careers and reputations to consider,
and so they had every reason to keep quiet. It's doubtful that
anyone would ever hire a doctor or a nurse who had faked a death
certificate, or a producer who had produced a crooked show. But
Terry was another matter—he might easily talk. And if it got out
that Benny had not died when he was supposed to, on May 17,
the police would start looking into his real death and that could
lead to discovery. The killer had to get Terry out of the way.

"Now here's how I imagine the chronology: Sometime after
Benny left the Chateau Marmont, and before the funeral the next
day, the killer—or to be more exact, someone the killer hired—
went down to the beach house at Trancas and murdered Benny.
From the police autopsy, by the way, we have learned the true
cause of death—Benny Hartman was smothered, possibly with a
plastic bag pulled tightly around his head.

"Next the killer sent his hired hand to the funeral at Forest
Lawn to show up in Benny's place at the rendezvous with Terry
Parker. Terry was stabbed in the back but he had enough strength
left to whisper one word when I got to him: *Ham.* I have been
puzzling over this word for months, but actually he meant it in
its most traditional metaphor—a theatrical ham. Someone who

hogs the stage and hams it up. Terry had no way of knowing, of course, that Benny was dead, and he must have believed Benny had hired the killer to get him out of the way so that Benny could win the award himself. Terry was trying to get out some sentence like: 'That big ham, Benny Hartman, is still alive! He's responsible for this!' But, of course, he had very little life left, and so he managed only one word. Really, when you think about it, it is the key word to this entire sorry affair: *ham.*"

To one side of the stage I saw Jayne nodding.

"At the time, unfortunately, this one word wasn't particularly helpful to either the police or myself in solving the crime—but the killer had no way of knowing that either. The killer must have been alarmed that Terry lived long enough to whisper a message, and just about everything else that he—or she—did after that was an attempt to confuse matters and throw us off track.

"Billy D'Amato's death was designed for nothing else but to muddy the waters. It was all show business—special effects, you might say. A cheap hood broke into my bedroom, threatened that Jayne and I would suffer terrible things if Billy did not win the award, and then ran away. Naturally, this guaranteed that I would go storming off angrily to Billy—but when I got there he was dead, with a knife in his back similar to the weapon that killed Terry Parker. A knife, I'm sorry to say, that was from a set I had given to Benny years ago and was reported stolen last Christmas. So now we were supposed to think that perhaps there was a serial killer on the loose sticking knives in famous comedians. Or maybe even that I did it!

"To add to the confusion, Gloria Hartman and the chauffeur, Bud Albertson, were doing their best to contest the will. Albertson, I need to tell you at this point, was Benny Hartman's illegitimate son, who had grown up with his mother in New Jersey and had arrived in California six years ago hoping his father would set him firmly on the path to fame and fortune. Benny, however, did no such thing—he gave Bud a menial job as his chauffeur, and told him to keep his mouth shut about their relationship. Most likely if Bud had been more clever and had pretended at least to be a loving son, his position would have improved with time. But Bud did the worst possible thing—he seduced the woman of the house, his young stepmother, Gloria, thereby earning his father's undying enmity. Bud is an angry, sullen young man and, as I say, not the brightest creature in the world. About the only clever move he has managed so far, I might add, is to make a full statement to the police this afternoon.

"Bud and Gloria both believed that they should inherit oodles of money, rather than what was actually left them in Benny's will—one dollar apiece. Benny may well have meant simply to teach his son and wife a lesson, to scare them into being nicer to him when he made his return from the dead. But when he was murdered, this pretend-will became the real thing, and Bud and Gloria did just about every crazy thing they could think of to overturn it. It was Bud, following Gloria's orders, who managed to get his hands on a wax dummy of Benny Hartman from Madame Tussaud's up in San Francisco. This was not difficult to arrange due to the fact that Bud had a friend who worked at the museum who was glad to help steal the wax figure for five hundred dollars now, and the promise of much more later when Bud received his supposed 'inheritance.' Bud had met his friend, by the way, during a brief prison stint back East.

"Gloria and Bud drove around town with the figure and finally left it on a park bench in Beverly Hills, doing their best to create some real confusion. They meant to retrieve the dummy, by the way, but unfortunately for them a secretary in Don Mulberry's office was passing by and picked the thing up in her car.

"Once again, it's important to say that Bud and Gloria were not exactly geniuses when it came to planning. They were simply trying every wild scheme they could think up to break the will. They were broke, there were creditors at their door, and they were hoping for more time. If they could confuse things enough, they might at least delay the probate of the estate and continue to live in the Beverly Hills house while they dreamed up some new scam.

"Jayne had a glimpse of the wax figure one night, as did several other people as well, and this created enough doubt that the LAPD was able to get a court order to exhume Benny's coffin. And *voila!*—when the coffin was opened, there was no Benny inside—just Pussycat Charlie. Now that the cat was out of the bag, so to speak, the killer thought he had nothing to lose by throwing a little smoke, actually producing the body of Benny Hartman and—after briefly thawing it out—leaving it in my backyard. The body was frozen solid—it had been placed in a freezer these several months to obscure the actual time of death. So now, along with all the other mysteries, we were left to wonder when exactly did Benny really die?

"There is one more unpleasant and extremely mysterious event left for me to describe: the killer hired a woman to impersonate Darlene Bronson, a maid who had worked in the Hartman residence a number of years ago. Her job was to kidnap Jayne and keep her out of the way for several days—a plan which became complicated by an entirely unplanned brush fire in the Malibu hills. There was only one reason for this kidnapping, but it was a big one—to make certain I did not cancel the show tonight, which in fact I was on the verge of doing. The killer achieved this goal by having Jayne make a recording that she would be killed if the show did not go on.

"I hope you can see how this kidnapping and subsequent demand that the show proceed as scheduled eliminates some of our suspects. Gloria and Bud, for example, very much wanted to *stop* the show so that the million-dollar prize would not be given away. But it does not let our producer friend, Jerry Williams, off the hook . . . nor a number of other people as well, sponsors and such who had money riding on tonight's production. But let's assume that Jerry is not the killer, nor the network executives whose careers are on the line . . . and let's ask ourselves, what did the killer have to gain by having this show go on the air? The answer, I should tell you, has already come to pass. The killer simply wanted to show the world the truth about Benny Hartman, exactly what sort of person he really was—a vain, conceited, irresponsible egomaniac, rather than the beloved figure the American public believed him to be. This was a crime of hatred, ladies and gentlemen. The killer wanted me, or some other celebrity, to open the envelope for the Funniest Person Alive, announce Benny's name, and have everyone realize that this entire thing has been a hoax from start to finish, set in motion by a most unfunny and unscrupulous man. Thanks to the killer, of course, Benny would not be bounding up on stage to accept the award, and so the joke, such as it was, would fall very flat.

"I won't drag this out any longer, because I'm certain that some of you who have been following this case closely have already figured out the identity of the killer. Really, it's very simple. Who knew everything about Benny Hartman to hate him so passionately? And why, in fact, did the killer go to such lengths to confuse matters with bodies in swimming pools and other theatrics? Because he was, in fact, Benny Hartman's closest associate, and one of the first people the police might suspect. It was only through this close association that the killer knew about the hoax, and even about Benny's appointment to meet Terry Parker at the funeral.

"The killer knew every intimate detail of life in the Hartman household. I am talking, of course, about P. Ellsworth Dodd. Or rather, as we knew him . . . Patrick Larson.

"And so this very complicated matter boils down to the most elementary crime of all—a crime of revenge. It is a classic, I'm afraid:

The butler did it!"

chapter 56

Jayne, Cass, and I were sitting in our dressing room backstage at Dorothy Chandler Pavilion waiting for word from Lieutenant Kripinsky regarding the whereabouts of Patrick Ellsworth Dodd, a.k.a. Patrick Larson.

I had finished up my onstage account of Patrick with as much information as I was able to provide: Here was a man who had once been a successful theatrical manager, and then was reduced to working for his biggest star as a butler . . . after that star had deserted his agency just as he was becoming famous and ready to launch into the bigtime. It was possible to imagine a smoldering resentment, a hatred ripening over many years, gradually becoming more twisted with time until it exploded into murder.

Patrick was clearly a complex character, a man willing to accept such a demeaning position from someone who had betrayed him. He was incredibly patient, playing the role of Benny's loyal butler for over thirty years before taking his revenge. And why, I wondered, had Benny kept such a person close at hand? Was it to remind himself of his humble origins and his great success in life? Perhaps Patrick would be willing to answer some of these questions . . . if we ever manage to find him. Unfortunately, this very bright and eccentric individual had managed to stay a few steps ahead of us so far.

There was a knock on the door. It was Lieutenant Kripinsky, and he looked about as gloomy as I'd ever seen him.

"Have you found him?" I asked.

He shook his head. "He's not at the Beverly Hills house, and he doesn't seem to be among the crowd here."

"Strange! I was betting he'd be here!" I said. "I thought he'd want to see the end of this . . . but maybe not. Perhaps the very idea of the Benny Hartman Comedy Awards was too much for him."

"He's probably long gone," the lieutenant agreed with a scowl. "This afternoon I learned from his bank that he withdrew six hundred thousand dollars in cash the day before yesterday. So he's been preparing to run."

"That's a lot of money for a butler to have sitting in his bank account!" Cass mentioned. He was sitting with his sprained ankle resting on a coffee table. The ankle was swollen and wrapped in an Ace bandage, but other than that, he seemed to have recovered from his tree-climbing accident.

"Well, Benny Hartman paid him a good salary for thirty years, and Patrick had virtually no expenses—he lived rent-free in the Beverly Hills mansion," the lieutenant said grumpily. "It seems he saved every penny. So yeah, apparently he's loaded."

"Lieutenant, why don't you sit down and let me get you a cup of tea," Jayne insisted.

"No," he grumped, "I'm too busy. I have to get back to work."

"Nonsense," Jayne told him. "Your officers are perfectly capable of running things in your absence for a few minutes. Now sit. You know, it's just struck me that I've never seen you laugh."

"*Laugh?*" he repeated in astonishment, taking over one of the armchairs. "You think an LAPD officer ever comes across anything even remotely a source of humor?"

"The problems we cause for ourselves—they're funny, if you look at them in a certain way," Jayne said.

He shook his head. "I never laugh," he announced somberly.

"Never?" she asked.

"Every day, I see robberies, murders, rapes, rip-offs, child molestations . . . believe me, there's nothing funny about it."

There wasn't much we could say to this, so we all sat in glum silence for a moment while Jayne made the lieutenant a cup of tea, using the hot water kettle in our dressing room.

"Well, as long as we're being so serious, I have a few questions," Cass said. "Like why in the world did that sleazeball, Murray, kill Gloria Hartman? That doesn't make any sense to me at all."

"Murray was just a hired hand. He was working for Patrick—

and it was Murray, of course, who actually carried out all the murders. He killed Benny Hartman, Parker, D'Amato, and finally, Mrs. Hartman," the lieutenant explained. "Patrick was too old to do anything quite so physical himself."

"Yes, but why Gloria?" Cass insisted.

"She and Bud found out too much," I explained. "She discovered that Patrick was behind the killings, and she was about to tell me this at the planetarium. She was hoping I could protect her—but unfortunately, she came to me too late."

"Probably you'll want to know *how* she found out about Patrick," the lieutenant said wearily, as though it was a great amount of trouble to tell. "Well, he left something incriminating behind in his room after Mrs. Hartman fired him, on that night you saw him getting drunk. Very careless of him, but probably he wasn't used to drinking so much. He left the case of kitchen knives you had given to Mr. Hartman years ago. Mrs. Hartman recognized it immediately, and put everything together in her mind. We know all this, by the way, because we have Bud downtown at the station, and he's blabbing like crazy."

"Bud and Gloria had a falling out, too," I added. "Over money. Bud didn't realize how truly broke Gloria was until just a few days ago, and then he exploded. He beat her up and Gloria was very afraid of him. She was trying to make a run for it with the photographs when he came back that day earlier than expected, and Gloria was forced to leave the green suitcase with Jayne, afraid of what Bud would do if he found out she was planning to split with the one thing they had of monetary value."

"I see Gloria as a very sad figure," Jayne said with a sigh. "Poor thing."

"Her luck certainly went sour," the lieutenant agreed. "Bud sent her off to the planetarium that afternoon, telling her to get those photographs back or else. Unfortunately, a few minutes after she left, Murray showed up at their motel and applied some heavy pressure. Bud didn't hold out very long—he told Murray where Gloria had gone, then Murray went to the planetarium and killed her. He had to silence her before she could tell Mr. Allen who the killer was."

"Wait a second!" Cass objected. "Two questions: First, how did

Murray find their motel? And second, why didn't he kill Bud as well? And another question, for good luck—why did Gloria go back to Bud at the motel after she left Jayne this morning? I thought Gloria had run away from Bud, stealing a car and everything.''

''Let's answer these one at a time,'' I suggested. ''First of all, you have to remember, Gloria and Bud were terrible conspirators. Gloria left the phone number of the motel on a pad of paper in her bedroom, and that's how Patrick knew where to send Murray. Murray actually told this to Bud in a gloating manner when he was threatening to bust his kneecaps. As for why Bud was able to survive—he simply got away after a struggle. Murray thought it was better to go after the lady for the time being, to stop her from telling me the truth. He took the green suitcase, by the way, out of sheer greed—it probably wasn't part of Patrick's plan. Murray apparently thought he might do a little blackmailing on his own after his job with Patrick was finished.''

''As for Gloria going back to Bud after she left me this morning, that's more complicated,'' Jayne said. ''I really think she felt lost without him, even after he beat her up. Some women are like that. Probably she thought if she could get the suitcase back, they could make up and get some blackmail money . . . and have a happy ending.''

''How sad,'' Cass said.

''By the way,'' the lieutenant said, ''Janet Dorfman has come out of her coma and it looks as if she's going to be all right. In the next couple of days, we'll send someone up to the hospital in Lake Tahoe and get a statement from her. All in all, this is ending up a fairly tidy case.''

''It will be tidier when you pick up Patrick,'' I suggested.

As if on cue, there was an urgent knocking on the dressing room door, and a uniformed cop stuck his face inside.

''We've found him, Lieutenant! He was here after all, and he almost got away—he's on the street outside. We have him surrounded!''

Lieutenant Kripinsky was about to hurry off, but he stopped unexpectedly before rushing out the door.

''You've earned the right to be in on the end of this case, Mr. Allen. You, too, Mrs. Allen.''

''How about me?'' Cass asked.

The lieutenant sighed. "Sure. If you can make it on that ankle, come along."

The scene outside on the sidewalk was a nasty one. Patrick, dressed in elegant evening clothes, had a knife at the throat of a young woman he was holding hostage. At least thirty cops had surrounded him in a large circle, their guns drawn. Nearby several hundred spectators were being kept away by another group of police. In the crowd I saw a friend, Channel 5 producer Bonnie Tiegel, giving instructions to a TV news cameraman.

"Please don't come any closer!" Patrick told the police. His voice was loud, but very calm and polite, given the circumstances.

"Can I give this a try?" I asked Lieutenant Kripinsky. "Patrick and I have something of a relationship."

Kripinsky nodded. "Be careful."

"Mr. Dodd," I said, stepping out into the ring of armed policemen. "It's Steve Allen."

"Mr. Allen . . . well, well! An unexpected pleasure. If you will be so kind, sir, I'd appreciate it if you'd convey to the authorities that I will slit this young woman's throat unless I am provided with a limousine immediately."

"Easy does it. Don't hurt the girl," I told him. The knife was held so closely to the young woman's throat that I could see a small trickle of blood; she looked terrified and was breathing in sharp little gasps.

"I'm in earnest about this, Mr. Allen. As I'm sure you will understand."

"Relax, Patrick. We'll get you the limousine," I told him.

"That's right, Dodd," Lieutenant Kripinsky added. "A car is on its way. It will take a moment."

"Very good," he said. "And please don't try anything funny. I did not come this far to take my revenge against that cruel son of a bitch to be thwarted at the last moment. I plan to escape and enjoy my old age in luxury."

"That's fine with us," I assured him. "But Patrick, just between you and me—did Benny really treat you so badly that you felt justified in killing him and three other people?"

"It's a shame about the others, but Benny had it coming, Mr. Allen. I created him out of nothing—he was only a dumb kid on the street when I met him, and I turned him into a star.

But just when we were set to really take off, he left me and signed with another agent. It simply wasn't what a gentleman does."

I raised an eyebrow. "You think a gentleman commits four murders?"

"If he must, Mr. Allen . . . if he must! Benny found me again thirty years ago when I was down and out, and he hired me as his butler as a kind of joke. It wasn't very nice, Mr. Allen . . . not nice at all. And every goddamned day thereafter—for years, for years, you understand—I was subjected to that man's meanness. Oh, he was all smiles and phony warmth to the public. And he fooled them, too. But to me and others who did anything, however slight, to displease him, he was vindictive. I pretended to be grateful for the job, but I was biding my time . . . and now I see my car has arrived, so you will excuse me."

A limousine had pulled up on the street about ten feet from where Patrick and his hostage were standing. Still facing us, and not taking the knife from the girl's throat, he pulled her back with him toward the waiting car.

And now we come to a very strange twist of our story: Directly behind P. Ellsworth Dodd, on the sidewalk, there happened to be a very common piece of refuse—a banana peel that probably had been dropped there earlier by one of the fans. To my astonishment, I saw that Patrick was moving backward directly toward this unseen, slippery object.

No, I thought, *this would be too impossibly ironic an ending, even for an ill-fated comedy show!*

We all watched—those of us who were facing Patrick and his hostage. Step-by-step, he moved upon an inexorable, slapstick path. And then at last, his right foot came down upon the banana peel and slipped out from beneath his body. With a sharp cry, he collapsed on the sidewalk, throwing the knife harmlessly into the air as he fell.

The police were upon him immediately, and the girl was safe.

To my surprise, I heard the sound of laughter. It was the gloomy Lieutenant Kripinsky, and he was laughing so hard there were tears running down his face as he slipped a pair of handcuffs around Patrick's wrists.